THE APPROACHING STORM

BY ALAN DEAN FOSTER

Published by The Ballantine Publishing Group

THE APPROACHING STORM

ALAN DEAN FOSTER

THE BALLANTINE PUBLISHING GROUP
NEW YORK

A Del Rey® Book
Published by The Ballantine Publishing Group

Copyright © 2002 by Lucasfilm Ltd. & ™.
All Rights Reserved. Used Under Authorization.

All rights reserved under International and Pan-American Copyright
Conventions. Published in the United States by The Ballantine Publishing
Group, a division of Random House, Inc., New York, and simultaneously in
Canada by Random House of Canada Limited, Toronto.

Del Rey is a registered trademark and the Del Rey colophon is a trademark of
Random House, Inc.

www.starwars.com
www.starwarskids.com
www.randomhouse.com/delrey/

Library of Congress Catalog Card Number: 2001096587

ISBN 0-345-44300-4

Manufactured in the United States of America

First Edition: February 2002

10 9 8 7 6 5 4 3 2 1

For Shelby Hettinger,
So that everyone will know you're not kidding,
From Uncle Alan

A LONG TIME AGO IN A GALAXY
FAR, FAR AWAY . . . .

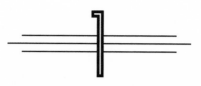

"It seems to me that mine is becoming a very important planet, Honorable Shu Mai."

The president of the Commerce Guild smiled thinly. "Small keys can unlock very big doors, Senator Mousul."

As they conversed, the dignified quartet strode slowly through the galaxy. Not the actual galaxy, of course, but an immense, intricately delineated, fully three-dimensional representation. It filled the entire private chamber. Stars glowed all around them, enveloping the strollers in a haze of soft, multihued refulgence. By reaching out and touching a planetary system, a visitor could summon forth a detailed, encyclopedic description of that system and its individual worlds: everything from species and population to minute characteristics of flora and fauna, economic statistics, and future prospects.

One of the strollers was a blue-skinned Twi'lek female who was quiet and contemplative of aspect. Her companion was a very important and readily recognizable Corellian industrialist. The president of the Commerce Guild was short and slender,

greenish of skin, with the typical coiffure for females of the Gossam species: a rising, upswept tailing. The fourth member of the
group, trailing elaborate robes woven from the most exotic materials to be found on his homeworld, was the Senator from the
world called Ansion. Despite his high standing, he looked nervous, like someone afraid of being watched. As for the Twi'lek
and the Corellian, they were clearly master and supplicant—
though the second was a very powerful supplicant indeed.

The president of the Commerce Guild halted. With a single,
expansive gesture she encompassed shimmering pinpoints of
light representing a thousand worlds and more. Amazing, she
thought, how trillions of sentient beings and entire civilizations
could be reduced to mere specks hovering in a single room. If
only the reality were as easy to organize and manage as was this
efficient, luminous depiction.

Given time and the assistance of carefully nurtured alliances,
she reflected confidently, it would be.

"Your forgiveness, noble lady," the Corellian murmured,
"but my associates and I also do not configure the importance of
this world called Ansion."

Shu Mai clapped her hands softly. "Excellent!"

Among her three companions, confusion readily crossed
species lines. "You find it satisfying that we do not see this place's
significance?" the female Twi'lek asked.

"Absolutely." A tolerant grin creased the Gossam's face. "If
you do not see it, then neither will our enemies. Pay attention,
and I will do more than make it evident—I will make it visible."

Turning, she reached into the pulsing panoply of worlds and
suns to pass the tips of the fingers of her right hand through a
small but centrally located star. With words and gestures, she
proceeded to manipulate the system she had singled out.

In response to her actions, a trio of laser-bright blue lines appeared, linking the first system to three others. "The Malarian Alliance. On the face of it, one of hundreds of such casual alliances." Her slim, deft fingers moved again. Yellow lines appeared, tying the first star to six additional systems. "Keitumite Mutual Military Treaty. Never invoked, but still in force." Her smile widened. She was enjoying herself. "Now, observe this." Her hands proceeded to play with the surrounding galographics like a musician strumming an expensive quintolium.

When at last Shu Mai finished, her three companions eyed her triumphant handiwork in silence. The four visitors were enclosed by a web of lines, straight and uncompromising: blue, yellow, gold, crimson—all the colors of the spectrum. Perhaps even, some dared to think, the colors of an empire.

And at the nexus of this web of intensely bright, unwavering lines that represented outstanding treaties and alliances, pacts and planetary partnerships, lay a single, suddenly far less insignificant world.

Ansion.

With a wave of one hand and a dismissive word from Shu Mai's lips, the elaborate network faded. It would not do to have someone not privy to the machinations of the group walk in unannounced and see what was being discussed. Awkward questions might ensue.

"Who would have suspected that a world such as this could lie at the center of so many interlocking treaties?" The blue-skinned female was suitably impressed.

"Precisely the point." Shu Mai inclined her head slightly in the female's direction. "There are other worlds that occupy comparable positions of strategic importance; worlds more heavily populated, thoroughly industrialized, and frequently mentioned as important players when the current unsettled state of affairs within the Republic is being discussed. In contrast, no one thinks to bring up Ansion. That is the beauty of it." Steepling her fingers, she glanced significantly at Senator Mousul.

"If we can get the Ansionians to commit to pulling out of the Republic, no one will really care. But because of their alliances, their withdrawal should be enough to sway their already vacillating partners in both the Malarian Alliance and the Keitumite Treaty to follow. You saw how many other systems are tied, in turn, to both of those pacts. The effect will be as of an avalanche; starting small, growing fast, and accelerating of its own accord. By the time the Senate knows what has hit it, forty systems or more will have withdrawn from the Republic, and we will be well on our way to solidifying the kind of changes we wish to see come about."

Mousul's fingers clenched tighter and tighter until whiteness showed beneath the skin. "That will be the spark that we need to propose the passage of extraordinary measures to cope with the emergency."

The Corellian industrialist was all but dancing with excitement. "It's wonderfully cunning, this plan you've devised! I know that the interests I represent will agree to send a force to Ansion immediately, to compel the inhabitants to withdraw from the Republic." For an instant, Senator Mousul looked alarmed.

"Which is exactly what we do not want them to do," Shu Mai countered sternly. "As I seem to recall, the Trade Federation already tried something similar elsewhere. The results were, shall we say, somewhat less than triumphant."

"Yes, well." The Corellian coughed uncomfortably into one hand. "There were unforeseen complications."

"That continue to resonate to this day." Shu Mai was unrelenting in her tone. "Don't you see? The beauty of this plan is the seeming insignificance of its linchpin. Send a fleet, or even a few ships, to Ansion, and you will immediately attract the attention of those forces that continue to frustrate us. Obviously, that is the last thing we wish. We want the Ansionian withdrawal to appear wholly natural, the result of internal decisions reached in the absence of external influences." She smiled benignly at Mousul.

"Will it be?" the Twi'lek asked pointedly.

Shu Mai eyed her approvingly. She would be useful, she knew. As would the others she had involved—if they could keep their wits about them.

It was Senator Mousul's turn to respond. "Like so many peoples, the Ansionians are divided as to whether they should remain within the Republic or step outside the corruption and sleaze that permeate it. Rest assured that there are among its citizens those who are sympathetic to our cause. I have taken care and expended considerable political capital to ensure that these elements are appropriately encouraged."

"How long?" the deceptively soft-voiced Twi'lek wanted to know.

"Before Ansion decides?" The Senator looked thoughtful. "Assuming the internal divisions continue to widen, I would expect a formal vote on whether to withdraw from the Republic within half a standard year."

The president of the Commerce Guild nodded approvingly. "At which point we can look on with satisfaction as those who have been traditionally allied to Ansion follow suit, and those allied to the allies fall in turn. Surely, as children all of you played with blocks? There is invariably one key block near the bottom that, if removed, will cause the entire structure to collapse.

"Ansion is that key. Remove that one block, and the rest of these systems will crumble." Her thoughts, as well as her gaze, seemed to focus on something outside the range of vision of her associates. "On the ruins of the old, decrepit Republic those of us with foresight will build a new political structure, perfect and gleaming. One without any weak links, free of the moralistic waste that encumbers and slows the appropriate development of a truly advanced society."

"And who will lead this new society?" The female Twi'lek's voice was tinged with just a touch of cynicism. "You?"

Shu Mai shrugged modestly. "My interests lie with the Commerce Guild. Who can say? That is something yet to be determined, is it not? The cause must succeed before leaders can be chosen. While I admit I would not turn down such a nomination, I believe there are others who are more qualified. Let us begin with small things."

"Like this Ansion." Having recovered from the previous mild reproach, the Corellian's enthusiasm had returned full strength. "What a pleasure it would be, what a wonderment, to at last be able to conduct business unencumbered by mountains of superfluous rules, regulations, and restrictions! Those I represent would be forever grateful."

"Yes, you would at last have the chance to secure the restrictive monopolies you so devoutly seek," Shu Mai observed dryly. "Don't worry. In return for your political and financial support, you and those you represent will receive everything they deserve."

The industrialist was not intimidated. "And of course," he added shrewdly, "this new political arrangement will open all manner of opportunities to the Commerce Guild."

Shu Mai gestured modestly. "We are always eager to take advantage of shifting political realities."

In the midst of mutual congratulations and expectations, she noticed that Senator Mousul was saying little.

"Something burrows in your thoughts like a worm with indigestion, Mousul. What is it?"

The Ansionian glanced back at his associate, a look of mild concern on his face. His large, slightly bulbous eyes stared evenly back at the president of the Commerce Guild. "You're sure no one else could winnow out the true nature of these plans for Ansion, Shu Mai?"

"None has thus far," the other replied pointedly.

Mousul straightened to his full height. "I flatter myself that I am intelligent enough to realize there are those who are smarter than me. They are the ones who concern me."

Stepping forward, Shu Mai put a reassuring hand on the Senator's shoulder. "You worry overmuch, Mousul." With her free hand and without regard for tact, Shu Mai gestured, and the point of light that was Ansion reappeared. "Ansion! Look at it. Small, backward, unimportant. If queried, I wager not one politician or merchant in a hundred could tell you anything much about it. No one except those of us in this room are aware of its potential significance."

Stymied by and angry at the casual venality and suffocating bureaucracy that had come to rule the Republic—and to complicate his business dealings—the Corellian industrialist could purchase entire companies and whole territories with a mere touch of his imprinting finger. But for all his wealth, he could not buy a glimpse into the future. At that moment, he would have gladly signed over a few billion for the answers to one or two questions.

"I hope you are right, Shu Mai. I hope you are right."

"Of course she is." Having agreed to this meeting somewhat reluctantly, the Twi'lek was feeling far more confident of the future following their host's detailed explanation. "I am both impressed and moved by the full scope and subtlety of President Shu Mai and Senator Mousul's strategy. As they have so eloquently pointed out, this world is far too unimportant to attract anything in the way of significant outside attention . . ."

"**H**aja, sweet scent—what're you hiding under that big ol' robe?"

Luminara Unduli did not look up at the large, unshaven, rough-hewn, and unpleasantly fragrant man or his equally coarse and malodorous companions. She treated their knowing grins, the eager forward tilt of their bodies, and their leering eyes with equal indifference—though their collective body odor was somewhat harder to ignore. Patiently, she raised the spoonful of hot stew to her lips, the lower of which was stained a permanent purplish black. A series of interlocking black diamonds tattooed her chin, while more intricate markings decorated the joints of her fingers. The olive color of her skin contrasted strikingly with the deep blue of her eyes.

These rose to regard the younger woman who was seated on the other side of the table. Barriss Offee's attention shifted between her teacher and the men crowding uncomfortably close around the two of them. Luminara smiled to herself. A good person, was Barriss. Observant and thoughtful, if occasionally impulsive. For now, the young woman held her peace, kept eating, and said nothing. A judicious reaction, the older woman knew. *She's letting me take the lead, as she should.*

The man who had voiced the impropriety whispered something to one of his friends. There was a ripple of crude, unpleasant laughter. Leaning closer, he put a hand on Luminara's cloth-draped shoulder. "I asked you a question, darlin'. Now, are you gonna show us what's under this lovely soft robe of yours, or d'you want us to take a peek ourselves?" An air of pheromone-charged expectation had gripped his companions. Huddled over their food, a few of the establishment's other diners turned to look, but none moved to voice outrage at what was happening or to interfere.

Spoon pausing before her lips, Luminara seemed to devote greater contemplation to its contents than to the insistent query. With a sigh, she finally downed the spoonful of stew and reached down with her free right hand. "I suppose if you really want to see . . ."

One of the men grinned broadly and nudged his hulking companion in the ribs. A couple of others crowded closer still, so that they were all but leaning over the table. Luminara pulled a portion of her outer robe aside, the intricate designs on the copper- and bronze-colored metal bands that covered her upper forearms glinting in the diffuse light of the tavern.

Beneath the robe was a metal and leather belt. Attached to the belt were several small and unexpectedly sophisticated examples of precision engineering. One of these was cylindrical, highly polished, and designed to fit comfortably in a closed hand. The aggressive spokesman for the group squinted at it, his expression slightly confused. Behind him, a couple of his heretofore hopeful cronies abandoned their leering expressions faster than a smuggler's ship making an emergency jump to hyperspace.

"Mathos preserve us! That's a Jedi lightsaber!"

Expressions falling like hard rain, the band of would-be aggressors began to back off, split up, and drift hurriedly away. Unexpectedly deserted, their erstwhile leader was unwilling to admit defeat so quickly. He stared at the gleaming metal cylinder.

"Not a chance, no. A 'Jedi' lightsaber, is it?" He glared belligerently at the suddenly enigmatic object of his attentions. "I suppose that would make you a 'Jedi Knight,' sweet splash? A lovely, lithe Jedi at that!" He snorted derisively. "Sure and that's no Jedi lightsaber, is it? Is it?" he growled insistently when she failed to respond.

Finishing another spoonful of her meal, Luminara Unduli carefully set the utensil down on her nearly empty plate, delicately patted both her decorated and her untouched lip with the supplied linen napkin, wiped her hands, and turned to face him. Blue eyes peered upward out of her fine-featured face, and she smiled coldly.

"You know how to find out," she informed him softly.

The big man started to say something, hesitated, reconsidered. The attractive woman's hands rested, palm downward, on her thighs. The lightsaber—it certainly *looked* like a Jedi lightsaber, he found himself thinking apprehensively—remained attached to her belt. Across the table, the younger woman continued to eat her meal as though nothing out of the ordinary was taking place.

Abruptly, the gruff intruder became aware of several things simultaneously. First, he was now completely alone. His formerly enthusiastic companions had slipped away, one by one. Second, by this time the woman seated before him was supposed to be anxious and afraid. Instead, she only looked bored and resigned. Third, he suddenly remembered that he had important business elsewhere.

"Uh, sorry," he found himself mumbling. "Didn't mean to bother you. Case of mistaken identity. Was looking for someone else." Turning, he hurried away from the table and toward the tavern's entrance, nearly tripping over a scraps bowl on the floor next to an unoccupied serving counter. Several of the other patrons watched him go. Others eyed the two women fixedly before finding reason to return to their own food and conversation.

Exhaling softly, Luminara turned back to the remnants of her meal. Making a face, she pushed the bowl and what remained of the meal away from her. The boorish intrusion had spoiled her appetite.

"You handled that well, Master Luminara." Barriss was finishing up her own food. The Padawan's perception might occasionally be lacking, but never her readiness to eat. "No noise, no fuss."

"As you grow older, you'll find that you occasionally have to deal with an excess of testosterone. Often on minor worlds like Ansion." She shook her head slowly. "I dislike such distractions."

Barriss smiled gaily. "Don't be so somber, Master. You can't do anything about physical attractiveness. Anyway, you've given them a story to tell, as well as a lesson."

Luminara shrugged. "If only those in charge of the local government, this so-called Unity of Community, were as easy to persuade to see reason."

"It will happen." Barriss rose swiftly. "I'm finished." Together, the two women paid for the meal and exited the establishment. Whispers, mutterings, and not a few awed words of admiration trailed in their wake.

"The populace has heard we're here to try to cement a permanent peace between the city folk of the Unity and the Alwari nomads. They're unaware of the far greater issues at stake. And we can't reveal the real reason for our presence here without alerting those who would oppose us to the fact that we know of their deeper intentions." Luminara drew her robe tighter around her. It was important to present as subdued yet impressive an appearance as possible. "Because we can't be completely honest, the locals don't trust us."

Barriss nodded. "The city people think we favor the nomads, and the nomads fear we're on the side of the city folk. I hate politics, Master Luminara." One hand fell to her side. "I prefer settling differences with a lightsaber. Much more straightforward." Her pretty face radiated a zest for life. She had not yet lived long enough to become inured to the new.

"It's difficult to persuade opposing sides of the rightness of your reasoning when they're both dead." Turning up one of Cuipernam's side streets, chaotic with traders and city folk of many different galactic species, Luminara spoke while scanning not only the avenue but also the flanking walls of commercial and residential buildings. "Anyone can handle a weapon. Reason is much more difficult to wield. Remember that the next time you're tempted to settle an argument with a lightsaber."

"I bet it's all the fault of the Trade Federation." Barriss eyed a stall dripping with jewelry: necklaces and earrings, rings and diadems, bracelets and hand-sculpted flash corneas. Such conventional personal ornamentation was forbidden to a Jedi. As one of her teachers had once explained to Barriss and her fellow

Padawans, "A Jedi's glow comes from within, not from the artificial augmentation of baubles and beads."

Still, that necklace of Searous hair and interwoven pikach stones was just *gorgeous*.

"What did you say, Barriss?"

"Nothing, Master. I was just expressing my dissatisfaction at the continuing scheming of the Trade Federation."

"Yes," Luminara agreed. "And the Commerce Guilds. They grow more powerful by the month, always sticking their money-hungry fingers in where they're not wanted, even if their immediate interests are not directly involved. Here on Ansion, they openly support the towns and cities that are loosely grouped together as the Unity of Community even though the law of the Republic guarantees the rights of nomadic groups like the Alwari to remain independent of such external influences. Their activities here only complicate an already difficult situation." They turned another corner. "As they do elsewhere."

Barriss nodded knowingly. "Everyone still remembers the Naboo incident. Why doesn't the Senate simply vote to reduce their trade concessions? *That* would settle them down a bit!"

Luminara had to fight to keep from smiling. Ah, the innocence of youth! Barriss was well meaning and a fine Padawan, but she was unsophisticated in the ways of governance.

"It's all very well to invoke ethics and morals, Barriss, but these days it's commerce that seems to rule the Republic. Sometimes the Commerce Guilds and the Trade Federation act like they're separate governments. They're very clever about it, though." Her expression twisted. "Fawning and bowing before emissaries of the Senate, issuing a steady stream of protestations of innocence: that Nute Gunray in particular is as slippery as a Notonian mudworm. Money equals power, and power buys votes. Yes, even in the Republic Senate. And they have powerful allies." Her thoughts turned inward. "It's not just money anymore. The Republic is a soiled sea roiled by dangerous currents. The Jedi Council fears that general dissatisfaction with the present state of governance is giving way to outright secession on many worlds."

Barriss stood a little taller as she strode along beside her Master. "At least everyone knows that the Jedi are above such matters, and aren't for sale."

"Not for sale, no." Luminara sank farther into preoccupation.

Barriss noted the change. "Something else troubles you, Master Luminara?"

The other woman mustered a smile. "Oh, sometimes one hears things. Odd stories, unaccredited rumors. These days such tales seem to run rampant. This political philosophy of a certain Count Dooku, for example."

Though always eager to display her knowledge, Barriss hesitated before responding. "I think I recognize the name, but not in connection with that title. Wasn't he the Jedi who—"

Stopping sharply, Luminara threw out a hand to halt her companion. Her eyes flicked rapidly from side to side and she was suddenly no longer introspective. Her every nerve was alert, every sense on edge. Before Barriss could question the reason for the action, the Jedi had her lightsaber out, activated, and fully extended before her. Without moving her head, she raised it to a challenge position. Having drawn and activated her own weapon in response to her Master's reaction, Barriss searched anxiously for the source of unease. Seeing nothing out of the ordinary, she glanced questioningly at her teacher.

Which was when the Hoguss plunged from above—to spit

itself neatly on Luminara's upraised lightsaber. There was a brief stink of burning flesh, the Jedi extracted the beam, and the startled Hoguss, its now useless killing ax locked in a powerful but lifeless grip, keeled over onto its side. The heavy body made a dull thump as it struck the ground.

"Back!" Luminara started to retreat, the now anxious and alerted Barriss guarding her Master's rear and flanks.

The attackers swarmed down from rooftops and out of second-story windows, came bursting through doorways and up out of otherwise empty crates; a veritable flash flood of seedy in-famy. Someone, Luminara mused grimly as she retreated, had gone to considerable trouble and expense to arrange this ambush. In the midst of genuine concern for herself and her Padawan, she had to admire the plotter's thoroughness. Whoever it was clearly knew they were dealing with more than a couple of female tourists out for a morning's sight-seeing.

The question was, how much did they know?

There are only two ways for non-Jedi to defeat Jedi in battle: lull them into a false sense of security, or overwhelm them with sheer force of numbers. Subtlety obviously being a notion for-eign to their present assailants, a diverse rabble of bloodthirsty but untrained individuals, their employer had opted for the latter approach. In the crowded, active streets, the large number of at-tackers had gone undetected by Luminara, their inimical feelings submerged among those of the greater crowd.

Now that the attack had begun, the Force throbbed with an enmity that was out in the open as dozens of well-armed hired assassins fought to get close enough to their rapidly withdrawing targets to deliver a few final, fatal blows. While the narrowness of the street and the aimless fleeing of panicked bystanders elimi-nated a clear line of retreat and kept the two women from sprinting to safety, it also prevented those of their attackers who were wielding firearms from setting up a clear shot at their intended targets. Had they been tacticians, those in front swinging blades and other less advanced devices would have stepped aside to give their more heavily armed comrades room in which to take aim. But a reward had been promised to the ones who made the actual kill. While this served to inspire the truculent rabble, it also made them reluctant to cooperate with one another in achieving their ultimate objective, lest it be a colleague who claimed the substantial bonus.

So it was that Luminara and Barriss were able to deflect bursts from blasters as well as blows struck by less technical weaponry such as long swords and knives. With high walls shielding them on either side and merchants and vendors continuing to run for cover, they had room in which to work. Bodies began to pile up in front of them, some intact, others missing significant portions of their anatomy, these having been neatly excised by whirling shafts of intensely colored energy.

Barriss's exuberance and occasional shouted challenge were complemented by Luminara's steady, silently ferocious work. Together, the two women not only kept their attackers at bay, but began to force them back. There is something in the hushed, frighteningly efficient aspect of a fighting Jedi that takes the heart out of an ordinary opponent. A would-be murderer has only to see a few blaster shots deflected by the anticipatory hum of a lightsaber to realize that there might be other less potentially lethal ways to make a living.

Then, just when the two women were on the verge of pushing the remaining attackers around a corner and back out into an open square where they could be more effectively scattered, a roar of anticipation rose above the fray as another two dozen assassins arrived. This mélange of humans and aliens was better dressed, better armed, and tended to fight more as a unit than those who had preceded them. A tiring Luminara realized suddenly that the previous hard fighting had never been intended to kill them, but only to wear them out. Steeling herself and shouting encouragement to a visibly downcast Barriss, she once more found herself retreating back down the narrow street they had nearly succeeded in escaping.

Drawing new courage from the arrival of fresh reinforcements, their surviving assailants redoubled their own attack. Jedi and Padawan were forced steadily backward.

Then there was no more backward. The side street dead-ended against a featureless courtyard wall. To anyone else it would have appeared unscalable. But a Jedi could find hand- and footholds where others would see only a smooth surface.

"Barriss!" Lightsaber whirling, Luminara indicated the reddish-colored barrier behind them. "Go up! I'll follow." Dropping to his knees, a man clad in tough leathers took careful aim with a blaster. Luminara blocked both his shots before taking one hand briefly off the lightsaber to gesture in his direction. Like a living thing, the dangerous weapon flew out of his hands, startling him so badly he fell backward onto his butt. Protected by his fellow assassins, he did not panic like a common killer but instead scrambled to recover the blaster. They couldn't keep this up forever, she knew.

"Up, I said!" Luminara did not have to turn to sense the unyielding wall behind her.

Barriss hesitated. "Master, you can cover me if I climb, but I can't do the same for you from the top of the wall." Lunging, she disarmed a serpentine Wetakk who was trying to slip in under her guard. Letting out a yelp of pain, it stepped back and switched the hooked blade it was holding to another hand, of which it still had five remaining. Without missing a breath, the Padawan added, "You can't climb and use your weapon, too!"

"I'll be all right," Luminara assured her, even as she wondered how she was going to make the ascent without being cut down from behind. But her first concern was for her Padawan, and not for herself. "That's an order, Barriss! Get up there. We have to get out of this confined space."

Reluctantly, Barriss took a last sweeping swing to clear the ground in front of her. Then she shut down her lightsaber, slipped it back onto her belt, pivoted, took a few steps, and leapt. The jump carried her partway up the wall, to which she clung like a spider. Finding seemingly invisible fingerholds, she began to ascend. Below and behind her, Luminara single-handedly held back the entire surging throng of eager killers.

Nearly at the top, Barriss looked back and down. Luminara was not only holding off her own assailants, but had moved forward to ensure that none of those in the back would have time to take aim at the climbing Padawan. Barriss hesitated.

"Master Luminara, there are too many! I can't protect you from up here."

The Jedi turned to respond. As she did so, she failed to see or sense a small Throbe standing behind a much larger human. The Throbe's blaster was small, its aim wild, but the undeflected shot still managed to graze the woman in the umber robes. Luminara staggered.

"Master!" Frantic, Barriss debated whether to ascend the remaining distance to the top of the wall or disobey her Master and drop back down to aid her. In the midst of her confusion, a subtle tremor ran through her mind. It was a disturbance in the Force, but one very different from anything they had experienced this dreadful morning. It was also surprisingly strong.

Yelling encouragement, the two men plunged past on either side of Luminara. Neither was physically imposing, though one had a build suggestive of considerable future development. Lightsabers flashing, they fell in among the bewildered band of assassins, their weapons dealing out havoc in bantha-sized doses.

To their credit, the attackers held their ground for another couple of moments. Then, their associates falling all around them, the survivors broke and fled. In less than a minute, the street was clear and the way back to the central square unobstructed. Letting go of the wall, Barriss dropped the considerable distance to the ground, to find herself facing an attractive young man who wore confidence like a handmade suit. Smiling cockily, he deactivated his lightsaber and regarded her appraisingly.

"I've been told that morning exercise is good for the soul as well as the body. Hello, Barriss Offee."

"Anakin Skywalker. Yes, I remember you from training." Automatically nodding her thanks, she hurried to her Master's side. The other newcomer was already examining Luminara's blaster wound.

"It's not serious."

Luminara pulled her garments closed rather more sharply than was necessary. "You're early, Obi-Wan," she told her colleague. "We weren't expecting you until the day after tomorrow."

"Our ship made good time." As the four emerged onto the square, Obi-Wan's gaze swept the open space. Presently, it was as void of inimical disturbance, as was the Force. He allowed himself to relax slightly. "Since we arrived early, we suspected there would be no one to meet us at the spaceport. So we decided to come looking for you. When you weren't at your stated residence, we decided to take a stroll to acquaint ourselves with the city. That's when I sensed the trouble. It drew us to you."

"Well, I certainly can't fault your timing." She smiled gratefully. It was the same intriguing smile that Obi-Wan remembered from working with her previously, framed as it was by its differently toned lips. "The situation was becoming awkward."

"Awkward!" Anakin declared. "Why, if Master Obi-Wan and I hadn't—" The look of disapproval the Jedi shot him was enough to destroy the observation in midsentence.

"Something I've been curious about ever since we were given this assignment." Barriss moved a little farther away from her counterpart and closer to the two senior Jedi. "Why are *four* of us needed here, to deal with what seems to me to be nothing more than a minor dispute among the native sentients?" Her impatience was palpable. "Earlier, you spoke of greater issues."

"You remember our discussions," Luminara explained patiently. "Well, the Alwari nomads think the Senate favors the city dwellers. The city folk are certain the galactic government will side with the nomads. Such perceptions of favoritism on the part of the Senate are dangerously close to persuading both groups that Ansion would be better off outside the Republic, where internal disputes could be settled without outside interference. Their representative in the Senate appears to be leaning in that direction. There is also evidence to support the contention that offworld elements are stirring the pot, hoping to induce Ansion to secede."

"It's only one world, and not a particularly important one at that," Barriss ventured.

Luminara nodded slowly. "True. But it's not Ansion itself that is so critical. Through a multiplicity of pacts and alliances, it could pull other systems out of the Republic as well. More systems than I, or the Jedi Council, likes to think about. Therefore, a way must be found to keep Ansion within the Republic. The best way to do that is to remove the suspicions that exist between the city dwellers and the nomads, and thereby solidify planetary representation. As outsiders representing the will of the Senate, we will find respect on Ansion, but no friends. While we are here, suspicion will be our constant companion. Given the fluid complexity of the situation, the matter of shifting alliances, the possible presence of outside agitators, and the seriousness of the potential ramifications, it was felt that two pairs of negotiators would make a greater and more immediate impression on the situation than one."

"I see now." There was much more at stake here, Barriss found herself thinking, than a disagreement between city folk and nomads. Had Luminara been instructed to conceal the real reason for their journey from her Padawan until now, or had Barriss simply been too preoccupied with her own training to see the larger issues? Like it or not, it appeared that she was going to have to pay more attention to galactic politics.

For example, why would forces beyond Ansion want to see it secede from the Republic badly enough to interfere in the planet's internal affairs? What could such unknown entities possibly have to gain by its withdrawal? There were thousands upon thousands of civilized worlds in the Republic. The departure of one, or even several, would mean little in the overall scheme of galactic governance. Or would it?

She felt sure she was missing some vital point, and the fact that she knew she was doing so was exceedingly frustrating. But she couldn't question Luminara further about it, because Obi-Wan was speaking.

"Someone or several someones beyond Ansion doesn't want these negotiations to succeed. They *want* Ansion to secede from the Republic, with all the problematic consequences that would ensue." Obi-Wan squinted at the sky, which had begun to threaten rain. "It would be useful to know who. We should have detained one of your attackers."

"They could have been common bandits," Anakin pointed out.

Luminara considered. "It's possible. Anyway, if Obi-Wan is right and that rabble was hired to prevent us from continuing with our mission, their employer would have kept those who attacked us in the dark as to his or her identity and purpose. Even if we had been successful in capturing one of them, an interrogation might well have been useless."

"Yes, that's so," the Padawan had to admit.

"So you were on Naboo, too?" Feeling left out of the conversation between the two older Jedi, Barriss turned curiously to her counterpart.

"I was." The pride in the younger man's voice was unapologetic. *He's a strange one,* she mused. Strange, but not unlikable. As stuffed full of internal conflicts as a momus bush was with seeds. But there was no denying that the Force was strong within him.

"How long have you been Master Luminara's Padawan?" he asked.

"Long enough to know that those who have their mouths open all the time generally have their ears shut."

"Oh great," Anakin muttered. "You're not going to spend all our time together speaking in aphorisms, are you?"

"At least I can talk about something besides myself," she shot back. "Somehow I don't think you scored well in modesty."

To her surprise, he was immediately contrite. "Was I just

talking about myself? I'm sorry." He indicated the two figures preceding them up the busy street. "Master Obi-Wan says that I suffer from a surfeit of impatience. I want to know, to do, *everything* right now. Yesterday. And I'm not very good at disguising the fact that I'd rather be elsewhere. This isn't a very exciting assignment."

She gestured back in the direction of the side street they had left piled high with bodies. "You're here less than a day and already you've been forced into life-or-death hand-to-hand combat. Your definition of *excitement* must be particularly eclectic."

He almost laughed. "And you have a really dry sense of humor. I'm sure we'll get along fine."

Reaching the commercial district on the other side of the square and plunging back into the surging crowds of humans and aliens, Barriss wasn't so certain. He was very sure of himself, this tall, blue-eyed Padawan. Maybe it was true what he said about wanting to know everything. His attitude was that he already did. Or was she mistaking confidence for arrogance?

Abruptly, he broke away from her. She watched as he stopped before a stall selling dried fruits and vegetables from the Kander region to the north of Cuipernam. When he returned without buying anything, she eyed him uncertainly.

"What was that all about? Did you see something that looked tasty but on closer inspection turned out not to be?"

"What?" He seemed suddenly preoccupied. "No. No, it wasn't the food at all." He glanced back at the simple food stand as they hurried to catch up with their teachers. "Didn't you see? That boy over there, the one in the vest and long pants, was arguing with his mother. Yelling at her." He shook his head dolefully. "Someday when he's older he'll regret having done that. I didn't tell him so directly, but I think I got the point across." He sank into deep contemplation. "People are so busy getting on with their lives they frequently forget what's really important."

What a strange Padawan, she mused, and what an even stranger young man. They were more or less the same age, yet in some ways he struck her as childlike, while in others he seemed much older than her. She wondered if she would have time enough to get to know him better. She wondered if anyone would have time enough to get to know him. She certainly hadn't, during their brief encounters at the Jedi Temple. Just then thunder boomed overhead, and for some reason she could not quite put a finger on she was afraid it signified the approach of more than just rain.

Ogomoor was not happy. Walking as slowly as was acceptable down the high hallway of the bossban's quarters, he tried his
best to ignore the sideways glances of busy servants, clerks, and
workers scurrying to and fro. Though as the bossban's majordomo he outranked them all, the lowliest among them exhibited
more confidence and contentment than he. Even the blue-green
Smotl known as Ib-Dunn, arms overflowing with hard communications larger than himself, bestowed a pitying look on the
majordomo as Ogomoor stepped over him without, characteris-
tically, disturbing so much as a single piece of the far smaller
worker's burden.

They had reason to pity him today, he knew, and he had reason to be pitied. Be they good or bad, it was his job to report in
person all major developments to Bossban Soergg the Hutt. Present news to be delivered being exceedingly unpleasant, Ogomoor had spent much of the morning devoutly praying for the
intercession of some fever-inducing, preferably highly contagious

disease. Regrettably, both he and the bossban remained in perfect health.

Whether that would allow him to weather the forthcoming meeting with Soergg remained open to much speculation—and some spirited informal wagering—among his coworkers. Not one among them failed to favor him with less than a genuinely sorrowful look. Amazing how quickly word of bad news spread among the lower ranks, he mused in one of the few moments when he was not drowning in self-pity.

Turning a corner, he found himself standing before the entrance to the bossban's office and inner sanctum. A pair of heavily armed Yuzzem flanked the doorway. They regarded him disdainfully, as though he were already flayed and dead. With a shrug, he announced himself via the comm unit. *Might as well get it over with,* he decided.

Bossban Soergg the Hutt was a grayish, heaving, flaccid lump of flesh and muscle only another Hutt could possibly find attractive. He had his back to the door and his hands folded in front of him, staring out the wide polarized window that gave a sweeping view of Lower Cuipernam. Off to one side, three of his concubines were playing bako. They were presently unchained. One was human, one Brogune, the other representative of a species Ogomoor to this day did not recognize. What Soergg did with them the majordomo could barely imagine. When the Brogune looked up and eyed him sadly, with all four eyes, no less, Ogomoor knew he was in deep mopak.

Soergg heaved himself around, turning away from the window. The tiny automated custodial droid scurried to keep up with the movement, efficient if not enthusiastic at its assigned task of doing nothing but cleaning up after the Hutt's trail of slime and tailings. Hands clasped over his prodigious gut, the Hutt glowered down at Ogomoor out of bulging, slitted eyes.

"So. You failed."

"Not I, Omnipotent One." Ogomoor bowed as low as was feasible, given the proximity of Hutt slime. "I hired only the best, those who were recommended to me. The failure was theirs, and that of those who recommended them. These unworthies I have already reprimanded. As for myself I was, as always, nothing more than your humble facilitator."

"*Hurrp!*" Caught directly in the line of fire, with no tactful means of dodging, Ogomoor was compelled to suffer the full force of the bossban's belch. The fetid emission staggered him, but he held his ground bravely. Fortunately, the consequent contortions of his digestive system were not readily visible. "Perhaps it was no one's fault."

So stunning, so atypical was this straightforwardly bland admission from Soergg that Ogomoor immediately suspected a trap. Warily, he tried to divine the bossban's true intent. "If there was failure, how can it be no one's fault, O Great One?"

A hand gestured diffidently. "Those fools who failed were told they would be dealing with one Jedi and her Padawan. Not two. Jedi strength multiplies exponentially. Fighting one is like fighting two. Dealing with two more akin to trying to handle eight. Fighting eight . . ." A quiver sludged in visible ripples the length of the Hutt's flesh. Ogomoor was duly impressed. Though he had never set eyes on one of the legendary Jedi in person, anything that could give Bossban Soergg the shudders was something to be avoided.

"The second pair was not supposed to arrive for another two days yet." Soergg was muttering to himself now, the words rum-

bling up from that vast abyss of a belly like methane gas bubbling
to the surface of a decomposing pond. "One would almost think
they had sensed the confrontation to come and accelerated their
arrival. This timing change is suspicious, and must be brought to
the attention of others."

"What others?" Ogomoor inquired, and was immediately
sorry he had done so.

Soergg glared down at him. "Why do you want to know,
underling?"

"I don't—not really." Ogomoor tried to shrink down into
his boots.

"Better for you, believe me. You would quake at the very
mention of certain names, certain organizations. Be content in
your ignorance and your minor status."

"Oh, I am, Your Corpulence, I am!" Privately, he wished he
knew who or what the bossban was talking about. The expectation of possible riches far outweighed any fear he might have felt.

"The situation was made worse," the Hutt was saying, "because trained Jedi can oft times sense threatening disturbances in
their vicinity. Because of this ability, they are infernally difficult to
ambush. Certain individuals will not be pleased by this turn of
events. There will be additional expense."

This time Ogomoor kept quiet.

Hutt movements are slow, but their minds are not. "Though
your mouth is closed, I see your brain working. The details of
this business are for me to know and you to forget." Noting his
bossban's irritation, Ogomoor forbore from inquiring how he
was supposed to forget something he had never been told.

"It may not matter. The representatives of the Unity grow
more displeased by the day with the continuing indecision of

Republic officials regarding the land claims of the nomads. I am informed that as with many current issues, Senate opinion is divided on the issue."

"Yes, yes, I know." Soergg grunted impressively. "It seems that the galaxy is now governed by confusion instead of consensus." A monstrous frown split his leathery face. "Bad for business, chaos is. That is why the Hutts have allied themselves, albeit quietly, with those forces that are working for change. For stability, the capitalist's friend." He wagged a finger at his assistant. "With luck, these Jedi will need time to accomplish anything. It will take more debate before this quarrel between the city folk and the Alwari can be settled. That gives us time, and opportunity, in which to still conclude this business in a satisfactory manner. It *must* be concluded in a satisfactory manner. The Jedi cannot be allowed to sway the opinion of the Unity representatives. The vote to pull Ansion out of the Republic must proceed!" Slobber trickled down the absent chin as a huge tongue licked thick lips. The custodial droid scuttled swiftly to catch the noxious drool before it could stain the floor.

"You cannot imagine," the Hutt added in dangerously low tones, "the extent of the repercussions if we fail to successfully carry out this contract. Those who have engaged us to carry out their wishes in this matter have a reputation for treating failure harshly, in ways that can only be imagined."

Ogomoor had all too vivid an imagination. "I will do my best, as always, Bossban. Still, four Jedi—"

"Two Jedi and two Padawans," Soergg corrected him. He looked suddenly wistful. Or at least as wistful as a Hutt could look. "Those pathetic malingerers you were forced to hire are all too typical of the quality available on outlying worlds such as Ansion. What is needed for this kind of work is a real, experienced professional. Someone whose work and experience falls outside the boundaries of Republic legalese. A proper bounty hunter, for example. Unfortunately, none such is to be found on Ansion." He sat brooding for a long moment.

"Slatt!" he finally exclaimed. "There is one good thing to come out of this fiasco, anyway. Thanks to the efforts of the Jedi, there are few survivors to claim their pay."

"Then if you are done with me, O Great One, I have much work to do." Ogomoor started to back out of the room. "The shipment of tweare skins from Aviprine is due to arrive—"

"Not so fast." Reluctantly, the majordomo was obliged to pause in his retreat. "I expect you to keep on top of this, Ogomoor. It's a wise merchant who misses no opportunity. Let's see some of that deviousness your tribe is famed for possessing. This business of putting a stop to Jedi interference takes precedence over everything else, including the shipment of tweare skins. I will expect regular reports. Whatever you need, requisition it and I will provide the necessary authorization. These visitors must be stopped, or there will be consequences for all of us! Do I make myself perfectly clear?"

Ogomoor bowed low. "Completely."

The Hutt puffed up importantly, like a toad much afflicted with pride. "I always do."

"To the greater edification of those of us who serve you, O Most Great and Wise Patron."

Having finally made good his flight from the room with rank and all body parts intact, Ogomoor resolutely ignored the multi-species giggling that followed him as he headed for his own office. There was nothing to worry about, he told himself. It was no big deal. All he had to do to retain his employer's trust and appreciation was oversee the demise of two Jedi Knights and their wily Padawans. Why, any country ignoramus could perform such a task using only half a brain.

Because that was what an angry Jedi would leave to him, a distraught Ogomoor knew. Still, there might be a way. What was it that overstuffed bag of smarmy suet had said? Something about the difficulty of sneaking up on and surprising a Jedi? Might there not be a way to counteract such a remarkable talent?

Or better yet, to outflank it?

"It didn't work." Soergg slumped before the comm station. The Hutt had considerable respect for the small biped whose hologram he was addressing. Not because of her personality, but because of Shu Mai's wide-ranging accomplishments in the field of commerce.

"What happened?" the president of the Commerce Guild asked curtly.

"The second Jedi and his Padawan arrived earlier than expected, and prevented the execution of the first." Soergg leaned closer to the comm. "The information I was given was faulty. Many hirelings were lost." He chuffed importantly. "I have incurred expenses."

Shu Mai was unforgiving. "Don't blame me for your failure. You were provided with the most up-to-date information available. Do you think tracking the movements of individual Jedi is like following a courtesan around a dance floor? They don't publicize their comings and goings, you know." Her apprehension was clear. "Now I have to pass this disagreeable information along to another. What do you plan to do to rectify this miserable failure?"

"The matter is being pursued. The Jedi will not be allowed to prevent Ansion's secession."

"Ansion is your chosen homeworld," Shu Mai reminded the Hutt. "Don't you care if it stays in the Republic or not?"

Soergg made a rude noise. "A Hutt's home is where his business interests lie."

The president of the Commerce Guild nodded. "Even the members of the Trade Federation are not so mercenary."

"Fine words, coming from the one whose organization covered up the niobarium pollution on Vorian Four."

Shu Mai's expression widened. "You know about that? For one with access to such restricted information, I would think the elimination of a couple of Jedi—and their Padawans—would be a simple matter."

"It would," Soergg agreed, "if I could get proper help. Can you not send me suitable individuals?"

Shu Mai shook her head. "I am under strict instructions to avoid any action that might draw additional attention from the Jedi Council. Sending in offworld professionals is precisely the kind of action that would do so. Our friend would be hard-pressed to explain away such an action. You will have to make do with what you can hire locally. I was assured that you could. That is why you were engaged."

"This is not an easy business," Soergg complained bitterly.

The president of the Commerce Guild leaned close to her holo pickup, so that her face filled the imager. "I will make you a deal, Hutt. Trade positions with me. I will take care of these meddlesome Jedi, and you come here and deal with the one to whom *I* must report."

Soergg thought about it—but not for very long. The Hutts had not achieved all that they had by being fools. Besides, there was always the possibility that if Shu Mai became too intemperate, too insistent, she could be bypassed. One could go over her head.

Did Soergg want to do that? He was not at all certain he really wished to know who was backing the impatient Commerce Guild. Not on a personal level, anyway.

"I sense agitation, anxiety, and outright hostility," Obi-Wan said.

Anakin trailing dutifully behind him, Obi-Wan led the way toward the municipal hall of the city of Cuipernam, where they were to meet formally for the first time with deputies of the Unity of Community—the loosely bound political entity that represented the scattered city-states of Ansion and was the closest thing the world they were visiting had to a recognizable planetary government. The same ersatz planetary government, he reminded himself, that was threatening to secede from the Republic—and as a consequence, possibly take dozens of other systems with it.

Luminara nodded. "In other words, a bunch of nervous politicians." She glanced over at Barriss. "There are certain constants that remain the same throughout the galaxy, my dear. The speed of light, the motion of muons, and the unwillingness of politicians to commit to anything that requires a leap of personal responsibility."

As always, the Padawan listened thoughtfully before responding. "Then how do we persuade them of the rightness of the galactic government's ways, and that it's in their best interests to remain a part of the Republic?"

"Sometimes it seems as if money works best." Obi-Wan's tone was quietly sardonic. "But regardless of what goes on in the Senate these days, that is not the way of the Jedi. Unlike politicians, we cannot offer to buy the loyalty of these people with promises of financial aid and elaborate development projects. Instead, we are restricted to the use of reason and common sense. If all goes well, they will respond to these as enthusiastically as they do to ready cash."

There was no need for guards or clerks to announce the visitors to the assembled representatives; they were expected. The municipal hall itself was impressive by Cuipernam standards: long and high, the upper reaches of the second story lined with scenes of Ansionian life rendered effectively in stained quartz. No doubt it served to impress petitioning citizens. On Coruscant, Obi-Wan reflected, it would not have drawn a curious yawn from a bored passing traveler. The difference in scale and aesthetics did not make him feel bigger or more important than the locals. Very early in his training, he had come to realize the insignificance and unimportance of mere physical achievements. Anyone could buy expensive attire and fancy accoutrements, live in a big house, command legions of servants both organic and mechanical. Wisdom was much harder to come by.

Nevertheless, the four visitors dutifully admired their surroundings, complimenting the female who came forward to extend them formal greetings. Seated at a long table cut from a single piece of purplish xellwood, seven delegates awaited them. Two were human, four indigenous Ansionian, and one Armalat.

Luminara studied the Ansionians carefully. Slightly shorter on average than humans, the dominant native species of Ansion was much slimmer, wiry and lean, with skin a pale yellow that was almost golden. Both genders were hairless except for a single startlingly dense brush of fur about fifteen centimeters wide and seven or eight high that ran from the top of their foreheads all the way down their backs to terminate in a fifteen-centimeter-long tail. Beneath their warm, well-made clothing the sweep of hair, which varied in color across the entire visible spectrum, was usually kept neatly trimmed. The large eyes with their small black pupils were usually red, sometimes shading to lighter tones of yellow or, in rarer instances, mauve. The numerous teeth were noticeably sharp. Though omnivorous, the Ansionians ate proportionately more meat than humans.

Particularly, she reminded herself, the Alwari.

There was no one in the chamber to represent the interests of the nomads, of course. They shunned the cities and towns, preferring their life out on the immense prairies that dominated much of Ansionian topography. After millennia of constant conflict between nomads and city folk, a tenuous peace had finally been established two hundred local years ago. Now the exigencies of interstellar politics threatened to tear that fragile concord to shreds and drag Ansion out of the Republic entirely.

The nomads wished to remain under the Republic's protection. Chafing against the weight of regulations and petty rules that seemed to pour forth from Coruscant in a never-ending stream, the urbanites were considering joining the nascent secessionist movement. The result was fresh estrangement between nomads and city dwellers. If they could reconcile these opposing views, Luminara knew, Ansion would probably stay within the Republic. As was ever the case through history, local conflicts threatened to expand beyond their boundaries. It was likely that neither side in this internal dispute truly grasped the far larger issues that were at stake. The intensifying argument between city dwellers and nomads had galactic ramifications.

Not only those who were bound to it through formal pact and treaty, but others, too, were watching to see what happened on Ansion. Due to its strategic location and entanglement of alliances, it was a key world in this part of the Republic. Remove a small plug from a dam holding back agitated waters, she knew, and an unexpectedly great flood can result.

The Ansionian who rose from behind the table gestured a formal local greeting. The other delegates, Luminara noted, did not rise.

"I am Ranjiyn. Like my colleagues, a representative of the Unity, of Ansion's city and town dwellers." Most Ansionians used only one name, she knew. His mane was dyed in alternating black and white stripes. He proceeded to introduce his fellow delegates. One did not have to be a master of the Force to note their wariness. When he had finished the introductions, he concluded, "We of the towns and cities welcome you, the representatives of the Jedi Council, to Ansion and extend to you all the hospitality and cooperation of which we are capable."

Fine words, Anakin thought. Master Obi-Wan had spent much time trying to satisfy his Padawan's curiosity about politics. One of the first things a student of that odious subject learned was that words were among the cheaper currencies employed by politicians, and therefore one they felt free to spend lavishly.

Meanwhile, Luminara was replying. She certainly was unusual for a Jedi, he thought. In her own way, she could be as intimidating as Obi-Wan. At least she was openly friendly and understanding, which was more than could be said for her by-the-book Padawan Barriss.

"On behalf of the Jedi Council, Obi-Wan Kenobi and I, Luminara Unduli, thank you for ourselves and our Padawans, Anakin Skywalker and Barriss Offee." She and her companions took seats on the other side of the beautiful table, opposite their hosts. "As you know, we are here to try to mediate this dispute between the urban inhabitants of your world and the Alwari nomads."

"Please." A tall, dignified older man waved one hand diffidently. "None of your Jedi subterfuges. We all know you are here to do anything and everything in your power to keep Ansion from voting to join the secessionist movement. Local quarrels of the kind to which you allude are not the purview of the Jedi Council." He smiled confidently. "In any event, they would not send four representatives to deal with what is essentially a minor internal problem."

"No conflict is minor to the Council," Obi-Wan responded. "We hope to see all citizens of the Republic living together in peace and contentment, wherever they may be, whatever species they may represent, whatever their local customs and lifestyles."

"Contentment!" Reaching under the table, one of the other Ansionians, a female with long vertical lines in her face and one clouded brown eye, pulled out a stack of data disks the size of a building stone and dropped them onto the highly polished surface. They landed with a dull boom. "Lifestyles! Do you know what this is, Jedi?" Before either Luminara or Obi-Wan could reply, she told them. "It's the latest bimonthly policy update from the Republic Senate. The latest only!" She gestured at the enormous stack as if it were some obscene sea creature that had suddenly expired on her desk and already begun to rot. "The yearly indices alone carry more data than the city library. Compliance, adherence, obedience: those are what the Senate is interested in these days. That, and preferential treatment for themselves and those they represent in matters of trade and commerce. The once-great galactic Republic has fallen under the sway of petty bureaucrats and self-seeking button pushers who seek only personal aggrandizement and advancement, not justice and fair dealing."

"The Senate's clear bias toward the Alwari proves this," de-

clared the female Ansionian seated next to her. "Senator Mousul
has kept us well informed."

"The Senate favors no social or ethnic group above another,"
Luminara countered. "That basic principle is enshrined in the
founding law of the Republic and has not changed."

"I happen to agree with the delegate," Obi-Wan declared
quietly.

Surprised and even a little startled, the room's occupants
shifted their attention to the other Jedi. Even Luminara was
taken aback.

"Pardon my eyes," Ranjiyn murmured, "but did you say you
agreed with Kandah?"

Obi-Wan nodded. "To deny that there are problems within
the Senate and the bureaucracy would be to deny the existence of
pulsating stars. Certainly there is confusion and disagreement.
Certainly there is bureaucratic infighting and conflict." His voice
rose slightly, though not in the general manner of other people.
It was full of controlled energy. "But the law of the Republic
stands, pure and inviolate. So long as all participating sentients
adhere to that, all will be well within the galaxy." His gaze fixed
on Kandah. "And on Ansion."

Seated at the end of the table because his massive legs would
not comfortably fit under it, Tolut the Armalat finally rose to
point one of his three thick fingers at Obi-Wan.

"Jedi obfuscation!" He glared out of small red eyes at his fellow delegates. "See not where this is leading or what is being
attempted? They try to fool us with clever words. Think all Ansionians are backworld dust riders, I wager!" Leaning forward over
the table, he rested the knuckles of his powerful hands on the
smooth purplish wood. Though strong and well made, the table
creaked under the weight of his several hundred kilos.

"Masters of the Force, are you? Masters of scheming and sneaky phrases, say I. Jedi mischief!"

"Please, Tolut." Ranjiyn tried to calm his far larger, highly agitated colleague. "Show some respect for the Force, if not for our visitors. Though we may disagree, we still—"

"*Pagh!* 'The Force.' You all bemused and intimidated by this Force nonsense." Green fingers stabbed at the silent visitors. "These are humanoids, like yourself. Sentients, like me. They bleed and die like any creatures of flesh and blood. Why should we continue to suffer beneath their burdensome rules? Their officials are corrupt, or ignorant of the needs of different species, or both. When a government becomes like an old sea creature, it should be treated like one." Thick, chisel-like teeth flashed. "Taken out and buried." Reaching across the table, he picked up in one hand the massive stack Kandah had brought forth and threw it across the room, where it slammed against a wall, disks scattering everywhere.

"Regulations! Restrictions! What can be done by peoples and what cannot. All words—words we of Ansion not write. This movement to leave the Republic we should join, say I and those who think like me. Free Ansion! And if the Alwari will not join us in this, we should deal with them as we have in the past."

Throughout the tirade, the visitors had sat silently. Now Anakin's hand strayed in the direction of his lightsaber. A hint of a smile from his Master was all that was necessary to still the movement. Not that Anakin cared particularly whether Ansion stayed in the Republic or not. The convoluted machinations of galactic politics were still a mystery to him. It was the insult to his Master that caused the anger to rise within him. Now he forced himself to remain calm—because his Master wished that he be so.

Obi-Wan Kenobi, he knew, was quite capable of taking care of himself.

The Jedi Knight started to rise, but somewhat to Anakin's surprise deferred to the woman seated next to him. "The Force is nothing to be so casually disparaged, my large friend," Luminara informed the Armalat. "Especially by one who has no understanding of it."

Once again showing his huge, flat white teeth in a broad grin, Tolut started around the table. Barriss and Anakin both tensed, but Obi-Wan sat quietly, indifferent to the approach of the massive, powerful Armalat. A small smile played across his face. Luminara rose and stepped away from her chair.

"Think you only Jedi know the Force?" Tolut snorted at his fellow delegates. "Anyone can know it. It only takes practice." Extending a huge hand, he gestured at the table. One of the several crystal carafes of water that had been placed there to slake the thirst of the participants trembled slightly, then rose half a meter off the surface. Sweat starting to seep from his cheeks in large, glossy beads, Tolut smiled triumphantly at his friends.

"See! With exercise and will, anyone can do what Jedi can do. Hardly reason for awe!"

"On the contrary," Luminara told him, "knowledge is always reason for awe." She did not raise her hand. She did not have to.

The carafe stopped trembling, steadied. As Luminara focused on it, it rose slowly until it reached the ceiling. Fascinated, the delegates could not take their eyes off it. Living as they did in a border world, none of them had previously had the opportunity to observe Jedi manipulation of the Force.

Like a bulbous crystal bird, the carafe drifted along the ceiling until it was poised directly above the Armalat. Grim-faced, he began to make ponderous, then frantic gestures in the hovering container's direction. These had absolutely no effect on the floating object. He might as well have been gesticulating in front of a mirror.

As smoothly as if manipulated by an experienced waiter, the carafe abruptly turned upside down and dumped its ice-cold contents on the increasingly frustrated alien. Glaring, he wiped water from his eyes and took a step toward the serene Jedi. Barriss reached for her lightsaber, only to be stilled by her Master, much as Obi-Wan had earlier restrained his own Padawan.

One by one, the remaining carafes leapt off the table to dash their contents in Tolut's face. Laughter began to rise from the remaining seated, and still dry, delegates, the humans chortling softly, the Ansionians emitting boisterous bellows that belied their wiry frames. The tension that had enveloped the summit like a smothering spiderweb promptly vanished.

"I hope," Luminara murmured as she turned away and resumed her seat, "that no one is particularly thirsty."

Sputtering and soaked, the big alien growled dangerously—and then a change washed over him. Dripping water from face, teeth, and now glistening leather attire, he stomped back to his chair and sat down in a somewhat soggy frump. Folding arms the size of a human's torso across his massive chest, he nodded slowly in the direction of the woman responsible for his aqueous humiliation.

"Tolut is big among his people. Don't always speak so good. But big doesn't always mean stupid. Tolut knows when he wrong. I defer to greater power. Was wrong about Jedi abilities."

Luminara favored him with a kindly smile. "There is no shame in admitting one does not know everything. It shows wisdom. That is a much more valued talent than physical strength—

or even the ability to influence the Force. You are to be commended, not condemned." She bowed her head slightly. "I congratulate you on the acuteness of your perception."

Tolut hesitated, at first uncertain if the Jedi was making fun of him. When he realized that the compliment was meant honestly, and came from the heart, his glower softened and his demeanor changed.

"Perhaps we of the Unity can work with you." A hint of his earlier belligerence threatened a return despite the lesson that had just been imparted. "But working with the Alwari is something else."

Leaning toward Anakin, Obi-Wan whispered softly. "And that, my young Padawan, was a demonstration of what is known as dynamic diplomacy."

Skywalker nodded briefly. "Example noted, Master." He studied the tranquil, beautiful face of Luminara Unduli afresh. He did not notice the "I-told-you-so" look on Barriss's face. Her expression strayed dangerously close to a smirk.

Wiping a last tear of amusement from the corner of one eye, Ranjiyn strove to recapture the serious tone that had preceded the watery demonstration. "It doesn't matter what you do. A thousand tapcaf tricks will not persuade the Alwari to allow us to jointly exploit the prairies. That is the only way we of the Unity will agree to remain bound by Republic law; if we are treated as equals everywhere on the planet, and not like people who are hemmed in forever in our towns. As it stands, the Alwari dominate by far the great bulk of the land, while we control the cities. If they are going to run bleating to the Senate every time we try to expand, then we are better off outside the Republic and free of its endless, pestiferous rules and regulations."

"It seems to me that would mean interminable local war,"

Anakin spoke out. At a look from Obi-Wan he thought further and added, "Or at least some form of continuous, running conflict between you and the Alwari."

"It would be debilitating for both of you," Barriss added as Luminara looked on approvingly.

From his seat, the tall, elder human male gestured resignedly. "Anything is better than being forced to bow beneath oppressive regulations that take a hundred years just to get out of committee. We have been assured by friends that if we were to announce our secession from the Republic, the kind of aid that we truly need—and that the Senate does not provide—would be readily forthcoming."

"What friends?" Obi-Wan inquired pleasantly. His tone made it sound as if the answer was of no particular consequence, but Anakin knew differently. He could see the slight tenseness in his Master's posture.

Whether the Ansionian representative detected it or not they never knew. In any event, he did not supply names.

Luminara filled the pause that ensued. "Anything may be better—except peace." She eyed each of the skeptical representatives in turn. "In our capacity as representatives of the Jedi Council, we have a proposition for you. If we can get the Alwari to agree to share dominion over half or more of the prairie lands they presently control, and to allow you to develop some of the resources that lie within those lands, will the people of the Unity agree to abide by the Republic law under which they have always lived, and to forget this dangerous talk of secession?"

At this unexpected and extraordinary offer, the delegates fell to murmuring among themselves. Their tone, their expressions, and their repressed excitement showed that they had not considered so sweeping a proposal before.

While they caucused, Obi-Wan leaned over to whisper to his colleague. "You promise much, Luminara."

She adjusted the thrown-back hood of her robe. "I spent a lot of time prior to arriving on this world studying the history of Ansion's peoples. Something extreme has to be done to break this local sociopolitical datajam. It's the only way to get these people thinking about something besides leaving the Republic." She smiled. "I thought laying out the possibility of a whole new, vast commercial opportunity before them would shake them up a little."

Obi-Wan studied the quietly deliberating delegates. The animation in their expressions and gestures was genuine, and not simply a display for the benefit of the four visitors.

"Looks like you've certainly done that." He added that small, sly smile with which she was rapidly becoming familiar. "Of course, if they accept, you've put us in the awkward position of having to deliver."

"Master Luminara always fulfills her promises." There was just a touch of sharpness in Barriss's voice.

"I've no doubt she does." Obi-Wan regarded the Padawan tolerantly. "It's getting these innumerable, fractious, quarrelsome nomads who call themselves the Alwari to abide by the proposed terms that concerns me."

Luminara interrupted the exchange with a slight nod. The delegates had concluded their vigorous conversation and once more sat facing the visitors.

"No one doubts that obtaining the agreement of the Alwari to such an accord would radically change the social dynamic that exists here." It was the third Ansionian representative, a female named Induran, who spoke. "And if such a treaty could be achieved, it would certainly tilt the opinion of many of those who

are presently inclined to favor secession from the Republic because they believe remaining in it does nothing for them." Her
large, convex eyes gazed unflinchingly at the Jedi. "However, the
likelihood of obtaining the hand of the Alwari to such an agreement the majority of us find doubtful in the extreme."

It was the formerly bellicose Tolut who rose to the visitors'
defense. "For those who can make it rain indoors, even such a
thing as rational dialogue with the Alwari may be possible."

Luminara smiled at the burly alien. Confrontational he might
be, but at least he was flexible enough to change his position
when the facts warranted his doing so. That was more than could
be said, so far, for his human and Ansionian colleagues—though
they were weakening. One could feel the subtle change in the
mental atmosphere in the chamber. It was as if, though fed up
with the convoluted workings and the oppressive bureaucracy of
the Republic, they *wanted* to believe in it. It was up to her and
Obi-Wan, together with their respective Padawans, to bring the
members of the delegation around.

Everything now hinged on gaining the full cooperation of
these Alwari nomads. Somehow she felt that was going to entail
more than sitting in a comfortable room performing tricks with
jugs of water.

"How do we find the Alwari?" Anakin queried, showing
impatience.

Luminara's gaze narrowed as she regarded the Padawan.
One could sense the strength of the Force within him, as well as
other potentialities. Though she knew little about him, she knew
that Obi-Wan Kenobi would not take on a Padawan who did not
show considerable promise. He was just the Jedi to rein such a
headstrong youth in, to take the sharp edges off the rough dia-
mond and polish him into a true Jedi. There was nothing wrong

with the Padawan's words, or with him speaking out. It was only that there was a fine line between confident and headstrong, between bold and arrogant. Glancing slightly to her right, she saw that Barriss visibly disapproved of her male counterpart. Well, the young woman would keep her doubts to herself—unless Skywalker provoked her. Barriss was reserved by nature, but she was not easily intimidated. Especially by another Padawan.

Ranjiyn did not hesitate. "Go east. Or west, or any other direction. Go away from civilization. Leave the cities behind." He ventured the thin Ansionian version of a smile. "You will find the Alwari. Or they will find *you*. I wish I could be there to watch you try to talk sense into them. That would be something to see."

"Something to see," Tolut grunted in agreement.

Luminara and Obi-Wan rose simultaneously. The conference was at an end. "You know our reputation," Obi-Wan said. "We have put it behind our words thousands of times before. This will be no different. Dealing with your Alwari can't be any more frustrating than trying to negotiate the traffic patterns on Coruscant." His expression twisted at the memory of his last visit. He didn't much care for intracity travel.

The mention of urban confusion further solidified the growing, if wary, rapport that had developed during the conference between visitors and delegates—which was of course precisely why he had alluded to it. Official business concluded, visitors and delegates alike chatted amiably for another hour, both sides grateful for the chance to learn something more of one another off the record and on a personal level. In particular, the now nearly dried-out Tolut had taken a special shine to Luminara. She tolerated the hulking delegate's proximity without concern. In the course of her career she had been required to make friends with far more obnoxious sentients.

While engaged in her own conversations, she noted with admiration how Obi-Wan Kenobi put others at ease. For all his vaunted skills and experience, his was a personality others found nonthreatening. His tone was understated, while his words fell on the ears of others as gently as a therapeutic massage. If he had not become a Jedi, she mused, he would have been a great credit to the diplomatic service.

But that would have meant a career in the very bureaucracy that they both decried, the consequences of whose blundering and stumbling they were both here to try to smooth over.

Barriss was doing her best to charm both Ranjiyn and the elder human representative, while Anakin was spouting a streak of self-assurance at the other human. The woman listened intently to everything he said, more engrossed in his words than Luminara would have expected. She would have listened in, but she had Tolut and the still-suspicious Kandah to try to win over. Anyway, if Anakin needed monitoring, that was Obi-Wan's job, not hers.

If only, she reflected, succeeding in their mission here could be reduced to a matter of choosing the right phrases. Unfortunately, she had been involved in too many disputes on too many unruly worlds to believe that the quandary of Ansion would be solved by shrewd words alone.

Delegate Kandah, of the Unity of Community that represented the urban citizens of Ansion, waited uneasily in the dark passageway. Beyond, the lights of Songoquin Street, with its chanting vendors and night-strolling patrons, beckoned. Like all her big-eyed kind, she was comfortable moving about even on moonless nights. But in such a restricted defile, with only one way in and out, even a night-sighted Ansionian might be for-given for wishing for a little more illumination.

"What have you for me?" Though she recognized the voice immediately, the abruptness of it snapping unannounced out of the darkness startled her. "What of the meeting between the visi-tors and the representatives of the Unity?"

"It went all too well." She did not know the identity of the contact with whom she was speaking, much less his name. She could not even be sure it was a he. None of that mattered. What was important was that he paid handsomely, without delay, and in untraceable credits. "The delegation was mistrustful and skep-tical at first. I did my personal best to sow confusion and dissent. But the Jedi are as clever with words as they are with the Force. I'm certain they have convinced that stupid Armalat to vote on their behalf. The others continue to vacillate." She proceeded to describe in detail the rest of the meeting.

"So the Jedi intend to try to persuade the Alwari to allow ex-ploration and development on up to half the traditional nomad prairie lands?" Incredulous laughter echoed from the shadows. "That would be something! They have no chance of doing so, of course."

"I would have thought so, too," she whispered into the gloom, "until I met them for myself and saw how they operate. They are subtle, as well as shrewd."

The voice hesitated before responding. "You don't mean to say you believe they might actually secure such an agreement with the Alwari?"

"I mean to say that these are true Jedi, and I am not qualified to predict *what* they might or might not accomplish. I *can* say that I would not bet against them—in anything."

"Jedi are famed as fighters, not talkers," the voice muttered uneasily.

"Is that so?" Kandah recalled more details of the conference. "These Knights and their Padawans are suavity made solid. As for what you say, how many Jedi have you seen in action? Of any kind?"

"Never mind what I have seen or not seen." The voice's owner was clearly irritated, though not with his supplier of information. "I must convey this information to my patron. He will know what to do."

Will he indeed? thought Kandah. *Better him than me.* All she had to do was deliver a report. She was glad her attempt to frustrate the Jedi's mission did not require that she go any farther.

"Your payment will be deposited in the usual manner." The voice spoke offhandedly, clearly preoccupied with all that the Unity delegate had told him. "As always, your good work is appreciated. When Ansion at last stands outside the Republic and free of its interference, you will receive your just reward. Your unfairly appropriated family estates in Korumdah will be restored to you."

"I am your humble servant," Kandah replied politely. Turning to leave, she hesitated. "What do you think your patron will do to try to stop these Jedi from succeeding in their task, now that the attempt at direct assassination has failed so ignobly?"

No reply was forthcoming from the darkness. Having swirled his dustcape securely around him, Ogomoor had already vanished into the night.

"So the Jedi intend to keep the Unity within the Republic by settling their differences with the Alwari. A bold plan."

"Also a stupid one, Your Greatness."

"Is it?" Soergg glanced over from the lounge on which he was relaxing. Outside, one of Ansion's small moons waxed ivory.

"It hasn't a chance of succeeding."

"Hasn't it?"

Sensing that he was rapidly losing argumentative ground, Ogomoor decided to change tactics. "What would you have me do?" He considered. "I could try to bribe one or more of them."

Huge, slitted eyes rolled ceilingward. "Bribe a Jedi! You really are ignorant, aren't you, Ogomoor?"

Swallowing both his suggestion and his pride, the major-domo replied deferentially, "Yes. I would be grateful if you would enlighten your humble servant."

"I will." Generating a disgusting squinching sound, the Hutt rolled onto his right side, the better to regard his employee. "Know this: Jedi cannot be bribed, connived, broken, or swayed from what they believe to be the right and true course of the way. At least, such has been my experience." He spat to one side, and the custodial droid rushed from its resting place to clean up the repulsive gob. "This is a shame, but many truths often are. Therefore, we must deal with them elsewise. Come close, and I will tell you how."

Must I? Ogomoor thought. But there was no more escaping the Hutt's breath than there was his orders.

I am not, Ogomoor reflected as he stood bravely absorbing the full force of that noxious miasma, *being paid enough for this.*

One of the advantages of living and working on Coruscant was that there were innumerable places to meet, if one did not want to be located. So it was that the little group found themselves in a small drinking establishment of no special reputation in an unfashionable part of Quadrant H-46. In such places, there was less of an immediate need to preserve one's anonymity. In any event, none of them was recognized by the other patrons as they wandered in.

"This places stinks of the working classes," Nemrileo, who hailed from the powerful world of Tanjay, sniffed. "It will hide the smell of treason."

Senator Mousul had to smile. "You talk of committing treason against the treasoners. Don't get your loyalties confused, Nemrileo. Now is not the time."

"You don't have to tell me about time." The man hunched lower over the table. "But this Ansion business is beginning to worry me."

"It should not." Mousul exuded assurance—an easy thing,

his questioner mused, since the interests supporting them had promised to back Mousul for the governorship of his entire sector once Ansion and its allies had withdrawn from the Republic. "I am confident that everything is proceeding as planned, and that within a very short time the dominant political force on my world, the Unity of cities and towns, will vote for full withdrawal from the Republic, thus setting in motion all that we hope for."

" 'Everything'?" said an alien female politician whose explosion of straw-colored fur threatened to burst forth from within her tight-fitting camouflaging suit. "That's not what I hear."

Mousul gestured indifferently. "A minor glitch. Nothing to be concerned about."

"I admire your assurance," the alien female declared. "Not everyone would be so casual upon learning of the arrival on their homeworld of two Jedi, together with their Padawans, in the midst of the most delicate negotiations over secession."

"I told you." Mousul's tone turned darker. "It is being dealt with."

"It had better be," Tam Uliss, a business associate from Ansion, declared. "My people are growing impatient. They are ready to move, have been for some time, and dislike having to wait upon the decision of a bunch of minor sentients from a decidedly minor world."

"The president of the Commerce Guild would not like to hear such talk."

"That's why we called this meeting," muttered the alien female politician. "So we could discuss possibilities without her." Her yellow eyes burned into his. "And if you weren't similarly interested, you wouldn't be here now."

The Senator raised a cautioning hand. "I said I would come to listen, and to apprise you of our progress in the Ansion matter.

I make no judgments. But if Shu Mai says we should restrain our interests until Ansion has declared for secession, then I believe we should listen to her."

"Should we?" Another of the group showed by his expression as much as by his words that he felt otherwise. "Can Shu Mai and the Commerce Guild truly be trusted?"

"You haven't met her," Mousul replied. "Be assured that she can. She has all our best interests at heart."

"Does she really?" Nemrileo was not so sure. "From what I've heard, she doesn't have a heart."

"I trust her," announced the female politician seated next to the cynic. "I know her from her work in our quadrant. What I *don't* trust are my own constituents."

There was laughter from around the private table. "Trust constituents . . ." ". . . how very droll!" As soon as the mirth had faded, Mousul spoke anew.

"I have been in touch with my principal contact on Ansion. He assures me the Jedi will be dealt with. Shu Mai continues to show confidence in this individual as well. There are social and commercial bonds that affirm our mutual contract. I suggest you all return to your positions and be of good cheer. All our hopes will be realized soon enough."

"To be at last free of the corruption and vices of this bloated, inert, so-called Republic!" Tam Uliss exclaimed. "Truly a dream to be wished."

The Senator looked around the circle. "We are all of the same opinion. And we are fortunate to have someone who believes in our cause as strongly as Shu Mai does to mediate for us with others who for now must remain nameless." He passed a hand over the table's response plate. "Now, let us all relax and have something to drink. It's rare enough that we're able to gather together like this."

Tension dissolved after the first few rounds of drinks. In the company of his fellow conspirators, Mousul was also able to relax. He would be more relaxed still after he reported to Shu Mai on the one member of their group whom he felt they could no longer trust. A lack of trust was a bad thing in a conspiracy. It poisoned the atmosphere of cooperation. It could prove fatal.

Especially to the individual in question.

Soergg was well pleased with the final plan that had been devised. It had been carefully thought out, honed and refined, until he could see nothing wrong with it. It possessed the twin virtues of simplicity and directness. He explained it assertively to Ogomoor. His majordomo listened carefully. Only when the Hutt had finished did the Ansionian timidly venture to comment.

"It certainly sounds most promising."

"Promising?" the bossban rumbled. "It's perfect!" He glowered down at the complaisant biped. "Isn't it?"

"Well, the only obstacle I see lies in this ability of the Jedi to intuit danger coming their way. To sense trouble as a disturbance in the Force."

Soergg nodded as much as one could who had no neck. "I am all too aware of the cursed Jedi abilities. So to carry out this plan I have engaged two who are immune to such Jedi perceptiveness. Two of your own kind who possess unique qualifications."

"Not to dispute your expertise, but how can any thinking, feeling sentients be impervious to Jedi acuity?"

"Meet them, Ogomoor, and judge for yourself." Looking off to one side, he clapped his large, flabby palms together and raised his voice. "Bulgan, Kyakhta—come and meet my majordomo!"

Expectant and curious, Ogomoor turned toward the doorway that led from the bossban's audience chamber to a side waiting room. The aspect of the two Ansionians who entered in response to Soergg's call did not fill him with overwhelming confidence.

One had a ripped and ragged mane of splotchy auburn and a crudely fashioned artificial arm. The other was completely shorn from head to spine, bald and pallid of skin, with a patch over one eye and a back permanently bent from some incurable childhood disease. Neither was especially tall or strong. Together, Ogomoor decided, the pair would have been hard-pressed to kidnap the offspring of an elderly water carrier.

So astonished was he by the sight of the forlorn duo that for a moment he forgot his fear of his employer. "Bossban, you're going to send *these* two to capture a Jedi?"

"Not a Jedi, Ogomoor. One of their Padawans. With one of the two youths in our custody, the Jedi will be forced to parley." He puffed himself up to his full, impressive—if loathsome—size. "We will demand they withdraw from all negotiations involving Ansion's domestic and galactic disputations, and that no new Jedi come to take their place. Once they agree to that, they will be helpless to affect the outcome of the vote for secession. One Jedi's word binds all Jedi." He all but rubbed his hands together. "This is even better than killing them. They will be forced to leave in disgrace and failure, with their tails tucked between their legs. At the same time, the Jedi Council will not rise up in rage against the deaths of several of their Order. They will simply have been outmaneuvered, and out-thought. By me." He puffed up so much that Ogomoor thought the Hutt might explode. Unfortunately, it remained nothing more than a wishful image. "Sometimes humiliation is more effective than death."

"I do not disagree, Bossban." Recovering some fortitude, Ogomoor indicated the two proposed hostage takers. The one called

Kyakhta was gaping openmouthed at the room's luxurious furnishings, while his bent-backed companion Bulgan stood staring blankly at the floor, flagrantly picking his single nostril. "But seriously, you are sending these two to overpower a Jedi Padawan?"

Instead of roaring, Soergg held his patience. "Look at them, Ogomoor. Take a good, close look. What do you see?" Clearly, the Hutt was enjoying his employee's bewilderment.

Dubiously, and without getting any closer than was absolutely necessary, the majordomo scrutinized the shiftless pair. Closer inspection did not produce encouragement. "At the risk of insulting your judgment, if not them, O Bossban, I would say that they appear to be slightly *felek*. Mentally deranged. Addled."

"Indeed they are. Just enough." Looking hugely pleased with himself, as well as more than usually huge, Soergg leaned back on his tail. "In the course of carrying out research for my many business interests, I have discovered that even a minor mental illness is sometimes sufficient to confuse perception of the Force in those who are capable of it. Psychosis acts like a fogged piece of transparisteel, distorting but not completely hiding what lies beyond." He gestured at his new hirelings. Bulgan smiled vacantly in response. "These two are indeed slightly mad. In their madness lies the secret of our success."

Enlightened, Ogomoor eyed the pair with fresh interest, if not increased respect. "I've been trying to place their garb. While they're obviously Alwari, I have to admit I don't recognize their clans."

"That is hardly surprising," Soergg grunted, "since they have no clans. Because of their physical and mental infirmities, they have been cast out. Sent to live in the hated cities, where they eke out a living doing whatever work comes their way." He beamed as much as a Hutt could beam. "With what I have agreed to pay them, they will do anything I ask. Anything! Even attempt to capture a Jedi Padawan." He snorted derisively. "Like so many, credits mean more to them than morals."

Including a people called the Hutts, Ogomoor thought.

"That's so, it is," declared Bulgan, speaking for the first time. His words were somewhat difficult to understand as he still had one finger up his nose.

"We'll do it." The elocution of his one-armed companion Kyakhta was somewhat better, being uninfracted by the kind of digital nasal blockage that was presently afflicting his companion. "We can do it." As Kyakhta spoke, Bulgan blinked his one good eye; the thick, opaque Ansionian lid flashing meaningfully from left to right.

"The Jedi will not be able to sense their approach." Soergg was visibly reveling in the inimitability of his plan.

"Not via the Force, perhaps, Bossban. But the humans still have eyes, and reactions more sharply honed than those of most sentients."

The Hutt nodded patiently, having thought it all out in advance. "Our friends here will flatch the snatch late in the day. Even Jedi require the occasional break from their duties. The four who trouble us have been observed taking in the sights of Cuipernam. As they do so, sometimes they separate. Jedi they may be, but they are still of two different genders. The females often seek out different things than the males. If a younger Padawan can be caught out a distance away from its Master, the abduction may be accomplished. Most Jedi, so it is said, rely on their senses to warn them when danger approaches. Sensing no danger in these two idiots, they will ignore them as they continue with their sight-seeing." With an imperious wave of one hand, he dismissed the two addled but willing kidnappers.

"Go now! You know where the visitors stay." He smiled unpleasantly. "Everyone knows, as they are official guests of the Unity delegation and the city council of Cuipernam. If you succeed, take the Padawan to the chosen place and wait there for my further orders."

Kyakhta turned and bowed. When Bulgan did not, his companion smacked the other clanless one on the back of his bald skull. Bulgan then turned and, being already bent, did not have to bow. But he did at least remove his finger from his nose. Together, they backed out of the room through the door that had granted them admittance. Ogomoor was still dubious—but a flicker of anticipation had begun to burn within him.

"An audacious plan, to be sure, Bossban. But risky."

"What risk?" Lumbering to his right, Soergg shoved a fist into a bowl filled with turgid liquid and fished out something the sight of which made Ogomoor blanch. Unrepentant, the Hutt tilted back his head, dropped the noisome contents of his closed hand into his cavernous maw of a mouth, and swallowed noisily, smacking his lips by way of appreciation. "The risk falls entirely on those two cretins. If they fail, the Jedi will surely kill them."

"And if they do not, but only wound and capture them? Artless as they are, they will surely tell the Jedi who hired them to attempt such a task."

Soergg's great belly heaved as he laughed. "Once they commence the operation, they are to report personally to me at prescribed intervals via closed-band comlink. Two nights ago, while they slept the sleep of the simple, I had my own physician install a small device in the neck of each. Should they fail to report" —he tapped one finger into an open, greasy palm—"I will remotely activate the devices. Before they can give away any incriminating information, the very compact explosive charges contained within will separate their heads from their shoulders. Rather messily, I'm afraid."

"What then, Great One?" Ogomoor was curious to know.

Soergg shrugged, fleshy ripples running in descending waves down his entire flaccid length. "Clanless imbeciles are cheap, even in Cuipernam. If these two fail, we will try again with another pair."

Kyakhta swirled the lightweight, waterproof robes more tightly around him, the better to hide his face. They were the robes of a member of the Pangay Ous. That was not his clan. He and Bulgan were Tasbir, of the Southern Hatagai. But it felt good to be back in clan gear even if it was not his own, even if it had not been earned.

The robes were necessary to allow them to blend in with the crowds that filled the bustling marketplace. Remembering the small device clipped to his waistband beneath the robes, he fingered it briefly, as per the instructions of their master the Hutt. Soergg had been most insistent that they call in regularly. After all, he had informed them, explaining how the explosive devices implanted in their necks worked, if they failed to check in at the appointed time, they would not live long enough to collect their pay. Kyakhta and Bulgan had been deeply touched by this intimate expression of the Hutt's concern for their welfare.

There were larger marketplaces on Ansion than Cuipernam's. In these days of modern intragalactic commerce, the majority of transactions involved little more than an exchange of numbers and symbols. But on many worlds, the old-style, traditional marketplace still retained a warm spot in the hearts of the local inhabitants. Trading by machine might be more efficient, and allow for an infinitely greater variety and volume of goods to be bartered, but there was no joy in it. The delights of doing business face to face remained one of life's small pleasures in an increasingly automated galactic civilization.

Besides, what did a local specialist vendor of marthan fruit need with the expense and complications of an electronic trading nexus? And how many visitors and gawkers and tourists would a portable information shifter draw to a community's downtown? Not to mention that face-to-face business provided a way to avoid many taxes. Among those inhabitants of Ansion who were heartily in favor of secession could be counted many notable merchants. It wasn't so much the taxes themselves that had caused them to distance themselves from the Republic—it was the endless and ever-growing list of rules and regulations. Though these concerns were shared throughout the Republic and had been passed on to the Senate by citizen representatives, like so much else, they seemed never to be acted upon. Isolated and coddled on distant Coruscant, the galactic government had grown ever more divorced from the needs and aspirations of the people it purported to govern.

Kyakhta and Bulgan moved easily through the crowds, though Kyakhta had to keep a close eye on his companion as they wended their way past one stall and shop after another. Innocent that he was, the bent-backed Bulgan had a disconcerting tendency to sample assorted wares without remembering that it was necessary to pay for them. They had no time for such nonsense today. They were on an important mission! Not as important as herding, or racing, or celebrating with one's clan, perhaps. But for two clanless ones such as themselves, important enough.

"There they are!" he whispered tersely as Bulgan bumped up behind him. The other strained to see out of his one good eye, straightening as much as he was able. Bulgan sniffed as he stared.

"Got no guards," he noted observantly. Bulgan was simple, but not quite so stupid as his outward appearance and attitude might suggest.

Kyakhta withheld the majority of his contempt. "Of course they got no guards, dimwit! What need do Jedi have for guards? It is *they* who guard *others*."

Bulgan frowned, looked around in confusion. "What others?"

Not bothering to reply and keeping his face hidden as much as possible, Kyakhta saw that the visitors were unaccompanied by a local guide. In keeping with their unassuming demeanor, he knew they would prefer to travel without even a small entourage. Nor would they wish to attract a crowd. That was good. For the work they intended to do, he and Bulgan wanted as few complications, and witnesses, as possible. His upper right arm was throbbing above the prosthetic, as it always did when he was nervous.

"Which one we take?" Bulgan had to move his head from side to side in order to see around eddying pedestrians who were not so much taller than he as straighter.

"I don't know. It's easy enough to tell the Padawans from their Jedi. They're much younger. I don't remember if there is a strength difference between human genders." He did not bother to ask if Bulgan recalled such a thing. Bulgan had trouble remembering what day it was, and sometimes his own name.

What did the Hutt Soergg want with a Jedi Padawan anyway, he wondered. Well, that was no business of his. He and Bulgan had only to carry out their task. Besides, thinking on more than one subject at a time hurt his head.

"Let's follow them," the bent one suggested. This was so obvious and sensible a notion that Kyakhta could hardly countenance its origin.

The Jedi visitors acted like any group of tourists, listening to the spoken explanations of their guide as they strolled through the marketplace, dutifully admiring the sights while occasionally pausing to taste samples of the local cuisine. Occasionally, one or two of them would pause to admire a handicraft or artwork, a neatly turned bracelet or glistening singing plant from the equatorial regions. They did not buy anything, Kyakhta noted. What use did a Jedi have for personal possessions when their Council kept them always on the move? But their roving lifestyle did not prevent them from looking and appreciating.

One of the Padawans stopped outside a shop that featured sanwiwood sculptures from the Niruu Plateau. The Niruu Alwari were famed for their woodwork. It was the young female, Kyakhta noted. The modestly windowed shop was one of many that fronted on the central marketplace itself, and therefore was more substantial than the temporary stalls and carts that filled the central square.

Go inside, he heard himself thinking urgently at the preoccupied Padawan. *Go on, go in. Admire the lovely pretties.* Next to him, Bulgan had gone silent, sensing that the moment might be near. In the midst of watching and waiting, Kyakhta did remember to finger the homing device at his waist.

After exchanging a few words with her equally youthful counterpart, the female Padawan entered. Her male colleague turned away and moved off, trailing the two older Jedi. The latter were locked in animated conversation. They appeared not to have noticed the momentary detour taken by one of their young apprentices.

"Now, quickly!" Forcing himself not to break into an eye-attracting lope, Kyakhta hurried forward.

The Winds of Whorh were with them. There was no one else in the shop: only the proprietor, a wizened old city dweller who looked nearly as well worn as some of her antique woodcarvings. No other customers. Keeping their robes as tight about their faces as possible, the two newcomers pretended to examine a ritual high-backed Nazay seat from Delgerhan. The Padawan was slim and did not appear to be especially muscular. But then, Kyakhta knew, Jedi did not depend on brute physical strength for their protection.

Gesturing to Bulgan, he waited while his friend carefully unfolded the polus net from beneath his robe. When Bulgan was ready, Kyakhta stepped up to the counter. Smiling patiently, the proprietress shuffled toward him. A last, quick glance in the direction of the marketplace showed that the entryway remained clear. There was no sign of the other visitors through the single large, transparent pane.

"Welcome to my modest place of doings, sir." Eyeing his robes, she added, "I see that you are Pangay Ous. You are a long way from your stretch of prairie, sir." A hint of uncertainty crept into her voice. "Yet you do not have the look about you of one who is of the Northern Bands. I see no identifying tattoo on your forehead, and your mane is—"

"But my body fragrance is of the Pangay Ous," he declared, interrupting her. "See?" Pulling the compact atomizer from beneath his robe, he shoved it forward and sprayed her right in the face, before she could object. She inhaled reflexively, her eyes rolled back, and she slumped to the floor, her chin banging against the counter as she dropped. So fast did the spray work that she did not even have time to look surprised.

"Haja!" he exclaimed, stepping back from the counter. "The poor lady has collapsed! It must be her hearts!"

"Here, let me have a look." Alerted to a possible emergency and wishing to be helpful, Barriss pushed forward. "I'm not that familiar with Ansionian physiology, but there are certain bipedal circulatory and respiratory constants that . . ."

Kyakhta moved aside, not listening to her incomprehensible medical jargon. He wouldn't have understood any of it anyway. Bulgan was already in motion. Another glance outside showed that the street was still devoid of Jedi. The Padawan had stepped behind the counter and was kneeling beside the fallen proprietress.

"Her vitals appear sound." She sounded a note of puzzlement. "I don't think it's serious. Perhaps only a fainting spell." She started to rise. "A little cool water on her face, I think. I wonder what could have caused her to go down like that, so sudden and silently?"

"Maybe this?" Thrusting the sprayer forward, Kyakhta caught the female with a full burst right in the face. If anything, having two nostrils instead of the normal one, she absorbed more of the mist than would an Ansionian. Her eyes flickered but did not roll back, and she started to reach for the lightsaber slung at her waist. Startled and beginning to panic, Kyakhta squirted her again, and then a third time, before she finally went down. In a testament to her training, she'd absorbed enough vapor to put out a whole squad of mounted warriors.

"Hurry, hurry!" Trying to divide his attention between the entrance and the now unconscious Padawan, he struggled with Bulgan to stuff the human female into the unbreakable sack they had brought with them. Finally lifting their bagged burden, which proved surprisingly heavy, they hurried toward the back of the establishment. As was typical with such better-off shops, it boasted a second, rear entrance. Uldas was with them—the dirty service alley was deserted. Remembering to finger the signaling device at his side, he led the way toward Jaaruls Street, the shielded and secure apartment waiting there, and safety. Excitement rose within him. They'd done it!

Now all they had to do was hold on to their captive, keep her alive and well, and await further instructions from Soergg. Compared to the abduction they had just carried out, such talk-work struck Kyakhta as not work at all.

No one questioned the contents of the lumpy sack the two Alwari lugged down alleys and back streets. Business was business, and a nomad's business was none but his own.

Luminara put down the beautifully enameled little mirror that had been cut from a single reflective mineral surface and looked around, frowning. Something didn't feel right. Something didn't feel normal. It took her a moment of searching, with both eyes and mind, both within and without, to realize what it was. She had not seen Barriss in some time.

Where had the Padawan gone? It wasn't like her to stray. A free-roaming Padawan had autonomy, but no access to greater knowledge. Kenobi took notice of her concern and moved to stand next to his colleague.

"Something amiss, Luminara?"

"I don't see Barriss, Obi-Wan. She usually hangs on my every word, as well as on those of whomever I happen to be with at the time."

He smiled reassuringly. "Then it's not surprising she's off somewhere. We've both been pretty quiet here these last few moments."

"Last time I saw her," Anakin put in, "she was looking at woodcarvings in a shop." Though he did not reach for his weapon, his natural protective instinct was instantly aroused.

Luminara's deep blue eyes met his. "Which shop?" she demanded.

"Not to worry, Master," Anakin told her. "I've kept an eye on the entryway ever since she stepped inside. She hasn't come out."

"Hasn't come out this way, you mean. It's probably nothing, and she dislikes it when I act more like a mother than a teacher, but Barriss absorbs and files sights very quickly. It's not like her to linger." Her eyes bored into the Padawan's. "Which shop?" she reiterated.

Sensing the seriousness in her manner, Anakin put aside any remaining vestige of flippancy, raised a hand, and pointed. "That one, over there." He followed close behind the two Jedi as they walked rapidly toward the establishment he'd identified.

The door was propped open, which was not surprising. No one acknowledged their entrance, which was.

"Barriss?" Luminara's anxiety rose as she moved rapidly through the shop, searching among the larger woodcarvings that crowded the back. A shout redirected her exploration.

"Luminara!" It was Obi-Wan. That in itself was alarming, because she had already noted that he hardly ever raised his voice. "Over here!"

He was cradling the head of the elderly Ansionian female against his right leg. Anakin looked on, his usual buoyancy gone, his expression stricken. "Water," Obi-Wan called tersely. Hunting hurriedly through a rear room, Anakin found a cooler half full of small polymer receptacles. Bringing one containing cold water forward, he handed it to his Master and watched while Obi-Wan lightly sprinkled the contents on the oldster's face. Her large eyes, the color of fine claret, blinked open moments later.

"Goodness me—by Nomgon's Arm!" She studied the alien human faces gazing worriedly down at her. "Who are you people?

What happened to me?" Using her hands to push herself into a sitting position, she added bewilderedly, "Why am I lying on the floor?"

Luminara studied her fixedly. "We were hoping you could tell us that."

Obi-Wan and Anakin helped the proprietress to her feet.

"This—this is my shop. My place. I was showing some wares to a customer." One hand went to her head and rubbed her graying brush of mane forward. "Alwari, he was. Said he was Pangay Ous, and wore the right raiment. But his manner was odd." Her face added wrinkles of distaste to those shaped by age. "There was another with him, I think. I remember because he was ugly, and yet his companion made him look handsome."

"A young human female, dressed like us," Luminara broke in. "Have you seen anyone like that?"

The elderly native blinked. "*Ou,* to be sure. Very attentive she was, though I suspect not intending to buy anything." She smiled, showing sharp Ansionian teeth. "When you've been in this business as long as I have, you can tell, even with different species."

"Where is she now?" Obi-Wan inquired in his soft yet commanding voice.

"Why—I don't know. I don't know where any of them are." The proprietress looked down and shook her head. "Last I remember, we were speaking of odors, and then . . ." She looked up blankly. "Then I opened my eyes, to see you three bending over me. What do you suppose could have? . . ."

"Masters! Out here!"

Responding to Anakin's call, the two Jedi hurried to the back of the shop and out the rear entrance whose door was now ajar. They found him standing in an alley, kneeling and pointing. The pavement was dry and thick with dust. The marks of the two sets of footprints were clear to see. Thank the Force, Obi-Wan thought, for the absence in the back alley of a muddling breeze.

"Ansionian footprints." Luminara looked up, glancing both ways down the alley. "By themselves, confirmation of nothing." She indicated the numerous other prints that marred the avenue's dusty coating. "Many feet have recently trod this path."

"But these begin right from the doorway," Anakin argued. "And see how deep they are compared to some of the others. As if the two who made these deeper ones might be carrying something." He gazed down the shadowed passageway. "All Ansionians are more or less the same size—and weight."

"Three go into the shop, two come out, and neither of those sets human." Obi-Wan was nodding approvingly. "You are learning to see beyond the obvious, Anakin. Would that you always continue to do so."

Luminara had shut her eyes tightly. Now they opened anew. "I cannot sense her presence anywhere. If she has been taken, I should be able to detect her distress. But there is nothing."

"She might be unconscious." Obi-Wan had moved farther out into the alley, the better to scan its most distant reaches. "If the two locals who took her intended her ill, they might have used the same method to knock her out that they used on the owner of the shop."

"Or she might be dead," Anakin pointed out. In another setting, among other people, his comment could have provoked angst or outrage. Neither Luminara nor Obi-Wan reacted, however. As Jedi, they were not offended by objectivity, no matter how sensitive the subject.

But within, Luminara was churning. While a Jedi might not show many emotions, that did not mean she did not have them.

"This is a sizable city. How are we going to find her?" She fought to keep the anger she felt in check.

"We could ask the city authorities for assistance," Anakin proposed helpfully.

Obi-Wan set the suggestion aside. "That's all we need now, at this delicate stage of negotiations. To confess to our hosts that one of our own has gone missing, and that we were helpless to prevent it. How much confidence in our perceived omnipotence do you think that admission would inspire?"

Anakin nodded understandingly. "I see what you mean, Master. Sometimes I am too direct."

"A common affliction of the inexperienced, for which you are not responsible." He looked back at Luminara. "We have to find her ourselves, no matter what her condition." His anxious colleague smiled tightly. "And quickly, lest our Ansionian hosts sense something is amiss."

Luminara indicated the shop. "First we'll get as detailed a description as we can of the two Alwari who were here at the same time as Barriss. Then I think we should split up, each of us taking a third of the city. Using this shop as a nexus, we'll fan out and sweep as much of the community as we can; asking questions, offering rewards locally, and striving to sense Barriss's presence."

"Obi-Wan, do you think the same people as those who were assaulting Master Luminara and Padawan Barriss when we arrived are behind this?" Anakin wondered.

"Impossible to say," the Jedi Knight replied. "There are so many factions opposing one another on this world that it could be the work of any one of them. And as you know, there are off-world interests at work here as well." In his quiet way, Anakin saw, Obi-Wan Kenobi was more than a little displeased. "This is all we need—to add heat to a flashpoint. But politics aren't important now. What matters is finding Barriss." He did not add "alive and well."

He did not have to.

NEWSBLINK (Coruscant News Network)—Nemrileo irm-Drocubac, representative from Tanjay VI, died yesterday when his aircar collided with a heavy-equipment delivery vehicle in south quadrant, section ninety-three, of the exclusive Bindai suburb where he lived. Questioned at the site, the pilot of the delivery craft declared that his vehicle's internal guidance system had suffered an undetected software failure that led directly to the fatal collision. Investigators on the scene were attempting to confirm this assertion, though their efforts have been complicated by the severe damage to both vehicles.

Representative from Tanjay irm-Drocubac leaves behind a wife and two children. Though active in the growing secessionist faction, and suspected of sympathies with the more extreme members of that movement, he was well respected by his colleagues and coworkers, as well as by his supporters on his homeworld. In accordance with Tanjay tradition, his ashes will be scattered tomorrow above the capital city where he lived and worked for the past fifteen years of his life.

A grieving Chancellor Palpatine is scheduled to deliver the eulogy.

(end transmission; end article)

"**F**or a young humanoid female, she weighs more than I would have expected." Kyakhta let out a tired whoosh of air as he and his companion set the sack down on the bed. In response to movement within, Bulgan released the seal at the top. Sitting up, Barriss shuffled the sack off her shoulders. It fell to her waist and, when she stood, to her feet. Her ankles were strapped together and her hands secured behind her back. A quick glance downward, then up at her captors, found her focusing on Kyakhta's smile.

"Looking for this, apprentice?" From a bag slung at his waist, he removed her service belt. It contained all of her personal gear, including her comlink and lightsaber. Shuffling over, Bulgan tentatively fingered the latter.

"Jedi lightsaber. Always want try one."

Kyakhta yanked the belt away, let it slip back into the open bag like a sedated snake. "Don't touch that, you idiot! Don't you remember briefing where Hutt warned about handling such devices? A Jedi lightsaber can be tuned to its owner's personal electrical field. Try activate this one, and you likely blow it to bits. Along with you your dumbself also."

"*Ou,* that right. Bulgan forget." Turning, he once more considered their bound captive. "Not much to look at, is it? I could break it in half easy."

"Only physically." Unable to run or gesture, Barriss sat down on the bed. "You obviously know who I am, what I represent. Are you aware that even as we speak there are three Jedi hunting furiously for me, and that they will not be happy when they find out what has happened?"

Kyakhta laughed while Bulgan chortled gruffly. "Let them look. They not find you here." He indicated the high smooth walls that enclosed them. "This a safe place, and in any case you not stay here long." Remembering, he flicked the switch on his call-in. "Already, others being notified. They come here, take you off our hands. Then we a little rich, and done with you as well."

Choosing not to dispute the claim, she continued quietly. "What do you, or whoever you work for, want with me?"

The two Alwari exchanged a look. "Not our business," Kyakhta finally replied. "Catching you our job. Questions not our job." He turned to leave the room. "Report in success now. I looking forward to it." He straightened. "Bossban don't think we can do it. Be nice surprise for him." His smile widened. "I think I make him wait a little while before I tell him so." He gave his companion a shove. "Watch her close, Bulgan. Beware Jedi tricks."

"No worry, Kyakhta." Hunched over but alert, the other Alwari settled himself on a bench opposite the shackled human. "Bulgan watch carefully."

Barriss stared as the single door closed heavily behind the

one who called himself Kyakhta. A loud *click* followed his exit. Without her lightsaber, she would not be able to penetrate the barrier, and her limited mastery of the Force was not sufficient to allow her to pierce it mentally. She was trapped until her friends could locate her. That they would do so she did not doubt. Only the time factor troubled her. Would there be enough of it before she was transferred from this place and handed over to whomever had arranged for her abduction? Of one thing she was certain: whoever it was was likely to be both more ruthless and more competent than her two comparatively simple Ansionian captors.

As time passed, she waited for her guard to grow tired, or to leave. He did neither. Nor was she able, try as she might, to influence his mind. That could be, she reflected, because according to every indication there was not much mind there to influence. That might explain why neither she nor her Master had sensed its hostile intentions.

They had used the unconscious shopkeeper to distract her attention. Upset with herself at falling for the diversion, she repressed the growing irritation. Anger was another kind of distraction, one she could not presently afford.

"Maybe bossban give Kyakhta and Bulgan bonus," her watcher observed aloud. "Jedi lightsaber would be nice. Then Bulgan go home, show to clan. They let Bulgan back in. And those who object," he made a swinging motion with one heavy hand, "Bulgan cut off their heads!"

"You speak fondly of your bossban." She made a conscious effort to appear and sound as helpless and resigned as possible. "Who might that imposing individual be?"

A slow smile spread across her guard's face. "Padawan try

fool Bulgan. No Jedi tricks here. Bulgan and Kyakhta little slow, maybe. But that not mean we stupid." Rising and lumbering forward, he loomed over her seated form; a broad-chested, bald-pated, threatening mass of muscle and bone, unusually massive for an Ansionian. "You think Bulgan stupid?"

"I did not say that, nor did I mean it," she responded soothingly. The Alwari backed off. "But I do see something else about you that I am sure of."

The hulking native's eyes narrowed dangerously. "What that? Careful be, Padawan human. Bulgan not afraid of you."

"I can see that. What I also see, and can sense in ways you cannot imagine, is that both you and your accomplice are in pain—and probably have been so for a long time."

Bulgan's brown, gold-flecked Ansionian eye bulged even wider than usual. "How—how you know that?"

"In addition to the usual Jedi training, many of us have our own specialties. Areas of learning that we are especially drawn toward. Myself, I am a practicing healer."

"But you human. Not Ansion."

"I know." Her tone was tender, reassuring—compelling. "And I can't fix your poor back, or give you a prosthetic to replace your missing eye. But the pain in your mind is akin to the pain nearly all warm-blood sentients experience. It arises from certain kinds of neural breakdowns and malfunctions. It's as if someone was trying to wire a very complex computer and all the necessary materials and components were laid out before her, but she wasn't quite sure how to link everything together. So she did a job that was a little too hasty. Do you understand anything of what I'm saying, Bulgan?"

The Alwari nodded slowly. "Bulgan not dumb. Bulgan

understand. *Haja,* that just how Bulgan feel most of the time. Not wired right." Tilting his head slightly to one side, he stared at her hard out of his one good eye. "Padawan can fix that?"

"I can't make any promises. But I can try."

"Fix pain in head." Her captor was clearly exerting a considerable mental effort. "No more pain here." He rubbed his forehead with his open palm. "That be a big thing. Bigger even, maybe, than credits." The effort at extended cogitation having exhausted his limited intellectual resources, he glared at her again. "How know Bulgan can trust you?"

"I give you my word as a Padawan, as a student of the Jedi arts, as one who has dedicated her life to their high ideals—and to mastering the skills of a healer."

Obviously torn, her captor took a deep breath, glanced circumspectly at the door, and then turned back to her. "You try fix Bulgan. But if you try trick, I—"

"I've given you my word," she interrupted him, forestalling his threat. "Besides, where could I go? The door is locked and barricaded from the outside. Or haven't you realized that you're locked in here with me?" She did not smile. "Your friend is taking no chances."

"Locked in?" He rubbed his bare skull, his hand passing to either side of where a dark mane would normally be. "Bulgan confused."

Immediately, she jumped on the opening thus offered. "Confusion comes from the pain you've been living with. Let me try to help you, Bulgan. Please. If I fail, it costs you nothing. Even if I succeed, you can still keep me in here because the door is locked from outside."

"That right. Padawan speak truth. *Ou,* you try."

Meeting his gaze evenly, she gestured toward her bound

wrists. "You have to untie me. To do this kind of work, I need my hands."

He was instantly wary. "What for? Jedi trick?"

"No. Please trust me, Bulgan. There are vastly more important things at stake here than my life, or the size of your future credit account. Are you familiar with the secessionist movement?"

The Ansionian made a negative gesture. "Only movement Bulgan know is in bowels." He thought a moment longer. "Kyakhta be unhappy," he muttered. Then he reluctantly stepped behind Barriss and passed a desealer across her wrists. The opaque bond that restrained them promptly dissolved, breaking down into cellulose, catalyst, and water. Relieved to have her hands free, she rubbed firmly at her wrists. As the circulation began returning, she beckoned for him to approach.

"Come here, Bulgan," she instructed him gently. He did so with head bowed, shuffling his feet like a child approaching its mother. A very strong, very dangerous child, she reminded herself. She did not have to ask him to lower his head farther. His poor bent spine had already placed it within reach. Extending both hands, palm downward, she tenderly cradled the sides of his skull, careful not to cover the aural openings. His flesh was warm to the touch—the normal Ansionian body temperature being several degrees higher than that of a human. Her eyes closed, and she began to concentrate.

A throbbing ran through her as her focus sharpened. An enduring, agonizing ache that through straining and training she made her own. She let herself flow outward toward it, surrounding it with the soothing balm that was her own harmonious inner self. Within the damaged, misfiring neurons that were the source of the native's ongoing hurt, the Force compelled a subtle

realignment of tissues, an almost imperceptible but physiologically critical alteration.

She stood holding him like that for several long, silent minutes: healer and patient locked together in that mysterious,
inscrutable mutual melding comprehensible only to another
master of the Jedi healing arts. Not until all felt normal and natural and *well* did she finally allow herself to withdraw from the
vulnerable state into which she had placed them both.

Opening her eyes, she found herself staring back at her captor.
But there was something different about him now: a faint but discernible change of posture, a glint instead of a dullness in his eye.
He straightened slightly, as much as his broken, permanently bent
back would allow, and looked slowly around the room.

"How do you feel?" she finally prompted him when no
words were forthcoming.

"Feel? Bulgan feel—I feel good. Very good." Making fists of
both three-fingered hands, he raised them toward the roof.
"Really exceptionally remarkably good! *Haja, jaha, ou ou!*" The
little dance he proceeded to perform, joyfully throwing his arms
repeatedly into the air all the while, lifted her hopes in concert
with his spirit.

Then he stopped, lowered his hands, and said to her in a notably different tone of voice than he had used before, "But you're
still my prisoner, Padawan." When she slumped, he grinned,
showing fine Ansionian teeth. "For about another minute."

"You mean? . . ." His intent became clear when he walked
over to her with a spring in his step that had been absent previously and bent to pass the desealer across her ankle bonds. They
dissolved promptly, allowing her to stand. Her feet and legs
numb from lack of use, she would have fallen had he not caught
her in his strong arms.

At which point the door clicked and Kyakhta entered the room.

To say that the senior Alwari was startled by the sight that greeted his bulging eyes was an understatement worthy of a senior tax collector. The sight of the Jedi Padawan unbound was disquieting enough. The sight of her slumped slightly in his partner's arms was a spectacle that constituted an irresolvable conundrum. If Bulgan did not with his first utterance say exactly the right thing, Kyakhta was ready to bolt back outside and lock them both back in.

Fortunately, the heretofore guileless Bulgan was now in a cerebral position to do so.

"She fixed me," he informed his companion simply and straightforwardly, tapping the side of his head. "Fixed me here. She can fix you, too."

"No promises," Barriss warned them both.

"Fix what?" Kyakhta had already taken a wary step backward. "I not broken. What do you mean, fix me?"

"Up here." Once more, the mentally mended Bulgan touched hand to head. "I have no more pain in my mind. I know you suffer from the same syndrome, my good friend. Let her work her Jedi healing on you."

Another step back. The door was within reach. Easy to dart back out into the hallway, slam the barrier shut, and seal the lock. But—what had happened to Bulgan in his absence? Kyakhta wondered. He hadn't been gone very long. Only a few minutes, and now his good, honest, dumb companion in mutual exile and disgrace was talking like an infernal city councilor! No, he corrected himself. Not like a councilor.

Like a true Alwari nomad: independent, confident, and free.

Three fingers hovered in the vicinity of the door. The Jedi

made no move to stop him, though he sensed she might have done so. "What this nonsense about 'Jedi healing'?"

"She worked it on me. Fixed my head, my mind. It doesn't hurt anymore, Kyakhta! I can think clearly again. My thoughts haven't been this free since I was a child and was thrown from that suubatar." His voice lowered. "That was the same throw, the bad dismount, that broke my back and stole my eye—and damaged my mind."

"But I . . ." Kyakhta was at a loss for words. In the face of the evidence, in the face of his friend's face, he was forced to accept a seemingly inconceivable reality.

There was another reality that would have to be faced, and quickly. Unbound hands outstretched, the Jedi was advancing slowly toward him.

"Let me help you, Kyakhta. I give you the same promise I made to Bulgan. Whether I can help you or not, I am still your prisoner."

That was true, Kyakhta realized. Dissolved bonds notwithstanding, he and his friend were still the ones in control here. Only they knew the way out of the building in which the cell was located. Only they could get her past the outer guards and security checkpoints. Of course, a Jedi Knight would probably make short work of such minor obstacles, but a Padawan still in training . . .

Unarguably, she had worked a marvel with Bulgan. Could she take away the similar pain that had afflicted him all his adult life; remove the regular, pounding waves of agony that daily stabbed through his brain? Wasn't it worth, if nothing else, a try?

"Go ahead," he told her, adding by way of warning, "if this a trick, the bossban may not receive you undamaged."

Paying no attention to the threat, she reached out and up to put her hands on the sides of his head and draw it toward her. Her fingers were cool against his skull, he realized, and there were too many of them, but otherwise her touch was inoffensive. Calming, even.

Several moments later, he was blinking back at her with the same awed realization that had not long before nearly overcome his companion. Unlike Bulgan, he did not throw his arms wildly in the air and dance small circles. Instead, he bowed. As performed by an Ansionian, it was a particularly graceful and supple gesture.

"I owe you my sanity, Padawan. For had you not interceded, I see surely now that the pain I have been living with would have led all too soon to utter madness, and eventually to death." Turning from her, he embraced his old companion-in-despair, long arms wrapping around Bulgan's broad shoulders, maned and bald head bobbing together in ardent, mutual exultation.

The joyous sight of the two Ansionians she had been able to heal did Barriss's heart good—but it was not getting her out of this place, or restoring her to her friends. "My name is Barriss Offee, my Master is the Jedi Luminara Unduli, and the sooner we find them, the better it will be for me and the safer, I suspect, it will be for you. For surely your employer will not be pleased to learn of the unexpected turn you have done him."

"Bossban Soergg!" Bulgan exclaimed. As soon as the words were out of his mouth, he looked askance at his companion. But Kyakhta was not upset at the unforced revelation.

"It doesn't matter now, Bulgan. I've just finished relaying news of our success to his headquarters. Someone else will have to inform him of this change in plans. We've cast our lot in with this female. Now she is going to have to deliver us from Soergg, instead of us delivering her to him." He eyed the Jedi expectantly. "Can you do that? We throw ourselves under your protection, without which we two who stand now clanless before you will surely be food for marauding shanhs before tomorrow's first light."

"Get me out of here in one piece," she assured them with a grim smile, "and I can promise you the gratitude of two Jedi Knights and a fellow Padawan—in addition to my own personal indebtedness." She started purposefully for the open doorway. "That's enough reassurance for almost anyone in the galaxy."

"Strange," Bulgan murmured as he followed his companion and their former captive toward the exit, "how clear thinking improves one's outlook on life. For the first time in a long, long while I begin to see myself as a person again, instead of a lowly source of jokes and cruel humor."

"I never saw you that way, my friend," Kyakhta called softly back to him as they quietly mounted the spiral staircase.

"Yes, you did," Bulgan shot back, "but I don't blame you for it. It wasn't your fault. It was all in the mind."

"Most cheap invective is." Feeling slightly naked without her service belt, Barriss followed Kyakhta upward. "Where is my gear?"

"In the storeroom. We'll get it for you before we leave."

There was one guard in the room. The Dorun sat in a deeply indented chair designed to accommodate his commodious backside. In his twinned tentacles, he held an oval reader. Both stalk-mounted oculars swiveled in Kyakhta's direction as the latter emerged from the stairwell.

"How beeth the prisoner?"

Kyakhta shrugged boredly as Bulgan emerged behind him. Barriss kept out of sight farther down in the stairwell. "Quiet. An unusual state of affairs, or so I have been told, for a humanoid female."

"Resignedeth to her fate by now, I wager." The Dorun returned to his viewing. Neither of his independently swiveling eyes noticed Bulgan picking up an empty chair. Both swiveling oculars dimmed when the powerful Alwari brought it down on the guard's head.

"Quickly now!" Entering a combination into a keypad, Kyakhta reached into the drawer that popped open in response and withdrew Barriss's service belt. Her lightsaber, she was relieved to note, was still fastened in place. As she was slipping the belt around her middle, she noticed Kyakhta fingering a small device secured at his own waist.

"What's that?"

"We have to call in our position at regular intervals," the Alwari explained dolefully, "or we'll die." He rubbed the back of his neck. "Bossban Soergg had explosive devices placed in our necks to ensure our compliance with his orders."

Barriss made what was, for a Padawan, a rude noise. "Typical of a Hutt. We certainly can't let him track us. Come, let me see."

Obediently, Kyakhta and Bulgan approached. Taking a scanner from her belt, she passed it carefully over the indicated spot on the back of Kyakhta's neck. It wasn't hard to find the inserted device. There was a perceptible bump under the skin just to the right of his mane.

Checking the scanner's reading, she entered a sequence and passed the compact instrument a second time over the Alwari's neck, then repeated the procedure with Bulgan. Satisfied, she headed cautiously for the outer door.

Kyakhta followed, once more rubbing his fingers over the

raised place. "The explosive is still there." Cleansed mind or not, he was still understandably uneasy at its presence.

Barriss studied the street outside. From everything she could see, traffic appeared normal. "I could cut them out, but I'd rather have it done neatly, and I don't have the tools with me. So I just deactivated them. They're harmless now. But we'd do well to move fast. Possibly the process of my deactivating them will result in notification of whoever is monitoring you for your boss-ban that something has gone wrong. I assume a rapid response will be forthcoming."

"Let's go, then." Pushing past her, Bulgan opened the door and stepped unflinchingly out onto the street. Kyakhta and their former prisoner followed.

"Central square, I think. The shop where you found me." Barriss followed Kyakhta's lead. "In looking for me, my companions will split up and begin their search from there." She fondled the closed-band comlink on her belt. "As soon as we're a safe distance away from here, I'll notify them of our destination, course, and that I'm okay." She smiled. "And of your change of heart, as well."

"Better to say change of mind." Everything that was previously familiar to him, Bulgan was now seeing out of new eyes. Harmless it might now be, having been rendered so by the Padawan, but the lethal packet embedded in his neck still itched. "Get rid of this as soon as possible."

"We will," Barriss assured him as they turned a corner onto a much busier thoroughfare. The presence of so many sentients around them eased her tension. "Until then, we'll simply tell anyone we meet to be careful what they say to you, because you happen to have an explosive personality."

Prior to her discerning ministrations, Bulgan would have

simply gaped dumbly at this remark. Now, both he and his friend Kyakhta had the pleasure of laughing at the joke.

It was the kind of pleasure that had been all too long denied them.

Sooner or later, a distraught Ogomoor felt, Bossban Soergg was going to grow tired of listening to his majordomo deliver bad news. When that happened, Ogomoor knew he had better be ready to run—or at least be standing well out of range of the Hutt's massive, powerful tail.

"Gone." Soergg lay on the resting divan in his sleeping quarters. He had been in the midst of his afternoon nap when Ogomoor, driven by urgency, had felt duty-bound to wake him. "Vanished. And those two morons with her."

"We do not know that they are with her, Great One. Only that she is missing, and so are they. The guard says he was attacked from behind, in all likelihood by one of them. Why would they suddenly decide to go with her?"

"Who knows?" The Hutt grunted as he slouched his sagging corpus off the divan and onto the floor. Immediately, a pair of tiny geril servants commenced the odious task of grooming the sluglike shape. Soergg ignored them as he scowled down at his subordinate. "I smell the stink of Jedi wiles behind this misfortune."

"The devices that were supposed to ensure the loyalty of the two abductors? . . ." Ogomoor left the question hanging.

"*Pagh!* I activated those as soon as you told me what had happened. Either those imbeciles are now headless, or else more Jedi sleight of hand is at work in this." As the gerils clung to his massive body, continuing their grooming without interruption, Soergg lumbered forward. Exhibiting courage he did not feel,

Ogomoor held his ground. His own head, he knew, remained attached to his shoulders only because of his continuing value to
the Hutt.

"Put out the word to every lowlife, criminal, lawbreaker, and
felon in Cuipernam. A thousand Republic credits to anyone who
brings the accursed Padawan back to me alive, or the head of a
dead Jedi. Hurry! We may still have a chance if she can be intercepted before she can rejoin her companions."

"I hear and obey, Bossban." Too relieved at the dismissal to
fear a shot in the back, Ogomoor whirled and fled unceremoni-
ously from the bedroom, his comlink already out and activated.

Behind him, the gerils reflexively sealed their nostrils as their
misshapen employer voided his disgust in an exceptionally ghastly
and malodorous manner.

What Ogomoor did not know was that his intimidating employer now had to report the failure to one far more important
than his Huttish self. Soergg did not fear that individual—but he
respected him. Almost as much as he respected the credits being
paid into his own local account in the service of furthering the
cause of Ansionian secession.

Who was behind the one making the payments? he often
wondered. Not that it really mattered. It was the money, the
credits, that were important. The Hutts had little interest in politics except insofar as these served their immediate interests. It
mattered not at all to Soergg whether Ansion and the worlds to
which it was tied via treaties and pacts remained within the Republic or pulled out.

Or even if something else, as yet unseen and unvoiced, arose
to take its place.

No one was surprised when Luminara was the first of the anxious searchers to find Barriss and her new allies. They met in the middle of a secondary marketplace. The two Alwari looked on with interest as Master and Padawan embraced unashamedly. Intent on the day-to-day grind of business, everyone else, shoppers and merchants alike, ignored them.

"And who might these two stalwart-looking locals be?" Luminara eyed the Alwari with interest. Kyakhta felt Jedi eyes burning into his own. For no reason at all, he began to shuffle his feet.

"My kidnappers, Master." At the look on Luminara's face, Barriss had to laugh. "Don't gauge them too harshly. Both suffered from cerebral infirmities. In return for my curing them, they helped me escape."

"A temporary escape, I'm obliged to remind you, Barriss," Bulgan said. Straining to see over the heads of vendors and customers alike, he was scanning the multitude for signs of imminent assault. "Even as you enjoy this happy moment, I'd wager my last good credit that Bossban Soergg is sending a host of cut-throats in pursuit of us all."

"Then we must hasten to leave." Pulling a comlink from her belt, Luminara addressed it briefly, listened to a reply, spoke again, and replaced it. "Obi-Wan and Anakin are hurrying to join us." She pointed. "We'll gather by the fountain on the far side of this square." Putting an arm around her Padawan's shoulders, she guided Barriss in that direction.

"I'm glad you've had a chance in the field to use your skill in the healing arts. In the future, I wish you would try to find practice subjects other than kidnappers. I should be upset with you for letting your guard down so badly, but I'm too happy to see you safe and returned to us to be angry."

They had to wait only a short while on the steps of the lorqual fountain before a swirl of robes in the crowd marked Obi-Wan's arrival. Anakin was not far behind him. Both greeted Barriss in the traditional Jedi fashion: ceremonial, yet affectionate.

Bulgan observed the proceedings in silence. Only when the formalities had been concluded did he venture to inquire, while swatting away a hovering green-winged pekz, "What are you going to do now?"

Luminara turned to him. "We have secured an agreement with the Unity of Community to make peace with the nomads, if the Alwari will consent to share a percentage of their traditional lands with the city folk. In return, the city folk will agree to provide the Alwari with all manner of advanced goods and services, and will not try to intrude on or otherwise alter the time-honored Alwari way of life. Each will respect the other and the Senate will stay, insofar as it is possible for bureaucrats to do so, out of Ansionian affairs. In return, Ansion will remain within the Republic, which will ensure its economic and political independence from the Commerce Guild. Among others." Her tone darkened. "Ansion will *not* become another Naboo."

Kyakhta scratched at the bare skin of his neck, careful not to irritate the explosive still buried there. "Sounds complicated to me."

"So it is," Obi-Wan admitted. "More complicated than should be necessary. But that's the way of things these days."

"Do you think the Alwari will accede to such a proposal?" Barriss was watching her friends and the crowd simultaneously.

The two nomads exchanged a look. "It depends on how it is put to them," Kyakhta finally decided. "If you can get the most prominent of the overclans, the Borokii, to agree, the others will follow their lead and fall into line. Among the Alwari, it has always been so."

Luminara nodded thoughtfully. "Then we must get their representatives to come to Cuipernam so we can talk with them in person."

Bulgan started to laugh, stopped when he saw that the Jedi was serious. "No chieftain of the Borokii will come within a hundred *huus* of Cuipernam, or any other city of the Unity. They don't trust the city folk, or their representatives. I speak now as a Tasbir of the Southern Hatagai. Albeit," he added painfully, "one who is presently clanless."

Leaning toward Obi-Wan, Luminara whispered something that soon had the other Jedi smiling and nodding. She turned back to Barriss's new friends. "If you are clanless," she said sternly, "it means you have nowhere to go. No responsibilities, no place to call home."

"*Haja,* that is all too true," Kyakhta exclaimed mournfully. "One who is clanless is as rootless as the blowing irgkul bush."

"Then," she continued, winking at Barriss, "you're free to work for us, to lead us to the Borokii."

"*Ou,* I suppose we . . ." Kyakhta paused, blinked, and stared back at the Jedi. As he did so, his mouth parted slightly, the thin lips moving farther and farther apart, showing more and more whiteness of tooth. "You mean—you would take on two such clanless ones as Bulgan and myself as your guides? Even after what we did to your Padawan?"

"That's in the past," Luminara told him. "And besides, Barriss says it wasn't really your fault, and that you're cured. I accept her conclusion on that."

"Guides for Jedi! Us!" Bulgan could hardly believe the change in their fortunes that had taken place in a single day—from working for a slime-tracker like Bossban Soergg to escorts for Jedi Knights.

The ever-wary Anakin leaned close to Obi-Wan. "Master, do you think it wise to place our trust and requirements in such as these?"

Obi-Wan pursed his lips. "I sense no danger in these two."

"Neither did Barriss," Anakin pointed out sagaciously, "until they abducted her."

"That was before she performed her healing. I think we shall be well looked after by this grateful pair. And they offer us an advantage we could not have hoped to obtain from the city folk: being Alwari themselves, they should find the right path and make the eventual necessary introductions as well or better than any others we could hire here in Cuipernam."

Anakin mulled this over. "Are in the final analysis all relationships between sentients ultimately reduced to politics of one kind or another, Master Obi-Wan?"

"It is thought so by many. Hence my continual attempts to

hammer into you the basic principles of skillful diplomacy. Who knows? One day they might serve you in personal as well as professional relationships."

That thought was sufficient to quiet the Padawan, and to set him on an entirely unrelated line of thinking. Meanwhile, the two older Jedi discussed details with their new guides as together they strode from the crowded square.

"The first thing," Luminara declared, "is to have these wicked devices removed from beneath your respective scalps."

"I know a healer who can do it in minutes, and will not be afraid to, now that they have been deactivated." Kyakhta flashed bright, sharp teeth at Barriss. "He is a fine craftsman, but he would never even have thought of treating us—before. To do so would have meant incurring the wrath of Bossban Soergg."

"Good." Luminara sidestepped a trio of wandering Mielps, bent down beneath the weight of shopping bags nearly as large as themselves. "Then we can hire a landspeeder, and proceed to—"

"No, no!" Bulgan cautioned her. "No landspeeders. We must take with us as few examples of galactic technology as possible. All Alwari are die-hard traditionalists. As you already know, this argument between them and the people of the towns centers largely on differences between long-established customs and new ways of doing things, of living. If you wish to gain the trust of the Borokii, to prove from the beginning that you do not favor the city folk, then you must approach them with reverence for the old ways."

Obi-Wan nodded amiably. "Very well then. No landspeeders. How do we travel?"

"For traversing the great prairies, there are many riding animals that are suitable."

Anakin made a face. "Animals!" He'd always been far more

comfortable working with machines. If they gave him enough time and access to sufficient equipment and spare parts, he could have built them a vehicle that would perform as required. But the native had been insistent—no landspeeders.

"By far the best is the suubatar." Kyakhta's enthusiasm was palpable. "If you can afford them, they are the preferred means of travel for Alwari highborn. Arriving in a camp atop one immediately marks the rider as a person of consequence. Not to mention taste."

Luminara considered. "The Jedi Council prefers that we travel modestly. We have at our disposal only limited means of exchange."

"I think we might manage it," Obi-Wan told her. "Given that we've been told to resolve this business as quickly as possible, no one should object to our spending a little to achieve that aim. The sooner we leave Cuipernam in search of these Borokii, the better our chances of quick success, and the safer we all will be."

"Riding a suubatar is like riding the wind." An eager Bulgan leapt over a dozing crowlyn. As he cleared its wide jaws, it pawed at him indifferently and went back to sleep.

Anakin shrugged. "I'm a champion Podracer. I'm afraid no organic riding steed, no matter how 'noble' it might be considered locally, is going to impress me very much."

But he was wrong.

If there was one thing advanced technology had largely eliminated from modern transportation, it was smell. The latter was present in abundance at the travel market, where an amazing variety of domesticated riding creatures was to be found. While the two older Jedi went with their new guides to find suitable animals, the pair of Padawans were placed on guard.

"I've already apologized to my Master for allowing myself to be abducted." As she spoke, Barriss's eyes were never still, regarding every vendor and shopper, every merchant and animal trainer, as a potential threat.

Having already been lulled once by the apparent tranquillity of his surroundings, Anakin was equally alert. He stood alongside his counterpart, wishing she were someone else but never less than properly and politely respectful of her already established bravery and talent.

"There's no need to be embarrassed. I've done plenty of stupid things in my life, too."

"I didn't say it was stupid." She turned away from him.

He hesitated momentarily. "Look, I'm sorry. We've managed to get off on the wrong foot somehow. All I can say in my defense is that I've got a lot on my mind."

"You're a Jedi Padawan. Of course you've got a lot on your mind." Eyeing a seuvhat driver heading purposefully in their direction, her hand strayed toward her lightsaber. When he turned his vehicle, her fingers fell away from the weapon.

"I mean I'm preoccupied." Reaching out, he put a hand on her shoulder, hoping the gesture would not be misconstrued. He needn't have worried. "If I hadn't been, if I'd been doing my job, I would have been paying more attention to the shop you went into. I might have followed up in time to prevent your abduction."

"The fault was mine, not yours. I was guilty of thinking of only one thing at a time. Besides," she added briskly, "if events had unfolded differently, I wouldn't have been able to help those two unfortunate Alwari, and we would still be looking for guides to take us to find this overclan. As Master Yoda says, there are many paths through life, so it is best to be happy with whichever one we finally decide to take."

"Ah yes, Master Yoda." He slipped deep into thought.

Along with watching the crowd for signs of trouble, she also stole occasional glances at her fellow Padawan. A hard one to read, this Anakin Skywalker. Strength boiled within him. Strength, and—other things. Already, she saw that he was far more complicated than anyone else she had trained with at the Temple. That in itself was unusual. Once chosen, a Jedi's path was straight and uncomplicated. That was not what she perceived within Anakin Skywalker.

"You said you were preoccupied," she finally said to him. "I sense that it's an unhappy preoccupation."

"Do you, now?" She couldn't decide if he was being sarcastic, or merely agreeable. Behind them, Jedi and guides continued to haggle for mounts. He found himself wishing they would get on with it. He was tired of this place, tired of this assignment. What did it matter if Ansion, or even several dozen allied worlds, seceded from the Republic? Given the current state of galactic governance and of the Senate, with its proven record of corruption and confusion, who could blame them? It might serve as a wake-up call to the rest of the Republic, a warning to clean things up or risk worse to come.

Strong thoughts for a Padawan. He smiled to himself. Obi-Wan was wrong. *I do think about the state of things, sometimes, and not just about myself.*

"Yes, I do," Barriss continued. She was not in the least intimidated by him. "With what are you so preoccupied, Anakin Skywalker? Why are you always so pensive?"

He thought about telling her the truth. In the end, he decided to explain only part of it. With a wave of one hand, he took in the travel market, the surrounding streets, the mixed throng of Ansionians and offworlders, and the city beyond.

"Why are we here? Master Obi-Wan has tried to explain it to me, but I'm afraid I'm not very sympathetic to the intricacies of politics. I find them difficult to understand, even irrelevant to life. Ever since I was a child, I've always had to be a direct sort of person." He looked over at her. "Where I grew up, the way I grew up, if you dissipated your energies, idled away your time, you didn't last long. You want my sincere opinion of this assignment?"

She nodded, watching him.

"It's a waste of time. A job for jabbering diplomats, not Jedi."

"I see. And what would you do if you were in charge, Anakin?"

He didn't hesitate. "I'd round up the leaders of both factions, city and nomad alike, lock them all in the same room, and tell them that if they didn't make peace within a week, the Republic would send a full task force and assume direct control of local affairs."

She was nodding slowly, an infuriatingly tranquil expression on her face. "And how would the Commerce Guild respond to that, given its extensive interests in this sector?"

"The Commerce Guild does what is profitable. War with the Republic is not profitable." He looked convinced. "That much I've learned."

"And if the Ansionian Unity of cities and towns, in consequence of this action of yours, makes good on its threat to join the new secessionist movement, and the other worlds that are allied to Ansion decide to join in—?"

"It wouldn't make any difference to people's daily lives. Trade would continue, everyday life on the worlds involved wouldn't change," he huffed.

"Are you so certain that you would risk thousands of lives to find out? And what would happen to the Alwari, who disagree with the present path of the Unity? Would not the Commerce Guild and its allies come down hard on them?"

"Well, I'm not sure that . . ." Under her relentless reasoning, his wall of certainty was beginning to crack.

She looked away from him, returned to studying the lively crowd. "Better, I think, to send a pair of Jedi and their Padawans to try to fix things. Far less threatening than a task force. Also cheaper, a course of action that always pleases the Senate."

He sighed. "You argue plausibly. But Ansion is such a nowhere world! Even Obi-Wan wonders if it is very important. He's spoken to me about it several times, as well as about what he thinks is wrong these days with the Republic itself."

"Flashpoints," she shot back. "Surely he has also spoken to you about flashpoints, and the need to stamp them out before they can grow into uncontainable conflagrations."

"Interminably." He sighed resignedly as he resumed surveying the crowd with her.

"It is a fair price." The mane of the Ansionian trader had been painted with alternating silver and black chevrons that ran down his spine to disappear beneath his low-cut collar. Convex lavender-hued eyes studied his clients blankly, giving away nothing. "Nowhere else in Cuipernam, or on the Sorr-ul-Paan Plateau, will you find six such splendid steeds of such grace and quality! Not for thrice the price!"

"Be not overinsistent," Kyakhta told him, "lest your incessant haranguing curdle the stomachs of my masters." Turning away from the broker, he lowered his voice as he and Bulgan conferenced with their new employers.

"He is right, Master Luminara. The price he asks is a fair one. Slightly high, perhaps, but the animals are in excellent condition."

"To ride such mounts!" Bulgan could hardly contain his anticipation.

"Give us a moment." Turning away, Luminara left the two Alwari to continue with the negotiations, although by now these were no more than a matter of trying to shave minuscule amounts off the broker's final offer. "What do you think, Obi-Wan?"

He surveyed the surrounding market, ever alert for signs of impending aggression. "I think we should rely on the native expertise of our new guides. After what your Padawan did for them, I believe they would cheat themselves before they would take advantage of her." A glance back showed the two Alwari still arguing agreeably with the seller. "Besides, I'm rather looking forward to riding one of the beasts. One of these days, I have a feeling I'll have no choice but to ride around in old skimmers and beat-up landspeeders." Looking up, he studied the clear blue sky.

Luminara eyed the Padawans. "There is still tension between Barriss and Anakin."

"Yes." Obi-Wan sighed. "I've noticed it, too. But they appear to be getting on better since her ordeal. A fine student, Barriss. The Force flows strongly within her."

"So it does, but not like it does in young Anakin. He is a wild river, your Padawan, full of repressed energy that needs channeling."

"He came unreasonably late to training, and was raised by his mother to a greater age than the usual apprentice."

Luminara looked again in the Padawans' direction. "He knew his mother? That is a bond Jedi apprentices do not normally bring with them. It presents all manner of potential complications and difficulties."

"I know. For that reason alone I would have not accepted him, but he was taken up by my own Master, Qui-Gon Jinn, whose dying wishes I vowed to respect. Among other matters that had to be dealt with subsequent to his passing, that meant dealing with and bringing along this unusually volatile youth."

"How has it gone?" she asked earnestly.

Obi-Wan stroked his beard absently. "He's often impetuous, which is worrying. Sometimes it carries over into impatience, which is dangerous. But he has gone through and survived a great deal, and he is an avid student of Jedi lore. There are subjects in which he excels, such as lightsaber combat. And he's a natural pilot. But he has little time for the intricacies of history or diplomacy, and politics positively make him ill. Yet he perseveres. A trait he gets, I believe, from his mother, whom Qui-Gon knew but briefly as a quiet yet strong-willed woman."

She nodded thoughtfully. "If anyone can turn such unwieldy raw material into a polished Jedi Knight, I suspect it is you, Obi-Wan. Many have the knowledge, but few the patience."

"You could do it, I think."

She regarded him straight on. Face to face, the two Jedi gazed into each other's eyes. Each saw something different but worthy there. Each saw something distinctive, even exceptional. When they finally looked away, it was simultaneously.

Turning, Obi-Wan moved to consult with the gently bickering Alwari. She watched him for a long, contemplative moment before turning back to resume her scrutiny of the crowd.

At Obi-Wan's urging, Kyakhta and Bulgan concluded their negotiations for the six animals. At the shoulder, the magnificent suubatars stood thrice the height of a human. They were six-legged, with long-splayed toes that seemed wholly out of place on a creature designed for running through open grasslands.

When Anakin pointed out this seeming evolutionary disparity to Kyakhta, the Alwari laughed.

"You'll see what they are for, Jedi Padawan!" Pulling back on the double set of reins, he effortlessly turned his own newly acquired mount.

The lightweight but thickly padded saddle was cinched between the front and middle shoulders. Between middle shoulders and rear haunches, a second swayback would accommodate a sizable pack of supplies. Having been negotiated for and priced, these were in the process of being loaded onto the complaisant animals by the merchant's busy underlings.

"Food, water, accessories: all has been acquired and accounted for, Master Barriss." Bulgan had his own booted, long-toed feet thrust forward in stirrups that were slung on either side of the suubatar's neck, instead of hanging downward. The smooth arch of the saddle behind him cradled his crippled back. "Ahhhh—*haja!*" he exclaimed with evident pleasure. "To sit like this brings back many memories."

Following Kyakhta's instructions, Luminara straddled her own mount. Despite its height, she had no trouble doing so. First, because it was presently crouched down awaiting its rider, and second, because the body was lean and narrow. The reason for the saddle became immediately apparent. Without it, one would be seated directly atop the line of protruding vertebrae.

"*Elup!*" Kyakhta barked. Starting from the front, the suubatar rose one set of legs at a time: front, middle, and finally rear. The reason for the high-arching leather curve at the back of the saddle was now clear. With no support behind her, the angle of ascent would have sent Luminara bouncing down the creature's spine all the way to the ground.

Though each boasted its own pattern of dark green stripes

set against short soft fur, all six animals were the same underlying light bronze color. The combination would allow them, despite their size and visibility, to blend in well with their prairie land surroundings. Expecting the suubatars to be typical grazing herbivorous creatures, Luminara was surprised to learn that they were in fact omnivores, able to survive on a wide variety of foods. Their long, slim jaws were hinged at the bottom, allowing for an enormous if narrow gape that could swallow astonishingly large fruits or prey in a single gulp. The four front canines protruded above and below the jaws, giving their owners a fearsome appearance that belied their placid nature.

"Of course, these are domesticated individuals," Bulgan told her, divining her thoughts. "Wild suubatars have been known to attack and destroy entire caravans."

"That's reassuring." Bobbing from side to side atop his patient mount, Anakin was struggling to maintain his balance. Kyakhta noted the trouble he was having and came alongside.

"You're sitting up too straight, Master Anakin. Lean back into the viann, the saddle support. There, that's it. See how your legs now thrust naturally into the forward stirrups?"

"But I can't see as well in this position," the Padawan complained, struggling to hang on to the double set of reins.

"I think we're high up enough to see anything of importance," Obi-Wan told him. He lay back in the saddle as one to the manner born. "Look on this as another unexpected episode in your education."

"I'd rather be educated in a late-model landspeeder," Anakin grumbled. But Kyakhta was right. The more he leaned back and trusted the saddle, the sturdier and more stable he felt. Maybe this wouldn't be so bad after all.

Could he trust himself to a strange, alien animal? The suu-batars were certainly handsome creatures, with their protruding silver-flecked eyes, single wide flaring nostril, and smooth skulls. Their ears were set flush against their skulls and unlike the Ansio-nians, they had no manes. The striped fur was short and dense, evolved to provide maximum insulation with minimum wind re-sistance. Tails were leg-length but as slender as the rest of the beast. Everything about the creatures spoke to one end.

Speed.

"Everyone ready?" Holding his steed's reins effortlessly in one hand, Kyakhta looked back at his companions. Bulgan sig-naled that the last of the supplies had been loaded. "Then let's go and find the Borokii!" Facing forward, he slapped his mount on the smooth back of its neck and shouted sharply, *"Elup!"*

The suubatar seemed to rise from the ground. In reality, it had simply launched into the requested gallop. The six-legged gait was extraordinarily smooth, Luminara noted delightedly. There was little sensation of jouncing or jolting. Leaning back in the saddle's viann, her fine, strong legs thrust calf-length into the deep leather stirrups, she watched the city fly past. Sluggish pedestrians had to scramble to get out of their way.

Far sooner than she expected, they sped beneath the high-arching Govialty Gate of the old city and found themselves on a dirt road leading westward. Kyakhta came pounding up along-side her. Despite what struck the Jedi as an extreme pace, she noted that his mount was not even breathing hard.

"Are you comfortable, then, Master Luminara?" The guide shouted to make himself heard.

"It's wonderful!" she yelled back. "Like riding on a cloud made of spun Dramassian silk!" Outside the city walls, they were exposed to the near-constant winds that circled the planet endlessly. Cool air rushed past her face, the suubatar's long, narrow, slightly triangular skull parting it like the prow of a ship.

A glance back showed Barriss hanging on for dear life, while Anakin's expression alternated between grim determination and youthful alarm. She would have laughed, had it not been unseemly. As for Obi-Wan Kenobi, he sat serenely in his embroidered saddle, arms crossed over his chest, eyes closed. His reins lay secured to the pommel-like brace in front of him. He might as well, she thought with some astonishment, have been sitting in a first-class seat on a starliner. She had known many Jedi, but never one so composed in the face of the unexpected.

"Kyakhta!" she called out to the rider galloping alongside her. "It's good to leave the city behind so swiftly, but aren't you concerned about overexerting our mounts? Won't this pace tire them quickly?"

"Overexerting? Tire?" From his saddle, he eyed her quizzically. Then realization dawned. "*Ou,* you do not understand. But that is reasonable. None of you have ever seen a suubatar before, much less ridden one." Pulling his slim legs and feet free of his stirrups, he stood up on the back of his pounding steed and looked back the way they had come, holding on to the crest of the viann for balance. "No one pursues us, but of one thing I'm sure: Bossban Soergg is not snoring this business away." Sitting back down and resuming his former riding posture, he smiled at her anew. "You're sure you are comfortable?"

"It feels almost natural. As I told you, I'm enjoying it."

He performed the Ansionian equivalent of a nod. "Then there's no need for us to continue dawdling here." Raising his voice and freeing his feet from the stirrups, he leaned forward once again and shouted, *"Elup!"* At the same time he kicked his mount sharply with his heels, making contact simultaneously on both front shoulders.

"By the Force!" Anakin exclaimed as he grabbed for something to brace himself with. Barriss started laughing wildly, the acceleration sending her cowl and the folds of her robes streaming backward like flames. Obi-Wan deigned to wake up.

Until then, it seemed, the suubatars had only been trotting. At Kyakhta's command, they broke into a six-legged sprint of such speed that their long-toed legs seemed not to touch the ground. When they did, six long powerful clawed toes dug into the hard-packed dirt and flung it backward. Thirty-six such digits propelled each ground-thundering suubatar forward at a velocity that left a thoroughly exhilarated Luminara momentarily breathless.

Which was not surprising, since they were now outpacing the wind.

Far behind them, a motley coterie of assorted thugs, brutes, and ruffians assembled atop the city wall by the very gate through which the Jedi and their guides had departed. Off in the distance, a very faint cloud of dust could be seen dissipating atop a low, rolling, grass-covered hill. To Ogomoor it might as well have been poison gas.

"That must be them." He turned to the hulking Varvvan standing at his side. "Get your people together. We're going after them."

"At that speed? You heard what the people in the market said. They're riding suubatars. Purebloods, at that." Behind them, the other members of the hastily assembled troop of cut-throats had begun to mutter among themselves.

"We'll take an airtruck. No suubatar can outpace an airtruck."

"Not outpace, no. But outmaneuver . . ." The Varvvan's

eyes leaned closer to Ogomoor's. "You ever try to corner an Al-wari mounted on a good suubatar? A quick way to die."

"*Bastasi!*" the impatient Ogomoor exclaimed. "As you will. What besides an airtruck will persuade you to follow my order and go after those six?"

The Varvvan considered, rubbing one eye as he studied the wispy remnants of the distant dust cloud. "Heavy weapons," he finally declared.

"Don't be stupid!" Ogomoor barked at the hireling. "Not even Bossban Soergg can engage heavy weapons in Cuipernam! There are some limitations that even he—*urk!*"

Clutching the squirming majordomo by the collar, the Varvvan had lifted him off the ground and was holding him in that position. "Don't—call—me—stupid."

Aware that he might have let his anger and annoyance get a teensy bit the better of him, Ogomoor hastened to calm the mercenary. "It was just a blurted exclamation—I meant nothing personal by it—now please let me down and—could you perhaps retract your eyeballs? They're oozing."

With a hiss, the Varvvan set him down. Straightening his jacket, Ogomoor turned to gaze longingly at the distant rise over which his quarry had disappeared. "Why the worry, anyway? The visitors are being led by a couple of clanless morons!"

Shouldering his compaction rifle, the Varvvan hissed again and turned away. His kind were brave, even fearless—but despite Ogomoor's assertion, they were not dumb.

"Say *you*. But I, and my associates, know only what we see. And what I see are four visitors and two escorts who do not ride like clanless morons." He started down the steps that led back to the city streets. "They ride like Alwari."

Frustrated beyond words, Ogomoor turned his attention

away from the useless mercenaries and back to the beginnings of the endless grasslands beyond Cuipernam. Where, he wailed silently, could he find assassins worthy of his orders? Where could he find beings willing to take up weapons against the unmentionable Jedi? Where could he find the kind of quality help that, at every turn, seemed to be denied him?

Most importantly of all, where could he find someone else to tell Soergg the Hutt that the Jedi and their Padawans had, once again, flown free of his intentions and beyond his reach?

Much to Ogomoor's surprise, Soergg listened quietly to his majordomo's report. "Once again, too late. Punctuality is the hallmark of the successful assassin."

"There was nothing I could do, Bossban. Those I had hired refused to pursue the fleeing Jedi."

"Yes, yes, so you told me." Soergg waved a dismissive hand. "Riding suubatars, you said. Given that, I'm not surprised at the lack of enthusiasm on the part of your puerile hirelings." He rubbed his vast chin, the flesh quivering like the sulfurous outfall of some particularly noxious thermal vent. "First a bungled killing, then a bungled kidnapping. The Jedi are on their guard now."

"They cannot be taken by surprise," Ogomoor added, unnecessarily.

"Perhaps." Huge slitted eyes looked past the assistant, toward distant places. "Certainly not by us."

"I don't understand, master."

Soergg did not reply. He was still gazing at that distant place, thinking Huttish thoughts.

I t was not merely beautiful out on the endless prairie that covered much of Ansion's landmass: it was magnificent. At least, Luminara thought so. Barriss agreed with her, while Obi-Wan was
impressed but noncommittal. As usual, Anakin wished himself
elsewhere, but refrained from saying so more than once a day.

"A year ago he would have been bemoaning his situation two
or three times a day," Obi-Wan pointed out that evening to Luminara. "I suppose it's a sign that he's maturing."

Nearby, Kyakhta and Bulgan were busy with the camp,
preparing food and making tea. Behind them, a ways off, the six
splendid suubatars had been set down for the night. Their legs
folded beneath their powerful, slender bodies, the graceful steeds
busied themselves browsing the grasses and grains that grew in
abundance all around them.

The prairies of Ansion were not all unbroken fields of grass.
Rivers cut erratically through the yellow-green flatlands while
rolling hills occasionally interrupted the monotony of the terrain.
There were clumps of forest filled with strange, intertwined trees

and brachiating fungi. Higher ridges were the bones of old volcanic vents and plugs. It was a strange landscape, an odd combination of different geologies jumbled together in a way Luminara had not encountered previously.

"Why is he so stressed all the time?" Leaning up against the viann of the saddle that the guides had uncinched and removed from her ruminating mount, she chewed on the stick of nut-flavored nutrient and waited for her tea to get hot.

The central campfire was reflected in Obi-Wan's eyes. "Anakin? As is common in such instances, there's more than one reason. For one thing, he feels obligated to excel. This is largely a product of his difficult upbringing, so different from that of the average Padawan. Also, he misses many things."

"Anyone who trains to become Jedi knows they will have to give up many things."

He nodded in agreement. "He fears he will never see his mother, whom he loves very much, ever again."

"That was a terrible mistake. Force-sensitive infants are removed from their families before they can form such dangerously lasting attachments." She sounded momentarily wistful. "I sometimes wonder what my own mother is doing, even at this moment, as we sit here discussing such things. I wonder if she is thinking the same thing about me." She looked away, off into the darkening prairie. "What about you, Obi-Wan? Do you ever think of your parents?"

"I have too much else to think about. Besides, every Jedi who is given charge of an apprentice has become a kind of parent. Being one leaves me with no time to think of my own. When such feelings do intrude, I find myself thinking of my teachers or Master Qui-Gon, and not my birth parents. Sometimes—sometimes I wonder if it isn't a flaw in Jedi training to take infants from their families."

"The proof of the truth lies in the success of the system. That, no one can doubt."

"I suppose," he replied. With a slight smile he added, "No Jedi would be a true devotee who didn't question the system, along with everything else."

She looked to her right, to the other side of the camp. "Your Anakin may be subject to many flaws, but an unwillingness to question things certainly isn't one of them. Will he ever see his mother again, do you think?" she asked thoughtfully.

"Who can say? If it were up to him, he would. But it's not up to him, any more than the direction of my future travelings are up to me. We go where the Council sends us. Better to ask such questions of Master Yoda than me." Again the sly smile. "Ask *him* if he thinks of his own birth parents."

She had to laugh. "Master Yoda's parents! Now we are talking of ancient history indeed." Her tone grew serious again. "Master Yoda has, so it is said, more important things on his mind these days."

He smiled thinly. "Always. This fermenting secessionist business foremost among them. Shifting, unpredictable alliances in the Senate itself. As for Anakin, there are other things occupying his thoughts besides his mother. I can sense the turmoil that bubbles inside him. But when I bring it up, he refuses to acknowledge that such disturbances even exist. Strange, how he is willing to question the validity of everything but his own inner uncertainties."

"Ah." Reaching down, she picked up the self-heating tumbler of hot Ansionian tea. It was black and sweet, with a distinctive tang of the open plains. Everything here tasted of the prairie, she was coming to realize. "Given so much powerful self-denial, do you really think he can become a full Jedi Knight?"

"I don't know. I really don't know. But I promised Master Qui-Gon that I would try my best to make it happen. To that end I have disagreed, before the Council, with Master Yoda himself. Yes, I have my doubts. But a promise is a promise. If Anakin succeeds in overcoming his own internal demons, he will make a great Jedi, and Master Qui-Gon's judgment will be vindicated."

"And you? What of your judgment, Obi-Wan?"

"I try not to make judgments." Rising, he dusted off his robe. "Anakin knows he has problems. I teach, I advise, I offer a sympathetic ear. But in the end, only Anakin can decide what Anakin will become. I think he knows that, but refuses to accept it. He wants me, or someone else, to make everything right, from his mother's condition to the condition of the galaxy." The smile widened slightly. "As you may have noted, he can be very headstrong when there is something that he wants."

"I would prefer to think 'resolute.' " She lowered the tumbler from her lips. Steam rose from the container, snaking slowly up in front of her face, blurring the distinct outlines of the tattoos on her chin. "What's the biggest problem? His mother? The deliberate pace of his education?"

"If I knew that, I would try to cure it. I think it is buried much deeper. So deep he isn't even aware of it himself. Someday it will come out." He turned and started to walk away. "When it does, I have a feeling it will make for some interesting times."

"Is that a feeling that emanates from the Force?" she called after him.

"No." Glancing back over his shoulder, he smiled one more time. "It's a feeling that emanates from Obi-Wan Kenobi."

She was alone only for a moment. Holding her own tumbler,

Barriss sat down beside her. The Padawan's gaze followed the re-treating Jedi. "What were you and Obi-Wan discussing, Master?"

Luminara leaned back against the comforting, supportive arc of the viann. On the other side of the camp, a suubatar bayed at one of the two half-moons that hung in the sky like the stolen earrings of an abdicated queen.

"Nothing of significance to you, my dear."

Unsatisfied with this response, but understanding that it meant she should probe no farther, Barriss tilted back her head to study the night sky. Brilliant with distant, steadily shining stars, it was unmarred by cloud or corruption. Unlike the aging, stumbling Republic, she reflected worriedly.

"So many stars, Master. So many planets, many with their own individual sentient species, cultures, attitudes. Some part of the Republic, others independent, still others as yet unexplored or undiscovered. I look forward to visiting as many of them as possible." Her eyes dropped to meet those of the older woman. "It's one of the main reasons I enjoy being a Jedi."

Luminara laughed. Her laugh was not soft and subtle, as one might have expected, but robust, even startling.

Barriss turned more serious.

"Are you lonely, Master Luminara?"

Soft sipping sounds came from the other woman's dark-stained lips as she swallowed the invigorating tea. The charming, inquisitive Barriss had never been one to hide her curiosity be-hind the veil of false subtlety. "All Jedi are lonely to one degree or another, Padawan. You'll learn that soon enough. The differ-ence lies in the degree. There are those who are more comfort-able with an ascetic lifestyle than others. Within the rules, there is some flexibility. You simply have to seek it out."

Barriss looked to the other side of the fire. "Is that what Anakin is trying to do? Find flexibility?"

Sensitive, she was, Luminara marveled. Her Padawan was going to make an exceptional healer. "He's certainly searching for something. Answers to questions he hasn't even formed yet. Whether he can find enough of them to make him happy remains to be seen. I've spoken to Obi-Wan about it. He isn't sure, either. He knows only that his Padawan has enormous potential."

Barriss rose. "Potential that goes unrealized is potential that might as well not exist in the first place."

From her recumbent position, Luminara looked up into the night. "Don't be so quick to judge, Barriss. Some of us suffer from greater uncertainties than others. I would as soon have Anakin Skywalker by my side in a fight as any Padawan I have ever met."

"In a fight, yes, Master. At other times . . ." She left the thought unfinished as she pivoted and walked back to her own sleeping place.

Luminara watched the young woman turn in. Had she herself ever been that restless, that uncertain? Leaning back, she scanned the stars anew. So many indeed, she mused, silently echoing her Padawan's observation. Each system with its own problems, each individual living therein with its own hopes and fears, triumphs and heartaches. Even now there might be dozens, hundreds of individual sentients, lying outside contemplating the night, wondering if another was feeling what they were feeling, gazing out across the light-years in search of enlightenment. Hoping.

Determinedly, she drained the last of the native tea and set the tumbler aside. The work of a Jedi was never done, whether it was bludgeoning recalcitrant planetary councils like the Ansionian Unity into seeing reason, fighting to hold the Republic together, or counseling distraught individual souls. Burdens enough for any one entity. She could deal with the exigencies. So, she knew, could Obi-Wan Kenobi. One day the same would be true for Barriss Offee. As for Anakin Skywalker, that remained to be seen.

Potential, Barriss had said. Was ever a word so fraught with confliction? As for Anakin's future happiness, where was it written that one had to be happy to perform well as a Jedi? Content, yes. Accepting, surely. But "happy"? Was *she* happy?

Focus on the task at hand, she told herself firmly. And the task at hand was not satisfying the curiosity of her apprentice, not trying to understand the puzzling Padawan Anakin Skywalker, not even supporting the aims and ideals of the Republic. No, the task at hand was to get a good night's rest in the absence of a comfortable bed. Turning onto her side, she pulled the thermosensitive blanket up to her neck, closed her eyes, and allowed herself to drift off into a deep and soothing sleep, where even a Jedi could, for a little while, openly and freely set aside all responsibilities.

The majordomo was impressed, but not sanguine. Bossban Soergg's plan was clever enough, but its success was far from guaranteed. Still, he admired several aspects of it, and said so, while keeping his criticisms to himself. It relied for success on a certain number of assumptions about the nomads. If there was one thing Ogomoor knew for certain about the nomads, it was that nothing was certain about them.

Still, it did not involve him risking his own neck, one aspect of the plan he heartily, if silently, applauded. He moved to implement it immediately. There was a good chance it would all come to naught, since it relied entirely on the advice of outsiders. As Soergg appeared to trust their opinions, Ogomoor had no choice but to go along with them.

If it worked, of course, the bossban would get everything he wanted, at no personal risk to himself. That was the beauty of it. Even better, when the truth came out, it would drive even deeper the wedge that already existed between the city folk of the Unity and the people of the plains. At that point, nothing and no one would be able to stop Ansion from pulling out of the Republic, with all the consequent actions the bossban seemed so eager to facilitate.

Personally, Ogomoor didn't see the significance of it one way or the other. In the Republic or out, what difference did it make to him? All he cared about was the size and integrity of his pay transfer.

With luck, and if all went as planned, they would have the results they sought in a week or two.

The water was wide, deep, and clear, but to Luminara's eyes the current was not threatening. Sitting on his mount alongside her, Kyakhta let its head drop the considerable distance to the ground to snag a few mouthfuls of the spotted zeka grass that grew there, and a pair of rodentlike coleacs as well. The bones of the latter being efficiently crunched provided a noisy counterpart to the guide's words.

"Torosogt River," he announced proudly. "We've made good time. Once across, we will truly be in the realm of the Al-wari. No towns beyond this place. No fault-finding, arrogant 'Unity.' "

"How long till we reach the Borokii?" she asked him.

Black pupils stared back at her out of dark-hued, protuberant orbs. "Impossible to tell. They have their traditional grazing grounds, but like any clan, the Borokii are always on the move."

"Too bad we couldn't find them with a seeker droid and put an aerial tracker on them," Anakin observed from behind them.

Kyakhta flashed sharp teeth in the Padawan's direction. "The Alwari choose to retain many of the old ways, but they are ever ready to make use of new developments that do not contradict tradition. Having always had weapons, they are happy to make use of better ones. They would use these to instantly shoot down any device sent to try to monitor them."

"Oh." Anakin accepted this explanation without argument. *When,* he thought to himself, *will I learn to see beyond the obvious?* While the latter might be an admirable trait in a Podracer, it would not do much to qualify him as a Jedi.

The party started forward again, Kyakhta's mount spitting out small bones as it walked. "You see the problem Unity emissaries face. How can they make treaties and commerce with the Alwari if the clans will not stay in one place long enough to talk to them? Yet it is these same traditional rights of the nomads that Republic law protects. No wonder the cities are considering banding together to join this proposed secessionist movement. If they succeed in pulling Ansion out of the Republic, then they can deal with the Alwari as they choose."

"And yet the Alwari think we may be here to support the claims of the Unity," Luminara responded.

Kyakhta eyed her with an intelligence unsuspected prior to Barriss's healing ministrations. "Isn't your primary task here to see that Ansion stays in the Republic?"

"Of course," she replied without hesitation.

"Then the Alwari are entitled to question the means by

which you might choose to make that happen. They'll know that they and their interests are not your priority."

"So do the delegates of the Unity." She sighed tiredly. "You see, Kyakhta? Both sides are already united by their common suspicion of our motives. Not exactly a firm foundation for mutual understanding, but it's a beginning."

The slope leading down from the last grasses to the river's edge was not acute enough to slow a crawling infant, much less the towering suubatars. The group paused on the bank while Kyakhta and Bulgan studied the flow with an eye toward picking the best place to cross. Finally, Bulgan started forward while Kyakhta directed their charges to hold back.

"The Torosogt runs deep, but Bulgan thinks he has found a sandbar shallow enough for the suubatars to walk most of the way. From there we will swim."

Luminara leaned forward in her saddle. "I suppose we could all do with a bath."

"No, no." A smiling Kyakhta hurried to correct the misunderstanding. "We don't swim. The suubatars will carry us." Ignoring the considerable distance to the ground, he leaned way over to indicate his steed's middle legs. "See—a suubatar's fur is short, but runs all the way to its feet and down between the toes. With six legs and long toes, suubatars are very good swimmers."

Luminara had to admit that a vision of swimming suubatars was one that had not occurred to her. As Kyakhta had pointed out, six churning legs would provide plenty of propulsion.

She had time to fill in the image while Bulgan made progress. Halfway across the river he stopped, turned in his saddle, and waved. By this time the water was up over his knees despite his high seat on the suubatar. Luminara wondered how deep the river ran on either side of the "shallow" sandbar. Giving her mount a perfectly enunciated *"Elup!,"* she found herself starting forward in tandem with Kyakhta.

Water rose gradually until it was up to her stirruped feet. As her mount was slightly larger than Bulgan's, she remained dry. Barriss and Anakin were not so fortunate. She could hear them both grumbling quietly behind her. As for Obi-Wan, when the water reached his feet, he simply pulled them out of the stirrups and crossed them atop the saddle. A spectator would have thought he'd been riding suubatars all his life.

Bulgan waited for them to catch up before resuming his own forward movement. There was a brief sensation of dropping, a quick bob upward, and she realized the suubatars were no longer walking. If anything, their swimming motion was even smoother than their remarkable gallop. While paddling effortlessly forward, they held their long, narrow skulls just above the surface. That did not mean no exertion was involved. The snorting of their single, wide nostril was clearly audible.

The water lapping against her feet and calves was cold and bracing. Looking down, she could see schools of streamlined, multilegged backswimmers riding the wake generated by her mount. The finger-length water breathers had their multiple limbs folded flat against their sides to conserve energy.

She was already focusing on the opposite shore when Bulgan's mount was suddenly thrown sharply to the right. The two Alwari let out a simultaneous, though different, curse and drew their weapons. Her hand went automatically to her lightsaber, but search as she might, she could see nothing like an enemy.

Then her own steed was slammed violently sideways. If not for her feet being jammed firmly into the stirrups, she would have been thrown right off the saddle and into the water. Despite her concentration, she was aware of everything that was happening around her—especially Kyakhta's sharp but inexplicable warning cry of "gairks!" *What was a gairk?* she wondered.

Then a warty, misshapen olive-green face emerged from the water entirely too close to her left foot, and her curiosity was instantly sated.

Full of bulges and protrusions, the maw of the gairk was unlike any oral cavity she had ever seen. There was no symmetry to it at all. The thick, blubbery lips seemed to wander all over the pebbly-skinned face. From behind these gaping lips rose a pair of large, protuberant, gray-green eyes. Lightsaber raised high, she swung at the bloated, bottom-dwelling monstrosity, but it had already dived back beneath the surface before the blow could make contact. Another of the ugly creatures surfaced a short distance away.

She found herself drowning not in water, but in a rising din. The hum of Jedi lightsabers was interspersed with the bellowing of kicking, snapping suubatars, the shouts of her companions, and the intermittent crackle of their guides' newly bought blasters. She ought to have been more afraid, she knew, or at least felt a greater degree of apprehension.

Most peculiar of all, as near as she could tell, the gairk had no teeth.

If they weren't carnivores, then why were they attacking the crossing party? Did they rely on some other less apparent mechanism to catch and devour prey? Certainly, she saw as her mount reared sharply to kick out with both clawed forefeet at a gairk that crossed its path, their mouths were large enough to swallow a human whole. But she saw no biting apparatus, no sharp talons, not even potentially poisonous spines. Yet Kyakhta and Bulgan were treating them as if they were nothing but fang and claw.

Then she heard a yelp. Whirling in her saddle without regard to her own safety, she looked back at Barriss's suubatar. It was still behind her, holding the same position as when they had started to ford the river. There was only one difference.

The animal's embossed saddle was empty.

Barriss surfaced not far away, easily visible in the swirling tide because she was waving with her activated lightsaber. Kyakhta cursed violently. It struck Luminara that the Padawan was being carried downstream faster than the turgid current warranted. She pointed this out to Bulgan.

"It's the gairks!" the despondent Alwari told her. "They're dragging her away!"

Luminara's expression twisted. "Dragging her? With what? They have no hands."

By way of answer, the guide opened his mouth to form a wide, gaping O. Suddenly chilled by more than the river water, Luminara understood.

The instant he'd seen Barriss knocked off her mount and swept downstream, Anakin had gone in after her. He hadn't thought about it. The action was entirely reflexive. He knew that if the circumstances had been reversed, she would now be the one swimming hard to catch up with him. When he saw that she was unaccountably receding away from him, he redoubled his stroke. He was a strong swimmer, having grown fond of the skill when he had been confined indoors during winter months. Before long he was close enough to exchange words.

"You okay?" he called out to her. "How are you, Barriss?"

"Wet," she shot back. "Very—wet."

"Can you swim with me to shore?" Raising a hand, he

STAR WARS: THE APPROACHING STORM ══════ 119

pointed to where the others were already beginning to emerge on the far bank.

"I'm afraid I can't," she told him. "This situation sucks." At his look of incomprehension, she gestured downward with her free hand. "I mean literally."

Taking a deep breath, he ducked under the surface. The crystal-clear water offered little in the way of obstruction to his vision. He saw her legs, kicking hard but driving her nowhere. Behind her in the water was a single gairk, mouth agape, gills expanded to the maximum. It was taking in water in a steady stream and expelling it through its gills as it applied suction to drag her steadily downstream. Bursting back to the surface, he gestured reassuringly.

"Hang on. I'll take care of this." Taking another deep breath, he dipped back down and swam straight toward the creature, ignoring her legs in passing.

It did not try to dodge. It didn't have to, since he found himself intercepted in midwater. Looking back, he saw that not one but three of the creatures had taken up positions behind him. No two of the twisted maws were exactly alike, but when the three put their heads together, the differently shaped jaws fit together like the pieces of a puzzle. They were now applying suction to him—in unison. A fourth joined in. He felt himself being drawn inexorably back toward that unified dark maw. It now struck him, as it had Luminara, that they had no teeth. They didn't need them. By joining their jaws together to create greater and greater amounts of suction, they literally inhaled their prey.

The technique was uncomplicated. Jolt travelers off larger, inconsumable crossers like the suubatars, get them in the water, drag them downstream away from help, and then ingest them at leisure. Only, he and Barriss were not helpless grass grazers. The need for air was becoming imperative. Kick as he might, he found himself unable to free himself from the force of that quadruple suction. What was it Obi-Wan had often told him? If you can't defy the storm, go with it.

Turning, he kicked not away from his assailants, but directly toward them. Dark maws yawned expectantly. Lack of oxygen was beginning to blur his vision when he drew close enough to strike out with the lightsaber. As their flesh was parted, the four conjoined gairks separated, and the drag on his body evaporated. With the last remaining oxygen in his lungs, he kicked for the surface, breaking it with a gasp and sucking gratefully at the fresh air. Nearby, he saw Barriss swimming not for the nearby shore, but toward him.

"You all right?" she inquired. She seemed unjustly composed.

"I was coming," he wheezed, wiping water from his face, "to rescue you."

"I appreciate the gesture," she responded courteously while continuing to tread water, "but I was really in no trouble."

Aware that their Masters and the two guides were watching from shore, he forced down the first retort that sprang to mind. "You didn't look like you were in no trouble. You were being pulled downstream."

"I know that. It was just a matter of getting turned around so that I could strike at the gairk." Her eyes bored unflinchingly into his own as she deactivated and resecured her lightsaber. "You could have stayed on your suubatar. Did you hear me yelling for help? Did I ask you to come in after me?"

His reply was curt. "I see. Well, now that I understand you a little better, I promise that you won't have to worry about it happening again." He started to kick toward shore.

She kept pace with him easily. "Don't misunderstand, Anakin. It was a gallant gesture, and I appreciate your willingness to risk yourself on my behalf." She chuckled softly, her laugh far more restrained than that of her Master. "Not to mention your willingness to get yourself soaked for me."

Stroking smoothly on his side, he looked down at himself. "I certainly did that, didn't I? You swim well."

She laughed again. "The Force is with me. Race you to shore."

"You're—" Before he could say "on," she had burst forward like an eel. He almost caught up to her, but her hands and feet touched the sandy beach an instant before his own.

Two solemn-faced Jedi were waiting to greet them.

"Well, you two are certainly a pretty sight." Luminara stood with hands on hips. "What happened, Barriss?"

Barriss looked away. "It was my fault. I leaned too far to one side to try to see what was going on up front, lost my balance, and fell. Then something started pulling at my back and clothing, and I found myself being dragged downcurrent. I could see that it was some kind of water creature, but in falling out of the saddle my robes became twisted around me. Wet, I had a difficult time unwrapping them before I could get to my lightsaber."

"Very good, Padawan," conceded Obi-Wan. He turned his attention to the other apprentice. "What's your excuse, Anakin?"

Moving one foot slightly in a nervous gesture his mother would have recognized instantly, the taller Padawan muttered uneasily, "I went in to help her. Once I reached her, I realized she didn't need my help. But I didn't know that at the time." Looking up, he met his Master's gaze. "All I had to go on was the evidence of my senses. They told me she'd been dumped in the water and might need help. I'm sorry if I did something wrong, or violated yet one more unfathomable Jedi rule."

Obi-Wan held his silence and his expression for a long moment—before breaking out into a wide grin. "Not only did you not violate any rules, Padawan—you did exactly what you should have done. You had no way of knowing your colleague's condition. Under such circumstances, to assume that she might need assistance is always the wisest course. Better to be berated by a live friend than absolved by a dead one."

For a moment, Anakin looked uncertain. Compliments from Obi-Wan were as rare as snow-crystal on Tattooine. When he realized that it was meant, and that both Barriss and Luminara were also smiling encouragingly at him, he finally relaxed. Anyway, he did not have much choice. It's hard to stay tense when one is dripping wet. Something about being soaked to the skin, with one's clothes hanging limp as seaweed from sodden limbs, is desperately debilitating to one's dignity.

"I just wanted to help," he muttered, unaware that had been his mantra since childhood.

"You can help yourself," Obi-Wan told him, "by getting out of those wet clothes and into your spare set." Turning, he regarded the line of waving grass that marched to the edge of the riverbank. "The wind's no warmer here than on the other side, and I'd rather you didn't get sick."

"I'll try not to, Master."

"Good." Obi-Wan stood squinting at the cloudless sky. "We don't have time to waste on illness, no matter how educational the experience."

Stripping off their clothes while their Masters unpacked their small personal kits, Anakin and Barriss dried themselves in the sun. The two guides attended to the patient suubatars and studied the visitors with academic interest.

"Haja," exclaimed Bulgan softly, "just look at them. They have no proper manes. Only a little fur on top of their heads."

"They have no true biting teeth," Kyakhta added. "Only those short, chisel-like white chips."

Bulgan stroked the snout of a resting suubatar. It snuffled appreciatively and pushed its muzzle harder against the guide's ministrating hand. "Look at their fingers. Too short to do any real work. And their toes—utterly useless!"

"And there are too many of them," Kyakhta noted. "Five on each—almost as many as on a suubatar! To look at them, one would think them more closely related to such animals than to thinking beings." He shook his head in an odd, sideways fashion. "One feels sadness for such deficiencies."

Bulgan sniffed through his single nostril. "It may be a good thing. The Highborn of the Borokii cannot help but pity them. The perception of pity is always a good place from which to begin negotiations."

His companion was not so sure. "Either that, or they will see them as abominations against the natural order and give orders to have them killed."

"They had better not try anything like that!" His one good eye blinking, Bulgan waxed indignant. "We owe these visitors, or at least the one called Barriss, for the restored health of our minds."

"Not to mention the fact," Kyakhta added as he rubbed the place where his artificial right arm joined his own flesh, "that if they die prematurely we will not get paid for this journey." Still eyeing the aliens, he wondered whether he and Bulgan might have time enough to dig in the beach for some vaoloi shells. Poached vaoloi would make a wonderful supplement to their supper.

Bulgan grunted and adjusted his eye patch. "I would rather sacrifice all our pay than the life of one friend."

Kyakhta's heavy eyelids closed halfway. "Bulgan, my friend, perhaps Barriss did not complete her Jedi healing on you. Perhaps you would benefit from seeking another treatment."

"It doesn't matter." Giving the suubatar he had been caressing a fond chuck under its sharp chin, Bulgan let the reins dangle down to his hand and started to lead it toward the best grass. "No one on this trip is going to die, anyway. We journey with Jedi Knights."

"That much cannot be disputed." But even as he agreed, Kyakhta thought back to how easily the one called Barriss had been dumped into the water by the aggressive gairk, and found himself wondering just how resilient and tough the aliens he and his friend were guiding were.

"They've left, you know."

Ogomoor relaxed in the chair. It was a fine apartment, expensively decorated and furnished. An apartment suitable for a long-term stay by a visiting dignitary. Its present owner poured himself a tall glass of something cold and lavender. Inwardly, Ogomoor shuddered. What perverse desire explained the human affection for iced liquids?

The member of the Unity delegation gestured with the bottle. "Can I offer you a glass? This is a fine vintage, properly fermented."

Ogomoor smiled in the human manner and politely declined. He could feel the chill from the bottle from where he sat.

With a shrug, the human put down the bottle, raised the glass, and drank. Ogomoor felt his insides shudder in sympathy.

"I know they've left. We all know. They've gone to try to make an agreement with the Alwari. What do you think of their chances?"

"I think they're as good as dead already. They've been gone for several days, with no word." He shifted uncomfortably in the human chair that made no allowance for his short tail.

"It's in the nature of Jedi not to open their mouths unless they have something significant to say. Speaking of which," he added as he sat down on the couch opposite, "why are you here?"

"In the interests of expediting a decision that is critical to the future of Ansion. My future. Your future. Every citizen's future."

The human delegate sipped at his drink. "Go on."

Ogomoor leaned forward, feeling relief as his tail popped out from beneath his backside. "The Unity Council was on the verge of voting on whether or not to withdraw from the Republic when these Jedi offworlders arrived."

"I know." The man was not pleased. That, at least, was a good sign, Ogomoor felt. "That's the Senate for you. Always sending in a Jedi or two when their own obtuse directives get ignored. Serves them right. You'd think they would have come to expect it by now."

"These Jedi have nothing to do with Ansion," Ogomoor persisted. "The many peoples of this world, settlers as well as indigenous, have always acted independently and in their own interests."

The delegate raised his glass in mock salute. "Here's to the Republic, of which we're still a part. Sorry, Ogomoor, but our independence only extends so far."

"Not if we secede. Others will join our action."

"Yes." The human sighed. "I've read the fine print in the treaties. They make us more important than we would otherwise be. Hence the attention of the Jedi."

"How were you intending to vote?" Ogomoor did his best not to seem too interested.

His attempt at disinterest did not fool the delegate. "You'd like to know that, wouldn't you? You and your master the Hutt, and his associates in galactic trade."

"Bossban Soergg has many friends, it is true." Ansionian eyes locked on human ones. "Not all are in business."

The delegate's expression, cordial enough up to now, suddenly turned withering. "Are you threatening me, Ogomoor? You and that overweight slug you call a boss?"

"Not at all," the visitor to the apartment replied quickly. "On the contrary, I am here to show my respect, as well as that of my bossban—and his associates. As residents of Ansion, we are all concerned for the future of our world." He smiled again. "Just because a couple of Jedi have arrived here does not mean we should stand around in awed stupefaction."

The human's gaze narrowed. "What are you getting at?"

Ogomoor made a gesture of indifference. "Why should the Unity sit and founder while waiting for the Jedi to return? Suppose, for example, they do not come back from the plains. They have gone to try to influence the Alwari. Suppose the Alwari influence *them?*"

The human's expression showed that he had not considered this line of reasoning. "If the Jedi don't come back—or come back changed . . . You're saying that after talking with the Alwari, they might be persuaded to favor the nomad point of view?"

Ogomoor looked away. "I didn't say that at all. It's only that in the Jedi's absence, there is nothing to prevent the Unity Council from moving forward instead of sitting still. Are we of Ansion nothing more than mewling infants, to sit around and wait on the movements of offworlders—be they Jedi or not?"

Nodding slowly, the human finished the last of his drink in one long, cold swallow. "What would you have me do?"

Ogomoor sniffed through his single, broad nostril. "Call the council back into session. Take the vote. If the Jedi object to the result, let them file a complaint with the Senate. Ansion already has a government—free of outside influences. What could be the harm in taking the vote?"

"That it could be overturned by the Senate."

Ogomoor nodded understandingly. "Votes are harder to overturn once they have been taken. If the Jedi were here, there would be reason not to call for the vote. But—they are not here." He gestured toward the window and, by implication, the plains beyond. "They have gone. By choice."

The delegate was silent for a long moment. When at last he looked back up at his visitor, there was hesitation in his voice. "It won't be an easy thing, what you ask. The Armalat in particular will object, and you know what they can be like."

Ogomoor gestured significantly. "Time overcomes stubbornness. The longer the Jedi remain away from Cuipernam, the greater will be the erosion of confidence in their abilities among the other members of the council. My bossban and his friends are relying on your known powers of persuasion."

"I still—I don't know," the human murmured, clearly wavering.

"Your efforts will not go unappreciated." Ogomoor rose, glad to be able to abandon the uncomfortable, ill-fitting chair. "Think about it. According to my bossban, changes are coming to the Republic. Changes beyond anything you or I can imagine." In passing his host on the way to the door, he leaned close and lowered his voice. "I am assured it would be most advantageous to be on one side of these changes rather than the other."

The human did not see his guest out. He didn't have the time, having been left with too much to think about.

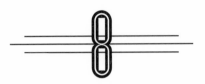

The assault by the gairk had done no harm, Luminara re-flected as they started across new prairie the following morning. It might even have done some good, alerting them to the fact that while they had left the minions of Barriss's would-be kidnapper behind, the planet Ansion presented dangers enough of its own.

While she and Obi-Wan rode on cloaked in the serenity that characterizes mature Jedi, their Padawans were less composed. The incident with the gairks had left them slightly jumpy. De-spite their comfortable, high perches on the backs of their suu-batars, high above the grasslands, they continued to regard everything that moved as a potential threat. Luminara observed Barriss's reactions with mild amusement while offering no com-ment. There was nothing like experience in the field to teach a budding Padawan when to jump and when to relax.

As for Anakin, at times he seemed almost eager for another attack, as if anxious for the opportunity to prove himself. Obi-Wan had spoken of the young man's skill with a lightsaber. But part of that skill, she knew, was knowing when *not* to use the weapon. Still, she found it hard to be critical of him. He wanted so badly to impress, to please.

The flock of ongun-nur provided an excellent lesson. They came swooping down out of the west, their enormous balloon-like wings darkening the sky. Anyone could have been excused for thinking that the huge flying creatures, with their long, rapierlike beaks and bright yellow eyes, represented a threat. At the sight of them commencing their dive, Anakin drew his lightsaber but did not activate it while Barriss made sure her own weapon was ready to draw.

The flock came steadily closer, making no attempt to swerve around the loping suubatars. Anakin's forefinger nervously caressed the ON switch of his lightsaber. Unable to stand it any longer, Barriss urged her mount forward until she drew alongside her teacher.

"Master Luminara, shouldn't we be doing something?" She indicated the oncoming flock. "Those things, whatever they are, are heading straight for us."

Luminara gestured, not at the plummeting ongun-nur, but at Kyakhta. "Look at our guides, Barriss. Do they look apprehensive?"

"No, Master, but that doesn't mean they are unafraid."

"You need to study different sentients more, my dear. Observe the intelligent natives of any world and see how they react to possible danger. Trust your own senses. By all means, keep alert. But there is no need to jump to conclusions, either." Raising a hand, Luminara indicated the dark flock that was almost upon them. "Just because something is large and intimidating in appearance does not mean it is dangerous. Look how the wind buffets them about."

It was true, Barriss saw. For all their great size, the ongun-nur were riding the wind, not manipulating it. They were rushing toward the band of travelers not intending to attack, but hoping they would get out of the way. At the last instant, the great flying creatures were able to alter their angle of descent just enough to carry them past the oncoming riders. So close did they pass that Barriss and Anakin found themselves ducking involuntarily. As they did so, she saw that the wings were paper-thin and the huge bodies swollen with air instead of muscle. The ongun-nur went where the wind took them, unable to fly against it. Seeing the suubatars and their riders heading in their direction, the members of the flock had probably been more frightened of them than the riders had any right to be of the ongun-nur.

It was an instructive visitation, one whose lesson Barriss immediately committed, as always, to memory. From then on, she paid more attention to the reactions of their guides than to whatever phenomenon manifested itself in the sky or in the grass. Similarly, she felt justified in increasing her vigilance when Kyakhta and Bulgan began to slow while sitting up straighter in their saddles.

Topping a rise, they found themselves looking down at a slight depression in the prairie. A sizable but shallow lake had formed there. Except for the center, it was filled with a peculiar spotted, multijointed, bluish reed. At one end of the lake an encampment had been established. A temporary corral held domesticated dorgum and larger, heavy-humped awiquod. Smoke rose from collapsible huts fashioned from imported composite materials. Each hut was tiled with anamorphic solar material that converted Ansion's abundant sunlight directly into power.

Luminara and Obi-Wan rode up to flank Kyakhta and Bulgan. Their guides were leaning forward to peer around the heads of their mounts as they contemplated the camp.

"Borokii?" Luminara asked hopefully.

"By the style of their camp, I would say they are Yiwa," Kyakhta informed her, "of the Qiemo Adrangar. Not an unimportant clan, such as the Eijin or Gaxun, but not an overclan like the Borokii or the Januul, either."

"If they have power," Obi-Wan wondered as he examined the solar huts, "why the need for campfires?"

"Tradition." Bulgan swiveled his crooked form around to focus his good eye on the man mounted next to him. "By now you should know, Jedi, how important that is to the Alwari—and to the success of your mission."

Obi-Wan accepted the mild reminder gracefully. A correction added to one's store of knowledge. It was a thing to be grateful for, not something to take offense at.

Kyakhta pointed. "They come to greet us. The Yiwa are a proud clan. They are constantly on the move, even more so than many of the Alwari. They may have news of the overclan Borokii for us—if they are willing to part with it."

"Why wouldn't they?" Luminara asked directly.

Bulgan blinked his one eye. "The Yiwa are a touchy people, quick to take offense."

"Then we'll be on our best behavior." Obi-Wan turned in his saddle. "Won't we, Anakin?"

His Padawan frowned uncertainly. "Why are you all looking at me?"

The Yiwa came pounding up the slight slope mounted on sadains. Stocky and powerful, the four-legged steeds had round faces with four eyes. In contrast to the suubatar, they boasted long, high ears that flared widely at the top. Unlike the swift suubatar, the sadain was built for pulling and for endurance, not for speed over distance. Those remarkable ears, Obi-Wan reflected as he saw the sunlight shine redly through their blood-rich membranes, would also serve to detect the presence of stalking shanhs and other potential predators of the Yiwa herds.

The welcoming party slowed. There were a dozen of them, decked out in suitably barbaric finery. Homemade bells and polished teeth taken from some of Ansion's less benign fauna alternated with flash colorpans and the latest glowals imported from other worlds of the Republic. The riders had painted their individual manes in a riot of colors and patterns, and the bare skin on either side at the top of each Yiwa head was tattooed in intricate traditional Ansionian patterns. Their appearance was a vivid mélange of the long-established and the contemporary—exactly what one would expect on a world like Ansion.

Two of them held comlinks that doubtless kept them in constant contact with the camp, while several of the riders pointedly displayed weapons that were anything but primitive.

Having the advantage of a much higher seat, Kyakhta nudged his suubatar forward a couple of paces and identified himself and his companions. The Yiwa listened stonily. Then one wearing a cape fashioned from two arc-striped shanh skins kicked his equally well-decorated sadain forward. His bulging red-brown eyes traveled suspiciously between Alwari and off-worlders. Luminara expected initial comments to be directed at her or her fellow humans. She was wrong. The crash training in the most frequently spoken local vernacular she and her companions had received prior to being dispatched to Ansion now proved its worth. The Yiwa dialect was harsh, but not incomprehensible.

"I am Mazong Yiwa. What are clanless ones doing riding suubatars?"

Kyakhta swallowed. Obi-Wan was shocked at the ease and speed with which the heretofore confident guide was intimidated.

"We beg your understanding, Highborn Mazong. Through no faults of our own, my friend and I," he indicated Bulgan, "have been forced to travel the trail of the outcast. We suffered greatly, and have only recently been restored to health, if not clan, by these wise and generous offworlders. They are representatives of the galactic Republic itself, come to treat with the overclan Borokii."

Leaning to his right, Mazong spit deliberately at the foot of Kyakhta's suubatar. The great animal did not move. Anakin started to tense but, seeing his Master apparently unconcerned, did his best to appear likewise.

"The matter of your casting out remains unknown to us. Why should we believe you, or invite you to partake of our hospitality?"

"If not us," Bulgan responded, "then do so for our friends. They are Jedi Knights."

There was a stir among the welcoming party. Luminara remembered what they had been told in Cuipernam. While the Alwari nomads chose to hew to their traditional way of life, that did not mean they were primitive or eschewed modern conveniences. The comlinks and solar-powered homes, the blaster rifles and sidearms they displayed, were proof enough of that.

Mazong's gaze roved among the humans. As he carried out his inspection, he shaded his eyes with one limber, three-fingered hand. Because of the protruding, convex nature of their eyes, Ansionians could not squint. In fact, Luminara had discovered in the marketplace, when the feat was performed by a human or another sighted creature capable of it, any Ansionian close enough to observe it would wince noticeably. The thought of squeezing an eyelid partway shut induced in them the same reaction a human would have upon being forced to listen to fingernails dragging across a piece of slate.

"I have heard of the Jedi." The leader of the Yiwa band kept his hands on the circlet of flexible metal that looped through the bump of cartilage above the huge single nostril of his sadain. "They are said to be honorable people. Unlike so many of those they work for." When none of the humans chose to react to this spur-of-the-moment provocation, Mazong grunted approvingly.

"If you seek an overclan, why trouble the Yiwa with your presence?" Behind him, his clanfolk stirred expectantly.

"You know how the Borokii move about, and how they would react to being tracked by machines." Kyakhta held his suubatar steady.

Mazong laughed, and several of his supporters smiled. "They would blow them out of the sky, along with any who came after them."

"*Haja*," Bulgan agreed. "So we seek them out in the time-honored way." He indicated the community by the lake. "A fine camp, but as usual, a temporary one. It is ever such for the Yiwa, as for all Alwari. In your recent traveling, have you come across any of the overclan?"

Trotting forward, a magnificently bedecked female whispered into one of Mazong's aural cavities. Indicating understanding, he looked back up at the visitors.

"This is no place for conversation. Come down to our camp. We will eat, and talk, and consider your needs." Looking past the two guides, he locked eyes with Luminara. "An agreeable color, blue. No indication of whether the individual behind it is likewise." Turning, he urged his sadain to a gallop. Yelling and waving their weapons, his clanfolk followed him.

The visitors trailed at a more sedate pace. "It doesn't seem too promising, Master." Having grown used to the staid attire of urban Ansionians, Barriss found herself captivated by the Yiwa's purposefully wild appearance.

"On the contrary, Padawan, a good merchant knows that getting a foot in the door before the servomotors can slam it shut is half the battle in making a sale."

They were guided to a transitory central square that had been created by placing half a dozen of the self-erecting huts in a semicircle facing the lake. Laughing and squealing children appeared from nowhere to flank the group, while the youthful equivalents of Anakin and Barriss stared in obvious envy at the two Padawans. Anakin did his best to stifle any incipient feelings of superiority. It was an ongoing problem with him that Obi-Wan had been at pains to point out on more than one occasion.

Their suubatars were taken away amid mutterings of admiration for such first-class mounts. Luminara had a momentary concern for their supplies, but Kyakhta reassured her.

"We are officially guests now, Master. To steal anything from us would be to breach ancient traditions of hospitality. The thief would be cast out permanently—if not fed to the shanhs. Worry not for your belongings."

She put a hand on his arm. "Forgive me for not trusting you, Kyakhta. I know you would have said something if there was any reason for concern."

They were led to the edge of the lake. A section of reeds had been cleared away to provide a clear view across the tranquil body of water. Small balls of black fluff darted among the reeds, chirping like runaway alarms. Intricately woven mats topped with thickly padded cushions had been set out on the bare ground. While the adults went about their business and children barely coming into their manes watched silently from a respectful distance, Mazong and two advisers sat cross-legged opposite their guests. Food and drink were provided. Luminara took one sip of the dark green liquid placed before her and immediately choked on the spicy concoction. A concerned Barriss was at her side in an instant.

Mazong grinned, then smiled, and finally had to place a long-fingered hand over his face to cover his muted laughter. His advisers did little better. The ice was broken, and none was the wiser for knowing that the Jedi had tolerated the strong local liquor without difficulty, only to fake her reaction for the very purpose of putting their hosts at ease.

That did not mean, however, that by gagging embarrassedly she had instantly gained their friendship and assistance.

One of the advisers, an elderly female whose sweeping arch of a mane had gone entirely gray, leaned forward. "Why should we help you find the overclan?" This anticipated question allowed Obi-Wan to launch into an explanation of their purpose in coming to Ansion. The Yiwa listened quietly, occasionally bending to eat or drink from the modest meal that had been set out before them.

When the Jedi had finished, the two advisers caucused, then whispered something to Mazong. He indicated agreement and turned back to the guests.

"Like all the Alwari, we dislike and remain ever suspicious of the motives of the city folk, even though we all do business with the Unity. What you ask would change relationships on our world forever." Raising a hand, he forestalled Luminara's comment. "However—that is not necessarily a bad thing. Time changes everything, and even the Alwari must adapt. But before we will ever agree to do so, we must have guarantees that our rights to our traditional way of life will be protected. We know there have been previous visitations by representatives of the Senate. Those we do not, and will never, trust. As for the Jedi"—once again Luminara found him staring at her—"we have heard that they are different. That they are honorable. That they are highbred. If you can prove this to us, to our satisfaction, then we will feel secure enough to at least point you in the direction of the Borokii."

Luminara and Obi-Wan whispered while their guides and the two Padawans looked on. When the older Jedi separated, it was Luminara who spoke.

"Ask of us what you will, noble Mazong, and if it is within our power to comply, we'll certainly do so."

Exclamations of satisfaction came from the chief and his advisers. *What kind of proof do they want?* Barriss found herself wondering. What kind of assurance could offworlders give to natives that would convince them of the genuine good intentions of their visitors?

Unsurprisingly, it was not what she would have expected.

Rising, Mazong gestured toward the camp. "Tonight we will have a proper feast. There will be entertainment. Among the Alwari, it is traditional for guests to provide it. We have never heard of representatives of your Senate deigning to do this. To us, this says that they have no souls. If the Jedi can show us that they, like the Yiwa, also have souls, then the Yiwa will believe they possess what their politicians are lacking."

Barriss's lower jaw dropped. To her surprise, Luminara was smiling agreeably. "We will meet your terms, noble Mazong. But I must warn you: aesthetics are not the first thing a Jedi masters. You may find our presentations less polished than those of your usual guests."

All but openly affable now, Mazong stepped forward to place a hand on her head. The long fingers reached to the back of her neck. "Whatever you do, it will have the virtue of novelty. For now, though, I have only one question, that has troubled me since first you arrived."

Looking up at the Yiwa, she felt only slightly concerned. "What is it?"

"Why," he asked frankly, "do you tattoo your chin and under-lip instead of the top of your head, as is proper?"

Intensely curious about everything around her, Luminara was struck by the flickering light from the portable glowrods that illuminated the mock central square. Nor was she shy in asking Mazong about the phenomenon.

"If you like, my friends and I can try to fix those lighting devices. Their internal schematics are fairly simple."

Mazong expressed confusion. "But there is nothing wrong with them."

She hesitated. "They should be supplying steady light. Constant illumination."

The Yiwa chieftain's response surprised her. He laughed. "*Ou,* we know that, O wise and observant Jedi. But we remember, and honor, the ways of our ancestors, who could hold such gatherings only by torchlight."

Realization dawned on her. The glowpoles had been deliberately modified to simulate the flickering of torchlight. Among the Yiwa, it appeared, retrogressive aesthetics took precedence over cutting-edge functionality. She wondered if they would find the same reverence for ritual among the overclan.

Her thermosensitive robes warded off the evening chill and kept out the ever-present wind as she took her place alongside

Obi-Wan and the two Padawans. Mazong sat down nearby, his two elderly female advisers close behind him. It seemed as if most of the clan had crowded around the open space. Hundreds of bulging Ansionian eyes glistened in the light from the glow-rods. On the far side of the encampment, torpid dorgum and irritable awiquod grunted and hissed as they jostled for space with the more high-strung sadains. A few deeper hisses, like steam escaping from a sauna, indicated the location of the travelers' suubatars.

For the second time since their arrival, food and drink had been laid out in copious quantities. Having already consumed samples of Yiwa fare, they found that the individual components of the lavish banquet had lost some of their exoticism. They were delivered straight from the transportable high-tech kitchen by lines of young Yiwa clad in guest-greeting finery. Kyakhta and Bulgan sat like regal potentates, still unable to quite believe their good fortune. Thanks to Barriss's healing and Jedi largesse, for two clanless vagabonds they had come a very long way in an exceedingly short time.

There was music, of a sort, produced by a quartet of seated Yiwa. Two played traditional handmade instruments, while their younger colleagues opted for free-form electronics. The result was a cross between the sublime and a porgrak in its final death throes. Luminara found her ears simultaneously outraged and captivated.

Beyond the music, there was no entertainment. That, she knew, was shortly to be provided by the clan's guests. If this was deemed acceptable, they would then hopefully receive useful answers to their questions. If spurned, they would have to find another, more amenable source of information as to the current whereabouts of the overclans.

At last nearly everyone had eaten their fill. The spiraling squeal from the local band faded away, losing itself in the vastness of the prairie night. Sipping on the needle-thin tube of a bulblike stuicer, Mazong turned expectantly to his company.

"And now, my friends, the time has come for you to prove to us that Jedi have not just ability, but inner essence, unlike the representatives of the great but soulless Senate."

"If I may suggest—" Kyakhta began. The chieftain shut him down with a sharp gesture.

"You may not suggest, clanless vagrant. The Yiwa remain uncertain about you." Looking back to the Jedi, he smiled. "Rest assured no matter how badly you do, we will not eat you. We do not keep every tradition."

"That's nice to know," Obi-Wan murmured. He wasn't concerned about whether or not he and his companions were considered suitable for consumption. He was worried about a dearth of information. If the Yiwa refused to help them, they might waste weeks searching for the Borokii. During that time, the mischief makers and would-be secessionists among the Unity were not likely to be idle.

It was also important that everything they did not only found favor with their hosts, but did not offend any of their inscrutable and closely held customs. Not knowing the details of these in advance, the Jedi could only proceed as best they could, while watching for any indications that their calculated response might be offending the Yiwa.

"I'll go first." Barriss rose abruptly to her feet. Moving to the center of the open space, which had been carpeted with a fresh flooring of clean quartz sand taken from the beach that fronted the lake, she turned to face her friends. There was a stir among the watching Yiwa. What would the flat-eyed, many-digited, maneless female visitor do? No one waited with more curiosity than Anakin.

Luminara gestured encouragingly at her Padawan. Nodding, Barriss reached down and removed the lightsaber from her belt. Immediately, several of the armed Yiwa went for their own weapons. Seeing that the other visitors remained seated and calm, a confident Mazong waved off his agitated sentries.

In the chill, still air of early night, Barriss's lightsaber blazed. She held it aloft, glowing perpendicularly, its soft hum rising above the approving murmurs of the watching Yiwa. Not exactly a dynamic performance, Anakin reflected, but certainly an arresting image. He wondered if their hosts would consider striking a pose sufficient to satisfy their requirements.

And then Barriss began to move.

Slowly at first, darting from left to right and back again, then north to south, her footprints laid out a design in the sand that marked the four points of the compass. The Yiwa saw right away what she was honoring with her movements. As a nomadic people, they were particularly appreciative. The Padawan moved faster and faster, gradually increasing the speed of her jumps until she was bouncing from point to point as if dancing atop a concealed trampoline. All the while she held her flaring lightsaber aloft, the spear of luminance piercing the night. The athleticism of the performance was a tribute to her conditioning. It went, Anakin decided admiringly, well beyond basic Jedi training.

Then, just when it seemed she could move no faster, she began to twirl the lightsaber. Spectators gasped softly, and there sounded the first hisses and whistles of genuine admiration.

It was a revelation to Anakin, who until now had never thought of the conventional Jedi lightsaber as anything but a weapon. That outside the fencing arena it could also be a thing of beauty had never occurred to him. But in Barriss's hands it was transformed from a lethal tool into an instrument of effulgent splendor.

Spinning rapidly now as she continued to skip between the four points of the compass, the beam of spectral energy fooled the eyes into seeing a solid ring of light above her head. She began to swing the lightsaber, creating a lambent disk first on her right side, then on her left. Leaping from north to south, she brought her knees up to her chest and passed the beam beneath her feet, drawing sharp inhalations of surprise and awe from her audience. Several times she repeated the dangerous jump. Looking on as intently as any Yiwa, Anakin knew that if she misjudged height or swing, she could easily cut her feet off at the ankles. A greater miscalculation could result in the loss of an arm, or a leg—or her head.

The potential deadliness of the dance added greatly to the suspense, and to the brilliance of the performance. Drawing to a conclusion, Barriss jumped straight toward Mazong, executed a double flip with the lightsaber whirling beneath her, and landed on her knees not an arm-length in front of him. To his considerable credit, the Yiwa chieftain did not flinch. But his eyes never left the spinning lightsaber.

Another bit of Alwari lore was imparted to the visitors as the assembled clan demonstrated their approval not only with hisses and whistles, but with a mass cracking of the knuckles of their lissome, long-fingered hands. Waves of popping swept over the gathering. As for Mazong, he quietly consulted with his advisers.

Breathing hard, her lightsaber deactivated and refastened to her belt, Barriss resumed her seat alongside her companions. Luminara leaned over to whisper to her Padawan.

"A fine exhibition, Barriss. But that last stunt was truly treacherous. It would make me unhappy to have to return to Cuipernam with you in less than one piece."

"I've practiced it before, Master." The Padawan was well pleased with herself. "I know it's a dangerous move, but we do want to make as strong an impression as possible on these people so that they'll help us."

"Striking off your own limb would certainly make an impression." Seeing the younger woman's expression fall, Luminara reached out and gave her an encouraging hug. "I don't mean to be overly critical. You did well. I'm proud of you."

"So am I." Obi-Wan glanced to his right, to the pensive young man seated next to him. "It's your turn, Anakin."

That snapped Anakin out of his introspection. "Me? But Master Obi-Wan, I can't do anything like that. I haven't been trained for it. I'm a fighter, not an artist. Nothing I could do would begin to approach Barriss's presentation."

"It doesn't have to approach it." Obi-Wan was patient with his Padawan. "But the chieftain clearly indicated he wanted to ascertain the existence of a soul in all of us. That means you, too, Anakin."

The younger man chewed his lower lip. "I don't suppose my sworn and witnessed statement to the effect that I have one would be sufficient?"

"I think not," Obi-Wan replied dryly. "Stand out there, Anakin, and show them some soul. I know that you have one. The Force overflows with beauty. Draw on it."

With great reluctance, Anakin unfolded his legs and stood. Aware of the many eyes on him, humanoid as well as Ansionian, he strode slowly to the center of the sand-paved clearing. What could he possibly do to convince these people of his inner nature, to show them that he was as much a feeling being as the gravity-defying Barriss? He had to do *something*. His Master had insisted on it.

He didn't want to be here, in this circle of light in the middle of a nowhere place on a nowhere world. He wanted to be on Coruscant, or home, or . . .

The one memory that overrode all others jarred something loose. Something from his childhood. It possessed the virtues of simplicity: a song; slow, sad, and melancholic, but full of affection for the one who was listening. His mother had sung it to him frequently, when money was scarce and when desert winds howled outside their simple dwelling. She would appreciate the words of that song, which he had struggled to sing back to her on numerous occasions. That opportunity had not presented itself for many years now, ever since he had left her and the world of his birth.

Now he imagined that she was here, standing before him, her comforting and reassuring face smiling warmly back at him. Since she was not here to sing along with him, to remind him of the words, he was forced to draw entirely on his memories.

As he imagined his mother standing there before him, everything else faded away: the expectant Mazong, the onlooking Yiwa, his companions, even Master Obi-Wan. Only she remained, and himself. The two of them, trading stanzas, singing back and forth to each other as they had when he was a child. He sang with increasing strength and confidence, his voice rising above the steady breeze that swept fitfully through the camp.

The simple but soaring melody from his youth rolled out across the attentive assembly, silencing the children and causing sadains and suubatars alike to turn their dozy ears in the direction of the central compound. It floated free and strong across the lake and among the reeds, to finally lose itself in the vastness of the northern prairie. None of the watchful Yiwa understood any of the words, but the strength of the young human's voice and the ardor with which he sang more than succeeded in conveying his loneliness. Even this was unnecessary. While the human's song was utterly different from their own edgier harmonies, like so much music it succeeded in reaching across the boundary between species.

It took Anakin a moment to realize that he had finished. Blinking, he scrutinized his diverse audience. Then the whistling began, and the hissing, and the coordinated knuckle cracking. He ought to have been pleased. Instead, he hurried to resume his place alongside his Master; head down, face flushed, trying and failing to hide his discomfiture. Someone was patting him approvingly on the back. It was Bulgan, bent and contorted, his face alight with pleasure.

"Good sounds, Master Anakin, good sounds!" He put one hand to an aural opening. "You please every Alwari."

"Was it all right?" Anakin asked hesitantly of the man seated next to him. To his surprise, he saw that his Master was eyeing him with uncommon approval.

"Just when I think I have you figured out, Anakin, you unleash another surprise on me. I had no idea you could sing like that."

"Neither did I, really," the Padawan replied shyly. "I managed to find some inspiration in an old memory."

"Sometimes that's the best source." Obi-Wan started to rise. It was his turn. "Something else interesting you yourself might not have noticed. When you sing, your voice drops considerably."

"I did notice that, Master." Anakin smiled and shrugged diffidently. "I guess it's still changing."

He watched while his teacher strode confidently to the center of the sands. What was Obi-Wan Kenobi going to do to reveal to the Yiwa his inner self? Anakin was as curious as any spectator. He had never seen Obi-Wan sing or dance, paint or sculpt. In point of fact, he felt, Obi-Wan Kenobi, Jedi Knight, was something of a dry personality. This in no way limited his skill as a teacher, Anakin knew.

Obi-Wan spent a moment mentally reviewing his knowledge of the local vernacular, making certain he could handle the Yiwa dialect. Then he folded his hands in front of him, cleared his throat, and began to speak. That was all. No acrobatic leaps à la the buoyant Padawan Barriss. No full-throated euphonious declamation of emotion like Anakin. He just—spoke.

But it was music nonetheless.

Like Barriss's gymnastic performance with the lightsaber, it was all new to Anakin. At first he, and many of the Yiwa, were restless, expecting something more expansive, more grandiose of gesture. If all the Jedi was going to do was talk, they might as well be doing something else. And in fact, some in the crowd did indeed start to drift away. But as Obi-Wan continued to declaim, his voice rising and falling in a sturdy, mellifluous tone that was somehow as entrancing as it was steady, they came back, reclaimed their places, and watched, and listened, as if the voice itself was as mesmerizing as the most powerful hypnotic drug.

Obi-Wan wove a tale that, like all great stories, began simply enough. Unpromisingly, even. But as details began to emerge, as profound truths could be discerned through the lens of adventure, it became impossible for anyone to leave. Try as they might, Yiwa young and old could not tear themselves away from the tale the Jedi told.

There was a hero, of course. And a heroine. And where both are present, there invariably arises a love story poignant and true. Greater issues than the feelings of the two lovers were at stake. The fate of millions lay in the balance, their very lives and the lives of their children dependent on the making of correct decisions, on choosing to fight for truth and justice. There was sacrifice and war, betrayal and revelation, greed and revenge, and in the end, as the fate of the two lovers hung suspended like a small weight from a thread, redemption. Beyond that, the humble storyteller could not see, could not say, a confession that provoked cries of unsatisfied frustration from his audience.

With a soft smile, Obi-Wan asked if they really wanted to hear how it all turned out. The chorus of concurrence that followed woke half the beasts in the corrals. Even Mazong, Anakin noted, had been sucked into the tale, and required closure.

Raising his hands, Obi-Wan requested and received a silence so complete that the small furry scratchers on the far side of the lake could be heard rubbing their abdomens against the rocks there. In a voice deliberately hushed, he resumed the story, his voice never rising but the words coming faster and faster, until his audience, leaning forward the better to hear and not miss a single word, threatened to collapse en masse onto the sand.

When he delivered the final surprise, there were shouts of joy and much appreciative laughter from the onlookers, followed by intense discussions of the tale just told. Ignoring these, Obi-Wan walked quietly back to his place and took his seat. So overcome were the Yiwa by the telling that they forgot to hiss or whistle or crack a single knuckle in appreciation. It didn't matter. There was no need for applause. Obi-Wan's saga had passed beyond the need for simple approval into the realm of complete acceptance.

"You enchanted everyone entirely, Master." Anakin hardly knew what to say. "Myself included."

Picking at the sand by his feet, the Jedi shrugged disarmingly. "Such is the power of story, my young Padawan."

Anakin considered this carefully, as he was learning to do with everything Obi-Wan Kenobi said. "You kept everyone in complete suspense. *Suspension* might be a better description. I never saw the happy ending coming and didn't expect it. Do all your stories have happy endings?"

Flicking a few grains of sand aside, Obi-Wan looked up at him sharply enough to give his apprentice an unexpected start. "Only time will tell that, Anakin Skywalker. In storytelling, nothing is a given, the astonishing becomes commonplace, and one learns to expect the unexpected. But when people of understanding and goodwill come together, a happy ending is usually assured."

The Padawan frowned uncertainly. "I was speaking of story-telling, Master. Not reality."

"One is but a reflection of the other, and sometimes it's difficult to tell which is the original and which the mirror image. There is much to be learned from stories that can't be taught by history." Obi-Wan smiled. "It's like making a cake. Much lies in the choosing of ingredients before the baking has even begun." Before Anakin could comment again, Obi-Wan had turned back to the center of the gathering. "We'll talk more about it later, if you like. For now, we need to show courtesy by giving our colleague Luminara the same kind of close attention as the Yiwa."

Unsatisfied but understanding, Anakin turned away from his Master to where Luminara had taken center stage. It wasn't much of a stage, he knew. The lighting was bad, the floor uneven, and one would flatter the audience by calling it unsophisticated, but she approached it as if it were the finest theater on Coruscant. She had spoken several times of feeling the chill carried by the wind that swept over the prairie, and so wore her long robes. Yiwa who had been astounded at Barriss's acrobatics, softened by Anakin's singing, and held spellbound by Obi-Wan's storytelling now waited and watched expectantly to see what the last of the visitors would do.

Luminara closed her eyes for a very long moment. Then she opened them and, kneeling, picked up a handful of sand. Straightening, she let it trickle out from between her fingers. Caught by the wind, the tiny grains formed a glittering whitish arc as they spilled from her hand. When she had emptied her palm, she slapped her hands gently together to brush away any remaining grains.

Some of the Yiwa began to stir. This polite acknowledgment of their environs was something the smallest children of the clan could do for themselves. There was merit in the recognition, but little in the way of enlightenment. Surely there was more to come!

There was. Kneeling again, Luminara picked up a second handful of sand, let it trickle from between her fingers. A few muted growls rose from the crowd. A concerned Barriss saw that Anakin was feeling the same confusion and uncertainty as herself. Nearby, Mazong frowned in disapproval. If anything, his advisers were even more discomfited. Only Obi-Wan appeared unworried. That in itself, she knew, was significant of nothing. He always looked that way.

She found herself leaning forward and squinting. There was something different, something odd, about the dribble of sand spilling from her Master's fingers. It took her a moment to figure out what it was. When she did, despite what she knew of her Master's capabilities, her mouth opened slightly.

The sand was falling *against* the wind.

It was just ordinary beach sand, drawn from the shores of the nearby lake, but in the delicate yet strong fingers of the Jedi, it became something magical. The light from the surrounding glow-poles caught the falling grains, turning mica to mirrors and quartz into polished gems. When the last particles had fallen from Luminara's fingers, they reversed direction. A few hushed cries of *"Haja!"* rose from the crowd as sand began to fall—upward.

Resembling a fragmented coil of wire, the column of grains began to wind itself around the Jedi, enclosing her in a slowly ascending spiral of sand. Like a serpent being born full grown, another column lifted itself from the ground to entwine her a second time. As the sparkling sand spirals rotated in opposite directions, they splintered into smaller and smaller threads, until Luminara was shrouded in multiple strings composed of shattered, water-worn specks. It was as if she were engulfed by thirty threadlike pillars of dancing diamonds.

She began to twirl, spinning slowly at first, balancing on one foot while the other pushed off and provided thrust. As she pirouetted, the glittering sand spirals responded, half turning with her, the other half rotating in the opposite direction. Though all was accomplished in complete silence, Barriss thought she heard music.

Faster and faster Luminara whirled, racing the rising sand. Centrifugal force threw the hem of her robes away from her legs. The spinning sands backed off accordingly. As she accelerated, her robes rose higher and higher.

A collective gasp erupted from the assembly. A blur of robes and sand, Luminara Unduli rose slightly from the ground. She continued to spin, her feet rising, until she was no more than a hand-length off the ground. Still rotating, she tilted forward, and began to spin and rotate simultaneously, holding her place in the air. It was as unique a demonstration of control over the Force as Barriss had ever seen, and certainly the most breathtaking.

Following her movements, the sand spirals rotated with her, until they formed a near-solid globe of shining, sparkling particles around the almost hidden body. There came a soft puff of air; the sound of a cloud exhaling. Luminara landed on her feet, hands outstretched, feet spread shoulder-width apart. The curtaining sphere of sand that had formed around her fell to the ground. Lowering her arms, she bowed her head once before walking back to rejoin her friends. As she resumed her seat, Obi-Wan inclined slightly in her direction.

"Okay, I'm impressed. How do you feel?"

"Dizzy." Smiling softly, Luminara blinked several times. Otherwise, she betrayed nothing of what she was feeling internally.

"Please, Master—what is the secret of the rotating trick?" Barriss very much wanted to know.

Turning her head slightly to face the eager Padawan, Luminara spoke through closely set lips. "The trick, my dear, is not to throw up. At least, not until one is well offstage."

There was no applause. No whistling, no hissing, no celebratory cracking of joints. In ones and twos, alone and in family groups, the clan Yiwa simply rose from their seats and melted away, returning to their collapsible homes and ceremonial fires. A number of armed males headed for their guard posts, to take up the nocturnal watch for shanhs and other predators that might try to prey on the slumbering herds. Sooner than expected, only the visitors were left, together with Mazong and his advisers.

"The clan has hosted many recitals by many guests," the chieftain of the Yiwa began, "but never in living memory have any been so diverse, so unexpected, and so remarkable."

"I didn't get a chance to show off my juggling," Bulgan muttered disappointedly. Kyakhta jabbed him in the ribs.

Mazong ignored the aside, pretending not to have heard it. "You have more than fulfilled your end of the bargain." His gaze fastened on Luminara. "I would give much to know how you did that."

"So would I," Anakin put in intently. "It would be useful in a fight."

Turning toward their host, Luminara launched into a discussion of the Force: what it was, how the Jedi made use of it, and the nature of its essence—dark as well as good. When she was finished, Mazong and his advisers nodded solemnly.

"You traffic in dangerous matters," he declared somberly.

"As with so much that holds great promise, there is always some danger," she replied. "Such as this proposed agreement be-

STAR WARS: THE APPROACHING STORM ══════ 153

tween the Unity of the town folk and the Alwari clans. But when it is treated with respect, the Force is ultimately a power for good. The same can be true of this concordance that we hope to achieve."

Mazong conferred with his advisers. The two elders appeared to have lightened up considerably, Barriss decided. As the chieftain finally turned back to his guests, she drew her clothing tighter around her. Though the winds of Ansion tended to diminish along with the daylight, they did not always cease entirely, and she was cold.

"We concur." He gestured magnanimously at Kyakhta and Bulgan. "We will give your guides such directions as will enable you to find the Borokii soonest. Clanless these two may be, but they raise themselves high by their choice of employers."

"How long until we reach their outlying factions?" Obi-Wan inquired.

"That cannot be foretold." As Mazong stood, his guests rose with him. "The Borokii are also Alwari. They may be encamped, as are the Yiwa. But if they are on the move, you will still have some tracking to do. We can only point you in the direction of their last known campsite." He smiled reassuringly. "Do not despair. With our directions you will find them far sooner than if you continued searching on your own."

"We thank you for your kindness, and for your hospitality," Luminara told him.

He responded with a gesture she did not know. "You have more than repaid us. Indeed, we are shamed by our suspicions."

"One never need apologize for caution." Obi-Wan stretched. A Jedi could go without sleep for an amazing length of time—but would not by choice. He was tired. They all were.

Anakin in particular could not get the Jedi Luminara's

presentation out of his head. It kept him preoccupied as he prepared for sleep and awake well into the morning hours. He
thought he had seen or read everything that could be done with
the Force. Once again, he had been shown the error of his assumptions. He could not imagine the amount of study and control it took to realize such a feat. The complexity of it, the skill
needed to simultaneously control one's body as well as thousands of individual grains of sand, was quite beyond him.

For now, he thought as he lay on his back in the visitors'
house. Though aware of his present limitations, his confidence in
his abilities was boundless. It was the same confidence that had
allowed him to survive a difficult childhood, had gained him the
skills necessary to master the intricacies of droid repair that had
made him so valuable to that winged reprobate Watto, and had
permitted him to participate in the liberation of Naboo from the
subjugation of the Trade Federation. It was the same confidence
that would one day enable him to achieve anything he wished.
Whatever that might be.

There was no celebration when they departed the following
morning. No chorus of young Yiwa lined up to serenade them
on their way. No line of mounted clanfolk escorted them northward, banners flying and horns tootling. The visitors were simply
given the requisite directions and sent on their way.

As they trotted off on their well-rested suubatars, Luminara
asked Bulgan about this absence of a departure ceremony. The
one-eyed Alwari gestured diffidently.

"The life of a nomad is a full one, though not so hard as in
the old days. There is little time for frivolities. There are animals
to care for, young to instruct, houses to be erected or broken

down for travel, elders to see to, food and water to be distributed to Alwari and animal alike. That's why rites like last night's are so important. Diversion is necessary, and respected, but only when there is time for it." He rode on in silence for a bit, then added, "You certainly left the Yiwa with a favorable impression of the Jedi Order." A long-fingered hand waved at the other mounted suubatar. "All of you did."

"We enjoyed it ourselves," she told him. "It's not often we're asked to reveal that side of our personas. Most of the time we find ourselves explaining Republic policy, or defending it, or preparing to do both. Believe me," she added forcefully, "few in the galaxy would better understand or sympathize with what you just said about the life of a nomad than would a Jedi."

The guide nodded gravely, then brightened. "But like the Alwari, you also know how to have fun!" When she failed to respond, he added hopefully, "Don't you?"

She sighed, shifting her position high atop the loping suubatar. "Sometimes I wonder. There are times when the words *fun* and *Jedi* seem to be mutually exclusive." Remembering something, she smiled. "Though I do remember a joke Master Mace Windu once played on Master Ki-Adi-Mundi. It had to do with three Padawans and the number of available eyeballs in the room . . ."

She proceeded to relate the tale to the interested Bulgan, who listened attentively. When she finished, he could only gesture helplessly, his face showing the strain of trying to comprehend the unfathomable.

"I'm sorry, Master Luminara, but I find nothing amusing in your story. I think maybe Jedi humor is as mysterious as Jedi strength." He was very earnest. "Perhaps one has to know the Force to understand the humor."

"I wouldn't think so." She rode on in silence for a while, then sniffed slightly. "Well, *I* thought it was funny."

They continued to make excellent time. Everyone's spirits had been raised by the encounter with the stolid but ultimately cooperative Yiwa, and they now had something in the way of a specific destination. At least, Barriss reflected as she relaxed in the saddle of her suubatar, they weren't galloping aimlessly over open prairie in the hope of accidentally bumping into the migrating overclan. Mazong's directions had been quite specific, though they still had to take into account his admonition that the Borokii might be on the move. She wondered how their habits and rituals would compare to those of the Yiwa. Within the numerous clans of the Alwari, Kyakhta had told her, there existed much differentiation.

They were traveling steadily north when their guides unexpectedly called a halt. Sitting up in her saddle, Barriss scanned their surroundings. The horizon was the same in every direction and had been for several days. Endless grassland, waving fields of native grains only rarely interrupted by clumps of small trees, an occasional depression holding water or mud, and the isolated hillock. Not a building of any kind, nor anything higher than a suubatar standing up on its rear and middle legs. So it was with interest she wondered why Kyakhta and Bulgan had brought them to a stop—and why they appeared more than a little apprehensive.

"What is it?" Luminara and Obi-Wan trotted forward to query their escorts. Attentive inspection of the four horizons left them no more enlightened as to the reason for the halt than it did their equally confused Padawans. "Why have we stopped here?"

"Listen." Both Alwari were leaning slightly forward in their seats, obviously straining to hear—what?

Luminara and her companions went quiet. Only the muted munching of the suubatars nibbling the tops off the ripe wild grains, the constant rustle of wind through the grasses, and the occasional querulous hooting of a kilk stalking soft-shelled arthropods broke the silence.

Then she heard it. Faint initially, like a first cousin to the wind itself. It strengthened slowly, a soft ripping sound approaching from the north, from the direction they were headed. It intensified until it became an audible buzzing, still muted but rising ominously in the distance. Peering hard in the direction of the ascending susurration, Luminara thought she could make out the first hints of a low, dark cloud.

The suubatars began to stir uneasily, throwing back their sharp-ridged skulls and pawing at the ground with middle and forefeet. She struggled to control her mount. At the same time, Kyakhta's eyes bulged with realization.

"Kyren!" he exclaimed fearfully.

"Quickly, my friends!" Bulgan was suddenly standing upright in his saddle, looking frantically in all directions. "We have to find shelter!"

"Shelter?" Obi-Wan held his seat, but began searching their immediate surroundings nonetheless. "Out here?"

"From what?" Barriss wanted to know. By now she, too, saw and heard the onrushing blur. "What's a kyren?"

Without suspending his search, Bulgan edged his steed closer to her own. "A flying creature that travels the plains of Ansion, migrating from region to region as it follows the seasons." He gestured downward. "When the grasses in one area mature and the heads of each stalk are ripe with seed, the kyren resumes its flight, eating until it is sated. Then it settles down to rest, and to breed. When the young are fledged, they take flight anew in search of further nourishment."

She blinked in the direction of the diffuse shadow on the horizon. "That can't be all one creature coming toward us."

"It's not," Bulgan disclosed apprehensively. "There are many more than one."

"I don't see why it matters." Anakin had moved forward to join the conversation. "What have we to fear from a flock of seed eaters? They *are* just seed eaters, aren't they?" he thought to add.

A strange expression came over the guide's face; strange even for a pop-eyed, long-maned, single-nostriled Ansionian. "Seed is their preferred food, yes. But once they have taken flight, they are unable, or unwilling, or simply disinterested in changing course. Nor will they fly higher to pass over anything unexpected in their path." He swallowed hard. "Rocks they will smash themselves into. Trees they will cut down. Living things like hootles, or suubatars, or cicien, they will eat their way through. Unless those creatures can somehow find a place to hide, or manage to get out of the way."

"Hootles or suubatars?" Barriss asked softly. "Or—people?" Somehow she wasn't surprised when Bulgan nodded solemnly.

Anakin's hand strayed to his belt. "We have lightsabers, and other weapons. Can't we stand and defend ourselves from these things? How big are they, anyway?"

Raising his long-fingered hands, Bulgan placed them on either side of his head. "This is the average of their wingspan."

"That's all?" Anakin frowned. "Then I don't see why you and Kyakhta are so concerned."

"How *many* of them are there?" Barriss asked. "In the average flock?"

Lowering his hands, the guide looked back at her. "No one knows. No one has ever been able to stay in one place long enough to count an average flock." He gestured toward the now rapidly darkening northern horizon. "I think this flock may be a little larger than average."

"Take a guess." The fingers of Anakin's right hand continued to hover in the vicinity of his lightsaber. "How many of these things are we likely to be facing?"

Turning in his saddle, Bulgan considered the horizon anew. "Not a conspicuously great number. But enough to pose a serious danger if we don't find cover quickly. No more than one or two hundred million, I would say."

Anakin's hand moved away from his lightsaber. " 'Hundred million'? 'One or two'?" The only shelter in sight was a trio of wolgiyn trees standing forlorn and isolated off to their right. They did not cast much of a shadow.

"This way!" Pointing forward and to his left, Kyakhta urged his mount in that same direction. The two Jedi Knights followed, with the Padawans bringing up the rear.

Barriss tried her best to conceal her unease. Instead of fleeing, they were riding straight into the oncoming adumbration. On a collision course, kyren flock and speeding travelers drew rapidly toward one another. Though she had never seen a kyren in her life, she trusted that Kyakhta had seen something more substantial than a mirage, and more solid than faint hope.

Several minutes of hard riding later, it was still impossible to make out individual kyren, but their collective screeching had come to dominate all other sounds on the prairie. Usually frightened of nothing, a pack of shanhs went racing past in the opposite direction. The fearsome carnivores were absolutely terrified. Terrified of something that cracked grass seed for breakfast, Luminara reflected. A small, lightweight, winged herbivore she could hold in the palm of one hand. The sight of the fleeing shanhs was anything but reassuring. As she had been instructed, she urged her suubatar faster, not wanting to fall behind. There were some instruments of nature even a Master of the Force could not stand against. One kyren, without question. A dozen, surely. A few hundred, perhaps. A few thousand? Questionable.

A hundred million of anything was too vast a number for even several Jedi to stand against. Even if the adversaries in question were nothing more than small, soft-bodied, seed-eating fliers.

By the time she finally saw where Kyakhta was leading them,

the collective cries of the millions upon millions of kyren were a steady stabbing in her ears. They blocked out the sun, creating their own eclipse, and their stench threatened to overwhelm her inundated sense of smell and send her reeling. Grimly, she clung to the reins of her mount and kept her feet jammed resolutely into the forward-facing stirrups. With one hand she pulled a bit of robe across her face to shut out a little of the dust and smell.

"There, that way!" Peering into the gathering darkness, she barely managed to hear Kyakhta's cry, and see where he was leading them.

Looming out of the gloom just ahead and towering above the grass, a crazy conglomeration of tilted pillars and columns took shape. Ranging in hue from a light tan to dark umber, more than anything else they resembled alien tombstones set in the middle of the open plain. The analogy was not encouraging. Roughly triangular in shape, each rose to a sharp point. Not all were perfectly vertical. Some thrust upward from the ground at marked angles, and several lay broken and shattered, having fallen over on their sides.

She later learned they were the mounds of the jijites, tiny creatures that lived in the soil and fed off the wide-ranging root systems of the numerous grasses. Constructed of tiny, even minuscule pebbles, they were bound together by a natural mortar extruded by specially designated jijite workers. Each pillar served to vent hot air from the living tunnels below the surface, cooling the jijites' immediate environment. They were also lookout towers from which farsighted jijites could keep watch on the surrounding plains—and on other, marauding members of their own kind. They were not insects, but a kind of collective small reptilian life-form.

No four-legged lookouts were visible now, peering

watchfully out of red, slitted eyes at the surrounding prairie. Having long since detected the oncoming kyren, they and their brethren had moved deep into the earth, down to multiple burrows safe from the onrushing swarm.

Luminara had to work hard to slow her speeding suubatar so that it wouldn't race past the aggregation of pillars. Shouting to make himself heard, Kyakhta indicated that they had to split up into groups of two, since even the largest of the columns could effectively shelter no more than that.

Obi-Wan didn't like the idea, but they had no choice, and no time for debate. True, they could have stayed together, clinging to one another for support and reassurance, but that would have meant tethering their mounts separately, with no riders to control them. They hurriedly dismounted.

"If one suubatar panics," Bulgan explained, putting his mouth close to Luminara's ear in order to make himself heard, "the rest may stampede with it. That's the way it is with all herd animals on the prairies. They rely on each other's reactions for protection from danger. If you are potential prey, it's better to bolt than to stand around assessing the situation for yourself." He clung tightly to the reins of his own steed. "If we don't stay with our mounts, we might well lose them." He nodded in Obi-Wan's direction. "I know you have the means for contacting Cuipernam and calling for rescue, but not even an armored landspeeder could force its way through a kyren flock. This is our only chance."

She indicated understanding. "I doubt we have time to call for help, anyway. Very well, Bulgan. We'll split up."

They discussed the situation quickly, with no wasted words. Much as Luminara wanted to stay with Barriss, and Obi-Wan with Anakin, it made more sense to pair each of the Padawans with one of the more experienced guides. The two Masters would take their own animals down behind the largest of the artificial pillars. Though the distance between columns was small, the sense of parting was disproportionately great.

As soon as she and Obi-Wan succeeded in persuading their animals to lie down behind the brown column, they took shelter themselves, huddling close together in the middle of the triangular pillar. The suubatars' reins had been wrapped around the stony column itself and secured in the manner hurriedly demonstrated by Kyakhta. When all was in readiness, she found that she had to smile. Her companion couldn't help but notice.

"I see that you've found a source of humor in our present situation. If it isn't private, I could use a touch of amusement myself."

Barely able to make herself understood above the deafening massed screeching that was now nearly on top of them, she nodded forward. "Years of difficult study spent mastering innumerable skills, more years of crisscrossing the galaxy in the service of the Republic, the accolades of peers, and here I am: relying on a rock for protection while staring at the oversized backsides of a pair of alien steeds."

Gazing himself at the pair of outsized behinds as he pressed himself back against the shielding stone, Obi-Wan soon found himself, despite their desperate situation, smiling uncontrollably.

The sky was now as dark as during a cloudy sunset. Something made a faint smacking sound behind the two huddled Jedi. It was followed by another, and then more, in rapid succession. Then the swarm began to pass by overhead, and the smacking noises became a steady dull battering and splatting against the other side of the pillar. Luminara found herself giving thanks to tiny burrowing creatures she had never seen. It was their regurgitative engineering that was providing protection for the travelers, and keeping them alive.

But for how long? The sound of airborne kyren slamming into the pillar rose in volume until the conglomeration of stone and cementlike saliva began to tremble against their backs. How far did the flock extend? How long would it take for it to pass over? Would their pillar, and those shielding their companions, be able to withstand the relentless pressure of hundreds, perhaps thousands, of kyren hurling themselves aimlessly against it?

Black shapes numbering in the tens of millions pelted past at high speed. In the crush of small bodies, it was impossible to make out individuals. The swarm was a cyclonic mass of wings, eyes, and gaping mouths. Something struck her right ankle and, Jedi restraint or not, she jumped slightly. Reaching down, Obi-Wan gently picked up the fluttering, hopping creature in both hands. Wings and body broken, it twitched for another minute before lying still against his palms.

Almost jet black, it had four membranous wings: two that spanned the Jedi's cupping hands and emerged from extended ribs, and two half the size that sprouted from its back. No wonder it could stay aloft for so long, Luminara reflected. If necessary, it could glide on the lower wings while being propelled forward by the top pair. A bright yellow splotch decorated each wing, perhaps an aid in identifying itself to its brethren while all were airborne. Instead of legs, it boasted a pair of thick, furry tufts that ran the length of its underside, like runners on a sled. Spending most of its time aloft, it evidently had little need for pedestrian locomotion.

The kyren's method of mass feeding was made clear by its mouth—a wide gape lined top and bottom with twin ridges of horn. The flock hurtled along, those flying low clipping the nourishing crests of grain without stopping, the sharp lower ridges of horn acting like tiny airborne scythes. As soon as they were sated, those soaring along near the underside of the flock would change places with their hungry brethren flying above or behind them. Riding in the middle or the top of the swarm, those that had eaten would digest their meals while still aloft. The cloud of kyren would remain in constant motion not only on its chosen forward path, but within itself as well.

Another appeared, flopping and fluttering its way helplessly along the ground. Stink aside, they really were rather cute, sad little creatures. Leaning forward slightly, Luminara looked to her right, past Obi-Wan.

"Barriss! Are you all right? Can you hear me?"

Her call was lost in the wail of wings. Nothing could be seen through the solid, continuous torrent of fliers; nothing could be heard above their ear-splitting screeching. Barriss, she remembered, was with Bulgan. It was not so much that Luminara was worried about her apprentice. Barriss had already proven on this mission that she could take care of herself. And the familiar slight disturbance in the Force indicated that her living presence was still strong. It was just that a glimpse of her familiar form would have been reassuring.

They sat scrunched up against the jijite pillar for what seemed like the entire morning, but in reality was less than an hour. The suubatars huddled against one another for comfort and protection, their long narrow heads resting plaintively on the ground. Kyren shot past on either side or overhead, too intent on maintaining their flight paths to swerve even slightly to left or right to nip at the grass that was bent beneath the weight of resting suubatar jaws.

The stone column that was the only protection for human

and steed alike continued to shudder beneath the impact of hundreds of suicidal bodies. With the airspace on all sides of them occupied, hemmed in above by tens of thousands of their brethren, the kyren that slammed into the pillar were compelled to sacrifice themselves out of instinct, and not a desire to commit mass suicide. They did not perish willingly: they simply had nowhere else to go. The sky was full.

After a while, the sound of bodies hitting the stone column began to fade, even though the blizzard of black shapes continued to thunder past unabated. Eventually, even that sound began to dissipate. Soon only thousands of kyren were rushing by the pillar. Then hundreds. The sky brightened, black giving way once more to blue. A few clouds appeared. Looking to his right, Obi-Wan could once more make out the seated forms of Barriss and Bulgan, seated behind their indomitable jijite shield.

When the last stragglers had passed and could be seen flapping madly southward in frantic attempts to keep up with the main flock, the travelers rose from their places of rest and protection for a joyful but solemn reunion. Tension had tired them, but any feelings of fatigue were more than offset by the relief they felt. No one had been hurt, although a curious Anakin had been struck in the face when he had tried to peer briefly around his and Kyakhta's protective column. A small scratch across his forehead was the only indication of the fortunately brief encounter with airborne kyren.

It was a worthwhile lesson. Sometimes danger came not from the powerful and overbearing, but from the small and the overlooked.

The meticulousness with which the mighty swarm had fed was remarkable to see. The only grass stalks that had been knocked down were those that had been trapped beneath the prone, resting suubatars. The kyren had not flattened a single section of prairie. Every stalk remained standing, but nearly all had been shorn of their ripened seed. As far as the eye could see, the grassland looked as if it had been given a clipping by the largest and most perfect of all mowers.

The reason for what had seemed at the time the premature cessation of flying bodies slamming against each pillar was soon apparent. A small mountain of kyren bodies, hundreds of them, formed a perfect line pointing northward from the back of each column. After a while, enough had died hurling themselves against the unyielding stone to form a soft, protective buffer between each pillar and the rest of the oncoming airborne horde. Ever curious, Obi-Wan picked one up, holding it by a limp wing, and turned to Bulgan.

"Seems to me these vast flocks would be an excellent source of available protein for traveling nomads. Are they good to eat?"

One eye or not, Bulgan managed to convey a complete response with a single disgusted expression. It was left to Kyakhta to elaborate.

"Even after a kyren is cooked, it tastes like boiled mud. All grease." He eyed Obi-Wan uncertainly. "Would the Jedi like to try some?"

Wrinkling up her face, Barriss made a sickened smacking sound. "Jedi prefer to learn things for themselves—but there are instances where it's better just to accept the wisdom of others." She looked slightly worried as she turned to her teacher. "Isn't that right, Master Luminara?"

"It is in this case," her Master responded without hesitation. "Besides, I'm not hungry." Gazing down at herself, she contemplated the side effects of being obliged to sit for an hour beneath millions of kyren passing by overhead. "What I am in need of is a bath." To this heartfelt observation neither Barriss, nor Anakin, nor even their two guides raised a single objection.

The smell was bad enough, but as they rode on they were forced to look at one another. It was not a pretty sight. At least, she mused, the mess was only discoloring and not toxic. Still, the discovery of a clear-running stream meandering through a shallow vale the next day was too tempting to pass up.

While their employers disrobed to their undergarments and waded into the water—Anakin, Barriss, and Luminara with a relieved rush, Obi-Wan patiently and with a bit more dignity—the two guides unloaded supplies and dirty tack from the patient suubatars. Only then did Kyakhta and Bulgan, urging the lofty mounts before them, join the humans in the river. Keeping their long snouts above water, the suubatars were able to walk out to the very center of the channel, submerging their grimy, soiled selves completely in the cleansing current.

In contrast, the bipeds stayed in the shallows, alternating cleaning themselves with conversing casually. Luminara luxuriated in the tepid tributary, lying back on the sun-warmed sand once she was finally clean and letting the water gently caress her weary body. Though Jedi were trained to tolerate the most extreme conditions, that did not mean they were immune to the occasional indulgence. It might not be a flavor-charged bath in a top-rated hotel on Coruscant, she reflected lazily as something small, blue, and harmless skittered past her through the water, but after days spent on the back of a suubatar, lying there in the bright sunshine within the warming embrace of the pellucid stream was akin to a choice slice of paradise.

Laughter broke out nearby. Obi-Wan had taken up a stance between the two Alwari. Using the Force, her colleague was directing a spray of river water onto the flanks of a pair of suubatar that had waded into the shallows. In an expression of sheer delight, the beasts were bobbing their heads rapidly up and down. Their lean, muscular flanks rippled under the invigorating water pressure.

Farther out in the stream, Anakin and Barriss were attempting to duplicate Obi-Wan's feat. Only, instead of directing jets of liquid at the wading suubatar, the two Padawans were squirting streams of Force-pressurized water at each other. Sitting up, her legs and hips still submerged, supporting herself on her hands, Luminara smiled to herself. If only Master Yoda could see to what use his earnest teachings were being put.

Sometimes, she thought, *you can be a bit too serious yourself.*

Lying back down in the water, she contemplated the single puffy white cloud that was presently scudding across an otherwise sapphire sky. Convinced her companions were occupied, and that no one was watching, she tentatively at first, and then with more enthusiasm, began trying to see how high she could fling water with her right foot.

With her great wealth, the president of the Commerce Guild could command entire legions of servants, thousands of workers, dozens of bodyguards. The multiple enterprises of her people spanned the civilized galaxy, reaching from one end of the Republic to another. She was universally acknowledged, even by her most fervent competitors, to be an individual of unusual intelligence and perspicacity. Usually, a few minutes was enough time to enable her to size up an opponent or a friend.

Take Senator Mousul. Talented but vain, loyal but self-centered, he had to be watched at all times. Not that Shu Mai thought him unreliable. The Senator was in too deep and had too much at stake to risk quitting now. Shu Mai had seen him at work in the Senate. Mousul could be a mesmerizing speaker. But outside the Senate, removed from his official position of power, he was just another Ansionian—and therefore had to be watched.

What was important was that they had the same view of the future, of where the diseased, tottering Republic was going. With the Senator's political acumen and alliances and the Commerce Guild's financial and commercial resources, there was nothing they could not accomplish. But not quite yet. The Republic was still powerful, its long-established institutions not quite weak enough to be ignored.

In matters of political policy she tended to defer to the Senator, though not always. Shu Mai respected her associate's opinions, just as Mousul believed the president of the Commerce Guild listened attentively to his advice. What the Senator sometimes failed to acknowledge was that he was by several orders of magnitude the junior partner in their mutual arrangement. Adept as he was at massaging the egos of fellow politicians, Mousul was content to let Shu Mai deal with the unseen one whose interests they represented.

The watercraft on which they were presently relaxing drifted freely on Savvam Lake, an exquisite body of water that, like everything else on Coruscant, was artificial in nature. It was a private playground of the very rich, lined with trees and genetically engineered flowers that bloomed year-round, filling the air with a hundred different scents. Other boats cruised sedately nearby, some larger than Shu Mai's, some smaller. She could have overawed them all, but preferred not to be conspicuous. The two were the only ones on the boat. Live servants had ears with which to listen. The pilot droids did not.

"Our supporters grow impatient." Mousul let the sun bake

his chest, its rays carefully filtered through the inconspicuous polarized shield that hovered above the boat. "Tam Uliss in particular worries me. He would not be as easy to deal with as was the unfortunate Nemrileo."

"Impatience is a potentially fatal disease." Rolling to her left, Shu Mai picked up the spiral tumbler of refreshment and sipped contentedly at its contents. "According to everything you tell me, events on Ansion are unfolding at a predictable and reasonable speed. The others must learn to contain their impulsiveness."

"It isn't easy, you know, to restrain people caught up in the grip of a new idea."

Raising her tumbler, Shu Mai gazed through the liquid-filled transparency. It colored the sunlight gold. "That's your job, my friend. I handle the guild, you keep the local political and business interests in check. We'll move only when the time is right."

Mousul bridled inwardly at what sounded like a directive. Outwardly, he smiled and nodded. For now, Shu Mai was in control. Let her dream her dreams of personal grandiosity. When Ansion seceded and Mousul was appointed sector governor, their positions would be reversed. Then it was Shu Mai and her guild that would come calling in search of favors. He met his smaller colleague's gaze evenly.

"These Jedi complicate matters. Whatever Uliss and the others think, no legitimate vote can go forward until they have been dealt with. I have been in regular contact with our agent there, and I've been assured as recently as yesterday that the visitors will be neutralized."

"They'd better be." With a soft grunt, Shu Mai leaned back in her chair. "If only the Jedi Knights could be brought around to our way of thinking. It would simplify everything greatly."

"Won't happen." Mousul stirred his drink with a finger,

activating a few more of the time-release narcotics swirling within. "The Jedi can't be bent."

The president of the Commerce Guild shrugged. "It may be that some are not so staunch as you believe."

Mousul blinked at his co-conspirator. "What do you mean?"

"Time will reveal all. Meanwhile, events on Ansion will unfold at their own speed. While they do, you and I must wait, and persuade the others to do likewise." She took a long swallow of her own, non-narcotic-infused drink.

Mousul grunted and went silent. Businessfolk like that brusque Tam Uliss simply did not understand. While it was true that life was transitory and the window of opportunity to do great things fleeting, they could not be rushed. To move too soon would be to risk everything. If Uliss and the rest would only be patient, the future would be handed to them.

Beneath the two, who rested and plotted and warmed themselves in Coruscant's beneficent sun, thousands of lesser beings toiled in the great interlocked buildings two hundred stories high whose roof was the lake known as Savvam.

If not for the small matter of their mission, the travelers would have chosen to spend another day and night at the tranquil, bucolic campsite. Sadly, as always, time insisted and duty called.

Following the route proposed by the Yiwa brought them to a line of high hills that stretched unbroken across the northern horizon. Kyakhta and Bulgan did not know their names, but a few of the prominences were almost high enough to be called mountains. Gentle of slope, with only a few isolated cliff faces but many water-worn undercuts and overhangs, they presented no barrier to the wonderfully long-legged suubatars. Still, to save time and preserve the strength of their mounts, the travelers chose to continue forward through one of several meandering gaps that cut through the range. None of these was particularly steep-sided, being more gully than gorge. Erosion, Luminara reflected, had long since worn down these old mountains.

Riding alongside Kyakhta, she noticed that the guide's attention was unusually fixed. "You see something that troubles you, Kyakhta?"

"No, Master Luminara. But the Alwari dislike this kind of country. We prefer flat lands, grassy plains, and open spaces. Being born to the wide prairies, we are uncomfortable in enclosed places." He indicated the gentle, grass-covered slope on his left. "My mind tells me there are few places up there in which to hide, my eyes tell me there are no dangers to be seen, but my heart is full of concerns hammered into me from childhood, when my mane was but a line of immature fuzz running down my back. Old suspicions die hard."

Scanning the same hillside, she tried to cheer the guide. "If it means anything, I don't see any likely source of trouble, either."

Which was because it could not be seen. Only felt.

Sweeping down through the undulating hills, the ever-present wind of Ansion was strengthened by the natural funneling effect of narrowing canyons and clefts. Wind speed did not reach gale force, but it grew strong enough to induce the travelers to cover their mouths and nostrils with protective cloth.

Bulgan suddenly sat up straight in his saddle. Or at least, as straight as his bent back would permit. No question that he saw something, Obi-Wan noted. The Jedi did not have a chance to ask what it was.

"Chawix!" Bulgan exclaimed. Reining in his suubatar, he began looking around wildly. Hearing his friend's warning cry,

Kyakhta turned his suubatar quickly toward the nearest of the overhangs they had passed.

"In here with your mounts, quickly!"

Unable to see any danger, Luminara nonetheless hurried to follow Kyakhta's lead. She barely had time to direct her own suubatar to its knees to allow her to dismount when the guide appeared in front of her.

"Stay here, Master Luminara." Looking back over his shoulder, he winced as something shot past the opening to the undercut. "I think we're safe in here, but if you go farther out, you might catch a gust of wind."

"What's wrong with that?" Having lowered the protective cloth from the front of her face, she was staring outside. There was nothing to be seen except the narrow gully they had been traversing and the rising slope of the hill on the other side.

"You might intercept a gust of wind carrying a chawix."

Obi-Wan had come over to join his colleague in studying the seemingly innocuous gulch. "What kind of animal is a chawix?"

"It's not an animal," the guide explained. "It's a plant." Turning, Kyakhta dropped into a crouch. As he approached the edge of the undercut and the first pebbles of the sun-washed gully, he dropped to his belly and beckoned them to follow.

Lying flat on the ground, they were able to watch as several, then dozens of what appeared to be large bundles of impossibly intertwined, ropelike branches came bounding past. Lightweight and propelled by the constant wind that blew down the gully, they would hit the ground, bounce into the air, and soar a substantial distance before touching down once more and bounding skyward once again.

"Not good to get hit by a chawix." With the two Padawans following him, Bulgan had slithered up alongside the prone Jedi.

STAR WARS: THE APPROACHING STORM ══════ 175

"I can see how it could be uncomfortable," Barriss mused aloud. She was interested, but not happy. Crawling flat on hard alien dirt was not one of her favorite pastimes. "But I don't see why it should cause anyone to panic."

"Maybe our friends worry about one of them striking a suubatar in the face." Anakin shielded his eyes against the dust and the glare as he watched the bundles of vinelike material come bouncing past their rocky shelter. "It looks like they might have some thorns."

As they looked on, a membibi emerged from its den on the far side of the ravine and started upwind, heading for another burrow. The small, four-legged insectivore was hairless, with splotchy pale white skin, a long whiplike tail, and a low-slung protruding snout it carried only a thumb-length above the ground.

Flying through the air, propelled aimlessly forward by the wind, a spinning chawix arced downward to land on top of the scurrying membibi. Luminara expected the plant to bounce off, as it had bounced off the rocky surface of the gully itself. It did not.

Sensing proximity to flesh, it extended a dozen or more thorns from fingernail to finger in length, like a feline extending its claws. Pierced by these multiple woody stilettos, the membibi gave a muted shriek and fell over onto its side, legs kicking. Within minutes it lay still. The chawix, its position secured by the thorns thrust deep into the animal's flesh, began to feed on the dead membibi. The onlookers safe beneath the overhang on the other side of the gully could see the pallid penetrating thorns darken as they sucked up the liquefied flesh of their victim.

"So the chawix is a carnivorous plant that uses the winds of Ansion to get around." Having carefully retreated to the back of the overhang, Obi-Wan kept his attention focused on the gully.

"I don't think a good pair of wind goggles would be much protection."

"The membibi certainly died quickly enough," Luminara pointed out.

Close to her, Bulgan grunted. "The feeding thorns hold within them a strong nerve poison. Membibi or person, it makes no difference to the chawix. Or to the poison."

"First the kyren, now the chawix. Both examples of mass subsistence that rely on steady, constant wind to help them feed." She shook her head. "I can see why on the plains of Ansion, a calm day would be a cause for celebration among the Alwari."

"We would be safer in the cities and towns," Kyakhta admitted. "But we would not be as free. And we would not be Alwari."

Bulgan indicated agreement. "I would rather live free among the perils of the prairie than safe in a cramped, smelly house in Cuipernam. And towns hold dangers of their own."

His friend hissed knowingly. "There are no Hutts on the open plains. Dearly would I love to see Soergg confronted by a few dozen flying chawix."

Bulgan nodded energetically. "The fat slimebag would feed a whole forest of chawix. On him, they'd grow big as trees!"

"This Soergg the Hutt," Luminara asked them, "the one who sent you to abduct Barriss: Did he ever tell you *why* he wanted her?"

The two Alwari exchanged a glance. "Our minds worked differently then, but no, I don't think he ever mentioned the reason."

Bulgan confirmed his friend's response. "I thought it was to hold her for ransom. That is the usual reason for carrying out a kidnapping, isn't it?"

"Not always." She looked to her left. "Obi-Wan?"

The other Jedi looked even more thoughtful than usual. "We know there are elements that would like to see us fail in our mission, that would dearly love to see Ansion and its allies secede from the Republic. First you and Barriss are attacked, then these two are ordered to abduct her."

"Not necessarily her." Bulgan indicated Luminara's Padawan. "We were told to take either of your apprentices."

Obi-Wan gestured impatiently. "It amounts to the same thing. A Hutt wouldn't dare to challenge the Order unless there was a substantial profit in it for him. That raises the interesting question of who paid this Soergg to carry out the kidnapping, and probably also the attack on you and Barriss."

"We have no proof the Hutt was involved in that," Luminara pointed out. "But it follows logically enough."

He nodded. "Having tried twice to stop us, it stands to reason he'll try again. We'll have to watch our step when we return to Cuipernam."

"You raise the question of the Hutt's employer, Obi-Wan." As she watched the last of the chawix tumble past outside their refuge, Luminara searched her memories. "There are many powerful elements among the secessionists. Clearly, some have grown bolder than others. If we could find out who hired the Hutt, we could make a case against them before the Senate. It would embarrass their cause."

He sighed softly. "You have more confidence in the Senate than I do, Luminara. First, they would appoint a panel to study the accusation. Then the panel would produce a report. The report would go to committee. The committee would issue a commentary based on the report. The commentary would be tabled until the Senate could find the time to vote on the report. Recommendations would follow based on the vote—unless it was

voted to send the report back to committee for further study."
He met her gaze evenly. "By that time, Ansion and its allies
could have seceded from the Republic, formed their own government, had a civil war, dissolved, and re-formed. One would
have to live as long as Master Yoda to see the final outcome."

Standing nearby, Anakin had listened in silence to the Jedi's
discussion. Master Obi-Wan was right, he knew. Put something
to the Senate, and nothing would ever be accomplished. That
was what the Jedi were best at, he decided: getting things done
without having to worry about the approval of the endlessly
garrulous, nonsensical debate of the Senate. Give him a clean
lightsaber over obfuscating words any day.

He moved slightly away from the others, leaning up against
the wall of the overhang, and gazed disinterestedly out at the
lethal plants that were still bounding past. There were fewer of
them now. He and his companions should be able to move soon.
Observing his isolation, Barriss moved to intrude upon it.

"You don't find wind-propelled carnivorous poison plants of
interest? Not many would be so quickly bored with otherworldly
wonders, Anakin."

He looked over at her. "It's not that, Barriss. I have other
things on my mind." Straightening, he stood away from the wall.
"I guess I'm just impatient to get this assignment over with." He
nodded in the direction of the gully. "For example, if we had a
landspeeder, we wouldn't have to worry about things like these
chawix. The kyren, maybe, but not chawix." One hand moved to
his lower back. "And my butt wouldn't hurt so much."

She smothered a smile. "Your saddle doesn't fit you?"

"Very little on this world fits me. I wish I was elsewhere."

"Strange world that, Elsewhere. I've heard a lot about it."

His expression changed. "Now you're making fun of me."

"No, I'm not," she insisted, though her tone and expression were ambivalent. "It's just that sometimes I think you're a little too self-centered to be a Jedi. A little too focused on what's good for and essential to Anakin Skywalker, as opposed to what's important to your colleagues and to the Republic."

" 'The Republic.' " He gestured toward where the two older Jedi were conversing with their guides. "You should hear Master Obi-Wan talk about the Republic, sometimes. About what's happening to it, what's going on in the government."

"You mean the talk of a secessionist movement?"

"That—and other things. Don't misunderstand. Master Obi-Wan is a true Jedi. Anyone can see that. He believes in everything the Jedi stand for and everything they do. The way I see it, that's very different from believing in the current government."

"Governments are always changing. They're a mutable organism." While she spoke, she continued to look on in fascination as the chawix slowly consumed the last of the unfortunate membibi. "And like any living thing, they are always growing and maturing."

"Or like any living thing, they die and are replaced. Believing in the Republic isn't the same as believing in the Senate."

"Ah—that overstuffed hothouse full of declamatory blowhards!"

He looked at her in sudden surprise. "I thought you disagreed with me."

"About the Republic and what it stands for? Yes. About the Senate, that's something else again. But politicians are not Jedi, Anakin, and Jedi are not politicians. It's the Council we report to, it's their directives that lead us, and unless that changes, I'm afraid I can't share your overweening cynicism regarding the state of the Republic."

"Your upbringing was different from mine. You haven't seen the things I have." He looked down at her. "You don't feel the kind of loss I do."

"No, that's true," she readily admitted. "I don't." Her tone softened from argumentative to curious. "What's it like, to know your mother? To grow up with one?"

He brushed past her, moving to rejoin the others. "It's a feeling of loss that's hard to describe. Just know that it hurts. You're better off without that hurt, Barriss. Nothing personal, but it's kind of private. Even Jedi are entitled to a few small privacies. Even Padawans." He forced a smile. "Anyway, that was a long time ago. Let's see if our good guides think it's safe for us to resume our journey."

There was more she wanted to ask him, but he was right. Thrown together for long periods at a time, Jedi and Padawan alike had a need for privacy. Curious and concerned though she might be, she was going to have to respect that. In their time together on Ansion, Anakin had done nothing to make her suspect his competence. Where Jedi teachings were concerned, he was as reliable and aware a fellow Padawan as she had ever met—if a bit strong-headed. What vexed her were these personal problems of his, inner quandaries that he only occasionally allowed to rise to the surface of his self, where others could perceive them.

She didn't want to quarrel with him, or accuse him. She wanted to help. But in order for her to be of any use, he would have to open up. If not to her, then to Obi-Wan. Clearly, there was much on his mind beyond a desire to do a good job and to eventually be promoted to the status of full Jedi Knight.

Perhaps with the passage of time, he might choose to confide in her more. Until then, she would try her best to monitor his shifting emotions, and to be there if he needed someone besides his teacher to talk to. Meanwhile, he would remain a bit of an enigma. She moved to join him and the others. If nothing else, he was certainly unique. That uniqueness gave him something to build on. But if he hoped to ever be promoted to full Jedi, he was going to have to sort out those problematic inner uncertainties.

She had never met such a thing as a conflicted Jedi. But then, she had never before met one who had been raised by his mother.

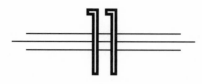

The chawix outbreak did not last long. Only long enough for a snack, a quick drink, and a brief rest, following which the travelers prepared for departure. It was when she was preparing to climb back onto the saddle of her mount that Barriss noticed the creature digging through the supply pack that was tied across the suubatar's second back. Momentarily startled by the unexpected sight, she froze.

It looked very much like any other Ansionian. The bright, convex eyes, the bipedal build, and the long, nimble fingers and toes were identical. But instead of the narrow mane that ran from the top of the head down the spine to terminate in a short tail, this intruder was completely covered in short, dense, dark brown and beige fur striped with dull yellow markings. Instead of a twitchy stub, its weaving tail was as long as her arm.

Most striking of all, it barely came up to her waist.

"Hey, stop that!" she yelled in all-purpose Ansionian.

Both arms laden with a trio of flexiwrapped foodpaks, the startled intruder looked up in response to her sudden shout.

Emitting a defiant squeal, it turned and leapt off the back of
the indifferent suubatar. Unhesitatingly, she raced around her
mount's front end. If the creature stayed where it was, it would
be trapped against the rear of the overhang. If she failed to intercept it and it ran outside, it would be highly visible and therefore
easy to track down on the slopes that bordered the gully.

As she rounded her mount's head, it lifted its snout to sniff
lazily at her, then closed its eyes and resumed its resting posture.
She expected to see the prowler huddled against the back wall, or
racing for the gulch beyond. What she saw instead was a pair of
legs vanishing beneath a protruding shelf of rock near the rear of
the overhang.

A quick backward glance showed her companions chatting or
preparing for departure. If the little thief thought he could hide
in a hole, he was very much mistaken. She was not so easily de-
ceived. Dropping to her knees, she went in after it. If she could
get a hand on one of those small feet, she was sure she could drag
the intruder back out.

Unexpectedly, the hole opened into a fissure that ran back
into the hill. Light filtered down from above. At that point she
hesitated. Cornering the thief in a dead-end recess was one
thing; chasing it down a slot canyon of unknown extent quite another. But—they needed every bit of their supplies. And every
second she lingered put more distance between herself and the
thief.

Determined not to let the prowler get away, she rose to her
feet and raced after it. If the rocky cleft branched off into multiple passages, she would have to terminate the chase and return,
defeated, to her companions. On the other hand, if it dead-
ended somewhere not far ahead, she would have the furry bandit
cornered.

Though clearly cut by running water, the crevice cooperated by not splitting into different branches. Agile though he was, the intruder was slowed by his ill-gotten burden. He never managed to slip entirely out of her sight. In fact, she was gaining on him noticeably when he suddenly turned to confront her. Jumping up and down, he proceeded to unload on her a series of furious squeals that she struggled to translate. The dialect was far more difficult to decipher than the comparatively sophisticated speech of the city, the idiom spoken by Kyakhta and Bulgan, or even the rough variant that was employed by the wandering Yiwa.

"Get back, get back, go away, go away, leave alone, leave alone!" In addition to these straightforward exclamations there were also numerous rapid-fire individual phrases that proved beyond her capacity to interpret, but whose general implication could be inferred from the vaguely obscene gestures that accompanied them. On careful consideration, Barriss did not believe any were intended to be flattering. Such imprecations and insults didn't bother her.

What did were the dozens of echoing comments and cries that emanated from the thief's cohorts, who by now lined both sides of the crevice's upper rim. Yelling and screaming, they hurled exceptionally inventive epithets down at her while their absconding colleague stood his ground and assumed a posture of unmistakable triumph.

The sight of them was as astonishing as it was unexpected. Despite their diminutive stature, proportionately slightly larger eyes, and full fur body covering, the similarities to the dominant Ansionian race were unmistakable. Her little thief and his comrades clearly represented a distinct branching of Kyakhta's and Bulgan's species, a dwarf genetic offshoot. Already she'd recog-

nized their speech as a variant of the Ansionian norm. Every one
of them, she noted, boasted a different pattern in its fur.

The cleft in the hill was a dead end, all right. For both thief
and pursuer. But he was the one with the swarm of allies. It occurred to her that not only did her companions not know she
was in trouble, they didn't even know where she was. Master
Luminara would be displeased. Cautiously reaching for her
lightsaber, Barriss hoped fervently that she would be able to
accept that displeasure in person.

"Hahaheehee!" With unflagging energy and enthusiasm, the
thief was jumping wildly up and down. "Tooqui fool you, fool
you! You trapped good now, you big back-bald bully-goo!
Squinty-eyes! Syrup-stink! What you do now now?"

That depended entirely, she knew, on what the thief's comrades did next. If she backed slowly down the crevice, retracing
her steps, would they track her retreat from above? Or would
they immediately lose interest in lieu of scrambling down to fight
one another over a share of their successful colleague's plunder?

The answer came in the form of a hail of stones. None was
particularly big, but she would only have to catch one fist-sized
rock between the eyes to be knocked senseless. Derived from her
training, her response was pure reflex. Raising a hand, she concentrated hard, hard.

The flung stones hit the sides of the narrow cleft. They struck
the floor at her feet. But none made contact with her. She was too
busy focusing on deflecting the missiles to wonder how long she
could maintain her concentration. Sweat began to bead on her
forehead. She couldn't spare the energy to yell for help. Given the
twists and turns in the cleft and the distance she'd come, she
doubted her shouts would be heard by her friends, anyway.

She was on her own.

Apart from the actual, very real danger, it was a strange feeling. This was the first time she had been attacked by herself, not counting the abduction in the Cuipernam shop. Involving as it had nothing more threatening than a soporific mist, that had been a relatively benign assault. This was completely different. The howling, gesticulating creatures on the gully rim above her were doing their utmost to split her skull.

Wouldn't they ever get tired? she wondered. The strain was beginning to tell. She felt herself growing dizzy from the effort. If they saw, or sensed, that she was weakening, they might redouble their efforts.

If she went down, it was entirely possible that nobody would find her. Words would have to be said over her demise in the absence of a body. Those she had known and studied with would grieve, wondering what had happened to her on distant, suddenly critical Ansion.

Just as she felt she was going to pass out from the strain, the barrage slowed, to finally cease altogether. Overhead, the assembled creatures turned from attacking her to jabbering excitedly at one another. Occasionally, one would point down at their intended target standing cornered below. At such moments she strove to project an air of complete confidence, even indifference. The pain in her head was beginning to fade. She saw one of her assailants shove another. A couple of fights broke out among the stone throwers—all long slapping fingers and angry tiny fists. Apparently, her assailants were a fractious bunch.

Hoping she remembered enough of the language course and still keeping a wary eye out for the odd hurled rock, she tilted her head back and addressed them forcefully.

"Listen to me!" Stunned debaters immediately ceased their

arguing. Several dozen wide-eyed faces turned to look down at her. "There's no need for us to fight. My friends and I mean you no harm. We're not from this world, from Ansion. We're humans, and we'd like to be friends. Understand? Friends." Turning slightly, she pointed back the way she'd come.

"Two of my companions are Jedi Knights. I and one other are their Padawans, their apprentices. We also have two Alwari guides with us."

She should have stopped with her own identification. At the mention of the guides, the assembled group resumed their leaping and howling—though not quite as vociferously as before, she noted. She struggled to keep up with the meanings of their overlapping cries.

"Hate Alwari! . . . Alwari bad, bad, bad! . . . No Alwari here! . . . Kill Alwari! . . . Alwari go away, away! . . ." A few picked up and brandished fresh stones.

She raised both hands. "Please, listen to me! The two Alwari who travel with us are not only from another part of this world, they're clanless! They are completely under the control of myself and my friends and will not harm you. We just want to be friends!"

The flourished stones were not set aside—but they were lowered. Once more the creatures lining the rim resumed their internal bickering. If not for their uninhibited belligerence, they really were quite attractive, she decided, in the diversity of their full-body fur. Eventually the squabbling diminished, though it didn't cease entirely. A gray-coated individual, clearly an elder, leaned over the rim of the crevice to peer down at her.

"You strange person, you is. What a 'Jedi Knight'?"

"What a 'human'?" exclaimed another, interrupting. Suddenly she was inundated by a volley not of stones, but of queries.

Wrestling with her limited local vocabulary, she did her best to answer them all.

Meanwhile, the singular thief who had triggered the confrontation stood with his back facing the cleft's dead end, still clutching his cumbersome spoils. "*Haja*—what about me? What about Tooqui?" He tried to raise one of the big foodpaks over his head but succeeded only in dropping it on his right foot. Now much more interested in asking questions of the tall stranger, his comrades ignored him. Putting down his burden, he began hopping about furiously, waving long-fingered fists at those gathered overhead.

"Listen to me! Talk to me, not this ugly beady-eyed one! *Jaja*, I'm talking to you, you noisy stupid heads! It's me, Tooqui! *Listen to me!*" In his uncontrolled rage at being ignored by his fellows, he was all but bouncing off the narrow enclosing walls.

Meanwhile, Barriss continued to reply to as many of the thief's now inquisitive companions as her limited knowledge of their language would allow. She learned that they were called Gwurran, that they lived in the caves and crevices that ran through these hills, and that they hated the Alwari nomads.

"Not all nomads are bad," Barriss told them. "The Alwari are like any other people. There are good people among them, and bad people. My kind, humans, are no different. There is good and bad in everyone."

"Nomads kill Gwurran," one of the tribespeople informed her. "Gwurran have to live here, in hill country, to survive."

"Not our nomads," she countered. "Like I told you, they come from far, far away. I'm sure they've never hurt a Gwurran in their lives. They may never even have seen one of your kind." Even as she said it, she fervently hoped it was true. It was hard to imagine the thoughtful Kyakhta or the kindly Bulgan ever showing such unreasoning hostility to a cousin, even in their formerly addled condition. "Why not come and see for yourselves? Come back with me and meet my friends. We'll have a party. You can try some interesting food."

Her assailants exchanged dawning glances. "Party?" someone murmured hopefully.

"Food?" exclaimed another expectantly.

". . . is anybody listen to me?" Having spent some time now bouncing off the walls, the Gwurran who called himself Tooqui was out of breath and out of energy. "This Tooqui talking. You know Tooqui. Tooqui who—" Dumping his ill-gotten gains indifferently to one side, the thief sat down on the gravel floor of the fissure and exhaled deeply. "Ah, *moojpuck!* Nobody care. Gwurran bunch of brainless bonehead stupids." Thrusting an accusing finger at Barriss, Tooqui raised what was left of his voice.

"This all you fault, you small-head outland big-lips! You twist word noises, make friends forget Tooqui. I hate you."

She walked toward the disheartened thief. Everyone on the rim above went suddenly quiet. As for the talkative Tooqui, seeing the much larger stranger approach, he picked up one of the foodpaks and backed up as far as he could.

"You keep away from Tooqui, you long-leg ugly bean thing! Tooqui fight you! Tooqui kill!"

Halting, she indicated the foodpak he held awkwardly in a throwing position. "Not with a few packets of dehydrated energy pudding, I don't think." To make herself less intimidating, she knelt, bringing her face as close to the Gwurran's level as she could manage. It was a risk. While concentrating on the thief, she couldn't keep an eye on his rock-armed comrades overhead. If they chose to bombard her while she was talking to him, she wouldn't be able to defend herself. But as Luminara had often told her, it was difficult to accomplish anything worthwhile without the taking of a risk.

Little did she know that at that very minute, on distant Coruscant, a group of extremely powerful and very determined individuals were contemplating that exact same conundrum—though for them, the stakes were inconceivably higher.

"I don't want to hurt you, Tooqui. I want us to be friends." She nodded up at his comrades who lined the top of the fissure. Some still held rocks in their small but strong three-fingered hands. She fought not to show her nervousness. "I want all of us to be friends."

The Gwurran hesitated, aware that his fellow tribesfolk were following with great interest the confrontation being played out below. "You not hurt Tooqui? You not angry with him?"

She smiled engagingly. "On the contrary, I admire you for what you did. I imagine it's not every Gwurran who would be so bold as to try to steal in broad daylight from a party of tall, strong offworlders like myself and my companions."

Though still uncertain and continuing to eye her guardedly, he slowly lowered the foodpak and moved away from the wall. "*Jaja,* that true so. Nobody but Tooqui brave or clever enough to do it." He came a little closer. "Tooqui bravest brave of all Gwurran."

"I don't doubt it," she responded, repressing a smile. "Actually, I think you're kind of friendly."

He took immediate offense, standing as tall as he could. This brought his face up to the level of the Padawan's stomach. "Tooqui not friendly! Tooqui most fierce ferocious slayer of all Gwurran enemies!"

"I'm sure you are," she agreed, reaching out to brush the fur on his forehead from back to front. He stumbled away from her, flailing irately at his head as he struggled to smooth down his ruffled fur.

"Don't do that! Don't touch Tooqui." Fur once more flattened and smoothed back, he glared up at her out of bulging, orange-tinted eyes. "Tooqui have much dignity."

"Sorry." She lowered her offending hand, palm upward. "Now, if you and I are going to be friends, Tooqui, and if you're going to join the party, you have to return what you took."

The Gwurran eyed the three foodpaks uncertainly. "Tooqui work hard for to steal this stuff."

"Take my word for it, you wouldn't like it anyway. At least, not until it's been properly rehydrated. If you'll come back with me, I'll see that you're the first one who gets to taste it."

"First one? Tooqui be first?" His single nostril sniffed at the pak he still held. "Tooqui *always* first."

In your own mind, anyway, you sly little sneak. "It's settled, then? You'll come back with me, we'll be friends, and we'll have a party?"

The Gwurran vacillated only a moment longer. Then he confidently placed first one foodpak and then the other two in Barriss's waiting arms.

"Tooqui consent to join you." Leaning back, he regarded his comrades on the rim above. "It okay okay now. Tooqui make stranger harmless. All Gwurran can come down safely safely now. We go to see what nasty ugly outlander strangers got to offer Gwurran."

Smiling to herself at the little brigand's bravado, Barriss waited while the rest of the chattering Gwurran, agile as spiders, scrambled down the walls of the fissure to join them. Tooqui's blustering notwithstanding, they largely ignored him as they pushed and shoved to get close to her, feeling her feet, her exposed lower arms, and her protective clothing. She put up with their innocent, wide-eyed curiosity for several minutes, until it threatened to become more intimate than she was prepared to tolerate. Then she shrugged them off and started back down the cleft, the three foodpaks slung over her left shoulder, accompanied by the entire tribe of chattering, jabbering, energized Gwurran.

Slender but strong fingers continued to tug at her as she walked, along with a continuous flow of questions.

"Where humans come from? . . . Why you so silly-tall? . . . What happened to rest of you hair? . . . How can you see see out of such small small flat flat eyes? . . . What this shiny-pretty on you waist? . . ."

"Don't touch that." She slapped the probing fingers away from her belt. The notion of a lightsaber in the hands of an unruly, combative, slightly rowdy Gwurran was more than a little unsettling. In the constricted confines of the fracture in the hillside, the riotous babble of the diminutive Ansionians was deafening.

"She can't just have disappeared into thin air!"

For the tenth, or maybe the twentieth time, Luminara ran through the list of possibilities. Barriss had gone walking outside the protective overhang and had managed to get herself lost. She had found something of interest and wandered off into the hills. Something vast and voracious had swooped down out of the sky and carried her off. She was attending to personal needs that were taking more time than usual.

The last seemed the most likely, but even allowing for a severe gastrointestinal upset, the Padawan ought to have reported back in by now. If nothing else, she should have used her comlink. That she hadn't done so suggested a number of possible explanations. The device was broken, its power pack had inexplicably gone dead, she had lost it off her belt somewhere and was even now searching some hillside for it, or—it had been forcibly taken from her. Who or what might be responsible for the latter Luminara could not imagine, but in the absence of solid facts, any and all possibilities had to be considered.

Movement made her turn. Obi-Wan, Anakin, and Kyakhta returned from searching the slopes outside their little refuge. "No sign of her anywhere." Anakin's tone was full of concern. "Would she have run somewhere instead of walking?"

"That would depend on the circumstances, wouldn't it?" Luminara was hard-pressed to keep anger and sarcasm out of her voice. She knew that Barriss's absence had nothing to do with Anakin. But the Padawan was Luminara's responsibility. If anything had happened to her . . .

Anakin had bristled at Luminara's tone, but held his peace. It was not his place to question a Jedi Knight, not even if she was being unreasonably abrupt. He could not yet talk back to someone like Luminara Unduli as an equal. Soon, though. Soon . . .

Bulgan looked up at her out of his one good eye. "We'll take the suubatars and make a spiraling sweep of these hills and gullies, Master Luminara. We can cover much more ground that way. Perhaps she has fallen into a hole in the rocks and hurt a leg."

A worried Luminara nodded absently. Sitting high up on the back of a suubatar would certainly provide a better view than was available from searching on foot. The implications of the Alwari's observation were distressing. If Barriss *had* fallen into a hole, and if the hole was big enough, and if she had been knocked unconscious, they might never find her.

That was when they heard a voice hailing them.

"Hey, everybody. I'm over here."

Racing around a pair of resting suubatars, they saw the object of everyone's present concern emerging on all fours from beneath a projecting slab of rock. The crawlway it concealed was exceedingly well hidden from anyone not standing directly in front of it and bending to look under the jutting stone.

"Barriss! Are you al—?" Slowing as she drew near, Luminara's expression quickly changed from open concern to a reproving scowl. "Where have you been, Padawan? We've been looking all over for you. And—are you hurt?"

"No, I'm fine." Rising from the crawlway, Barriss brushed dust from her hands and stretched. "And so are our new friends."

Luminara was not alone in taking a couple of surprised steps backward as a veritable deluge of noisy, jabbering, furry bipeds spewed from the concealed crawlway. In an instant, they were investigating Barriss's companions with the same candid zeal and lack of discretion they had shown toward her.

"Suubatar," one shouted as it clambered up onto the back of Kyakhta's mount. Glowering his irritation, the guide hurried toward it.

"You, little fella! Get down from there! Get down just now!"

Sitting atop the unconcerned suubatar's middle shoulders, the brown and blue Gwurran made energetic faces down at the aggravated guide. "*Nyngwah nooglik,* goofy-talking no-hair outlander darling! You make make me!"

"Why you little! . . ." Kyakhta would have started up after the taunting pygmy, but Luminara called him back.

"Never mind that one now, Kyakhta."

"But Master Luminara, it is—"

"I said, never mind. Come and meet these people."

"People?" Muttering under his breath, Kyakhta reluctantly complied with the Jedi's order. "These are not people. These are dirt crawlers."

As Barriss proceeded to explain the reasons for her extended absence, Luminara was soon mollified. The Padawan's tale was brief but intriguing.

". . . and so I convinced Tooqui here to return what he'd taken, and to bring along his whole tribe with him." Barriss eyed her teacher hesitantly. "I promised them a kind of a party."

Luminara frowned. "This is not a pleasure trip, Padawan. Obi-Wan, what do you think about this?"

The other Jedi considered. After a moment, somewhat unexpectedly, he grinned. "A Padawan's promise does not bind a Jedi, but that doesn't mean it should not be honored. We don't have musicians, and speaking for myself, I feel I've already done enough entertaining on this journey. But we can certainly show them some things, and let them try a taste of our food. Maybe they'll consider accepting a little education about the galaxy at large in place of singing and dancing. Perhaps that'll be enough entertainment for this get-together to qualify as a 'party.'"

Actually, it did not matter what the travelers did: the Gwurran seemed to find everything and anything about the humans most amusing. Whether it was demonstrating technical gear, or exposing their differently toned furless flesh, or matching five comparatively thick human fingers against three slimmer Ansionian ones, the tribe was utterly enthralled. Wholly devoid of tact, they crawled over everything: travelers, dozing suubatars, and supply packs alike. But there were no more attempts at petty theft. When one adolescent attempted to make off with a plasticine pack covering, she was roundly chastised by several of the adults. Luminara was gratified to see that friendship, if not comprehensive understanding, had been established.

At least, it had been established between human and Gwurran. The two petulant Alwari guides observed the proceedings in bad-tempered silence, tolerant of the tribe's antics but less than enthusiastic—to the point that Luminara felt compelled to question them about their reticence.

"Why the attitude, my friends?" she asked them. "Is it that you've had bad dealings with people like this before?"

"I've never seen creatures like this before." Kyakhta remained scrunched up against his softly breathing suubatar, as if he was afraid a bunch of the Gwurran were going to hoist the huge animal up onto their shoulders and walk off with it. "Don't know their kind, don't think I want to know."

"Alwari keep away from hilly places like this," Bulgan added, "so it's not surprising my clan has never encountered such as these."

"But they're not so very different from you," she pointed out. "They're much smaller, true. That should make them less of a threat, not more. So what if their eyes are slightly bigger in proportion to their faces than yours are, and unlike the Alwari they're completely covered in fur? They speak a variant of your language, and they look and act like the representatives of many other tribes we saw in Cuipernam."

"Not Alwari," the normally equable Bulgan argued. "Ignorant little savages is what they are."

"Ah, I see." She turned to watch the merriment as Obi-Wan demonstrated how a self-heating foodpak worked. Squeals of delight followed by energetic conversation rose from his furry audience. "So the Alwari are educated, sophisticated, forward-

looking beings, while these Gwurran are primitive ignora-
muses?" The guides' ensuing silence was answer enough.

Nodding knowingly, Luminara eyed each of them in turn.
"Isn't that how the city folk of Ansion look upon the Alwari?"

Kyakhta looked confused. As for Bulgan, his face contorted
as he struggled to get a handle on the concept. Then he looked
at his friend and companion. If it was possible for an Alwari to
look sheepish, both guides succeeded.

"You are a good teacher, Master Luminara." Kyakhta rose
from his resting position. "Instead of yelling and screaming, you
let those you are instructing come to the truth at their own
speed, by their own road." Looking past her, both he and Bulgan
contemplated the frenetically active but good-natured Gwurran
from a new perspective. "Maybe you're right. Maybe they are
just curious, and not a tribe that lives by stealing."

"Give them a chance. That's all that's being asked here. Like
Barriss gave you and Bulgan a chance."

"That is fair enough." Gesturing positively, Kyakhta moved
off to see if they could help with Obi-Wan's demonstrations.
Watching them go, Luminara felt she had struck a small blow for
the kind of tolerance and understanding that would be needed to
make for a just and strong planetary government.

And for a durable Republic as well, she told herself as she
watched Barriss at work.

"But we're not nomads." The Padawan was trying to explain
the nature and purpose of the Jedi Knights to a small cluster of
attentive but obviously confused Gwurran.

"Sure sure you are," argued one of the tribe. "You tell us
what Jedi folk do: travel travel all the time, go from this place to
that place to next place, always on the moving, never staying

same place very long." She looked to her multihued companions for support. "That a nomad."

"It's true that some of us do seem never to put down any roots," Luminara admitted. "But others do live for a long time in one place. If you rise to a position on the Jedi Council, for example, you find yourself spending most of your time on Coruscant."

"What a Coruscant?" one of the other Gwurran asked.

"Another whole world, like Ansion," Barriss explained.

The tribesfolk exchanged puzzled looks. "What an Ansion?" one finally inquired ingenuously. With a resigned sigh, Barriss did her best to try to explain the concept of multiple worlds. It would have been easier at night, with stars in the sky. Clearly, the horizons of the Gwurran were far more limited than those of the Alwari.

Much of the remainder of the day, when the travelers should have been galloping through the hills and across the open prairie beyond, was spent educating and entertaining the Gwurran, who were passionate in their desire to learn, to explore every new object and idea. What they needed, Luminara decided, was not a casual visit but a permanent school, to at least bring them up to the educational level of the taller nomads they so disliked. Starting with physical and intellectual disadvantages, they needed proportionately more help. When they returned to Cuipernam, she resolved to mention it to the proper authorities. Failing local interest, there were societies and organizations within the Republic specifically designed to help isolated ethnic groups like the Gwurran.

Also, she and Obi-Wan determined that, despite the genuine affability exhibited by the little Ansionians, the onset of night might prove just a tad too tempting for the more acquisitive

among them. Better for all concerned to remove any opportunity
to stray by leaving while the sun was still up. While the overhang
in the gully offered an appealing campsite, they would find a way
to manage out on the open prairie.

So they bade their farewells and promised to send others to
teach and assist the Gwurran. It was as they were making final
preparations for departure that Luminara felt a tug at her pant
leg. Looking down, she saw a Gwurran she recognized. It was
Tooqui, the enterprising and unusually bold would-be thief who
had led a persistent Barriss to his tribe.

"What is it, Tooqui?" she inquired politely. "We're almost
ready to go, you know."

"Tooqui know." He slapped both long-fingered hands
against the striped brown and black fur that covered his chest.
"Tooqui bravest of all Gwurran. The best fighter, the smartest,
the most handsomest, the—"

"Yes, you're a fine representative of your tribe, Tooqui." Luminara agreed absently as she checked the supply pack harness of
her patient suubatar. "I'm sure they're very proud of you."

"*Pifgah!*" he exclaimed sharply. "Gwurran multiple stupids!
Got no dreams, no purposes, no goals. Happy living in holes in
hills." The little thief managed the difficult task of appearing to
strut while standing still. "Tooqui want more. Tooqui got to
have more." Bulbous red-orange eyes gazed up at her. "I want
go with you."

That put pause to her inspection. Squatting, she gazed
apologetically into those oversized, staring eyes. "Tooqui, you
can't come with us. You know that."

"Know what? Don't know that." The Gwurran was not in
the least intimidated by the much bigger Jedi. "Tooqui know

only what he can see. See that you have plenty room on great big riding suubatars for little guy like Tooqui. I fight hard, don't eat much. Usually."

She had to smile. "You mean, usually you fight hard, or usually you don't eat much?"

Taking a step back, he kicked angrily at the ground. "Don't word-game Tooqui! I not stupid stupid like these other ground-burrowers! Tooqui smart smart."

"Smart enough to steal from us when we're sleeping?" she inquired pointedly.

Placing his right hand over his face and his left over the back of his head, he declaimed as sonorously as his small stature would permit. "May Tooqui shrivel in the sun if he ever take a grain crumb from his new friends without asking. May his insides spill out on the ground and run run away like worm suckers. May all his relatives burn in grass fire that cleans the open places and—"

"All right, all right." She was laughing softly despite herself. "I get the picture." Although she had the feeling that Tooqui wouldn't particularly mind if certain of his relatives *did* happen to meet an untimely and unpleasant end. "You're brave and true. But we still can't take you with us. As Barriss has already told you and your fellows, we're engaged in a difficult and dangerous mission and have no time to look after guests."

"Tooqui take care of self! You see see. Tooqui not afraid of danger." Once more he slapped himself on the chest. "Tooqui eat danger for morning meal! Make good pet, too."

She blinked. "Pet? You're an intelligent being, Tooqui. You can't be a pet."

"Why not? Gwurran keep small yirans and sometimes omohts as pets. They get free food, free living place, protection from shanhs and other things that want eat them. Seem seem like pretty good deal to me. If I intelligent like you say, then not I smart enough to choose what I want to be?"

"It's not that." The last thing she would have expected was for the glib Gwurran to confuse her with subtle academic argument. "It just—it wouldn't be proper, that's all."

"If I intelligent enough choose for myself, then where be improperness?" He smiled, showing miniature versions of the same sharp teeth as their guides. "That intelligent Tooqui's choice: I want want go with you new friends as pet. Learn about Ansion world-ball. Maybe other world-balls, too. Learn much, then come back and help Gwurran."

Not only was the proposal rational, it was downright noble, Luminara mused—although Tooqui doubtless had personal motives as well. How was she going to put him off? Jedi were taught to use logic and reason on those who disagreed with them, not to terminate an awkward dispute by saying, "Because I say so."

"Jedi can't have pets," she finally declared in exasperation.

"Where does it say that in the regulations, Master?" It was Barriss, injecting herself into the debate at the worst possible time. Luminara glared at her Padawan.

"I'm sure it says something of the kind somewhere. Anyway, we're not equipped to accommodate guests."

"Tooqui equip self." Putting a hand in Barriss's, the Gwurran smiled innocently. "See? Good pet, yes yes?"

"Please!" Turning to resume her final packing check, Luminara grumbled as she struggled to secure a strap seal. "If you want to take responsibility for him, Barriss, then I suppose he can come along." She looked back sharply. "But if you cause us the least trouble, Tooqui, if you slow us down or impede our work in any way, then you have to leave leave. It's back to the hills for you, and no arguments. Agreed?"

Repeating his hands-over-face-and-head gesture, the eager Gwurran replied without hesitation. "If I cause any impede-thing, may I rot rot slowly in decaying water. May all my fur turn purple and I sick sick turn myself inside out. May I chew on my feet and—"

"Just keep him quiet," an exasperated Luminara instructed her Padawan. "And away from me."

"He'll be good." Bending over, Barriss patted the Gwurran on his furry pate. "Won't you, Tooqui?"

"Good as a Gwurran can be be," he told her genially.

Somehow, Luminara did not find that pledge particularly reassuring.

Obi-Wan was indifferent to, if not openly amused by, the antics of the newest member of their party, while Anakin was quietly pleased. The Gwurran was someone new to talk to, even if his vocabulary was limited and tended to repetition. He and Barriss took turns looking after Tooqui who, true to his word, needed very little looking after at all. The energetic native helped with everything, from unpacking the suubatars at night to gathering fuel for the campfire to learning how to operate simple devices such as the compact firestarter and watermaker. He was a fast learner, eager to know everything about anything. Or everything everything, as he habitually put it.

Only the Alwari guides were displeased by his presence among them. They did not exactly shun him, because they knew that would displease their employers. But neither did they go out of their way to assist in his instruction, or to become fast friends. The gulf that existed between Alwari and Gwurran was inexplicable to Luminara, as they both sprang from the same ancestors. Physically, they differed significantly only in size and hirsuteness.

To someone used to dealing on a daily basis with representatives of different species who differed far more radically in their physical appearance, the continuing enmity displayed by the two guides was hard to understand. Hopefully, traveling together would eventually oblige Kyakhta and Bulgan to view their smallish cousin in a better light.

At present there wasn't much of the latter, as the sun was beginning to rise over the northern horizon. It was the same horizon they had been riding toward for days; flat and grassy. A pack of shanhs had shadowed them for a night and a day, but sensing no weakness in either suubatars or their riders, had given up and drifted off in search of easier prey.

"Something moving from east to west along the horizon," Kyakhta called out. Though still waking up, everyone immediately turned in that direction.

Obi-Wan had his electrobinoculars out and was gazing at the indicated spot, trying to resolve the distant movement.

"Borokii?" Anakin inquired hopefully.

Lowering the powerful scanning device, the Jedi replied uncertainly. "I don't know. Kyakhta and Bulgan will tell us. But I have a feeling not. From what we've been told, the overclans are like the Yiwa, like all Alwari, in that they're herding nomads." He nodded in the direction of distant movement. "Whoever these are, they seem to be more advanced than that." He urged his mount forward. "Or at least, they choose to travel with far more in the way of material goods. I don't see any signs of a domesticated herd. No dorgum, no awiquod—nothing but draft animals. That means that whatever they are, they're not the Borokii."

Obi-Wan's assessment turned out to be correct. The procession that was advancing in their direction was not the sought-after preeminent overclan. Not only did it not include any herd animals such as they had encountered among the Yiwa, but it was also loud to the point of boisterousness. It was Bulgan who eventually identified the clanging, noisy procession as soon as it had drawn near enough to be recognized.

"It's a Qulun clan. The Qulun are traders. They operate freely among both the Alwari and the city folk. Though no one likes them very much, there's a need for them out on the plains, in the absence of shops and communications. Oft times they have very interesting things for sale."

"What do they accept in return?" Obi-Wan asked the guide.

Bulgan licked his lower teeth. "Besides money? All manner of goods. Cuts of dried meat from the Alwari herds. Fruits and vegetables gathered from remote parts of Ansion. Wonderful handcrafted items made mostly by the females of each clan. Only the best."

The Jedi indicated his understanding. In a Republic long since sated with the commonplace, exotic foodstuffs were much sought-after items. So were handicrafts. Bored with machine-made goods, the wealthy and the curious were always willing to pay high prices for unique handmade items that hailed from distant worlds with strange names.

"See." Bulgan rose slightly in his saddle. "They're coming out to greet us."

The three riders who broke away from the main column headed straight toward the group of travelers, who responded by slowing to meet them. Otherwise the suubatars would have easily outdistanced the powerful but much shorter sadains. Falling in line alongside Luminara's and Barriss's mounts, the trio of Qulun flashed wide smiles and waved energetic greetings. It was a notably less confrontational meeting than the earlier one

with the Yiwa. No weapons were prominently displayed, no suspicious glances were directed toward the newcomers. Not that
their eyes, the Jedi noted, were unbusy. They missed nothing,
least of all the overstuffed supply packs strapped to the second
back of each animal.

Riding with Barriss while clambering back and forth along
the length of her suubatar from head to tail, Tooqui kept up a
steady stream of muted chatter. "Strange people these. Tooqui
never *see* before. Not known to Gwurran." Tilting back his head,
he sniffed of the prairie air with his single wide nostril. "Smell
different from Alwari."

"They look different, too," she commented. "Their cos-
tumes, the tack on their sadains, the way their procession is
organized are very dissimilar from the Yiwa. What do you think,
Tooqui?"

The Gwurran's eagerness never flagged. "More food for
Tooqui's head. More new things to see and learn about."

"Well, if you *talk talk* all the time you won't be able to concentrate on those new things, and neither will I. How about
keeping quiet for a while?"

"Tooqui quiet? Two things that not go together." He settled
himself down close to her, taking up minimal space on the edge
of the saddle. "But master command, so Tooqui must obey." He
smiled. "Tooqui good pet always."

"Sarcasm is not a quality many people desire to have in their
'pets.' "

"Their *loss loss*." But as she requested, the Gwurran kept his
mouth closed, and despite the obvious strain, settled for observing the newcomers in silence.

Save for their far louder, more garish attire, two of the riders
could have passed unnoticed among the Yiwa. Not their leader,

though, for such he obviously was. This generously propor-
tioned individual clearly put a strain on his chosen sadain. Unlike
his companions, or for that matter Kyakhta, he had no mane running from the top of his head down his back. Looking at him,
Luminara suspected his smooth pate was the result of an intentional close shave as opposed to natural fur loss as in Bulgan's
case. In its way, his bald head, gleaming in the morning sun, was
as distinctive as his girth. For all that, he rode gracefully atop his
hardworking steed.

"Welcome, offworlders! The Qulun bid you welcome!"

Luminara tried to remember how many spaceports Ansion
boasted. Clearly these traders, or at least their leader, had visited
one or more where he had enjoyed the opportunity to encounter
sentients from other parts of the Republic.

"Thankings for your greeting," Kyakhta responded formally.
"We ride north."

"So we see." Performing a wondrously gravity-defying stunt,
the portly leader bowed without falling off his mount. "I am
Baiuntu, chief trader of this clan faction. What seek a mix of offworlders and Alwari in the north country?"

Appreciative of the chief's description of him as Alwari,
Kyakhta replied with good grace. "The Borokii."

"Borokii! What do offworlders seek among the overclan?"

Leaning slightly outward from his saddle, Obi-Wan replied
with a question of his own while simultaneously ignoring the
chieftain's. "Can you help us?"

"Perhaps, perhaps." Forgoing the reins of his sadain along
with his query, the chief extended both heavy arms wide. Luminara watched in fascination. Baiuntu was the first truly portly Ansionian she had seen. "Tonight you dine with us. The Qulun are
always keen on company. New faces mean new news."

"And potential new customers," Anakin murmured across to Barriss, "though I wouldn't see that as a reason not to chat with them."

"It's not up to us." Though she professed disinterest, Barriss hoped the Masters would consent to the Qulun leader's request. It would be yet another chance to learn more about Ansionian society—and besides, the food would be fresh.

Obi-Wan and Luminara saw no reason not to stop and spend the night among the effervescent traders. So long as each side kept to its own camp, security could be maintained, and there was the implication that the Qulun might be able to narrow down and therefore speed the search for the elusive Borokii. To Barriss's surprise, Tooqui stayed close to her instead of straying. For reasons of his own, he continued to be uncharacteristically closemouthed, speaking only when none of the Qulun was around. When she inquired as to the reason behind his unusual silence, he had his usual ready answer.

"Qulun think Tooqui simple dumb dumb pet. Is good position to do trading from."

"We're not here to trade." She eyed him warningly. "We're here to make friends, and to maybe learn more about the where-abouts of the overclan. That's all."

The Gwurran looked hurt. "Tooqui not want much. Something to eat, maybe, or little baby-toy for small Gwurran, or simple weapon to overawe bully Gwurran with."

"Never mind that," she told him firmly. "Talk to them or keep quiet, that's up to you. But—no talk of trading." She wore a knowing expression. "Pets don't engage in trade."

"No, but their masters do," he countered without hesitation. "Maybe if silly-fun stupid-face pet do funny tricks for master, grateful Barriss buy little trinket-thing for poor poor Tooqui?"

"I'll think about it," she replied without further comment. Urging her mount forward at a faster pace forced the Gwurran to shut up and concentrate on holding on.

Riding importantly in the lead, Baiuntu led the visitors to the top of the ridge where the Qulun were making camp. Self-erecting dwellings were already unfolding walls and roofs while busy adolescents attached heating equipment and atmospheric water condensers. Automatic braces secured the temporary structures, which were designed to be put up and taken down every day, against the ubiquitous wind. Wonderfully decorated with enamels, painted mirrors, and all manner of eye candy, one pair of these distinctive structures drew Luminara's attention even before they were fully assembled.

"Trading rooms," Bulgan explained in response to her question. "The more eye-catching, the better." He passed a hand across both eyes, the Ansionian equivalent of winking. "Dazzle a customer; that's one of the hallmarks of the Qulun. Blinded buyers are agreeable buyers."

She rode easily on her well-padded saddle, the suubatar striding along effortlessly beneath her. "Are you saying that the Qulun cheat in their dealings?"

"*Haja,* no, Master Luminara. They are like any merchants, be they fixed in place as they are in the city or fully mobile as out here on the prairie. Some are wholly honorable while others are outright bandits. One can't say one has truly done dealing until one has dealt with them. To many traders, *shady* and *clever* have freely interchangeable meanings."

"Well, we're not on a shopping excursion, so it shouldn't matter." Rising up slightly from her saddle, she surveyed the surrounding plains. "Why are they setting up shop here? This country isn't exactly crawling with customers."

The Alwari gestured nonchalantly. "They are opening up only a couple of their many shops. No doubt they hope buyers will materialize from out of the grass." He chuckled the by now familiar Ansionian laugh, adding a few sharp knuckle cracks for emphasis. "Without a shop or two open for business, the Qulun would probably be uncomfortable. For fear of missing even one potential customer, they would lose sleep."

The welcome they received certainly stood out in contrast to how they had been greeted by the initially mistrustful Yiwa. Though weapons were visible, they were not brandished in the newcomers' direction. The visitors' steeds were given pride of place in the clan's corral, along with the best water and fodder. Luminara found herself and her friends directed to a large portable structure whose interior turned out to be lined with thick carpets, self-adjusting cushions, and all manner of conveniences one would not expect to find in the middle of the northern Ansionian plains. Anything they asked for that the Qulun could provide was provided—free of charge. Obi-Wan was not surprised at the modest largesse. Such tactics were a universal means for softening up potential customers.

Barriss and Anakin didn't concern themselves with such mundanities, preferring to leave the details of the encounter to their Masters. Instead, they allowed themselves to relax and enjoy the exotic food and drink, the entertaining lightwick sculptures, and the petite perfumed dance pixies that looped endlessly about the room. In contrast, Tooqui was unnaturally subdued. The little Gwurran certainly enjoyed himself, availing himself as readily as his human friends of the flush of small luxuries. But surrounded by so many unusually eager tall strangers, he was cautious in his movements, and kept his opinions to himself.

Baiuntu was delighted to have offworld visitors. "I have met many in my dealings," he told them that evening as they shared the comforts of the designated visitors' house.

"In Cuipernam?" Anakin was munching on something blue-green, plump, and delicious.

"In Cuipernam," their host boasted, "and in Doigon, and Flerauw. A smattering of your own kind as well as a most interesting variety of others." He rested both pudgy, long-fingered hands on his imposing belly. "Merchants are a species unto themselves, it seems. Shape has nothing to do with it. The Qulun realized this from the first time a vessel from another world set down here to trade."

As he declaimed, he kept popping small purple things into his mouth. They crunched noisily against his hard palate. Detecting what he thought was some slight movement among them before they disappeared down the chieftan's gullet, Anakin decided not to ask what they were. While there was a time for Jedi boldness, there were also occasions when it was better to exercise restraint.

"Then you feel that the Qulun have benefited from Ansion's membership in the Republic?" Luminara inquired encouragingly.

Their host made a face. "I would rather talk business than politics, but since you ask—yes, I do."

"And your clanfolk feel similarly?" Obi-Wan sipped at something sweet, warm, and refreshing.

"That I cannot say. Most are not so sophisticated in such matters as Baiuntu. Like all true Qulun, they will give their allegiance to whomever they believe will make them the most money."

"So they can be bought," Anakin commented. Obi-Wan gave the Padawan a sharp look, but the younger man only shrugged, seeing nothing wrong with the question. His teacher should know by now that his Padawan was nothing if not direct.

Certainly their host took no offense. "Any merchant can be bought, my large, furless young friend. That is the nature of business, is it not? To the Qulun, loyalty is just another commodity. For the moment, we are happy to see Ansion fully represented in the Republic. As to what tomorrow may bring, who am I to say?" Grunting with the effort, he leaned back against his pile of supporting cushions. Multiple tiny sensors and equally minuscule motors shifted mass within each cushion to provide the necessary response.

"An honest response, anyway," Luminara murmured to Barriss. "I suppose we can't expect any better from such people. They're only living according to their traditions."

"Tradition seems to mean everything on this planet." Barriss sampled another of the numerous drinks that had been set before her. Like everything else she had tried, it was delicious. Movement off to her right made her turn. Her diminutive friend was ambling toward the doorway.

"Tooqui, where are you going?"

"Too much much light for Tooqui. Too much talk talk. Go for walk. Back later."

"Fine," she told him, adding after a moment's thought, "Don't steal anything."

He responded with a gesture whose meaning she would have demanded to know had he not already disappeared. One of the guards stationed outside made a move to intercept him, but the Gwurran was too quick, vanishing into the night and the camp.

Now that was a bit odd, Barriss thought. Why would they try to keep Tooqui from leaving? She relaxed and leaned back against the cushions. Probably worried about him running loose and getting into trouble. Knowing Tooqui, she could sympathize with their hosts.

A stylishly clad and elaborately coiffured female brought forth an elegant rectangular case filled with delicate, tightly stoppered bottles. Each was unique, having been fashioned from a different natural gemstone. The server's attire left her back completely uncovered in a sweeping open V, the better to show off her golden, black-striped mane all the way to her short stub of a tail. Glistening bows and light-emitting sparklies had been artfully woven into the exposed fur. At the chief's direction, she bent to proffer the assortment to Luminara and Obi-Wan.

"These are essences from the Dzavak Lakes district, far to the west of here." Baiuntu spoke pridefully. "You will not find the like anywhere in Cuipernam. I would champion them in a contest of fine perfumes against any scents acquired anywhere in the Republic." He waved a thick-fingered hand encouragingly. "Go on, go on! Try them. The paluruvu—that's the violet-hued liquid in the bottle at the end of the display—is particularly flamboyant. A couple of drops of the pure essence blended with clear water will make a large flagon of expensive perfume." He smiled broadly.

"The Alwari may be prairie-dwelling nomads, but they are not uncivilized. Like the Qulun, they, too, enjoy the finer things. These essences are among our best sellers. After days spent traveling the open plains in the company of a great many reeking herd and draft animals, a well-off Alwari couple is grateful for the opportunity to moderate the natural bouquet within their home."

Tentatively, Luminara tried a whiff of several of the different extracts. All were outstanding, but true to Baiuntu's word, the paluruvu was exceptional.

"Wonderful," she declared as she passed the tray to Obi-Wan. His sampling was more perfunctory than hers, but he, too, had to admit that the assortment was the equal of anything he had encountered on Coruscant or any other equally sophisticated world of the Republic.

By the time Barriss and Anakin took their turn, the room was awash in a spectacular swirl of scents. These cloaked the atmosphere entirely, drowning out any hint of corralled animals or bustling clanfolk. As Luminara looked on, Baiuntu yawned hugely. Come to think of it, she was feeling quite weary herself. It *had* been a long day. Straightening, she prepared to excuse herself and her companions. That was the first inkling she had that something was wrong.

She couldn't straighten.

In fact, she could not even sit up. Her taut, lean muscles seemed to have turned to mush, to have buckled into the cushions and pillows that supported them. Her head swam, and she felt like she was melting into the floor. Out of rapidly blurring eyes she saw Obi-Wan rise and attempt to draw his lightsaber. His fingers clutched futilely in its vicinity. Even if he had succeeded in drawing and activating the weapon, there was no one to fight. Their host was already wheezing away sonorously, his hands clasped across his most un-Ansionian belly. The eye-catching essence presenter was lying nearby, her lithe form sound asleep at his feet.

"Something's—Barriss!" Attempting to shout, Luminara produced only a loud whisper. Her Padawan did not hear her. Barriss lay sprawled on her own cushioning divan, head back, mouth open, and limbs akimbo. Not far away, Anakin Skywalker lay facedown a body-length or two from the entrance to the visitors' house. A house, Luminara saw through a thickening haze, whose doors had been firmly and surreptitiously shut tight. To keep them in, she wondered? Or to seal in the striking, swirling mélange of fragrances? It amounted, she realized, to the same thing.

Paluruvu not only excited the sense of smell, she thought woozily. It also must contain the powerful sedative that was rendering her and her companions senseless. But if the result was intentional, why would Baiuntu subject himself and the female who had offered it up to the same sleep-inducing effects? Struggling to crawl toward the door, she tried to draw her own weapon. The effort was to no avail. Her brain no longer seemed capable of establishing contact with her fingers.

Nearby, Obi-Wan dropped to his knees and looked over at her. His expression was blank, drugged. As she stared, his eyes closed and he fell over onto his side. On the far side of the room, Kyakhta and Bulgan snorted loudly in the familiar wheezing, hissing Ansionian manner. Exerting a tremendous effort, Anakin Skywalker rose to his feet and rushed at the shuttered entrance. Through the increasingly dense haze that was clogging her thoughts, she marveled at the attempt. The youth must have an enormous reservoir of willpower, she decided.

Unfortunately, all of it was expended in reaching the door. By the time he struck it, Anakin's legs were barely able to hold him erect. The doors shuddered, but held firm. Retreating, he reached for his lightsaber, turned a slow, confused circle, and sat down. His eyes closed and he fell over onto his side. She was now the only one in the room who was still conscious.

Of course Baiuntu would subject himself and the serving female to the effects of the immobilizing perfume, she found herself thinking. How better to put someone you wanted to poison at ease than by partaking of that same poison yourself? If nothing else, it suggested that the narcotizing procedure was not fatal. Baiuntu might be the type to join his intended victims in sleep, but not in death.

She saw it all clearly now. They had been lured in and rendered helpless—but for what purpose, to what end? Soon other Qulun would doubtless open up the room, wait for the tranquilizing mist drifting within to dissipate, and then assist their chief and the unconscious female. As for the clan's erstwhile "guests," what was to be done with them remained a matter of some speculation. Speculation she could not track to a logical conclusion, because she was tired, so tired, and at the moment nothing could possibly feel any better, nothing could conceivably matter more, than a good night's sleep.

A part of her brain screamed at her to keep awake, to stay alert. Fighting the perfume's effects, she managed to lift her head off the cushions. It was a last, defiant gesture. Even Jedi training could be overcome. Perhaps not by force of arms. But a lightsaber was useless against the delectable, all-pervasive, irresistible fragrance of essence of paluruvu . . .

"**T**here's the grotty little dyzat! Get him!"

Tooqui didn't know why the two Qulun were chasing him, but he didn't hang around to find out. Both clan members were brandishing strange, foreign weapons, and even though he didn't know what they were or what they could do, he decided right away that it would be better not to wait around to see.

Something bad must have happened. If Master Barriss was all right, she wouldn't stand for him being chased like this, by screaming, wild-eyed, angry Qulun. The last time he had seen her, she and her endlessly interesting friends were relaxing in the company of the Qulun chief. Everyone seemed to be getting along wonderfully well well. What had happened to change that?

True, the traders were Qulun, not Alwari. But they were still people of the plains, not the hills. Perhaps they were after all no more trustworthy than a bunch of roving, slobbering Alwari, the dorgum-herding *snigvolds*.

If that was the case, then Master Barriss too might for sure be in danger. She and her teachers were very powerful, but they were not gods. They were not as strong as Miywondl, the wind, or Kapchenaga, the thunder. They were only people. Bigger than the Gwurran, maybe a little smarter, but just people. They could be broken, and deaded. The Qulun were people, too. That meant they also knew of different ways of killing.

But if there had been killing, surely he would have heard something. From what he had seen, Master Barriss and her companions were not the kind to go down without a fight. Had they been tricked somehow? Many were the tales told in the tribal canyons on dark nights of the tricks shrewd trader folk sometimes played on unsuspecting visitors.

Something bright and hot singed the hair on the crest of his mane. He accelerated, running as hard and fast as he could. Though the Qulun people had longer legs, they were accustomed to riding and selling. If there was one thing the Gwurran knew how to do and did well, it was running. Faces peered out at him from the outlandish fold-up flat-sided dwellings. Alerted by all the commotion, a few of their occupants tried to catch him. He dodged them all, as if he were playing a game of blo-bi with his family-friendlies. No game this, though. The bright-hotness spat by him again. This time it missed him completely, momentarily illuminating the night sky above his head.

Then he was clear of the camp, his legs pumping as he raced out onto the open prairie. The high grass slowed him down somewhat, but it would also help hide him. He thought he was safe—until he heard the clumping of sadain feet coming up fast behind him.

"This way!" a Qulun shouted. "I saw the dyzat over this way!"

I am not a dyzat! he wanted to turn and yell. However, he was also smart enough to know that the moment of foolish defiance might very well cost him his life. Frantically, he hunted for someplace to go to ground. But there were no familiar hills here, no friendly clefts or crevices down which to duck. The voices of the pursuing Qulun drew closer. Any moment now and they would be right on top of him. Lights lit the night in his wake. More mechanical magic, acquired from traders in the cities. He wondered if he would live long enough to set eyes on one of those people-filled, magical, mysterious places only a very few Gwurran had ever visited.

That was when he saw the kholot burrow. The entrance was just big enough for him to squeeze into. Panting hard, he wriggled himself through the opening and started down the incline on his belly. Would the Qulun think to look for him under the ground, or just on top of it? The burrow widened slightly, allowing him to crawl faster. When it opened into an oval chamber three times his size, he knew he had reached the end. Muted by the intervening earth, the shouts and cries of the patrolling Qulun sounded more distant than they were. It would have been a perfect hiding place, except for one complication.

It was already occupied by a family of kholot.

He froze. The kholot ate grasses and grains and leaves, not Gwurran. At least, he hoped so. Flat of face and covered in prickly olive-green fur, the two adults regarded him warily. Thankfully, there were no cubs in the burrow. If there had been, he probably wouldn't have made it this far. Each adult was almost as big as he was. Their teeth, unfortunately, were much bigger: wide, heavy-duty incisors designed for slicing through large clumps of grass. If their blunt-snouted owners were so inclined, they could also slice right through his face.

He held his breath as they approached, snuffling and grunting, and tried not to tremble too much as they sniffed him over and up and all around. Eyes shut tight, he tried to imagine himself a piece of dorgum dung that had accidentally rolled down into their burrow. The sounds of tromping sadains and their Qulun riders still reached him from above. He did not know how much longer he could remain motionless.

With a last disdainful sniff that at another time the terrified Tooqui might have taken as an insult, the pair of kholot pushed past him and headed up the tunnel. Their reaction was more than passing strange. Surely he couldn't smell bad enough to force them to vacate their burrow? Then he remembered the time spent in the Qulun visitors' house, swathed in foreign smells and peculiar aromas. Evidently enough of that had adhered to his fur not only to drive the kholot out, but to keep them from biting him. Smell bad, taste bad, the two burrowing grazers had apparently decided.

There was an excited yell from above, followed by a sharp crackling sound and a pained yowl from one of the kholot. Emerging from the burrow, it had been mistaken for his quarry by one of the patrolling Qulun. As soon as the unfortunate grazer had been identified, the other Qulun had a good laugh at their trigger-happy comrade's expense. Turning himself around in the cramped chamber, Tooqui put his head partway up the tunnel and listened intently.

"Enough of this. It's late, and I'm tired. I don't care what Baiuntu says."

"Same here," declared another Qulun firmly, reining in his sadain. "Let's tell him we caught and killed the runaway, and be done with it."

"It's alone out here, without food or water or supplies. The prairie will finish it off."

This confident exchange was followed by the sound of many

sadain feet moving swiftly away. Even so, Tooqui remained hidden in the burrow until he was certain it was safe to emerge.

When he finally did so, tired and dirty but alive, there was no sign of his pursuers. Finding a rock, he climbed just high enough to see over the tops of the windswept grass. The Qulun were breaking camp, and in the middle of the night at that. They must be very anxious about something to do that, he knew. As far as Tooqui knew, no nomads had ever been observed breaking camp in the middle of the night.

Were Master Barriss and her friends still alive? And if they weren't, what did it matter to him? He was alone, without food or weapons or water, several days' run from the nearest hill country of the Gwurran. Hugging himself against the chill night wind, he took stock of his surroundings. The open plains were no place for a nervous little Gwurran! Every sound made him twitch, every hint of movement caused him to jump. What if there were shanhs out here, shadowing the traders' caravan? If they picked up his scent, he wouldn't last as long as a lace-winged birru in a windstorm.

Even if he wanted to help, there was nothing he could do. The best thing for him would be to start back home right now. If he was lucky, if he found some water and some things to eat along the way, and if nothing ate *him* along the way, he might make it back to the country of the Gwurran in a few days. He would have an exciting, dramatic tale to tell. The young ones would gaze up at him with awe, while their sometimes condescending elders would be forced to acknowledge, however grudgingly, his considerable accomplishments. For the rest of his life, he would be a big big among his people.

And yet—and yet, there was the matter of Master Barriss, who instead of shooting him as a thief had befriended him, and had interceded on his behalf when he had expressed his longing to travel beyond the traditional Gwurran homeland. Wasn't that what he was doing now? Of course, when he had made that request, he hadn't envisioned anything like this happening. No one, not even the human Barriss, would blame him for heading home as fast as his long-toed feet could carry him.

I have to know, he finally decided. He at least had to know. If Master Barriss and the others had been killed, then he could start for home with a clear conscience. On the other hand, if they were still alive . . .

If they were still alive, he suspected that his life was going to get even more complicated than it already was. He should be looking forward to that, he tried to tell himself. Hadn't he said as much to the humans? That Tooqui was the bravest, the fiercest, the smartest, the most most of all the Gwurran? At the time, he'd wondered if any of them had believed him. Certainly those two miserable dim dim stucky-up clanless Alwari, Kyakhta and Bulgan, had not. Imagine to see their faces—if they were still alive, he reminded himself—when Tooqui, the very same Tooqui they had mocked and derided, showed up to rescue-save their sorry short-tailed ugly behinds! The image filled him, if not with courage, then at least with nerve.

Tooqui would show them! Tooqui would show them all. Determined now, he prepared to track the roving Qulun clan. He would shadow them from afar, waiting to see what there was to see, waiting to learn whatever could be learned. It was just as he'd said. He *was* the boldest, the toughest, the most resourceful of all the Gwurran!

Alone and weaponless against an entire Qulun clan, with only a debilitating feeling of helplessness for company, he knew he would have to be even more than that.

*   *   *

She sensed that her head was still attached to her shoulders, but that was about the only good thing Luminara could be certain of when she finally regained consciousness. Her arms were tightly tied behind her, and her legs bound at thigh, calf, and ankle. Daylight was all she could detect through the soft, permeable hood that covered her head. She could breathe, but only through her nose, as the gag that had been expertly positioned in her mouth kept her from enunciating anything more eloquent than a grunt.

Still, that was enough to provoke answering grunts from nearby. She thought she recognized Obi-Wan, and Barriss. Anakin she wasn't certain about, but the muffled, high-pitched Ansionian noises most likely originated from Kyakhta and Bulgan. Evaluating different tones finally convinced her that Anakin, too, was among the imprisoned.

A voice that was not smothered by a gag quieted the communal mumbling.

"Good morning, my honorable guests. I have to thank you for what is going to prove a most profitable evening. For me, not for you," Baiuntu concluded contentedly. "The Borokii overclan you seek lies but a few days' ride north of here, but you won't get to meet with them. Instead, we've embarked on a leisurely journey to the city of Dashbalar, where my clan always does good business." Luminara could hear him striding back and forth in front of them, preposterously parading his triumph before prisoners unable to see.

"I'm sure you're wondering what's going to happen to you. You should relax. *Haja,* I would not think of harming you! To do so would be to violate every tenet of Qulun hospitality." Luminara could sense, if not see, him grinning. "There are many means by which word can travel quickly over the plains. It is said that if the return to Cuipernam of certain offworld visitors could be delayed for two parts of a breeding cycle, a great reward would be paid. These visitors were carefully described. You can therefore imagine my surprise and delight when you appeared outside our camp, asking for directions to the Borokii. I was overjoyed when you agreed to accept my hospitality. You will now have the opportunity to experience it at length."

She felt him approach. His musky body odor grew stronger, and his tone darkened. "While I was told not to harm you, but only to delay your return to the city, I must warn you: don't make me angry by trying anything that might impact on my profits. As we travel, you will be kept comfortable. But several of my best people will be watching you at all times. At the first sign of Jedi tricks, the perpetrator will be shot. Yes, we ignorant people of the plains know about the Force. Don't make me have to do anything we will both regret." Luminara sensed the return of the smile as he stepped away from her. "It would devalue my clan's reputation as traders."

Somewhere close by, she could hear Anakin growling incomprehensibly through his gag and hood.

"Now, now," Baiuntu protested, "I can't understand a word you're saying. Though I think the essence of it is clear enough. I am something of an expert on essences, as you by now must appreciate. When the time comes for the giving of food and water, you will be taken care of one at a time. Believe me, I respect the abilities of the Jedi as much as anyone. My people and I will take no chances with you. To that end I have seen to it that the comlinks you brought with you have been destroyed beyond any hope of repair. So even should you succeed in freeing yourselves, there will be no calling for help from the despised, if profitable, city folk." Luminara could feel his heavy footsteps receding as he turned to exit the room.

"Very soon now this visitors' house, the last of our camp still standing, will be taken down and packed on its transport. Another mobile facility has been reserved especially for you. While I regret that I cannot trust you to enjoy the passing scenery, you will at least be able to smell it. Enjoy the cool breeze of the prairie, my valued guests. And please, no theatrical attempts to escape. I would take it personally."

As soon as one of us gets loose, you'll take something *personally,* Luminara thought furiously. She forced herself to remain calm, to fall back on her training. Every Jedi knows that anger muddies clear thinking, and that revenge is, at best, an archaic waste of energy.

Someone didn't want them returning soon to Cuipernam. How long was two parts of a breeding cycle? What would be the point in holding them captive and then letting them go? Behind the blinding cloth, her eyes widened slightly.

The Unity Council! She and Obi-Wan had promised them an agreement with the Alwari. When they failed to return within a reasonable period of time, the position of those on the council in favor of secession would grow steadily stronger. Would they vote for secession without waiting for the Jedi to report? Like any politicians, the council representatives had constituencies to answer to. They wouldn't wait forever. They might not even wait longer than two parts of a breeding cycle.

Certainly someone thought that was the case. Who stood to gain the most by preventing the Jedi from completing their mission? Who, besides the already committed secessionists? Who had sponsored the attack against her and Barriss, and then had directed the Padawan's abduction?

Though her nostrils were not as sensitive as those of a suu-batar, she felt sure she smelled the distant presence of essence of a Hutt.

Once they returned to Cuipernam, they would have to have a few words with this Soergg individual, she thought grimly. Some rather harsh words. What particularly interested Luminara, as it was sure to interest the Jedi Council, was the ominously greater question of who was behind the Hutt. But before they could confront Soergg, they had to free themselves from the gilded captivity of the avaricious Qulun—and do so quickly.

Tooqui watched from within the high grass as the Qulun broke camp. Houses and the couple of trading buildings were neatly folded in upon themselves, goods stowed, the miscellany of a nomad clan carefully packed away. Trailing the procession were spare sadains and, more importantly, the six riding suu-batars that were owned by his new friends. When the caravan be-gan to move out, he moved with them, tailing the procession from a distance. Gradually, he became bolder, slipping progres-sively closer to the convoy. Greater proximity enabled him to pick out individuals while still keeping under cover.

He recognized a number of the clanfolk. Foremost among them was the rotund Baiuntu. The chieftain rode in the front of the procession, borne aloft on a platform decorated with colored streamers that snapped briskly in the steady breeze, handmade wind organs, Qulun pennants, and gaudy advertisements for the clan's trade goods. So occupied was Tooqui with monitoring the clan's movements and keeping hidden that he almost forgot why he was risking his life to do so.

But he jumped for joy when, later that afternoon, his friends were brought out of a transport pulled by eight sadains. One at a time, they were exposed to the wind, sun, and fresh air. After a modest interval, each was returned to the concealment of the transport, and his or her place on the front bench seat taken by another. Trembling with excitement, he watched and counted patiently. They were all there: the four Jedi as well as the two spiteful-talky Alwari. Based on what he could see from his hiding place in the grass, none of them appeared to have been harmed. They were hooded, gagged, and bound securely enough to control even a Jedi. Blob-butt Baiuntu might be a lie-liar and a sneak, but he certainly knew what he was doing.

How in the name of the rain gods was he going to free them? Tooqui wondered. First he would have to slip into their camp. Then he would somehow have to deal with guards. Qulun guards, bigger and stronger than himself. He had nothing to use for a weapon except rocks. Assuming he could manage to reach their transport undetected and take care of any sentinels, he would still need enough time to free all four of his friends, and maybe maybe the two Alwari as well. Afterward, they would have to recover their special personal things, take back their suubatars, and ride off intact and unharmed into the grasslands. Ten Tooquis would not be enough to do such a thing, and there was only one of him.

Wishing for more would gain him nothing, he knew. The Gwurran were a tough tribe. They had not survived inhospitable country and forbidding fauna through dint of heavy wishing. Where resources were lacking, they found acceptable substitutes, or devised their own.

That was it, he knew. He had some hasty devising to do. Reason and logic might all seem to lead toward inevitable failure, but Tooqui was able to compensate for his small self with an outsized ego. If nothing else, his own boastfulness would not let him fail.

Now, if only he could find a way to make the Qulun understand that.

Every step, every forward lurch of the plodding sadains he was following took him farther from home, from the safety of familiar hills and the warmth of the Gwurran tribe. He tried not to think about how far he was from everything he knew. Water was not a problem, rain having collected in small pools and depressions in the hard-packed prairie dirt. But he had to spend time searching for food, and then would have to hurry to catch back up to the steadily advancing caravan. Days passed in this fashion, then another, and another. Tired and filthy and homesick, he nevertheless somehow managed to keep up with the procession.

Yet another evening saw him no closer to a possible way of rescuing his friends than when he had hidden in the kholot burrow. As night fell, tired and hungry he once again sought shelter from marauding predators, and found himself having to move farther and farther away from the encampment. He regretted the loss of light from the camp's glowpoles, even if they could only be safely viewed from a distance. But safety was more important than a cheery glow in the night. If not a burrow, or a high tree, he would have to find some big rocks he could squeeze between before he allowed himself to rest.

What he encountered instead was a distant rumbling and booming. *"Ou, pifgot!"* he mumbled. As if his present situation wasn't bad enough, now it was going to rain. Pretty hard, too, judging by the smell of it. Wind swirled around him as if suddenly unsure of what direction to take, and the taste of impending moisture was heavy on the night air. Kapchenaga boomed off to the north, announcing his advance with steady earthward thrusts of the Light-That-Burned.

Behind him, the camp would be bracing itself for the arrival of the approaching storm: sealing house joints, fastening windows, fastening windows, securing livestock, and rolling up pennants and advertisements. The Qulun and their prisoners would wait out the storm safe and snug within sturdy shelters, warmed by hot food and imported offworld heaters. Meanwhile he, Tooqui, would be lucky to find a dry burrow not already occupied by some inhospitable creature.

An overhang beneath a rock would be better, he knew as he continued searching. Not as warm as a burrow, but far less likely to already be claimed for the night. Unlike an Alwari or a human, he had his coat of fur to keep him warm. At least the rain that was coming would mask his scent from roving meat eaters.

There, in front of him in the darkness—an unexpected ridge of hills. Just in time, too, judging from the rising wind. Already, fast-moving clouds were beginning to block out the stars and the light of Ansion's first ascending moon. Thunder was sounding more frequently now, and the first fat raindrops began to slap at the grass. Blinking away drip-drops, he headed for a gap between the nearest hills. A flash of Kapchenaga's breath briefly lit up the sky. Tooqui froze. These were not hills he was silently approaching. He knew that was the case not only because of what he had seen in that split second of illumination, but because the hill he was nearest to had turned a baleful eye in his direction.

Lorqual.

So startled was he that he couldn't decide whether to curl up on the ground, turn and run, or simply topple over unconscious. As a consequence, he did none of these. Instead, he just stood where he was, staring, as the rain began to fall in earnest. The sound of it pattering against the grass was familiar and soothing, but did nothing to remove the threat of the moaning mountains that loomed massively before him.

And he had almost gone strolling blithely in among them, he realized in shock.

The lorqual were, at least insofar as the Gwurran knew, the biggest inhabitants of the plains. Though they stood only slightly taller at their two sets of shoulders than did the suubatar, the lorqual were far more massive. A single mature adult would weigh as much as four suubatars. Their strange, stiff, brown and beige fur stuck straight out from their sides, giving them a bristly appearance. Half a dozen solid, bony knobs protruded from each massive skull. In rutting season, the sound of adult bull lorqual smashing into each other head to head could be heard across vast sweeps of prairie. Each of six feet terminated in an equal number of powerful horn-shielded toes: three facing forward and three back, a design perfectly suited to supporting the creature's great weight.

In contrast to their immense size, they had only two comparatively small eyes, one on either side of the blocky skull. But the single nostril opening was large enough for a Gwurran to hide within. Mounted on the end of a short, flexible snout that was constantly testing the air, it provided all necessary warning of possible danger.

Not that anything could really threaten a herd of lorqual, Tooqui knew. Even the young, once they were a couple of weeks old, were too big and powerful for anything less than a full pack of prowling shanhs to attack. Usually they were intolerant of intruders in their midst. But they ignored him. Huddled together as they were, he realized, they must be preoccupied with the impending squall. The rain that was falling would also serve to conceal his presence from them, masking his smell.

Lightning was flashing more frequently now, allowing him a better view of the herd. He judged it to be sizable, though it was impossible to gauge its full extent. He could not see over or around a single lorqual, much less the dozen or so immediately in front of him. These might constitute the entire herd, or there might be a dozen more animals lined up behind them, bony heads pressed against bristling flanks and hindmosts.

That was when he had the idea. It could as easily kill him as make him a hero. But after three days of hard scrambling through high grass, over rocky places, and down clammy mud holes, it was the first idea he'd had. That it might also be his last weighed heavily on him. It very likely might not even work.

Bending, he made a Gwurran gathering basket out of the driest grass he could find. It was something taught to every young member of the tribe, so he had no trouble performing the task in the dark, his nimble fingers weaving the grass stems together with the effortlessness of long practice. Advancing slowly and carefully through the falling rain so as not to disturb the highly sensitive lorqual, he began searching for something else. Even in the rain, it did not take long for him to find what he wanted: a basketful of stones, each somewhat rounded, and each of a size to fit comfortably in his long-fingered hand.

The easy part of his idea fulfilled, he now had no choice but to proceed to the much more difficult—and dangerous.

Still moving slowly and patiently, frequently wiping rainwater from his protuberant eyes, he tried to pick out one lorqual that looked a little drowsier than the others. In the darkness and rain, it was impossible. It might have been just as difficult in the daytime, he knew. One lorqual looked, and acted, pretty much like any other lorqual. If he kept dithering, though, he might abandon the idea entirely, and then where would he be?

With the nearest animal as likely a candidate as the next, he crept as close as he dared. Slipping the basket of stones over one arm, he grabbed hold of the lorqual's wet bristles and pulled himself up off the ground. When the creature did not react, he began to climb. The closer he got to the top, the greater his confidence in his chances of reaching the monster's back without getting stomped.

Then he was there, on top, balancing carefully on the animal's wet middle shoulders. Keeping his step as light as possible, he made his way forward between upthrust bristles that were not unlike prairie grass until he found himself in the natural saddle between the creature's first and second set of shoulders. It still had not reacted in any way to his presence. Damp and cold, soaked by the now pounding rain, Tooqui found himself encouraged by his not-so-insignificant triumph. He did not waste time congratulating himself. What he had accomplished so far was nothing compared to what still had to be done.

Assuming a standing position behind the lorqual's neck, he braced his feet as best he could, took one of the stones from the basket, and prepared himself. He did not have to wait long. Two shafts of the Light-That-Burns brillianted the underside of fast-moving clouds. More nervous than usual because of the now raging storm, the herd stirred uneasily. Thunder boomed. As it did so, he took careful aim and threw the first stone.

It struck its intended target just above the left eye. Letting out a startled howl of distress that sounded like a moaning moon, the lorqual next to the one on which he was standing rose and kicked out with its front legs, keeping the middle and rear pairs firmly planted on the ground. A distressed bellowing rose from those huddled nearby. A second stone flung in the wake of the first struck another member of the assembled herd. It also jerked and kicked out. A third rock hit the biggest lorqual of all right in the eye.

The herd began to surge back and forth, uncertain how to react or what to do next. Among the animals clustered around Tooqui, panic began to spread like a wave, ripples of alarm racing toward the outer edges of the mob. He kept chucking stones, continuing to agitate those animals within his throwing range. The mewling roar grew steadily louder, rising even above the rolling thunder and driving rain.

Confused and uncertain, fearful and concerned, lorqual bumped up against jittery lorqual. Then Kapchenaga lent a hand in the form of several bolts of the Light-That-Burns. With the last, closest strike, the herd abandoned all semblance of restraint. They began to move. Slowly at first, but rapidly picking up speed. Rain splattering against his eyes, Tooqui did his best to point them in the right direction with his carefully lobbed stones. When the last of these had been cast, he grabbed hold of a double handful of neck bristles and hung on for dear life. For his own, and for those of his friends. He had no choice anyway. Had he tried to slip clear of his gigantic mount, he would have been flattened like a bug. Beneath him, the earth itself trembled under the impact of the quickening lorqual.

The Qulun encampment was silent, dark save for the usual all-night glowpoles that were set out to show any nocturnal amblers the way between structures. Thunder rattled the raindrops, then resounded again.

A picket suddenly blew a distress call on his horn. Multiplying alarms reverberated throughout the camp. Everyone woke up; some quickly, others more slowly, wiping at their wide eyes. Within the visitors' transport, Luminara tried to mumble a question through her gag but failed to make herself understood. She sensed movement all around her as her equally securely bound friends struggled to sit up. There was no mistaking the reality of the disturbance, though. The turbulence was not in the Force—it was in the ground itself.

Buckling his loose-legged pants around him, a rapidly awakening Baiuntu was bawling orders in every direction. Around him, throughout the camp, all was loosely organized chaos. There was no time to get the sadains hitched to the transports, little enough to wake everyone. Under his direction, riders began to assemble. They had one chance to save everything the clan had worked for. Brandishing weapons, they charged out into the storm to try to split the stampede.

Rising above the storm, the cries of squealing sadains, trampled riders, and injured lorqual combined to create an agonized cacophony the likes of which had not been heard on that section of prairie in some time. No single shot, not even one from a modern pistol, could bring down a rampaging, panicky lorqual. But several such shots could wound severely, and more could force one of the great beasts to change direction in the hope of avoiding further injury. As the Qulun dashed back and forth in front of them, firing selectively and making as much noise as they could, the stampede began to slow, the lorqual's jittery conviction to unravel. Without breaking stride, several of the great beasts angled away from the stinging riders who had appeared in front of them, changing course slightly to the west. Others broke clear of the herd to thunder a little more to the east. Split down the middle, the bulk of the herd rumbled off to either side of the encampment.

But a number of lorqual, hysterical beyond feeling the shots the Qulun riders aimed at them, continued to plunge blindly forward. Two were brought down by multiple bursts from the Qulun's prized imported laser weapons. Two more were not, and in seconds found themselves in among the campsite.

Gigantic six-toed feet trampled trade goods and outbuild-ings, fracturing lightweight composite walls and sending those huddled within fleeing screaming into the rain-swept night. Great horned heads swung from side to side, tossing Qulun and animals flying. Crazed by dread, driven by lightning, and bleed-ing from gunshots, the lorqual smashed their way through the fractured, splintering, increasingly chaotic camp.

There were no longer any guards outside the visitors' trans-port. Like the rest of the clan, they had rushed to the assistance of their friends and families, desperate to save lives and liveli-hoods. Scrambling up the front of the transport, a dripping-wet Tooqui let himself inside. Within, sitting up and struggling with their bonds, were his friends; to all outward appearances they were still safe and unharmed. That much he had expected. All Qulun traders worthy of the clan name would do their best to ensure that their goods were not damaged.

Searching for something stronger than bare fingers to work with, he found the strange offworlder equipment neatly stacked and labeled in an unlocked storage case near the front of the transport. Reaching first for one of the lightsabers, he thought better of it and settled instead for a small, versatile Alwari blade that belonged to Bulgan. A knife, he knew how to use. Small but strong hands went to work on Barriss's bonds. When the Padawan's hood was pulled off and she saw who had come to rescue them, she hardly knew what to say. Which was just as well, since she remained gagged while Tooqui started in on her wrists and ankles.

"Tooqui tell truth." The Gwurran jabbered away nonstop as he worked. "Tooqui bravest of his people. The strongest, the fiercest, the wisest—"

"The most talkative," Barriss interrupted him when she

could finally remove the gag. Freed, she found that she was unable to move. Days of tight bondage had left her muscles cramped, the nerves tingling. Jedi schooling helped her restore her circulation far more rapidly than an untrained prisoner would have been able to manage. The busy Tooqui told her where their gear was stored. With two of them working together, they soon had Obi-Wan, Luminara, and Anakin untied.

Something slammed into the left side of the transport and nearly knocked it over on its side. Rising above wind and rain, a stentorian moaning reached them from outside. It was accompanied by the ragged shouts of thoroughly unnerved Qulun.

"What was *that*?" Anakin demanded to know as he rubbed circulation back into his legs. Even more than his lightsaber, he wanted to feel a certain Qulun chieftain's thick neck under his fingers. Obi-Wan would not approve of such thoughts, but there were times when Anakin was more than a little tempted to set aside the teachings of his Master. Now was one of them. Just give him the chance to throttle that fat sack of duplicity Baiuntu, and he would happily do proper penance later.

"Lorqual." Tooqui was sawing away at the material binding Kyakhta's ankles. "To fight fight Qulun, Tooqui need big stick." He looked up long enough to smile smugly. "Lorqual herd big stick. Tooqui stampede them this way."

Kyakhta gaped down at the Gwurran. "You stampeded a whole herd of lorqual toward us? We could've all been flattened!" As if attesting to the validity of the guide's observation, something banged hard into the transport a second time.

The Gwurran glanced over at the guide. "Big-mouth Alwari maybe should flatten mouth-lips a little. Also sit still, otherwise possible Tooqui have accident and cut off toes."

"Listen, you little—*ou*, watch what you're doing down there!"

Within moments every one of them stood tall once again, their equipment and their freedom restored. Lightsaber in hand, Luminara moved guardedly to the front of the transport and peered out. Glowpoles rocked in their stands and frightened Qulun ran to and fro, while the pelting rain continued to obscure much of what might otherwise be seen. Looming above all was the swaying, head-swinging, immense bulk of a single badly disoriented and very angry lorqual.

Force, she thought. If that was *one* lorqual, what must a stampede of them look like? Glancing back, she caught sight of the agitated but determined form of Tooqui, squeezed in among the others.

"Whatever happens from now on, Tooqui, I want you to know that I and Obi-Wan and our Padawans think you are very brave indeed."

"Not just brave. *Brave* brave!" The Gwurran started to step forward, then shrank back as the rampaging lorqual head-butted a sizable water cistern in their direction. It exploded against the ground nearby, adding a little more liquid to the wind-driven downpour. "But right now, just a little scared scared."

"With good reason." Obi-Wan had moved up alongside Luminara to scrutinize their immediate surroundings. "If they haven't broken free or been injured by these lorqual, we should try to reach our suubatars."

"The suubatars will be all right, Master Obi-Wan." Bulgan spoke from behind the Jedi. "They are too valuable for the Qulun to lose. They will have sent lookouts to watch over them and keep them safe from the stampede. And if they stand together, suubatars are big enough to turn even lorqual."

The Jedi nodded. "Then we should have a few guards to deal with."

"That's fine, Master." Crouched close behind his teacher, Anakin gripped his lightsaber tightly. "Having been tied up for so long, I could use a little recreation—excuse me, exercise."

Barriss frowned at her counterpart. "You're not preaching payback, are you, Anakin?"

"Of course not," he shot back. "I'm just saying that if someone gets in my way, at this point I'm not in the mood to pause and discuss the situation politely."

Huddled within the transport, they waited until the way was clear. Then the time for debate was at an end. With Tooqui, Obi-Wan, and Luminara taking the lead, the party of former prisoners sidled out of the battered transport and began working their way back toward the rear of the Qulun encampment. Along the way they encountered few of the traders. Those they did come across were mostly terrified females and children doing their best to stay clear of the amok lorqual. They had neither the time nor the inclination to concern themselves with escaping prisoners.

Fury and confusion swirled all around them, the chaos compounded by the still-potent storm. Despite this, they reached the corral area located at the back of the encampment without incident. Crouching low beside a storage transport sealed tightly against storm and intrusion, they carried out a swift inspection of the enclosure. Their suubatars were up and pacing nervously. The travelers' supply packs, Luminara noted, were still strapped to the restless beasts' backs.

"I make out three sentries—no, four," she whispered tautly to Obi-Wan.

He nodded tersely. "That's all I can see." Raising an arm, he gestured wordlessly.

Beckoning to Barriss, Luminara moved off around the back

of the feed-carrying transport. Obi-Wan and Anakin headed in the other direction. As they parted, Barriss remembered her fellow Padawan's earlier words. His expression belied what he had told her. Trailing close behind Obi-Wan, Anakin looked entirely too eager for what was to come.

The two Alwari waited next to the transport with Tooqui. As they did, gazing out into the turbulent night, Bulgan suddenly remembered something. Turning to face their diminutive companion, he slowly dropped to his knees and placed head and hands on the chill, damp ground, eyes facing the mud, rain-slicked mane arcing skyward. Recognizing what his friend was up to, Kyakhta did likewise—though he grumbled as he performed the traditional genuflection. Tooqui looked on with satisfaction.

"Okay okays. Get up now, silly softhead dip-dips." Both guides rose, wiping away grime and rain. "Tooqui have trader deal for you now." His eyes flashed in the intermittent light. "You no call Tooqui dumb savage anymore, and Tooqui no call you dippy stupid stupid blockhead dimwit numbskull—"

Wiping water from his good eye, Bulgan cut their savior off in midsuggestion. "We understand what you are saying, Tooqui. That's fair enough." Using a sharp elbow, he jabbed his companion in his tightly curved Ansionian ribs. "Isn't it, Kyakhta?"

"*Haja,* I suppose," the other guide mumbled reluctantly.

Content, their furry companion turned to look back at the darkened corral. "That better. Tooqui would have gone to help get suubatars back, but Jedi want him stay here to look look after you two, keep you safe."

Bulgan reached out just in time to prevent Kyakhta's long fingers from digging themselves into the Gwurran's short, wet fur.

*   *   *

Undimmed by the pounding rain, shafts of bright artificial light illuminated opposite sides of the corral. They wove graceful, elegant arcs of luminous lethality that were clearly visible through the darkness and damp. Slipping through the fence, Obi-Wan gestured silently toward the farther of the two guards standing watch on their side of the perimeter. Both Qulun were hardened from years of fighting off marauding predators and raiding clans. Their senses were sharp, their fighting skills acute.

The one who turned first overcame his surprise at the sight of the two oncoming humans in time to raise his rifle and fire a single burst. Deflected by the unnaturally swift parry of Obi-Wan's lightsaber, the bolt went flaring off into the night. Before the sentry could get off a second shot, the Jedi had taken him down.

At first, Obi-Wan thought his Padawan might be having some trouble with the other guard. When he saw that Anakin was only toying with him, the Jedi frowned and started toward the battling pair. As soon as he saw his Master approaching, Anakin finished off his opponent with a quick cut to the neck. The Qulun collapsed into the muddy, short grass.

Deactivating his lightsaber, Obi-Wan looked down at the dead Ansionian, then up at his Padawan. Though a burst of lightning threw their faces and bodies into sharp relief, it could not illuminate the tension between them.

"What was that about, Padawan?" The Jedi's voice was perfectly uninflected.

"Nothing, Master." His face a mask of innocence, Anakin belted his lightsaber. "He was faster than I thought."

Kenobi considered his pupil in silence. Then he nodded, once. "Have a care, Anakin, lest next time your opponent is even faster than that." Stepping past the Padawan, he gestured curtly. "Come on. We've lost too much time here already."

A sharp whistle drew Luminara and Barriss to them. "Any trouble?" As he spoke, Obi-Wan glanced not at Luminara but in the direction of her Padawan.

The other Jedi shook her head. Water spilled down her face, droplets clinging to her tattooed lower lip.

"Good fighters, these. More seasoned than those who jumped us in Cuipernam." She nodded to Barriss. Holding up her left hand, the Padawan showed a small cut. Blood seeped from the wound, but the rain would cleanse it, and it would quickly heal.

Taking a step forward, Anakin eyed it appraisingly. "Have to learn to keep your distance. Especially when you don't know how your opponent is armed."

"I don't have your reach," she snapped brusquely. "I suppose you'd be happy to show me some tips?"

He surprised her. "No. I tried that once before, already. In more water than this. Remember?" So saying, he started toward his nervously pawing suubatar. Confused, she watched him for a moment before heading for her own mount. Now, she decided, was not the time to try to analyze Anakin Skywalker or his singular personality. She wondered if any time would ever be the right time.

Silently, the group mounted their restless suubatars. As they did so, both Kyakhta and Bulgan took note of the lifeless bodies of the four Qulun sentinels.

Luminara's animal reared nervously on its hind and middle legs and she fought to control it while staying in the saddle. A few weeks ago, she would surely have been thrown. But with time had come experience, and with experience, confidence.

Getting the towering beast back under control, she followed the guides as they urged their mounts northward. Firm hands and proper guidance restored to them, the bounding suubatars cleared the electrified barrier of the portable corral easily. Then they were out in the rain, racing northward across the prairie. Somewhere ahead lay the elusive overclan, and the closing stages of their mission.

Soergg had succeeded in seriously delaying them and throwing them off their timetable. Hopefully, the Hutt had not delayed them too much. As she let her suubatar carry her off into the night, Luminara prayed that the Unity representatives would keep to their promise to wait until the Jedi returned before holding the vote on whether or not to take Ansion out of the Republic. From experience and studies she knew that such a vote, once concluded, would be almost impossible to reverse.

Behind them, a furious Baiuntu saw what was happening and attempted to rally a few of his clanfolk. His hopes of mounting a pursuit were dashed by the sight of numerous panicky Qulun still running wildly through their lorqual-devastated encampment.

"You idiots! Gather yourselves. Collect your wits!" His sadain bounding and rearing beneath him, he fought to control it while assembling a chase party around him. Preoccupied with the escaping prisoners and the loss of the fee they represented, he did not see what was bearing down on him. But his sadain did, and bucked him off so that it could escape.

"You miserable, worthless! . . ." Sitting on the ground in the grass and mud, the Qulun chieftain was beside himself. What a night! And it had begun so promisingly. Heaving himself to his feet, he slapped irately at his mud-spattered clothing. A glance revealed that he was alone. The offworlders had gone, though by what means they had escaped he could not imagine. Had he held them long enough to collect the payment promised by the Hutt? It remained a possibility. The effort of holding the Jedi might still prove worth the effort. As for the thrice-cursed herd of lorqual, it had finally departed, no doubt to reassemble placidly somewhere just south of the camp it had just reduced to chaos. And he was here, out in the grass, facing a short but muddy walk back to his bed.

Well, he had led his clan through worse. Not for nothing had he acquired a reputation as a perspicacious leader as well as a shrewd trader. There would be other days, other opportunities for profit. A wise merchant knows how to resign himself to loss as well as how to anticipate profit. Everything depended on whether they had delayed the offworlders long enough to satisfy the city merchant. He started back toward the light of the camp's remaining intact glowpoles.

Something coughed softly behind him.

He took another step, and it coughed again. Turning sharply, fingers shaking, he fumbled frantically for his blaster, the fine one he had acquired at the annual trade fair in distant Piyanzi. His fingers came up empty.

The weapon must have spilled from its holster when he had been thrown by the accursed sadain.

Dropping to his knees, he ignored the mud and the rain as he commenced a furious search for his blaster. *Ou,* there it was, lying in the grass not far from where he had been standing. All would be well now, if not as well as it had been when the sun had set. Relieved, he reached for the gun. As he did so, a trio of closely set eyes materialized just above it. Flashing red murder, they were flanked by another trinity of eyes, and another, and still another. Gritting his teeth, he made a lunge for the blaster. For such a big individual, Baiuntu was quick, very quick.

But not nearly so quick as a shanh.

Morning brought with it a change in the weather as well as in everyone's outlook. Cleansed by the previous night's tempest, the plains wore rain-swept freshness like a coat of new lacquer. The sun shone down soothingly, small winged seed-crackers chittered vividly as they flitted from grass to copse, and even the usually imperturbable suubatars ran with a youthful spring in their sextuple step. No doubt the riders would have enjoyed the morning even more had they not been exhausted from riding all night.

Still, the brisk morning air was undeniably invigorating. Standing up on his saddle, maintaining perfect balance as his mount loped along beneath him, Obi-Wan proceeded to run through a series of stretching exercises. The two Padawans observed the demonstration admiringly. Anakin knew that if he were to try such a stunt, he'd be picking himself out of the grass within minutes. What Obi-Wan was doing demanded perfect coordination, complete confidence in his own abilities, and nerves of steel. But then, his teacher was well known for his mastery of the mysteries of the body's neuromuscular complexities.

Riding close alongside, Luminara occasionally glanced in the direction of the other Jedi Knight. She could have matched his movements, but preferred to rest. Before long she turned her attention back to the prairie ahead. There was a question or two that needed to be asked of their guides. Gently spurring her suubatar, she accelerated away from Kenobi and up to join them.

That left Obi-Wan alone to contemplate the gently rolling grassland in front of them. As was always the case on a new world, there was plenty to study: geology and climate as well as the more immediate flora and fauna.

Unbeknownst to him, Anakin continued to observe his mentor from a distance. Most of the time, he reflected, it was impossible to tell what the Master was thinking. Was that the fate of all Jedi—to gradually grow solitary, withdrawn, and distant? Looking at the young woman riding along beside him, it was difficult to envision such a melancholic transformation overtaking the spirited and energetic Barriss. His fellow Padawan was full of life. And to be fair, he told himself, Luminara Unduli was far more animated than Obi-Wan. Was it only male Jedi, then, who were destined to live lives of endless solemn introspection?

That would not happen to him, he vowed silently. Whatever the future brought, he resolved it would not include the life of dour reserve that seemed to afflict Master Obi-Wan. He recalled the marvelous, spirited storytelling performance his teacher had put on for the enthralled Yiwa. Was he judging Obi-Wan too harshly? Was it the Jedi's fault that he had never felt the kind of stirrings that moved his Padawan to stare for hours on end at the night sky and call out in silence to a certain distant star? His teachings told him to be compassionate when faced with the deprivation of others. Even a student could spare sympathy for a teacher, he decided. Then and there he resolved to always keep that in mind when arguing with Obi-Wan.

If I should ever forget this vow, he concluded firmly, *it will be because I am no longer the person I have chosen to be.*

"You did well last night."

"What?" Aware that he had been sunk deep in thought, he made a point of smiling broadly at his amiable if sometimes exasperating interrogator. "Did well at what?"

Having turned toward him, Barriss was riding effortlessly sidesaddle. "When we were escaping the Qulun, and particularly during the unfortunate business of recovering our mounts. I saw what you did."

He responded uninterestedly. "I did what Master Obi-Wan told me to do. What I had to do."

"That's the second time I've seen you wield a lightsaber. You're very strong." Unconsciously, she felt her hand where it had been cut. That kind of experience would teach her not to relax and lower her guard, she told herself firmly, even in the face of a seemingly inferior opponent.

"I've practiced hard." Raising its front, then its middle, and finally its hind legs, his suubatar cleared a low ridge of gray stone. "There are those who say you can define a Jedi by his skill with a lightsaber. I want my ability to be respected. Respect forestalls fights."

She smiled. "Watching you, one would almost think you could give Master Yoda a good contest."

That made him blink. "Master Yoda? You must be joking."

Her smile vanished. "Why would I joke about such a thing?

Master Yoda is reputed to be the greatest lightsaber master ever. Don't tell me you never had a fighting class with him?"

"Of course I had classes with him. And I agree that he's a fine teacher—of technique. Even if he does have to stand on a platform so that his students can see him. His dexterity is amazing to see, especially considering his lack of reach." Earnestness crept into his voice. "That's just schooling, Barriss. It's all theory and supposition. Even if it's being taught by Master Yoda. It's not real fighting."

This time, instead of replying immediately, she gave his observations some thought. "What makes you think Master Yoda has never used a lightsaber in an actual fight?"

He almost laughed out loud, then thought better of it. Obi-Wan and Luminara might overhear, and choose to inquire as to the source of so much hilarity. Anakin's explanation, he knew, would not go down well with his teacher. Like all other Jedi, Obi-Wan revered the grand Master. Certain subjects, Obi-Wan would lecture him tirelessly, were not appropriate subjects for humor.

That didn't mean he was going to ignore his companion's question.

"Come on, Barriss. Master Yoda, engaged in serious dueling outside the fencing arena? Can you actually envision such a contest?" Of the images that sprang to mind at such a thought, each was more amusing than the next. "Who could he reasonably be expected to fight? Someone Tooqui's size, maybe?"

"It's not the size of the Jedi or the amount of power running through her lightsaber, but the strength of her heart."

Anakin nodded knowingly. "Give me size and power any day, and keep your heart." His response verged on blasphemy, he knew, but he was curious to see how the other Padawan would react.

She handled it more calmly than he expected. "You should

be ashamed to say such things, Anakin Skywalker. How can you question the proficiency of Master Yoda?"

"I'm not questioning his proficiency," Anakin shot back. "I can't, because I've attended his teaching sessions. There's no one faster or more adept with a lightsaber—in a classroom. All I'm saying is that teaching technique is not the same as using it in battle. Besides, Master Yoda is—well, he's not young. As for questioning anything at all, a good Jedi is supposed to question *everything*. Self-assurance is the best kind."

"It's good that you think so," she retorted. "It means you'll never have to worry about ever making a mistake."

"We all make mistakes," he countered. "That's what questioning is supposed to help prevent." He tapped himself on the chest. "I question everything that comes my way. Right now we've got whole systems questioning the way the Republic is run. Ansion is just one of them, and it's being watched closely by all the others."

She eyed him intently. "Are you doing that, too, Anakin? Are you questioning the way the Republic is being governed?"

"I'd be the odd one out if I wasn't." He gestured past the head of his galloping mount. "Even Master Obi-Wan has reservations. About corruption, about the direction the government is taking, about the directions it's *not* taking because it's becoming more and more bogged down in bureaucratic twaddle—sure I have questions. Don't you?"

Straightening in her saddle, she shook her head tersely. "I don't have time to waste on political disputations. I'm too busy doing my job as Padawan, trying to secure promotion to Jedi. That's enough work to occupy anyone. Or at least I thought so." She stared hard at him. "You're lucky you have room enough in your thoughts to be bothered with galactic affairs of state."

And other things, he wanted to tell her, but did not. Although being thrown together in adversity had given him a grudging admiration for his colleague, and for her skills, he still did not trust her entirely. Anything he told her, he was certain, she was likely to pass straight on to her Master. Which Luminara would then tell Obi-Wan. So much for confiding, he thought. Some things were better kept to oneself.

Each time he engaged in such a verbal confrontation, it reinforced the belief that he was somehow different. Different from Barriss as much as from Luminara or even Obi-Wan. His mother had always told him as much. He wished he could talk to her now, seek her sage advice on a number of matters, not least of which was the one that threatened to consume him. And to think, he mused as he rode on, that there was a time when people thought serious separation meant finding themselves on opposite sides of the same planet. That was so long ago, so ancient a time, that it was almost impossible to imagine, back when people counted distances in physical lengths instead of time lengths.

They paused for the night by one of the innumerable small streams that notched the grasslands. There had been no sign of pursuit by Baiuntu's Qulun. Either they had suffered so seriously from the nocturnal stampede of the lorqual that they were unable to mount a chase, or else they had decided that it was not worth hunting prisoners who could strike back without being seen.

"There's another possibility, too," Kyakhta pointed out when the matter was broached. "The closer we draw to the overclan, the less inclined a lesser clan like the Qulun would be to risk interfering."

"What matters is that we seem to be safe." Obi-Wan squinted at the setting sun. "Still, we'll mount guard tonight. Just to be sure."

Anakin was glad when his turn came to stand watch. It was

late, after midnight Ansion time, when Barriss came to shake him awake. A touch was all that was necessary.

"Nothing to report." She whispered so as not to wake the others. As he rose and donned his upper clothing, she was already slipping tiredly into her sleep sack. "You don't see anything out there, but you can hear it moving around. This world is full of furtive night sounds that live in the grass." He couldn't be certain, but he thought she was asleep before she closed her eyes.

The lookout location had been carefully chosen by their Alwari guides. It was the highest point near their campsite, and only a very slight rise at that: a mere hiccup in the ground. Still, it provided the nearest thing to an actual vantage point within walking distance of the stream. Finding a firm, comfortable place to stand, he settled down to wait out his three-hour shift.

Most individuals would have found the duty unutterably boring. Not Anakin. Raised by a single parent, without any siblings, he was used to being by himself. For a long time as a child, machines had been his only company. Idly, he wondered what had happened to that protocol droid he had been cobbling together out of spare parts. And there was no telling what a certain garrulous winged merchant named Watto might be up to. He wondered what the taciturn big-nosed bug was doing these days. He found himself shaking his head at the memory. If anyone was entitled to act a little strange now and again, it was Anakin Skywalker. Who else could claim a greedy, oversized Toydarian as the nearest thing to a father figure?

Except for the absence of walls, there really wasn't much difference between retreating to the back of a machine shop and standing alone on an alien prairie, beneath an alien sky. One of Ansion's two moons was up and the other still rising, a pair of curved slivers glowing silver against a background of black velvet.

They were framed by a scattering of stars like diamonds. So many worlds, so many questions—with many of the latter focused upon the world on which he was presently standing.

Something rustled in the high grass. Glancing sharply in that direction, he saw nothing. As Barriss had told him prior to retiring, this planet was full of tiny, creeping night sounds. Entire communities of lesser local life lived out their lives below the crests of the waving wild grains without ever exposing themselves to sight or daylight. One could only wonder at what kind of havoc a stampede of lorqual would wreak on such hidden animal societies.

Probably not much, he told himself. Out here, in these wild open spaces, nature accommodated the needs of the small as well as the large. Tooqui's tribe was a good example of that. Plucky little soul, that Tooqui. Annoying and overly inquisitive, to be sure, but as bold as his boastings. Having been forced to live most of his life on boldness alone, Anakin greatly admired the quality in others.

An hour passed before he was again disturbed by rustling noises. Each day added another couple of previously unencountered native species to his growing catalog of Ansionian life, but the register of nocturnal creatures was, for obvious reasons, considerably smaller. Having nothing else to do, he decided he might as well try to find out what was making the soft sounds in the grass. Whatever it was, it sounded conveniently close.

Turning to his left, he crouched slightly and began to move deeper into the tall prairie. The crackling noise came again, closer still. A small group of local animals, he concluded, busily gathering fallen grass seed under cover of night. It would be interesting to learn what they looked like. At least one of them sounded like it might be of fairly good size, perhaps even as big as Tooqui.

Surprised in midstalk, the shanh exploded from its place of concealment. It didn't growl. Like so many of Ansion's indigenous life-forms, it hissed. The hiss of a shanh was not like that of an intelligent Alwari, however, or some of the endearing creatures that roamed the vast open plains. It was a low, sinister blast of air—fury made audible.

Front and middle paws slammed into Anakin's chest, knocking him backward and down. In an instant, the shanh's heavy, fang-laden jaws would have been on his throat. There was no time to think, no time to decide what to do next, no time to ponder a best course of action.

As the shanh's jaws descended, Anakin rolled madly to his right. The predator's upper row of backward-curving, serrated teeth slammed into bare dirt instead of his neck. Furious, the lithe, muscular carnivore turned to face its prey, all six legs working, single nostril flared wide, convex red eyes floating like small livid moons against the dark mass of the brute's front shoulders.

Scuttling backward on hands and feet, Anakin tried to focus the Force while reaching urgently for his lightsaber. Drawing it from his belt, he activated the beam—and had it slapped from his right hand by one triclawed paw. Landing in nearby grass, the device struck on its control side—and switched off. That was what came, a small part of him reflected, of trying to do two things at once without knowing how. A true Jedi could do that. Painfully, he was once again made aware of how much he had yet to learn.

If he didn't do something quickly, his learning days would be at a premature end.

Weaponless, he rose slowly to his feet. Hissing expectantly, the shanh watched him without blinking. Unlike the Padawan, it was not constrained by a need to think. Muscles bunching tight beneath short, striped fur, maw agape, it leapt.

Shorn of his only physical weapon, Anakin fell back on what remained to him. Concentrating as he had never concentrated

STAR WARS: THE APPROACHING STORM

before, he threw one hand out in front of him, fingers splayed, and focused.

His command of the Force was not yet sufficient to allow him to knock the charging shanh backward, but it was strong enough to deflect the lethal leap to one side. As it flew past him, it struck out with front and middle claws. One set raked Anakin's shoulder as he threw himself out of the way. He did not cry out.

Blood streamed from his torn shoulder. The wound was painful and messy but not deep. Enraged and confused, the shanh landed on all sixes and immediately whirled to launch itself anew. As it did so, Anakin made a dive for his lightsaber. His fingers closing around the metal cylinder, lying on his stomach, he started to turn to face his furiously hissing adversary. The shanh was a big male; powerful, fast, and hungry. He knew he would only have time for one strike. But with the lightsaber, that should be enough.

As he started to turn, something landed hard on his right wrist, pinning it to the ground. Wincing at the pain, he looked up—to find himself staring straight into a second pair of brilliantly reflective red eyes. Not an arm-length away, they narrowed as they bored into his own. His heart dropped toward his diaphragm.

The shanh's mate had arrived to join the party.

An enormous weight landed on his back. Everything was happening too fast. Using the Force against the shanh had been one thing, but now there were two of them. If he tried to throw off the male now crouching on his back, the female was likely to bite his face off. If he pushed at her and freed his hand and lightsaber, the male would have time to shred his back with its claws, or lock its jaws on his neck. Even as he formulated the thought, he knew he was spending too much time thinking.

The male shanh emitted a rising hiss, a tormented sound un-like anything it had given voice to so far. At the same time, the weight on the Padawan's back was removed. The shanh had stepped off him, for what reason Anakin could not imagine. Thus reduced to a single adversary, he shoved hard with the Force. Grunting in surprise, the female was knocked sideways several body-lengths. Arm freed, he activated his lightsaber.

Before he could bring it into play, the stunned but still reactive female leapt. She was met in midbound by a downward sweeping arc of light that caught her just behind the head. There was a single, sharp hiss of surprise and pain, a sudden smell of burned flesh, and she landed on him belly-first. Using his muscles he rose on hands and knees and shook the heavy weight off his back.

The big male shanh was lying nearby, motionless, smoke rising from its seared skull. Standing next to it was a single familiar shape. Though not inherently tall, in Anakin's sweat-stung eyes the looming figure assumed the proportions of a giant. The outsized image vanished in the smile the slowly turning figure bestowed on him.

"Small sounds often mask large sources." Clad only in her sleeping attire, Luminara Unduli deactivated her lightsaber and let it fall to her side. "A good lookout needs to listen with more than his or her ears, Anakin Skywalker. Reality is rife with disguises."

Breathing hard, he rose shakily to his feet and bowed his head once, hastily. "Thank you for my life, Master Luminara."

She accepted his thanks with a nearly imperceptible dip of her own head. "Your life is your own, Anakin, and not mine to give or take." He thought he detected a twinkle in her eye. "I merely helped preserve it." Approaching, she startled him by casually slipping an arm around his back. The feel of it was astonishingly comforting. It reminded him of something nearly forgotten. "Come with me. I'll stand the rest of your shift."

"But you're not due to come on for another hour yet," he protested.

Once more, she flashed that warming, knowing smile at him. "For some strange reason, I'm suddenly wide awake. It's all right, Padawan. Consider this just another learning experience. One you will learn from—won't you?"

It was a rhetorical question, one he knew he did not have to acknowledge. But he did anyway.

"When one hears the sound of a lightsaber springing to life in the middle of the night in a strange place on a strange world, one knows it is not being triggered for purposes of amusement. I believe I reached you just in time."

Feeling better with every step, he nodded agreement. "If anyone wants to ask me, I think I can tell them all they want to know about the collaborative attack tactics of the stalking shanh."

"Probably more than they would want to know." They were already back at the camp. Her arm slid off his back. "Get some sleep, Anakin. Don't worry about me. I'm used to this sort of thing."

It would have been churlish of him to protest further. Finding his bed, he fell rather than lay back onto it, not even bothering to slip into the sack. Not far away, Kyakhta and Bulgan slept on. Another shape moved slightly, awake but not rising from its bed. Bending down close to him, Luminara murmured something to Obi-Wan, who listened closely, nodded once, and lay back down. Anakin waited for the disapproval that was to come. Thankfully, his teacher was wise enough, or empathetic enough, to say nothing. In truth, no additional commentary was necessary.

That didn't stop Barriss from looking up from her own place of rest. She didn't say anything—just stared at him. He stood it for as long as he could, which was about a minute.

"All right, all right," he muttered. "Go ahead and say it."

"Say what?" she asked innocently. There was as much mischief in her expression as in her voice.

"You know." He fumbled irritably with his bedding. "That I was derelict in my duty. That I was daydreaming in the middle of the night. That I didn't pay attention to what I was doing. Whatever."

"I was just wondering if you were okay."

He remembered his shoulder. His anger at himself had temporarily masked the pain. Now it returned, full force. He was glad of the burning sensation, opening himself to it, welcoming it. He deserved it. Just as he deserved whatever condemnation Barriss might now choose to bestow.

That, however, was not her intent. "I wonder if Master Yoda, who only knows lightsaber *technique*, would have been caught off guard like that." Leaving him with a last smile, she rolled over to resume her own interrupted sleep.

An angry retort sprang immediately to mind, but he did not give voice to it. She was right, of course. More than right. She had given him something else to think about, something more to ponder. Turning onto his back, wincing at the fiery pain in his shoulder, he considered the stars from a different perspective than he had earlier that night.

There was more to mastering the Force than moving objects from point to point. One had to be conscious of it at all times, not just in moments of danger. It was not armor, always present to protect those who knew something of its ways. It responded only to conscious effort, to awareness. That was his problem, he realized. He was aware only part of the time.

It wouldn't happen again, he swore. From now on, he would be with the Force at all times, rather than waiting for it to be with him. Yet again, it had been brought home to him how much he did not yet know.

Fortunately, he was a fast learner.

They had gathered not in the formal surroundings of the city's municipal hall, but in the garden of the abode of Kandah, one of the Unity delegates who would vote on whether or not to pull Ansion out of the Republic. Enclosed on four sides by the two stories of the residence itself, the courtyard was alive with flowers and fountains. Like the house, everything had been paid for from the profits Kandah's family had acquired through years of trade. Those profits would have been much higher, she reflected as she watched her fellow representatives stroll the meandering pathways, had they not been subject to the confiscatory and arbitrary taxes of the Republic.

If all went well, those obstacles to even greater wealth would soon be removed.

The courtyard had been designed as a place of refuge from the noise and activity of the city beyond. Today it provided privacy of a different sort to the gathering of representatives and their aides. The latter were gradually dismissed, until only the senior officials remained, holding their refreshments and questions until all could assemble together beside a translucent fountain spewing scented water.

"It's premature." This from Garil Volune, one of the human delegates. "They haven't been gone that long."

"Be realistic, Volune," declared one of the male Ansionians. "They should have been back by now." He gestured toward the main street outside the courtyard and the house. "They should have been back days ago."

"The Jedi wouldn't abandon us," another delegate insisted. "It's not their way. Even if their attempt to make the Alwari see reason failed, they would return to tell us so."

Delegate Fargane, tallest and most educated of the four native Ansionians present, waved his tumbler angrily. "They have comlinks. They should have contacted us by now. Whether to speak of success or failure matters not so much to me. I ask only that those who desire my vote be polite." An irritated hissing noise emanated from his single nostril. "I can stand to be proven wrong, *but I don't like being ignored.*"

Towering over them all, Tolut offered a dissenting opinion. "Maybe they are having trouble with their comlinks."

Volune looked up at him in disbelief. The smaller human delegate was not intimidated by the bulky Armalat. "All *four* of them?"

Tolut gestured petulantly. He was no happier with the continuing lack of contact on the part of the visiting Jedi than were his colleagues. "We don't know that they each carry one. Maybe they only took two with them. Two could break."

"Comlinks just don't break down like that." Kandah took a deep breath. "If these Jedi are as competent as their kind are rumored to be, one would think they would carry necessary replacement parts, or spares. Yet still we hear nothing from them."

"Probably because they've failed to do what they intended to do, are too embarrassed to face you and admit it, and have already left Ansion to report their failure to their aged superiors."

Everyone else turned to look in the speaker's direction. Tun Dameerd, another delegate, responded. "Unlike the rest of us, you are not a chosen representative of the Ansionian populace, Ogomoor, and are here only as an invited guest. It's not your place to comment on these ongoing negotiations."

"What negotiations?" Blithely ignoring the admonition, Ogomoor set his drink aside and spread his long, three-fingered hands wide. "These Jedi came here and asked you to delay your vote on the matter of secession so that they might strike a bargain with the Alwari enabling everyone on Ansion to live within the suffocating strictures of the Republic. You graciously consented to give them this chance."

He turned a slow circle, presenting himself to each of them in turn. "What has been the result? More delay, more obfuscation, more of what the Republic has given Ansion for decades. If that isn't proof enough that it's time for a real change, I don't know what is." Feigning indifference, he picked up his glass again. "Of course, as you say, I'm only here as an observer. But I do know that there are many who eagerly await the outcome of your eventual vote. A positive outcome."

"Your bossban, for example?" Volune eyed the majordomo sarcastically.

Ogomoor was not upset. "Naturally, Soergg looks forward to the day when he and his kind can conduct business in this part of the galaxy openly and without being crushed beneath the onerous burden of outdated Republic rules and regulations."

"I didn't know a Hutt could bend," Dameerd quipped. Mild

laughter rose from the delegates—but not from all of them, Ogomoor noted. He and his bossban had allies here.

"You can joke," Kandah observed icily, "but my family's commerce and the businesses of those who supported my election to this position have suffered mightily under the Republic's sluggishness and indifference. I say it's time we moved forward! We've delayed long enough. Call for the vote!"

Fargane raised his own glass. "Kandah is right. I flatter myself that I might live long enough to see it."

Volune's lips tightened and he shook his head. "I agree that the Republic has lost its way. I agree that our pleas for relief from oppressive laws and taxes are too often ignored. But the Senate *has* responded to our complaints." He looked around at his fellow delegates. "Do you not all agree that if the Jedi can make this peace between the Unity of towns and cities and the Alwari that Ansion will be better off under the laws of the Republic than outside them?"

The discussion that followed was heated, and short. Once again it was Kandah who spoke up. "Of course we are agreed on that." She ignored the look of surprise on Ogomoor's face. "If we were not, we would have gone ahead and taken the vote the same day the Jedi arrived. But we have no peace with the Alwari. We have no agreement. And with each day that passes, our assurances of support from the Malarians and the Keitumites that they will follow our lead diminishes. It is critical that this matter be *decided*."

Into the silence that followed, Volune offered a compromise. "We cannot vote today in any case. The proper procedures are not in place. I am willing, albeit reluctantly, as the chosen representative of my constituency, to set a date on which the vote to

secede or not to secede shall be taken." He looked at the Ansionian on his right. "Will this satisfy the venerable Fargane?"

The eldest Ansionian present paused, then gestured affirmatively. "It will."

Volune turned back to the others. "Then let us settle on a
date and a time, and not deviate from that. If the Jedi return before then, we will hear them out. If they do not, then we will go
ahead and take the vote, and they will have only themselves to
blame for their lack of a timely response."

The proposal was too reasonable for even Tolut to object to,
and the Armalat found himself making the suggestion unani-
mous. For his part, Ogomoor knew that Bossban Soergg and his
supporters would be well pleased. The date chosen was not as
soon as might have been wished, but neither was it uncon-
scionably far in the future. Tolut might be a problem, but the Armalat's vote could be ignored. Following today's gathering,
Ogomoor would be able to report back that, besides Kandah,
Fargane and at least one other delegate would be likely to vote in
favor of withdrawal from the Republic. The votes of the others
were not yet a certainty. The transposition of certain large sums
of credits to untraceable banking accounts might yet have to take
place prior to the formal vote in order to ensure that Ansion
opted for secession.

In the interim, he and his bossban had little else to worry
about. Because to all intents and purposes, the Qulun Baiuntu
was doing his work very well indeed.

Morning saw the group of fast-moving travelers slow as
Kyakhta rejoined them. The guide had ridden on slightly ahead.
Now he returned at a gallop, visibly excited, bulging eyes aglow.

"Found them!" he announced proudly as he turned his suubatar. He extended his artificial arm to point. "Just over the next rise."

"At last," Luminara murmured. "You're certain it's the Borokii?"

The Alwari gestured emphatically. "No mistaking it, Master Luminara. They are in full ceremonial camp, pennants flying. The overclan Borokii, most influential of all the Alwari clans."

In truth, it was a more impressive sight than any of them had expected. Having been exposed to the nomad encampments of the Yiwa and the Qulun, the travelers believed they had some idea of what to expect. Neither of those previous encounters prepared them for what greeted their eyes as their suubatars topped the crest of the low ridge.

Spread out before them were not dozens of recently unfolded and erected portable structures, but hundreds. Several boasting sophisticated energy arrays for the generation of power must have required dozens of draft animals to pull them, Luminara reflected. Thousands of Borokii of all ages milled about within the vast, elaborate camp. Beyond, uncountable thousands of herd animals grazed peacefully within perimeters patrolled by sadain-mounted handlers. The din of their passive moaning and mewling, a kind of rising *urrr* noise, dominated the sounds of the camp. Here, just as they had been told, resided the supreme power of the Alwari. Where the Borokii led, the rest of the Alwari would follow.

"Surepp," Bulgan explained in response to her query concerning the herd. "Males are the blue ones with the darker neck ruffs and coiled antlers, females are green and slightly larger but without the ruffs."

Sitting up straight in her saddle, she let her gaze rove over the impressive panorama. "I've never seen an animal with three eyes lined up vertically like that, instead of in the usual horizontal position."

"Top eye keeps watch for flying predators, middle eye tracks fellow surepp, and the bottom eye monitors the ground for food and obstacles." Bulgan shifted in his seat, the side of his face with the one good eye leaning, as always, slightly forward. "That way the surepp miss nothing."

"I see. I suppose it makes sense for an animal that's standing still, but they must have terrible peripheral vision."

The guide nodded. "That is so, but they don't need it. When you almost always have another surepp on either side of you plus others in front and back, you don't have to see from side to side. Only up and down."

"What about the ones who find themselves pushed to the edge of the herd?"

"They can turn their heads to see to the side, and use their sense of smell. They can still see from side to side, just not as well as a dorgum or awiquod. Because of their numbers, surepp are much harder for hunters like the shanh to take than dorgum or awiquod, which are more likely to graze slightly apart from one another." He nudged his mount forward, and the suubatar broke into a slow walk. "That's why the richer clans like the Borokii prefer them."

"What are they good for?" Barriss asked from nearby.

"Everything. Meat, milk, hides, wool. Their teeth and antlers were once used to make tools. Nowadays, those kind of utensils are imported, so the bony material is used for expensive handicrafts." He smiled. "I'm sure you'll see examples of everything once we're inside the camp."

Up in the lead, Kyakhta raised his long-fingered prosthetic. "Riders are coming."

Unsurprisingly, there were six of them, six by now being readily recognized by the travelers as a number of significance for all Ansionians. More richly attired than Yiwa or Qulun, their lightweight armor gleamed in the sun. Two of the pickets held poles of imported carbonite composite atop which the Borokii standard snapped briskly in the morning breeze. In addition to traditional long knives, two of them wore Malarian laser pistols. Clearly, at least some of what they had heard about the overclans was true, Luminara saw. The Borokii had wealth, and the acumen to know how to spend it.

Curiosity overcoming his natural reserve, the leader of the half a dozen riders impelled his equally impressively attired sadain forward, halting in front of the lead suubatars. The considerable difference in the heights of their respective mounts forced him to look up at the visitors. To his credit, he did not seem in the least intimidated. He was also, Luminara decided, openly friendly—at least on the surface. But then, she knew, the powerful can afford to be magnanimous.

"Greetings, offworlders and friends." The Borokii briefly pressed one hand across his eyes and the other over his chest. "I am Bayaar of the Situng Borokii. Welcome to our camp. What do you wish of the overclan?"

While Obi-Wan explained their purpose, Luminara continued to study the pickets. Looking for any indication of hostile intent, she found only confidence and a professional readiness. Unlike the Yiwa, for example, these people were not suspicious or afraid of strangers. With thousands of fellow clanfolk to back them up, they didn't have to be. That did not mean they were indifferent to potential threats, or lazy. While their leader listened courteously to Obi-Wan, the members of his troop sat imperiously in their saddles. But their eyes were always moving.

Bayaar did not have to retire to mull a response when Obi-Wan had finished. "This is not something to which I can speak. I am an outrider—a sentinel, and sentinels do not make decisions of such magnitude."

Obi-Wan smiled in that slight, knowing way of his and nodded understandingly. "As a kind of sentinel myself, I appreciate your position."

"We will convey the news of your arrival, as well as your reasons for seeking out the Borokii, to the Council of Elders. Meanwhile, I invite you to follow me, and experience Borokii hospitality." So saying, he neatly turned his mount and started back down the gentle slope toward the bustling, milling encampment. Splitting up, the rest of his troop assumed flanking positions on either side of the line of visitors. They were an escort, Luminara saw, meant to honor, not threaten. The latter would have been difficult for the pickets to do in any case, given the disparity in size between their sadains and the visitors' suubatars.

The differences between the Borokii encampment and anything the travelers had encountered thus far were both striking and immediately apparent. Though entirely mobile, the community had been laid out like a permanent town, with temporary streets and designated areas for residential, commercial, and manufacturing activities. The latter consisted largely of processing large numbers of surepp carcasses for export. This was not unexpected. Something, Luminara knew, had to pay for all the imported structures and high technology that was on prominent display.

They drew plenty of stares but no impolite comment. Once more she noted how the lack of discernible suspicion was in stark contrast to their reception by the Yiwa. Given the power and reputation of the Borokii, coupled with the size of the nomad community, that was not so surprising. Clearly, here were a people who felt themselves secure, and deserving of the exalted position of *overclan*.

Still, she exchanged a meaningful glance with Obi-Wan when they were brought to a halt outside what Bayaar identified as the visitors' house. The last "visitors' house" they had stayed in had not proved very accommodating.

Apprised of their concerns, Kyakhta hastened to reassure the Jedi. "These are not mistrustful Yiwa or double-dealing Qulun. Since the Borokii are strong enough not to fear the challenge of outsiders, they are also secure enough to welcome them. And they have a reputation for courtesy to uphold." He indicated the building before them. "I think we will be safe here."

In response, Luminara instructed her suubatar to kneel. Climbing off, she watched while one of Bayaar's troops took the beast in hand, guiding it back down the street by its reins. Others took charge of their remaining mounts.

"What about our supplies?" Anakin inquired aloud.

"Your property will not be touched." Bayaar was not insulted by the query. After all, these were not only outsiders, they were offworlders. It was to be expected they would be unfamiliar with Borokii ways. Trying to decide whether Luminara or Obi-Wan was the leader of the visitors, he found himself unable to do so, and settled for addressing them simultaneously.

Having been informed of the nature of their purpose in seeking out the overclan, he tried to keep a neutral tone in his voice, even though personally he was not sanguine about the strangers' aspirations.

"I will convey your request to the Council of Elders. Meanwhile, you will be made comfortable, and be given food and drink."

"Do you think they'll give us an audience, your council?"
Luminara was quite taken by this dignified warrior-sentinel, who
thus far had demonstrated both courtesy and curiosity. Not that
he could by any means be considered an ally, but he at least
struck her as sympathetic.

"It's not for me to say. I am only a sentinel." Placing hands
over eyes and chest, he departed, leaving the visitors to wait for a
formal response. Hopefully, she mused, it would not be long in
coming. Councils of every type and species had a distressing tendency to dawdle until a consensus could be reached. With luck
the Borokii, a people used to being always on the move, would
be more responsive.

Everything they experienced during the next several hours
spoke to the strength of the overclan. The food was better, the
drinks richer, the trimmings and trappings of the visitors' house
in every way more lavish than anything they had previously encountered on Ansion. Truth be told, they enjoyed themselves.
After their dubious encounters with the Yiwa and the Qulun, it
was a relief to be able to relax in pleasant surroundings reasonably confident they would not be set upon at any moment by potential assailants. Both Kyakhta and Bulgan were convinced of
that much, though Tooqui remained as chary as always. As to the
possible response they would receive from the Borokii Council of
Elders, the two guides could offer no opinion.

Bayaar was back well before evening. If the swiftness of his
return was encouraging, his words were not. At best, they were
ambiguous.

"The council will greet you," the sentinel informed them.

Barriss's face broke out into a wide smile. "We're all set,
then."

As she spoke, Bayaar turned his attention to her. "I am not

entirely certain what you mean by that, but I think you are confident too soon. When I say that the council will greet you, that is all they will do. Not to do so would be ill mannered."

Obi-Wan worked to interpret their host's meaning, as opposed to his words. "Are you saying they will receive us, but not listen to our proposal?"

Bayaar nodded. "In order for that to happen, you must present the council with an appropriate conventional offering of their choosing."

"Oh, well then." Obi-Wan relaxed slightly. "What would satisfy the council? We have access to some funds that can be used for trade. If something more substantial is required . . ." He left the question open.

"Actually, the council requests that you present them with something smaller." Bayaar let his gaze travel over the group. Having encountered only a few human traders before, he was fascinated by their tiny, squinched-up eyes and individual follicular variations. "They wish one of you to hand them a handful of wool taken from the ruff of a mature white male surepp."

"That's all?" Anakin blurted. Obi-Wan threw his Padawan a warning glance, but a very mild one. He was himself surprised by the seemingly unpretentious nature of the request.

Which was why he was immediately wary.

"Where can we purchase some of this wool?"

"You cannot buy it." Bayaar was uncomfortable in the position of diplomatic go-between. He would much rather have been out on the prairie, patrolling a picket line, weapon in hand. "One of you must take it, by hand, in the traditional manner and without the use of any marvelous offworld devices or other forms of assistance such as a suubatar mount, from the back of a white surepp."

Tooqui made a face. "Don't like this idea. Too many many surepp gots too many many big feet."

Leaning over, Barriss whispered to her fellow Padawan. "I don't like this either, Anakin. Just a handful of wool? It seems too easy. The surepp are domesticated herd animals, therefore they can't be too hard to work with. How hard can it be to catch one and snip off a handful of ruff?"

He nodded uncertainly. "I know. Maybe that *is* all there is to it. Just because it's a custom doesn't mean it has to be difficult, or dangerous."

She indicated their Masters, who were conferring between themselves. "I have a feeling we'll know soon enough."

Standing away from Luminara, Obi-Wan again addressed their host. "We'll be happy to comply with the council's request." He hesitated. "I take it that wool from one of the surepp in the Borokii herd will suffice, and that we don't have to go looking for a wild one?"

"That is correct. It is allowed to cut from the ruff of a herd animal."

"Then we're wasting time. There's still ample daylight outside. If you'd be so kind as to escort us?"

Bayaar sighed. Plainly, these strangers had no idea what they were being asked to do. *Haja,* they would find out soon enough.

"Come with me."

The stroll through the nomad town was interesting, and Bayaar was happy to point out highlights and explain the sights. Before too long they found themselves on the outskirts of the bustling community, gazing across strands of recently unspooled, electrically charged superconducting lines at thousands and thousands of Borokii surepp. The herd was an impressive sight, mewling and moaning as it nibbled at the high grass. Grazing close together guaranteed safety, if not much room for individuals to move about. Catching a male and cutting off a handful of its neck ruff might require a healthy sprint on the part of the would-be wool trimmer, but it wasn't as if a lengthy dash across the plains was going to be necessary. There was only one problem. Bayaar had told them that the council demanded a handful of white wool.

The fur of every one of the dozens, of the hundreds, of surepp within view was mostly either blue or green. There was not a white animal in sight. Not even one that was a pale green. Luminara was quick to point this seeming discrepancy out to their host.

Bayaar looked embarrassed. "I don't make the laws. I am only serving as a vehicle for the council's directives."

"How can we cut white wool from an animal that doesn't exist?" Obi-Wan indicated the milling herd.

"It does," Bayaar told them. "The albino surepp is very real, and there are some in the Borokii herd."

Luminara's gaze narrowed as she studied their discomfited host. "There are thousands of animals foraging out there. How many is 'some'?"

Bayaar turned away, visibly uncomfortable. "Two."

Letting out a long sigh, Barriss found herself nodding knowingly. "I *knew* it sounded too easy."

"Without transport, I don't see how we're expected to do this." Anakin was visibly upset. The Borokii council had set the visitors a seemingly impossible task. Addressing himself to Bayaar, he asked dispiritedly, "What do the Borokii do with their herds at night?" He indicated the electrically charged conductors that kept the herd separated from the town. "The other Alwari we've seen round their animals up and keep them in temporary corrals, the better to watch over them and protect them from nocturnal predators." Both Obi-Wan and Luminara eyed him favorably, and he tried not to show how pleased he was at their approval.

"The Borokii do the same," Bayaar acknowledged, "though on a much larger scale than other Alwari." He indicated the softly humming barrier. "This keeps the surepp contented and together after dark, while outriders like myself keep shanhs and others away from the corral. The surepp cannot leap over the barrier, but a hungry shanh could."

"You said 'together.' " Luminara's mind was working. "How close together?"

"Very close." Holding his hands out in front of him, Bayaar brought the slender palms almost to the point of touching. "This close. Crowded up against one another, the surepp feel safe and secure. They sleep standing up."

Barriss studied the herd. "Packed that closely together, they'd have to."

Luminara nodded thoughtfully. "With the animals concentrated in one place, it would be much easier to find the white ones than during the day, when the herd is spread out over hills and vales like they are now." She eyed the polite sentinel unblinkingly. "How would the surepp be likely to react to someone moving among them?"

He had to smile. "I see what you're thinking. It is a dangerous notion. It *is* possible to walk among sleepy surepp without panicking them, but one has to be very careful. They are nervous creatures, easily agitated. If they feel disturbed, or threatened, or even nothing more than uneasy, their mood and manner can change abruptly. Anyone trying to walk between individuals could find himself gored by an abruptly irritated male, or crushed between many suddenly shifting bodies."

After a quick glance at his colleague, Obi-Wan spoke up once more. "Is there anything else you can tell us that would help us to single out these rare white surepp? Do they tend to congregate in any single place, any one part of the herd?"

"Actually, they do," Bayaar admitted. "Unfortunately, because they stand out so prominently, they naturally tend to seek the safest place—which is in the exact middle of the herd."

Surveying the thousands of large, healthy creatures that covered the nearby grassland all the way to the horizon and beyond, Barriss tried to imagine worming her way through a densely packed mass of them while striving constantly not to annoy or alarm a single one. In contrast to Obi-Wan's earlier optimism, she found herself tending to agree with Anakin. When confronted with the reality of the immense, easily agitated herd, the task that had seemed so simple at first was looking more and more impossible. Given a landspeeder, now, or a confident suubatar, or any other means of transportation capable of rising above the horned heads of the massed beasts, the task set before them would be worth contemplating. But the Council of Elders' instructions, as relayed to them by the sympathetic Bayaar, were all too straightforward: no offworld technology could be employed in the carrying out of the undertaking, and no mounts could be ridden into the herd. No suubatars, not even a smaller sadain.

It didn't matter. They didn't have a landspeeder anyway. A mastery of the Force would enable one to rise momentarily above a small part of the herd, but it would not permit long-term personal levitation. Something else would have to be tried. She tried to imagine stepping through the electrified barrier and walking all the way to the center of the herd, past thousands of closely packed animals, any one of which could turn on the intruder at any moment. A single snort of alarm might be enough to set them off. Once deep within the herd, there would be no chance of escaping from a stampede. An intruder would go down beneath thousands of hooves and a million tons of surepp mass.

She wasn't the only one who was stumped for a solution to the problem. "We'll come back here at evening time, just before sunset," Obi-Wan informed their host. "At least," he muttered more softly, "whatever we eventually try and whoever tries it will have a better chance of locating one of the albino animals when the members of the herd have clustered together for the night."

"And since we're not allowed to use advanced technology, we'll need a Borokii knife." Luminara spoke absently, as if her thoughts were focused elsewhere. "To cut the wool."

Back in the visitors' house, there was much discussion of possible ways to get around the council's stipulation. Getting around it seemed the most practical approach, since fulfilling the request as put forward seemed, on the face of it, unachievable. Numerous suggestions were proposed, debated, and just as rapidly discarded. The approach of evening found them no nearer a clear-cut solution than when they had begun talking.

With Bayaar once more guiding them, they returned to the outskirts of the provisional corral. Much to his distress, the sentinel had been appointed to take charge of and see to the needs of the visitors. No diplomat, he was uncomfortable with the assignment, but resigned himself to carrying it out to the best of his ability.

A considerable source of his unease arose from the stipulation the council had placed on the strangers. He found that he rather liked the squinty-eyed offworlders. It would make him unhappy to see any of them injured, or worse, trampled to death. He could not see how they were going to fulfill the council's requirement without that coming to pass. Perhaps, he thought, they would simply accede to the hopelessness of the situation, have a pleasant but inconsequential meeting with the elders, and continue on their way.

He could not read their alien expressions, but those of their guides did not lead him to believe that the offworlders possessed some special magic that was going to enable them to fulfill the council's demand.

Standing close to the fence line, the visitors studied the assembled surepp attentively. Herded together for the night, the burly, powerful animals were already beginning to settle down. Settling down, however, did not mean they were unaware of or indifferent to their surroundings. A single bellow by one would be enough to alert every fellow surepp to any perceived danger.

Having learned of the demand that had been placed on the visitors, a small crowd had gathered, more hopeful of seeing a trampling than anything else. Though it was beneath a warrior of Bayaar's stature, others of his clan had no hesitation about placing bets on the chances of the strangers' success. The only problem was that those wagering against the visitors had to give long odds in order to get any action at all.

He frowned. What was the taller female doing? Removing her outer clothes struck him as a most peculiar approach to entering the densely packed herd. If he was the one about to attempt the suicidal endeavor, he would want to have on as many layers of clothing as possible, to protect himself from thrusting horns, pounding feet, and the hard ground itself.

When the female finally finished, she was wearing only her strange, alien undergarments. In the light of the setting sun, he found them most peculiar. Still, they no doubt suited such an oddly formed biped. Concern for his guests was almost out-weighed by his curiosity to see what they were going to do next.

Obi-Wan stood looking into his colleague's eyes while arguing quietly with her. "I don't think this is a very good idea, Luminara."

"Neither do I, Master," Barriss added apprehensively.

Luminara nodded, glanced across at the last member of their little group. "And what about you, Anakin? You haven't said anything since I ventured the idea."

Asked for his opinion, the tall Padawan didn't hesitate. "I couldn't do it, that's for sure. It sounds crazy."

Luminara smiled. "But you know that I'm not crazy, don't you, Anakin?"

He nodded. "When I was a child, I did plenty of things that were called crazy. Everybody thought I was crazy to take part in professional Podracing. But I did, and I'm still alive." He stood a little taller. "The Force was with me."

"Luck was with you," Barriss murmured tartly, but so low that no one else could hear.

"So you think I should go ahead with this?" Luminara asked him.

Anakin hesitated. "It's not for me to say. If Obi-Wan agrees . . ." His voice trailed off without finishing.

She turned her attention back to the other Jedi. "Obi-Wan has already said he doesn't think it's a very good idea. Does Obi-Wan have a better idea?"

The Jedi hesitated for the briefest of instants, then gave a slight shrug. "I tend to side with Barriss in this—but no, I don't have a better idea."

"We need that piece of wool if we're going to get the Borokii to listen to us."

"I know, I know." Obi-Wan looked unhappy. "Are you sure you can do this, Luminara?"

"Of course I'm not sure I can." As she spoke, she was making certain the sharp, ceremonial Borokii knife Bayaar had loaned her was securely fastened to her narrow waistband. "But like you, I can't think of anything else to try. This is the best I could come up with." She smiled reassuringly. "We can't convince the Council of Elders to persuade the rest of the Alwari to agree to our position if we never get to speak to them."

"While your death might convince them of our sincerity, and of the importance the Republic attaches to our mission here, that's still no guarantee they'll agree to listen to the rest of us."

"Then you'll find other ways of convincing them of our sincerity," she told him. Reaching out, she put a hand on his shoulder. "Whatever happens here, now, may the Force be with you always, Obi-Wan Kenobi."

Stepping closer, he gave her a firm hug. "Not only will the Force be with me, Luminara Unduli, I expect you to be with me for a while longer yet as well." He indicated their Padawans. "You wouldn't go and leave me with not one but two Padawans to look after, would you?"

Her smile broadened. "I think you would manage to cope with the challenge, Obi-Wan."

"Master. . . ," Barriss began. Turning, the Jedi put a reassuring hand on her Padawan's shoulder.

"Not everything is assured in advance, my dear." Her hand slid off the strong shoulder. "I know what I'm doing. I just don't know what the surepp are going to do." Taking a couple of steps back, she took a deep breath and nodded at Bayaar.

It was not for him to try to dissuade the offworlder. He had already done all he properly could to apprise her of the danger she had chosen to face. Raising a hand high, he signaled to his right. Down the fence line, the operator in charge of this section of the corral responded with a gesture of acknowledgment. Something went softly *ssizzt*.

"The barrier here has been shut down," he told the visitors. "If you really mean to do this thing, you have to do it now."

"I know," Luminara replied. Whereupon she stepped carefully through the unelectrified fence line, gathered herself, and leapt onto the back of the nearest surepp.

Rising above the twilight clamor from the town and the communal mewling and burbling of the tightly packed beasts, the collective intake of breath from the audience of watching Borokii was plainly audible. Their astonishment was paralleled by that of the two Padawans, even though they had been given some idea of what to expect.

Exhibiting the strength of a weight lifter, the agility of a gymnast, and the training of a Jedi adept, Luminara sped not through the herd but *over* it. Across it, rather, Anakin thought as he looked on in amazement and admiration. Touching down only long enough to kick off and launch herself to another expansive, woolly spine, Luminara raced across the backs of the Borokii herd, heading for its approximate heart. Occasionally, disturbed by the contact, a sleepy surepp would look up in surprise. Unable to discern any threat or danger, it would then lower its head and return to its quiet dozing.

While her friends were able to monitor her progress via their macrobinoculars, Kyakhta, Bulgan, Tooqui, Bayaar, and the other observing Borokii could only strain to see with their eyes. Unable to stand the suspense, the sentinel finally sidled over next to the offworlder called Obi-Wan.

"How is your friend doing?" he found himself asking. "She is still alive, or you would have reacted."

"Moving fast." Obi-Wan spoke without lowering the device. "Back and forth. Fast enough that I couldn't keep her in focus, but this viewing device does it for me."

What seemed like hours but were in reality only minutes passed in tense silence before the Jedi murmured softly but excitedly, "There!" His voice rose despite his efforts to keep it under control. "She's got it!"

"So soon?" Bayaar was all but struck dumb with astonishment. "She moves very swiftly indeed, your female."

"Not my female," Obi-Wan hurriedly corrected him. "We are colleagues, equals. Like you and your fellow warriors."

"Ah," murmured Bayaar without quite understanding the offworlder.

"Yes, she's quick," Obi-Wan added. "On her way back now." Suddenly he jerked visibly, lowered the macrobinoculars from his eyes, then raised them again.

"What? What's happening?" Turning toward the herd, Bayaar strained to see. His night vision was excellent, but no match for the advanced viewer. "I think I see some disturbance."

"She slipped." The offworlder's voice was not quite as neutral as before. "Slipped and fell. I—I can't see her anymore." A rising mewling reached them from the place within the massed herd where Luminara had gone down. Even without aid, he could see that several animals were stirring uneasily. Beside them, others were waking from their evening torpor.

There was no time to discuss alternatives. They had to act before the disturbance spread.

"We're going after her," he told the two attentive Padawans. Though he could see the anxiety writ large in their expressions, there was no time to reassure them, no time for coddling.

"Concentrate," he ordered them. "Concentrate as hard as you ever have concentrated. Focus. And stay together." Taking Barriss's hand in his right and Anakin's in his left, Obi-Wan led them through the barrier.

Pushed, pressed by the focusing of the Force from not one but three trained individuals, the surepp gave way. Mewling and hissing, they parted to make a path for the striding offworlders. Triple eyes glared angrily at the bipeds, furious at the intrusion. But something kept them at bay, prevented them from trampling the trio beneath massed, sharp-toed feet.

If any of them lost heart, Obi-Wan knew, if either Padawan panicked or lost concentration, he and whoever remained focused might not be able to sustain the intensity necessary to hold the surging, increasingly restless herd back. He tried to will his own mastery into the two learners, to lend some of his own strength to each of them. Yet as they marched deliberately forward, ever deeper into the herd, a strange thing happened.

While Barriss held her own, Anakin seemed to grow stronger. It was as if, faced by the challenge and the very real proximity of death, the Force grew within him. Obi-Wan did not entirely understand what was happening, but at the moment he was far too preoccupied to examine the phenomenon. Right then, one thing and only one mattered.

They found Luminara lying unconscious on the ground, a trickle of blood trailing from her forehead. A quick glance showed Obi-Wan that the injury was not deep. Still, he could not see what she might have suffered internally when she fell. A muscular trill ran through his fingers where he held Barriss's. He could see the concern in her face, could feel the distress. But Barriss Offee was her Master's student. As a healer, she might have been expected to drop immediately to the ground to begin ministering to her Master. As an incipient Jedi, she knew that what mattered now was not individual healing, but sustaining the Force against the powerful animals that were hissing and pawing at the ground all around them.

Displaying his physical as well as mental strength, Anakin hoisted the unconscious Jedi onto his shoulders. Together, they turned and began to retrace their steps. A growing section of the herd had been alerted to the presence of intruders in their midst. Even though no danger had manifested itself, and none among the herd had been attacked, the surepp were increasingly edgy.

It became harder and harder to hold them back. Perspiration streamed down Obi-Wan's face. Though he had the help of Barriss and Anakin, the Force was centered on him, and it was up to him to maintain the energy that continued to hold the surepp back. He could see the barrier now, not far in front of them. The good-natured Bayaar was staring at him anxiously, wanting to encourage the visitor but not daring to shout his support. Standing well behind him, the rest of the Borokii who had come out to watch whispered fearfully among themselves.

Something bumped up against Obi-Wan, nearly knocking him off his feet. For an instant, his concentration faltered under the impact of the heavy surepp flank. Barriss shot him a look of alarm while confusion replaced confidence on Anakin's face. Atop his shoulders, Luminara stirred uneasily. If she cried out . . .

Then an exhausted Obi-Wan was through the quiescent barrier, and Anakin was handing his burden across. The waiting Kyakhta and Bulgan took her, Tooqui helping as much as he could. Together, they placed her gently on the ground, laying her on her back. Barriss was at her side in an instant, running sensitive, trained fingers over her Master's forehead, using part of her robe to wipe the blood from Luminara's face. Beneath the Padawan's gentle ministrations, the unconscious Jedi moaned softly.

Behind them, something bawled loudly. There was the sound of bone striking flesh. Anakin Skywalker half tumbled, half flew through the tangling barrier under the impact of the surepp's head-butt. He hit the ground hard, nearly knocking a startled Tooqui over in the process, rolled, and ended up on his belly. Obi-Wan eyed him anxiously as a crackling sound filled the night air. A surepp yelped, then another, as they made contact with the reactivated barrier and hastily retreated.

"Anything broken?" Obi-Wan inquired solicitously.

Wincing, Anakin struggled to his feet. "Only my dignity, Master." He nodded in the direction of the prone Luminara. "How is she?"

Barriss looked up at him. "I sense no internal damage, but I can't be certain."

Luminara's eyes opened. She blinked a couple of times and did not smile. "Help me to my feet."

"Master Luminara," Barriss began, "I'm not sure it's wise for you to—"

"It probably wasn't wise for me to go into that herd, either," Luminara declared painfully as she straightened. With Obi-Wan assisting on one side and Anakin on the other, she was soon standing among them. "But it had to be done." She gestured apologetically to Bayaar. "I'm afraid I lost your knife."

"What happened?" Obi-Wan asked her.

"It's not exactly like running a training course at the Temple. Every surepp back was different, yet I didn't have time to study where I was going to place my feet. I just had to run, and not linger, and hope. Everything was going well until I landed on an animal that was unexpectedly wet. It must have been grooming itself, or spent a lot of time being groomed by others. I slipped, and before I could catch myself, my head hit the ground." She smiled at each of them in turn. "Thank you for coming after me."

"You had no choice but to do what you did," Obi-Wan told her. "When you went down, we had no choice but to come after you."

"And I thought the Jedi were the masters of choice," Anakin murmured. "So much for that maxim."

Barriss's eyes widened slightly, then she slumped. "And we still have to find a way to get the fur, if we're going to get the Borokii elders to talk to us."

As she brought her hand down from her forehead, Luminara's lower, tattooed lip curled slightly upward. "You forget, Padawan: I was on my way *back* to you." Her expression fell. "Unless it slipped out when I went down." Reaching into her lower undergarment, she felt around anxiously for a moment. Then, slowly, her smile returned.

In her fingers she held the requisite tuft of fur from the albino surepp. It was the color of dirty snow.

Turning to Bayaar, she displayed the small, seemingly insignificant prize that had nearly been bought at so high a price. "You saw how it happened," she told the sentinel. Behind him, other Borokii were crowding around, each eager for a glimpse of proof of the extraordinary accomplishment. "It was done as demanded. Will the Council of Elders confer with us now?"

The sentinel gestured approvingly. "I fail to see why they would not. This is a moment I will remember for my grandchildren, as you may do the same for yours."

"Jedi do not have children." Surrounded by her friends, she started back through the Borokii encampment toward the distant visitors' house.

Bayaar watched them go. They were very powerful indeed, these offworlders. Masters of a great many talents, not to mention the Force itself. Therefore it seemed strange that one should feel sorry for them.

But he did.

Her posture straightened and her stride lengthened as they walked through the encampment. Curious Borokii, busy with nocturnal tasks, turned to follow their progress. Anakin and Barriss, Obi-Wan and Kyakhta, Bulgan and Tooqui, all crowded around her, offering tender congratulatory pats and touches or, in the manner of the two Alwari, caresses that were exotic and lingering but in no way invasive. Meanwhile Tooqui did his best to express his own relief by clinging occasionally to one of the Jedi's bare legs—a position that incidentally kept him from being pushed aside by the others. Restrained by his status and outside the group, Bayaar nonetheless made a point of offering traditional Borokii congratulations.

"Here." Still breathing hard and gulping for air as they stopped outside the visitors' house, the utterly fatigued Jedi thrust the clump of albino wool into their host's hands. "Give this to your elders. Tell them who it's from and how it came to be in your possession." Turning away from the solemn, respectful sentinel she took a step toward the entrance—and slumped into the supportive arms of her friends.

"The Force is a wondrous thing, but you can't bathe in it. I'm sure roasted surepp tastes wonderful, but when alive they smell like any herd of densely packed herbivores. Crucial meeting or not, I've got to have a bath before I can think of presenting myself to even a junior elder!"

As they helped her up the stairs into the visitors' house, numerous Borokii, having learned of what had just transpired, had assembled outside to stare at the offworlders. Their whispered comments were full of admiration, their unwavering gazes unobtrusive. A reverent Bulgan carried the Jedi's bundle of outer clothing. His and Kyakhta's admiration for the female offworlder, which up to now had been considerable, no longer knew any bounds.

While the notion of entirely immersing oneself in a tub or pool of water as a means of relaxation quite escaped the Borokii, they were more than willing to provide the means necessary for the visitors to indulge themselves. It was hardly an expensive request. While Barriss attended to the needs of her weary teacher and the ever-inquisitive Tooqui hovered nearby making a minor pest of himself, the other members of the group settled down to a late-evening meal and contemplation of the day to come.

Much good conversation and laughter filled the visitors' house of the Situng Borokii that night, followed by preparations for sleep that were carried out with more enthusiasm than usual. As Barriss had surmised, Luminara's injury was not serious, and was effectively treated. Tomorrow would hopefully see a meeting with the Council of Elders and, if fortune was with them, the successful conclusion of the Jedi mission to Ansion. It was with such expectations in mind that each of them in due course retired to his or her dry, comfortable, Borokii-style bed. Even the seemingly perpetual internal spring that powered Tooqui finally ran down, and the little Gwurran collapsed into deep sleep with nary a word of good night to anyone.

Lying on his overstuffed sleeping pad, Obi-Wan contemplated Luminara's already softly sleeping form in light of what she had accomplished earlier that evening. He did not think he could have done it. His particular talents lay elsewhere. The sight of her vaulting from the back of one surepp to another, never lingering long enough for her presence to unduly alarm a single beast, knowing that a single slip might mean certain death despite anything Jedi training could do, had aroused in him the kind of admiration one normally reserved for the actions of those on the Jedi Council. He wanted very much to ask her exactly how she had managed certain seemingly impossible moves.

But not tonight, he told himself firmly. This night was for savoring the accomplishments of the day and for anticipating the achievements to be realized tomorrow. Time enough later to deal with other thoughts, other matters.

Nearby, Anakin Skywalker relaxed for the first time in weeks. If Master Luminara's feat was followed, as Master Obi-Wan believed, by a successful meeting with the Borokii Council of Elders, then they would at least be able to return to Cuipernam and from there to civilization. A result devoutly to be wished, because anything that took him away from Ansion brought him closer to where he really wanted to be.

Thoughts swirling in anticipation of the successful end of their mission, he allowed himself, for the first time in many days, to drift slowly into a sleep that was as contented as it was deep.

While there was plenty of convivial chatter and casual conversation when the group gathered this time, all of the conspirators wore their concerns like jewelry. Despite the overweening air of gaiety, one could cut the tension inside the transport with a knife. Large enough to carry fifty passengers in luxury and comfort, the vehicle was presently conveying half that number, together with their attendant serving droids.

Below, the endless world-city that was Coruscant gleamed golden in the morning sun as the planet's star rose over the distant, irregular horizon of towers and domes. None of the passengers was pleased with the timing of the convocation, but all had agreed to it. There was dissension within the movement, and it had to be resolved. For many of the participants, the time for talking was done with. Those arguing in favor of moving forward *now* were making their case forcefully, even brusquely. To them, it was not a matter of moving too fast. It was simply that as far as they were concerned, the time for waiting was at an end.

That certainly seemed to be the majority opinion inside the transparisteel-enclosed passenger compartment. As tumblers clinked and expensively attired individuals saluted one another on their forthcoming triumph, one would have thought the articles of secession had already been signed and disseminated. Laughter rose above the small talk as jokes were swapped that described the eagerly anticipated reactions of certain well-known and heartily disliked politicians to the declaration that was to come.

Among the revelers were a handful who did not join in the hasty celebration. Most notable among these was a prominent Shu Mai of mild aspect and conciliatory demeanor. Idly, she peered out through the protective transparisteel at the unending panorama of residences and factories, gardens and urban facilities sliding past beneath them. The morning sky was full of similar, if far less well-appointed vehicles, carrying people to and from their places of work and habitation. Billions of them on Coruscant alone, trillions more scattered across the galaxy, the fate of all about to be altered to one degree or another by the decision the handful of sentients in this one transport were on the verge of rendering.

It was a great responsibility, she knew. Too much, really, for one individual to ponder. But she was prepared to do so. As president of the Commerce Guild, she was charged with making such decisions. Sooner or later, all sentients were compelled to confront their destiny. Most turned away from it. She intended to fully embrace her own.

Someone had to step forward and say what needed to be said. The victory celebration was getting out of hand—especially in the absence of any victory. Working her way to the back of the compartment, Shu Mai stepped up on a small stool. It wasn't much of a platform, but then, this was not the guild she was addressing, either.

"It's too soon!" Shu Mai proclaimed, loud enough to be heard above the babble but without shouting.

Conversation faded quickly. Everyone turned to look at her.

"Too soon," she added in a softer yet still steely tone, "to reveal our real intentions, and ourselves."

"Excuse me, Shu Mai," declared a slim but powerful humanoid who stood in the senate for three inhabited worlds, "but not only is it not too soon, *hssst*, it is overdue. We have waited for this moment long enough." The subsequent rising murmur showed just how much support this opinion held among the assembled.

Shu Mai was not intimidated. She never was. The easily intimidated did not become president of an organization like the Commerce Guild. "Everything we have worked for is at stake here. All our preparations, our carefully laid-out plans, are at last beginning to coalesce. Nothing will shatter our mutual dream more than to show ourselves prematurely."

"Nothing will cost us fickle support among those systems still wavering more than delaying unnecessarily," came a contradictory shout from the back of the group. The supportive murmuring rose afresh, even stronger this time.

Shu Mai raised both hands for silence. As she was one of their own, they conceded her their attention: out of respect not for her insistence, but for the power she wielded with the Guild. Beyond the transparisteel canopy, a judicial speeder drew close, checking on the luxury vehicle. Though the aerial transport was sealed as tight against external surveillance techniques as modern technology could make it, she waited until the speeder accelerated out of sight.

"My friends, you all know me. You know of my devotion and that of the rest of the guild to the cause. We have worked together, planned together, kept secret from the Senate together our carefully designed intentions for many years now. It is the wise animal who waits until the fruit is ripe before eating. Pluck it too soon, and sickness can be the result."

A squat, muscular figure pushed its way to the forefront of the group to confront the speaker directly. Shu Mai found herself looking down at Tam Uliss.

"Wait too long, and the fruit rots." The industrialist was not smiling. "We need to move. It *feels* right."

Shu Mai stepped down off her dais. "And are you now basing your decisions on your *feelings*, my friend?"

"Not of the Force, no. But I know people." Uliss gestured behind him, at the attentive crowd. "I know these people. They've waited and worked long and hard for this moment. So have I."

"I would be the last one here to deny everyone their moment," Shu Mai replied softly. "I just want to make sure it's the right moment." Off to one side, Senator Mousul nodded somber agreement. Looking past Tam Uliss, Shu Mai raised her voice again. "We *have* to wait for Ansion to declare for secession. Ansion is still the key. Public disgust with the corruption and bureaucracy of the Republic runs high, but even the most sensitive explosive needs a fuse to set it off. Ansion's withdrawal will serve as the detonator, and its interlocking alliances will bring the Malarians and the Keitumites with it. It will be the excuse we need to move."

"The movement is strong enough now," the industrialist objected. "We *could* continue to wait on Ansion and the others, yes. But in so doing we might well lose other, equally vital support. Once we move, Ansion will follow docilely enough."

"Are you sure of that, my friend? Are you certain? Even as we stand here conversing, there are Jedi on Ansion." Confused mutterings from the group showed that by no means everyone present was aware of what was happening on that key world. "Jedi working to ensure that Ansion, and by inference the Malarians and the Keitumites, remain within the Republic."

Uliss's gaze narrowed. "You and Senator Mousul told me they were being dealt with."

"So they are," Shu Mai assured him. "But where Jedi are involved, nothing is certain until it is done. As soon as the Senator receives word that their efforts have been countered and that the delegates to the Unity of towns and cities on Ansion have voted for secession, we move. But not before. We need Ansion and the others to declare for withdrawal before we can confidently implement the rest of our plans."

"No," someone else in the back insisted. "No more waiting.

Enough waiting! What matters this week or the next? I say we move now! Ansion and the others *will* follow. Jedi or no Jedi!"

" 'Jedi or no Jedi'?" Shu Mai's echo of the insistent speaker's proclamation was drowned out by supporting yells and exclamations of approval. "Very well then: since the majority of you are clearly in favor of taking action, I have no choice but to concede to the wishes of the majority." Cheers in several languages filled the compartment. "I ask only that you wait another few days."

"A few days?" someone blurted. "What difference could a few days make? We move to a turning point in the history of the Republic!"

Nearby, the voice of an anxious Senator Mousul rose above the ensuing clamor for action. "As you say, what difference could a few days make?"

Confronting his stolid co-conspirators, Uliss smiled condescendingly. "Since a few days will not make any difference, we will grant them. But," he added loudly to forestall the incipient rush of protests from those who supported his position, "*only* a few days. If after that time has elapsed Ansion still has not voted, we set in motion that which we have worked toward for so long." His eyes locked on Shu Mai's. "Those who do not wish to move with us will have only themselves to blame if they find themselves left behind."

It was not a threat—not in so many words. The president of the Commerce Guild's response was a smile of her own. "I could call for a vote on this here and now, but I am neither blind nor deaf. I see and hear how the wind is blowing. Never let it be said that I was a poor listener. We are agreed, then. We wait a few more days. That should be time enough." Raising her gaze, she looked past the unwavering industrialist to scan the rest of the expectant group. "I hereby acknowledge your wishes, my friends, and will deal with them, for the betterment of everything we seek!"

Gibes turned to cheers. Shu Mai nodded complacently. She was used to such approbation, and anticipated receiving more of it in the future. A great deal more.

Meanwhile, she and Senator Mousul had much to do. The obstinate Tam Uliss had all but guaranteed it.

It was hard to believe after all they had gone through that the moment, if not of truth, then at least of debating it, had finally come. Though their clothing was made to repel dirt and grime, it had not been designed to cope with days of hard riding on the back of a giant suubatar, not to mention everything else they had experienced.

Nonetheless, with the help of Bayaar and others of the clan, the four offworlders managed to render themselves reasonably presentable. When the time came to go before the Borokii Council of Elders, Luminara was convinced they presented as imposing a portrait of roaming Jedi as circumstances would permit.

Decorated with pennants, intricate weavings, and imported hangings of worked metal and composite, the meetinghouse of the Borokii sat off by itself awaiting their presence. The elders were already inside, waiting to hear what the visitors who had successfully shorn the fur of the white surepp had to say. Though honor guards drawn from the best fighters of the clan flanked the entrance, they kept their weapons sheathed. After the extraordinary display of skill the night before, not even the bravest among them had any desire to challenge the strangers' remarkable, lightning-fast reflexes.

Pausing outside the entrance, Luminara turned to their guides. "You three will have to wait out here. You don't represent the Republic Senate, and we can't risk any distractions during the meeting."

Kyakhta and Bulgan indicated understanding. The Gwurran understood also, but that didn't keep him from objecting.

"Tooqui no distraction! Tooqui keep quiet, say say nothing, mouth become like closed cleft in rock, speak no words unless asked, can be as quiet as a—"

Reaching out and down, she put a forefinger against the upper edge of his lipless mouth. "I know you can, Tooqui. But this is our mission, and our time. We'll tell you all about it when we come out."

The Gwurran folded his furry arms across his chest and sniffed, his single wide nostril rising slightly. "Humans no need blabbermouth Tooqui when come out. Human squinchy-faces easy to read as gogomar entrails!"

"Hear that?" Anakin murmured to an expectant Barriss. "You've got a face like gogomar guts."

"Thanks," she replied flatly as they turned to enter the temporary structure. "You're no prince of the realm yourself."

It was meant as a returning jest, but as she stepped past him it was just as well she did not see the look that came over his face.

The council consisted of twelve elders of both sexes. They sat on a semicircle of slightly raised, carpeted divans facing the entrance. With a few exceptions, every mane in the room was either white or gray, though some showed striking black spots or stripes. As the offworlders arrived, one particularly aged Borokii raised a hand in greeting, all three fingers spread wide.

"We welcome you to this council of the overclan, and will listen to whatever you have to say. Questions will be asked. It is to be hoped that answers will be imparted."

It was that simple, that straightforward. Obi-Wan made the

presentation, repeating what they had already told the Yiwa, the Qulun, and the Gwurran, explaining why they had come to Ansion and why it was so important that the Alwari reach agreement with the Senate's proposal. Telling them that not only the future of Ansion depended on what they decided here today, but perhaps that of the Republic as well. There was no need for embellishment or fancy oratory. That was not the Jedi way, in any case. Such trimmings and flourishes were the province of professional diplomats. Though Obi-Wan was a fine speaker, he disliked superfluities.

When he was finished, he stepped back and took a seat next to Luminara on a settee provided for the purpose. As befitted their status, Barriss and Anakin sat behind their teachers.

His presentation was followed by a good deal of muted but vigorous conversation among the members of the council. One female elder looked up to ask a question worthy of the Qulun.

"We understand what the Alwari are supposed to get if we agree to this proposal. What does the Senate obtain?"

"Assurance that the law will be respected, and that Ansion will remain within the Republic," Luminara replied without hesitation. "As goes Ansion, so will go the Malarians and the Keitumites. The integrity of the Republic will be preserved."

"But Ansion is not a powerful world," another of the elders pointed out. "Why so much attention to our internal problems, our border disputes with the people of the Unity, and so on?"

"A small crack can lead to the collapse of a huge dam," Obi-Wan told him. "True, Ansion itself is not powerful. But it is entangled in powerful alliances. These need to be preserved within the framework of the Republic."

"We have heard little of this secessionist talk that seems to so inflame many of the city folk," another of the senior Borokii commented.

"Just as well that you don't," Obi-Wan told the speaker. "When Ansion declares its intent to remain within the Republic, it will all blow over. Such movements have manifested themselves before. The history of the Republic is full of them, and all that remains of them today are their names."

But this one was different, he had been told. Far more sinister. Potent outside forces were at work, stirring up discontent and trouble on multiple worlds. His briefing from the Jedi Council had spoken of rumblings on Coruscant itself. Still, there was no need to tell the elders more than they needed to know. The situation was delicate enough without invoking the dangers that existed on other worlds.

Another elder was speaking. "If we agree to what you ask, how can we be assured the city folk of the Unity will not go back on their word?"

"The Republic will guarantee the arrangements between you," Luminara told them, to which she added quickly, to forestall intimations of rising laughter, "and so will the Council of Jedi Knights." That announcement was met with murmurs of evident satisfaction. "We will also see to it that you are not taken advantage of by the incursions of the Commerce Guild, the Trade Federation, or anyone else."

There were more questions; some general and friendly, others pointed and challenging. When at last there was nothing more to be said, the senior elder of the Situng Borokii raised a shaky hand.

"Retire in peace, friends from another prairie. We will give you your answer before the setting of the sun. Rest assured it will not be given in haste, nor thoughtlessly." Looking to right and left, she regarded her fellow elders. "This is a decision that will affect not only the Borokii, but every member of every clan, from the newborn to the dying. It must be taken with care."

As was so often the case in matters of diplomacy, the summit itself was much easier to deal with than the waiting that ensued. There was nothing for the offworlders to do but retire to the visitors' house. As they waited, they were badgered by Tooqui and to a lesser extent by the equally inquisitive Kyakhta and Bulgan for details of the meeting. The Gwurran in particular was especially entertaining or annoying, depending on one's mood of the moment.

When Bayaar finally entered, everyone turned immediately in his direction. Taken momentarily aback by the attention, his expression was unreadable. When at last he spoke, it was with uncharacteristic solemnity.

"The elders are ready to see you again." He stepped aside. "Please come with me."

The two Jedi exchanged a glance, then followed the sentinel out the door. As before, Anakin and Barriss trailed behind, conversing softly among themselves.

"So they've come to a decision." Anakin shortened his stride so Barriss could keep up. "About time."

"Always impatient, you are," she told him, mimicking Master Yoda. "Better to live a calmer life and a longer one, it is."

"No calm in my life have I had, say I," he shot back without missing a beat. His smile was unreadable. "I wouldn't know how to react if I wasn't on edge most of the time."

Glowpoles showed the way to the meetinghouse. Not candles or oil lamps but modern illuminators brightened the interior. The visitors arranged themselves before the council. A few of the elders had changed positions from where they had been seated previously. Whether that had any significance or not, Luminara did not know.

Kyakhta and Bulgan might have been able to shed some light on the seating switch, but the guides were not here.

Once again, in confronting the Ansionians, the Jedi were on their own.

The senior female present began cordially enough. "All this day we have been considering your request. From what we have heard, and from our conversation with you, we of the Borokii believe that the word of the Jedi can be trusted." Luminara allowed herself to feel a modicum of accomplishment.

"We therefore," the female continued, "have decided to accede to everything you ask. We of the Borokii will make this peace with the city folk of the Unity, and Ansion will remain within the Republic."

Nearby, Luminara could see Anakin nudge Barriss expectantly. Both Padawans could not keep themselves from grinning joyfully. Obi-Wan's expression, on the other hand, never changed.

"In return for this, we ask only that you do one thing for us," the female said.

"If it is within our ability," Luminara replied guardedly.

The senior male took up the dialogue. "You have already shown that you are quick and skilled, with abilities that exceed those of even the most skilled Borokii. The Jedi are known, even here, as supreme fighters." When he leaned forward, she noted that what remained of his mane was entirely gray. "Our traditional enemies, the Januul overclan, are encamped not far from here. Help us deal with them once and for all, and you will have earned the friendship and concordance of the Situng Borokii forever! This is our price for doing what you ask of us."

The smiles vanished from the faces of the two Padawans. Had she been standing, Luminara would have been rocked back on her heels. Of all the requests the Borokii might have put to them,

of all the challenges and demands, they had chosen one that the
Jedi could not possibly grant. It was absolutely forbidden for Jedi
to take sides in an internal dispute among individual ethnic, clan,
family, or political groups. If the Order was ever seen to be favor-
ing one or another on matters that were no province of the Republic as a whole, its vaunted reputation for evenhandedness
would be lost. There was no way they could help the Borokii fight
and defeat these Januul—no way under the sun. Any sun.

But if they said as much, then the Borokii would refuse to enter into the carefully crafted agreement with the Unity of Ansion's urban dwellers. Seeing nothing ahead for them within the
laws of the Republic but continued conflict with the peoples of
the plains, the delegates of the Unity, in turn, would likely vote
to secede.

It was an impossible conundrum, impossible. A glance
showed that Anakin and Barriss realized it as well.

Obi-Wan, on the other hand, was nodding solemnly. "Of
course we agree. We will be glad to help you to deal with your
traditional enemies."

Anakin's lower jaw dropped as he gaped at his master. As for
Barriss, it was the first time in her apprenticeship that she had
ever seen Master Luminara shocked.

The Borokii council was visibly pleased. "Then it is agreed."
The elders rose, some more slowly than others. A few had to be
helped to their feet. "The bond is forged. We march tomorrow."
One by one they filed out of the meetinghouse. When the last
had departed, the visitors followed.

They were barely out of the building when Luminara and the
Padawans crowded close around Obi-Wan.

"What are you thinking?" a disbelieving Luminara asked
him. "How could you promise that? You know we can't take

sides in this kind of dispute." Her voice was tight with frustration and confusion. "We don't have time for this!"

The Jedi did not appear in the least upset by her accusatory tone. "We had no choice, Luminara. Either we agreed to help them, or they were going to refuse to sign the treaty we've brought with us. They said as much."

"But Master," Anakin put in, "the first Januul we kill will prove to this other overclan that the Jedi Knights side with the Borokii. When that happens, the Januul will become *our* enemies as well. If we help the Borokii defeat them, the Januul survivors will not honor any agreement we put before them."

"And like the Borokii," an anxious Barriss added, "these Januul must have many allies among the Alwari. They'll also refuse to go along with the treaty."

"The Padawans are right." Luminara was uncharacteristically mystified. Obi-Wan's ready agreement to the demands of the Borokii elders had left her angry as well as confused. "It doesn't matter which side we favor in this: Borokii or Januul. Once we've demonstrated partisanship, we've lost a significant number of the Alwari. For the concordance with the Unity of the city and townsfolk to work, all the Alwari clans need to be on board."

"If you'll give me a chance, I'll try to explain," Obi-Wan murmured when the flurry of accusations finally died down. As they turned a corner, the visitors' house loomed just ahead, with its promise of privacy, rest, and refreshment.

"I hope you can, Obi-Wan," she muttered, "or none of us is going to get much sleep this night."

Though he felt that he knew his teacher better than any of his companions, Anakin still had no idea what his Master could have been thinking when he had consented to the elders' request.

"What's to explain, Master Obi-Wan? Either we help these

Borokii, as you say we are forced to do in order to gain their co-operation, or else we do not. There are only the two choices."

Looking over at his bewildered Padawan, Obi-Wan Kenobi ventured that knowing, thin smile of his and replied softly, "No—there is another."

It was a march of several days to the Januul camp. It would have taken much longer had the entire Borokii clan made the move, but only warriors undertook the trek. When at last they ascended a long, low hill overlooking their destination, Luminara saw that the Januul encampment was laid out much the same as that of the Borokii. With its herds and neatly aligned temporary structures, it appeared to be of similar extent.

As the designated official contact between the offworlders and the clan, Bayaar rode alongside the visitors. "The Januul and the Borokii have been at odds for as long as anyone can remember," he told his new friends. "Who should have preeminence among the Alwari has been cause for fighting for hundreds of years." He looked up at her from the back of his sadain. "While as a warrior of the Situung Borokii I look forward to victory today, I am personally sorry the elders saw fit to involve you in this."

"Not as sorry as we are," she told him as she directed her suubatar to kneel. Dismounting, she moved to join her companions in the forefront of the Borokii line.

Below, the Januul had assembled on the near side of the small river that formed the western border of their camp. Despite the best attempts of the Borokii to achieve surprise, skilled Januul outriders had detected the approach of the column of warriors a day earlier. Drawn up in three lines opposite the hill, the soldiers of the other overclan stood ready to meet their traditional enemy.

Beyond, within the camp, controlled chaos was the order of

the day. Businesses were being shut tight, children herded into homes, and groups of reserves positioned among the many mobile buildings. Farther out on the prairie, the great herds of surepp were being watched over by armed adolescents too young to participate directly in the anticipated forthcoming battle.

Many were going to die this day, Bayaar knew as he surveyed the Borokii's opponent. But with the help of the powerful offworlders, his clan would prevail. Today's battle, he felt instinctively, would decide which clan among the Alwari was going to predominate for a long time to come.

Studying the Januul multitude drawn up before them, Luminara made a hasty estimate of their numbers. Less than a thousand, she guessed, but all of them well armed and clad in striking, hand-worked armor. Standing alongside her, Obi-Wan concurred with her assessment.

"No heavy weapons." He leaned slightly forward as he carefully scrutinized the tightly packed lines of warriors. "No laser cannons, no launchers of any size." He remarked on this to Bayaar.

Their friend looked horrified. "*Haja*, no! If either the Borokii or the Januul were to employ such deadly offworld devices, one clan or the other might well win this and all other similar confrontations, but they would be shunned by every other clan on the planet. Besides, such an escalation would mean that the opposing side would have to acquire similar weapons to defend itself. And then where would the proud Alwari be?"

"Staring down the barrel of self-extermination," Anakin ventured from nearby. Though he would never have admitted to it, he personally found the barbaric display, with armored Ansionians riding equally flamboyantly garbed sadains and a few magnificently invested suubatars, oddly beguiling. From a purely academic point of view, of course, he hastened to assure himself. While today's

confrontation might mean a great deal to its Ansionian participants, to him it was only another episode in his education.

Barring, of course, the possibility that he and his friends
might die.

"So these are the Januul." Luminara indicated the massed
warriors. "They are pretty impressive."

"Along with the Situng Borokii, the Hovsgol Januul have always been one of the overclans, yes," Bayaar admitted. "But with
your help, the matter of who reigns truly supreme among the Alwari will finally be settled."

"I hope so," Obi-Wan told him quietly. "That's what we're
here today to decide. By setting an example for both the Borokii
and the Januul."

Now, that seemed a strange thing to say, Bayaar thought. But
then, the flat-eyed offworlders often seemed to speak in riddles.

Having been ordered to stay out of the fight and remain back
with the noncombatants, Kyakhta and Bulgan were in an agony
of frustration. They had promised their lives to the offworlders
who had helped them, and yet now they would be forced to
stand and watch as their new friends risked their lives on behalf of
fellow Alwari. It was almost too much to bear. Tooqui, on the
other hand, had no difficulty whatsoever in agreeing to stay out
of the forthcoming fight.

"There are only four of them." From their vantage point
slightly higher up on the hill overlooking the river and the Januul
encampment, Kyakhta strained to see. "Strong and skilled as they
are, how can our friends possibly make a difference in the midst
of a battle among so many?"

"I don't know." Bulgan rubbed nervously at his eye patch. "But
you know as well as I that these offworlders are full of surprises."

"Tooqui know what going happen." The two much bigger

Alwari turned to look down at him. "Jedi going do something stupid stupid." He moved to the edge of the slight overlook, trying to keep Barriss in view.

Frowning, Kyakhta was sorely tempted to smack the little Gwurran. "You're lucky Master Luminara ordered me not to hit you. You should show some respect. Whatever happens, I'm sure they're not going to allow themselves to be killed. Their mission here is too important to them."

Tooqui looked back up at him. "Who say somethings about them get killed? Tooqui not say that." The Gwurran returned his attention to the unfolding spectacle below. "Tooqui say they do stupid stupid. Maybe they think of something stupid stupid to do all over stupid stupid heads of Alwari."

The guides exchanged a confused glance with the equally puzzled Bayaar. Then, realizing that it was a waste of time to try to make sense of something as patently nonsensical as Gwurran gibberish, they all moved to the edge of the slight overlook the better to follow the proceedings unfolding below.

Up close, the savage spectacle was even more impressive than it was from the top of the hill. Having arrayed themselves in their triple defensive line opposite the Borokii force, the assembled Januul presented a panoply of pugnacious attire and attitude. War paint adorned their faces, bare heads, and rippling manes. Leather and composite armor was festooned with individual, family, and clan ornamentation. In addition to traditional bows and arrows, throwing spears, and swords, they carried imported blasters and rifles. Their grim expressions were those of people bent on defeating any attackers, no matter the possible cost.

Forming a solid line opposite the arrivals, the soldiers of the Borokii offered a no-less-striking display. Flaunting attitude as well as weapons, individual warriors jostled for position, each heavily armed male striving to gain a place near the front. Clan leaders mounted on rearing sadains took up forward positions, shouting instructions to their troops. The air was thick with anticipation and the Ansionian equivalent of adrenaline. Gazing down from the crest of the hill, the apprehensive Kyakhta and Bulgan saw that full, unrestrained combat could break out at any moment. Standing between them, Tooqui was unnaturally silent.

Unexpectedly, the screeches and cries and shouted imprecations arising from both massed forces died down. Heads were craned and weapons lowered. The center of the Borokii line parted. Advancing in single file, the two Jedi Knights and their Padawans marched out into the center of the budding battlefield. Up on the hill Kyakhta, Bulgan, and Tooqui held their collective breath.

A number of the Borokii murmured expectantly among themselves. Although only a few of them had seen what the offworlders had accomplished among their surepp several nights before, by now most had heard about it. As for the Januul, they were sufficiently puzzled by the offworlders' unexpected appearance to wonder aloud at their presence in this place. Given the flat-eyed, maneless aliens' precarious position directly in front of the Borokii line, their intentions were clear enough to every soldier of the Januul. No matter. The offworlders would die as readily as any *snigvold* Borokii.

Having halted halfway between the two opposing hosts, Luminara and Barriss turned around to face the massed Borokii. While a grim-faced Anakin confronted the Januul, Obi-Wan raised his voice. The Borokii waited expectantly for their offworld ally to throw down the formal challenge. Turning a slow circle as he spoke, the Jedi addressed not just the Januul, but both of the assembled armies.

"Listen to me! I am Obi-Wan Kenobi, a Knight of the Jedi Order. Standing here with me are the Jedi Knight Luminara Unduli and her Padawan Barriss Offee. Beside me also is my Padawan Anakin Skywalker. We have come to your world to make a lasting concord between the Alwari and the city folk of the Unity of Communities, so that the people of Ansion may remain within the galactic Republic confident that its laws and regulations will be applied equally and fairly to all." Raising an arm, he encompassed the sky with a single wave. "Out there, beyond Ansion, greater forces than you can imagine are at work. Enormous issues of vital importance to every sentient in the galaxy are moving toward resolution. Ansion is a vital part and parcel of what is happening." Still turning slowly as he spoke, he lowered his arm.

"We have come here because we know that wherever the Borokii and the Januul lead, the rest of the Alwari will follow. We ask that your elders, the elders of both sides, sit down with us and discuss these matters anew. Matters that are of greater import than those you propose to kill yourselves over today." Among the massed Borokii, an uncomfortable stirring had begun. What kind of challenge was this for an ally to put to an enemy?

"You must learn to work together," Obi-Wan continued. "*With* each other, as well as with those who dwell in the towns and cities. If you do not," he concluded, "then you risk losing that which you fight for to greedy meddlers from outside like the Commerce Guild—and others, who see Ansion and its people as nothing more than a pawn in a greater game."

Save for some confused murmuring in the ranks of the Borokii, silence greeted his speech. Then a Januul officer advanced on his ornamented mount. Pointing a ceremonial sword at the calm, composed human, he replied angrily.

"We know nothing of which you speak, offworlder!"

Obi-Wan responded serenely. "Of course you don't. That's because you have yet to hear us. Give us that chance."

Behind him, a Borokii leader moved forward. "What kind of assistance is this? What happens here today doesn't involve other worlds, offworlder. Attend to the business at hand, as you promised the elders!"

"Ansion is part of the Republic," Luminara replied. "Within the Republic, all quarrels are the business of the Senate. And the Jedi Council."

The Borokii reacted with a smirk. "So instead of helping us, you've decided to save us from ourselves? So be it, then. We don't need your help. The Borokii have always taken care of themselves." A defiant cry rose from the massed fighters assembled behind him.

It was matched by a challenging shout from the Januul, whose officer was not finished with the visitors. "Get out of the way, offworlders! We will settle this as we always have, in the traditional manner. Whatever your intentions, it is too late now to interfere. The Borokii have come, and we are ready for them." Raising his sword, he let out a wild, high-pitched whooping no human could have replicated, and urged his sadain forward.

Concentrating hard, raising a hand to aid in mental focus, Obi-Wan thrust his open palm sharply in the direction of the charging officer. It was as if the sadain had run into a wall. Despite its six legs it went down in a heap, more baffled than hurt. Sent flying over the blunt, stunned head, its rider landed hard on the grassy ground. The impact sent his sword flying from his three fingers. With a cry, the line of eager Januul immediately behind him raised their weapons and surged forward. Bellowing and hissing defiance, the Borokii responded in kind.

Arrows came flying, spears were flung, and most dangerous of

all, blasters were brought into play. Anything that came near the
Jedi was deflected by lightsabers that seemed to spin and whirl as
rapidly as the lightning itself. Missiles sent flying overhead were
deflected by judicious and skilled application of the Force.

Three Januul tried to jump Luminara. Three strokes of her
lightsaber disarmed the first, melted the blade of the second, and
knocked down the heavy club wielded by the third. She was
too busy to acknowledge their stunned stares. Weaponless, they
backed slowly away from the olive-skinned dervish, retreating
toward their own line. In this they were accompanied by more and
more of their companions as Luminara and her comrades methodi-
cally neutralized one group of bewildered warriors after another.

Firing blasters, a pair of furious Borokii rushed Anakin. Instead of fleeing, he advanced toward his attackers, the blade of
his lightsaber deflecting one shot after another. Two quick
strokes swept the weapons from their hands. It would have been
a simple matter to bring the lightsaber around, cutting off both
their arms with a single swift stroke. But Obi-Wan's instructions
as they had marched from the Borokii line out onto the field of
battle had been explicit.

"No maiming and no killing," the Jedi had instructed him.
"It's hard to win hearts and minds when you're cutting off heads
and hands."

Further forcefulness wasn't necessary anyway, he saw. Certainly not to convince the two who had so boldly charged him.
Without a glance at their expensive and now useless pistols, they
fled back to the safety of the Borokii line.

Another ten minutes or so of ferocious futility finally impressed
upon Januul and Borokii alike that the fight was over. Or rather,
that it was useless to try to engage in one. In all their mutual history, in all their experience of combat, neither side had ever

heard of a three-way battle. It was outside their experience, and
they had no way of coping with it. Especially since the third party
battled either side with equal zeal.

No, that wasn't quite right. The offworlders had not actually
attacked anyone. It was they who had been assaulted, for presum-
ing they could dictate the rules of battle to the proud warriors of
the overclans. Since that was precisely what they had done, both
sides had no choice but to fall back and rethink the unprecedented
situation. Especially since a good many of their finest weapons had
already been destroyed by the offworlders. And there were only
four of the maneless interlopers. Only four!

Nor was it lost on either side that the strangers had harmed
not a single combatant. They had liquidated only weapons.
Where was the guarantee that if the fight was resumed this would
continue to be the case? Disarmed warriors looked askance at
one another and gave voice to their unease. If they couldn't put
down even one of the offworlders with blasters it was unlikely
they would be able to do better with a traditional weapon like a
sword or a spear.

Perhaps, a few among them began to suggest tentatively, it
might be better to listen to what the visitors had to say. Listen to
the offworlders, let the surepp of both sides grow fat, and wait.
They could always resume the ancient argument between them
at a later date.

The Januul ranks parted to allow the emergence of a dignified, senior figure. Breathing hard, lightsaber held firmly in both
hands, Barriss reflected that he was certainly old enough to be an
elder. In response, an individual more withered than any warrior
but still straight of back and proud of posture stepped out from
among the massed Borokii. The two elders regarded each other

across the field of battle with an equal measure of distaste and re-spect. When they spoke, it was to accede to reality.

With the visitors having stated their case most admirably for an urgent meeting with not just one but both Councils of Elders, the Borokii senior invited the four offworlders back to the meetinghouse. This invitation was promptly countered by the elder Januul. It was unthinkable that such an important gathering should take place in a Borokii dwelling. Stepping his mount neatly sideways, the Januul indicated that the visitors should follow him down to the main camp below.

The result of these seemingly benign invitations was contra-dictory: both sides threatened to resume fighting over the new issue of who should host the forthcoming peaceful get-together. Visibly annoyed, Luminara decreed that the summit would be held in neither camp. A new building, using components pro-vided by both sides, should be erected right where they were currently standing. That way neither overclan could claim para-mountcy over the proceedings.

The Borokii agreed, grudgingly. The Januul concurred, reluc-tantly. Well aware of the hundreds of convex eyes upon them, the four offworlders turned and strode off the field of battle. They did their best to give the impression that nothing exceptional had occurred, and that the sensation they had caused was all in a day's work for representatives of the Jedi Council.

But in reality, they were each and every one of them dead tired. There is nothing more challenging or exhausting for a skilled fighter than engaging in combat while striving not to kill, but to preserve the life of, your opponent.

Especially when those opponents are frantically doing their best to annihilate one another.

Though the Borokii elders felt betrayed by their erstwhile offworld allies, they had no recourse now but to participate in the new meeting. For their part, the Januul were intensely suspicious of the entire business.

"You lied to us!" the senior Borokii male thundered accusingly, indifferent to what the attendant Januul might think. "You broke your solemn bond!"

"Not at all," Obi-Wan replied quietly. "You asked us to help you deal with your traditional enemies, the Januul. That is exactly what we did." His slight smile widened. "Nothing was ever said about helping you defeat them."

Mouth open, angry retort at the ready, the elder found himself hesitating. Eventually, he resumed his seat on the carpeted dais. On his right, a senior female tittered and cracked her knuckles—but softly. The Januul elders simply looked confused.

In the end, it was the realization that both sides felt equally put upon by the Jedi that led to their eventual reconciliation, at least within the terms of the proferred treaty. Only later, Luminara reflected, would they come to see that both sides had gained something: from making peace with each other as well as with the Unity of city and town folk. And most important of all, by agreeing to a plan that would see Ansion remaining, once and for all, within the Republic and under its laws.

Personally, Bayaar was delighted with the outcome. He had expected to lose many friends that day, among both his clan and the offworlders. Who could have foreseen such an outcome?

"I am told that the two councils have agreed to everything you have asked. The accord will be finalized tonight in the traditional manner, during a feast in which both Borokii and Januul will participate." If he'd had lips, he would have smacked them. "Those who are fortunate enough to be invited will have something exceptional to remember! Both clans also have a gift for you, though I was not told what it was."

There was no cheering, no shouting within the visitors' house. Only weary, satisfied smiles, and the knowledge of a job well done. Had their training not been adequate, had the three-way battle lasted much longer, any of them could have been seriously injured, or even killed. Now, quiet congratulations were exchanged, and relieved Master complimented joyful Padawan.

No one was more delighted than Anakin. He had enjoyed the opportunity to do battle with something besides words, though he would never have admitted as much. Especially not to Master Obi-Wan. They would be going back to Cuipernam now, not a moment too soon, and from there to Coruscant to present their report in person to the Jedi Council. After that, unless another crisis somewhere in the galaxy required their immediate attention, they would be granted a period of rest. If he could just manage the matter of transportation, and if Master Obi-Wan concurred, he knew exactly how and where he was going to spend his.

The feast was everything Bayaar had promised, a consuming spectacle of sight, sound, food, and drink. They next morning they bid farewell to their new friends among the Januul and the Borokii. Racing toward distant Cuipernam they should have been able to relax, but could not. In the absence of their comlinks, destroyed by the Qulun chieftain Baiuntu, they could not inform anyone, most importantly the delegates of the Unity, of their success. They had, as the ancient aphorism went, no time to lose.

Kyakhta and Bulgan rode proudly out front, full of pride at having participated in so momentous a moment in the history of the Alwari. As had become his habit, Tooqui traveled with Barriss, scrambling all over her towering suubatar from head to hindquarters. The patient steed tolerated the Gwurran's antics without complaint.

"A great accomplishment, Master." Her suubatar loping along effortlessly alongside Luminara's, Barriss spoke from her saddle. Experience had made her comfortable with the rocking motion, and she rode with the ease of a prosperous merchant.

"An accomplishment." Luminara was willing to concede that much. "A job well done. 'Greatness' is a description best reserved for the ages. Everyone thinks their own achievements worthy of memorializing, but time tends to treat such things unkindly. After a hundred years, most such 'accomplishments' have been marginalized. In a thousand, they are generally forgotten." Seeing the look on the Padawan's face, she made an effort to sound more upbeat.

"That doesn't mean what we did here was unimportant. *Our*

history is only yesterday, and yesterdays matter. Besides, we are none of us historians. Who is to say what is crucial to the history of civilization and what isn't? Not ordinary Jedi. That's for the Council and professional historians to decide. What *is* important is that we accomplished what we came all this way to do, and that as few sentients as possible died in the realizing of it."

Barriss spent a moment digesting this. Then her smile returned. "Whatever else anyone says about what we did here, I think holding off not one but two opposing armies without killing anyone on either side qualifies as something special. You were amazing, Master. Most of the time I was too busy to watch, but I had glimpses enough. I've never seen anyone so calm and so fearless under such pressure."

"Calm? Fearless?" Luminara laughed. "There were moments when I was scared to death, Padawan. The trick at such times is not to show it. Always know where in your mental closet you've hung your bravery, Barriss, so you can put it on whenever you need it."

She nodded. "I will remember that, Master."

And she always would, Luminara knew. A fine apprentice, Barriss. Tending a bit to the pessimistic at times, but a devoted student. Not like that Anakin Skywalker. Greater potential there, but also greater uncertainty. She had observed him during the battle. More than any other non-Jedi she had ever known, she would have wanted him defending her back. It was what he might do *after* such battles that concerned her. More than a bit of an enigma, that young man. That was not only her opinion. Obi-Wan had indicated as much to her on more than one occasion. But he had also insisted that the boy held within him the potential for greatness.

Well, as she had just more or less told Barriss, that was one of those outcomes only time could decide. Skywalker was not her responsibility, and she was glad of it. She was not sure she would have been as patient with him as was Obi-Wan. An unusual teacher for an unusual student, she reflected. She urged her suu-batar to lengthen its stride slightly.

Unity delegate Fargane's stomach was not all that was growl-ing. The senior delegate was tired. Tired, and angry. He missed his home in distant Hurkaset, he missed his relatives, and the family business never did as well without him around to dispense the worldly advice of which he was a master. It was all the fault of these representatives of the turgid, pompous Republic Senate. These "Jedi." Prior to their arrival on Ansion, delegate Ranjiyn had declared that their reputation preceded them. Well, *haja,* as far as Fargane was concerned, their reputation had receded with them. They had been accorded respect and greeted as potential saviors of the peace, only to vanish into the endless plains of Ansion.

It was time to make a decision. Though he was still not cer-tain which way he intended to vote, he was certain of one thing: that vote was long overdue. He said as much to his colleagues.

"They are still out there somewhere," delegate Tolut in-sisted. "We should maybe wait a little longer." Standing by the third-floor window, the bulky Armalat gazed pensively north-ward. Even his patience was beginning to wear thin. During their only encounter, the Jedi had impressed him mightily. But clever parlor tricks were no substitute for substance. Where were they—and more important, where was the treaty they had promised that would at last settle long-standing matters of disagreement between the city folk of the Unity and the Alwari nomads?

"I'll tell you where they are." Everyone turned toward the

speaker. As official observer for a coalition of Cuipernam merchants, Ogomoor had no power to affect the proceedings of the Unity Council. He could only offer an opinion. But as day after day continued to pass with neither sign nor word from the visiting Jedi, his views acquired greater and greater weight.

"They've gone."

The human delegate Dameerd frowned. "You mean they've left Ansion?"

Soergg's majordomo feigned indifference. "Who knows? I mean that they are no longer with us. There are other ports besides Cuipernam, and a good ship can touch down anywhere. Perhaps they've gone back to Coruscant, or perhaps they're dead. Either way, they've failed to deliver on what they promised: the acceptance by the Alwari of a new social understanding on Ansion." He gestured meaningfully. "How much longer will you delay? However you vote on this matter of secession, this eternal uncertainty is bad for business."

"I am in full agreement with you there," Fargane huffed.

Ranjiyn eyed the senior delegate respectfully. "I concede that a decision should be made. Ansion's future waits on those of us gathered here."

A conflicted Tolut tried to stall. "Can't we give these well-meaning visitors a little more time?"

"Who says they are well meaning?" Kandah snapped. "Shall we let them define themselves? They serve other masters. The Jedi Council, the Republic Senate, perhaps others. They do as they are told. If they have been told to leave without speaking to us, I would not be surprised. It would be characteristic of the kind of long-winded political maneuvering so typical of the Senate." Her voice rose angrily. "I don't like being treated in this manner!"

"By the end of the week, then." Ranjiyn was insistent. "I say that if we have not heard anything from them by then, we should take the vote."

"Well!" muttered Volune aloud. "A decision at last. While I tend to agree with Fargane that too much time has been wasted on this matter already, I will accede to that timetable." He looked over at the senior delegate, human eyes meeting those of the slightly shorter Ansionian. "Fargane?"

The representative made a gurgling noise in his throat. "More time wasted. *Haja*, very well. But no longer," he concluded warningly. "Tolut?"

The Armalat turned from where he had been staring out the window. "These Jedi are good people, I believe. But who knows what they have been told to do, or what has happened to them? They presume too much." The heavy head gestured affirmatively. "The end of the week. It is agreed."

It was so decided. No more delays, no more excuses. Jedi or no Jedi, treaty or no treaty, they each of them had responsibilities to their individual constituencies, whose citizens had been clamoring for a final decision on the matter of secession. Concerned communications had come as well from offworld, from the Malarians and the Keitumites, whose own futures were so closely and formally tied to that of their Ansionian allies.

Ogomoor was delighted. The end of the week was farther away than his master would have liked, but neither was it next solstice. Soergg and whoever he was working for would be much pleased.

The majordomo was much pleased with himself.

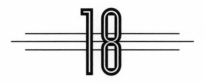

Ogomoor had just delivered a minor bit of good financial news to his bossban and was on his way out of the lounging chamber and back to his office when Soergg erupted behind him.

"It's not possible!" the Hutt bellowed into the commdroid, whose job it was to hover close to the massive, lumpy head during business hours.

Adroit fellow that he was, Ogomoor was able to divine several things simultaneously from his master's exclamation. First, when someone declares loudly and violently that something is not possible, it is probably an accomplished fact. Second, things that are supposed to be not possible that become reality almost always imply negative consequences. And third, there was no point in hurrying from the room because in all probability he would immediately receive an order to return.

All this flashed through the majordomo's mind in an instant; just long enough for him to mentally prepare himself. Soergg continued listening to whoever was on the other end of the transmission. The Hutt's huge eyes bulged and veins throbbed on his neck region and head. He must be upset indeed, Ogomoor knew, for those blood-carrying tubes to force themselves to the surface through so much intervening fat.

He listened patiently if uneasily. Patently, his bossban was not receiving good news. As bad news traveled rapidly down the chain of command through the Hutt's many enterprises, it was his destiny to be among the first to share in it. Occasionally, Soergg would interject a comment or two into the largely one-sided conversation. As the Hutt continued to listen, these rapidly grew both stronger and more profane in tone.

When at last the transmission ended, the enraged bossban swung furiously at the mechanical deliverer of bad news. A heavy hand smacked the guiltless hovering droid into the nearby wall. It crackled once before falling to the ground, shattered. Ogomoor swallowed hard. If the Hutt was angry enough to sacrifice expensive equipment on the altar of his rage, it did not bode well for his organic, more easily broken, subordinates. The major-domo took care to remain well out of the Hutt's reach.

Soergg was not in the mood to mince words, even at the sacrifice of his beloved sarcasm. "Those accursed Jedi are back!"

"Back?" Ogomoor looked blank. "Back where?"

Vast yellow eyes glared down at him, and Ogomoor was glad he had not moved any closer. "Back here, you idiot!"

Genuinely taken aback, the first assistant gaped at his master. "Here? In Cuipernam?"

"No," Soergg growled dangerously. "In my sleeping quarters." Voicing a curt command, he called forth another comm-droid from the cabinet in which they were stored in multiples. "They're at the city inn where they stayed subsequent to their initial arrival. At least we retain one competent informant! Get over there. Take whatever you need. Hire whomever you need.

Maybe, just maybe, they're too tired to ask questions and will retire for the rest of the day. If not—if it appears they are coming
out and heading for the Cuipernam municipal complex—stop
them. Do whatever you must. But keep them from reaching the
complex. *They must not be allowed to interfere with the vote of the
Unity delegation.* Not now. Not when we are so close to achieving everything we have worked for." The Hutt made a visible
effort to calm himself as he checked the newly activated comm-
droid's chronometer.

"Hold the Jedi until sunset. After sunset the vote will have
been taken and it won't matter what they do. But prior to the
setting of this benighted planet's sun, none of them must be allowed to reach the municipal hall."

"Yes, Bossban. You said I should do whatever I must." He
hesitated. "If I have to take steps, they might be in full view of
the populace."

"*Cross-spit the populace!* We will deal with any adverse public reactions later. It is not local reaction I am concerned with." Grunting, he leaned toward his majordomo. "Do you understand?"

"Yes, Bossban," Ogomoor replied somberly.

"Then what are you doing standing here oozing mental flu-
ids? Go. *Now.*"

Ogomoor went.

The manager was a Dbarian; all tentacles, warts, and worry.
That it was astonished to see them again, alive and well, was a
given. Suffice to say that its flexible unsegmented extensions
turned bright blue with surprise.

Were there rooms available for its honored guests? Did one
eat a loomas head-first? And could the manager possibly notify
the Unity delegation that the visiting Jedi had returned, with a

signed treaty not only from the Alwari overclan but the Januul as well?

The Dbarian executed its kind's equivalent of a frown. "You mean, honored guests, that you have not yet informed the delegation of this important achievement?"

Tired but happy, Luminara shook her head by way of response. "Our comlinks were lost during our sojourn on the plains, and neither the Borokii nor the Januul employ them." She smiled. "Tradition."

"But . . ." The Dbarian's chromophores were flashing different shades of maroon, indicating bewilderment. "The Unity delegation is voting on the matter of secession from the Republic *today.*"

"Today?" Anakin pushed right up among the manager's serpentine limbs. "But we haven't made our report to them yet. Surely they wouldn't vote on so important a matter without waiting to hear from us?"

Behind him, Obi-Wan was thinking fast and hard. "The sentiment for secession is strong among certain Ansionian factions, and we know they are being encouraged by offworld elements. Enemies of the Republic could very well have used our recent lack of communication to press for a vote." He eyed the manager intently. "You said that the voting session is to be held today. *What time today?*"

"That I do not know, honored guest. It is not something an innkeeper needs to keep track of. But the whole city knows about the vote. It was publicly announced, and is no secret. I believe—I believe it was scheduled for later this afternoon. Yes," he declared with growing confidence. "Just before sunset."

The Jedi relaxed. "Then we have time." He indicated the

instrumentation arrayed behind the manager. "I'll need to borrow a comlink until we can replace our own."

"Certainly, honored guest." Making sure it was fully charged, the manager passed one over. Reciting the relevant activation code, Obi-Wan immediately requested a connection to Unity delegate Ranjiyn.

There was no response. He tried again, and a third time.

Luminara looked questioningly at her colleague. "What's wrong, Obi-Wan?"

"I tried delegate Ranjiyn's personal contact sequence. Then Tolut's, and finally the venerable Fargane's. I received an automated message that was the same for each. 'United Ouruvot Communications regrets that all city transmission frequencies are temporarily off-line due to an equipment failure.'" He turned sharply to examine the entrance to the inn. "I fear that those who would keep us from delivering our report to the Unity delegation know we are here. I can feel it."

His companions were instantly on alert. Kyakhta and Bulgan saw to their own weapons while Tooqui found himself watching anything that moved. Behind them, the manager had been trying the inn's own facilities. Every attempt to communicate outside the building itself produced the same apologetic automated response.

"Are you saying, honored guests, that someone has ordered the shutdown of all city communications in Cuipernam just to keep you from speaking to the Unity delegation?" Its chromophores flared an intense pink.

"Until the vote is taken, anyway." Obi-Wan had already started for the doorway. "Don't concern yourself about it, innkeeper. I have a feeling that by nightfall your communications will be back on-line." His expression was grim as he glanced over at Luminara, who was matching him stride for stride. "We still have time, but we need to move quickly." With their anxious, alert Padawans behind them and their Alwari guides bringing up the rear, the two Jedi exited the inn and turned sharply up the main boulevard.

Exactly three minutes after their departure, the communications problems at the inn where they had planned to stay were rendered moot by a terrific explosion that caused the sturdy structure to completely implode.

As luck would have it, there wasn't a vehicle to be seen out on the street. Pleading vital Republic need, Luminara and Obi-Wan would have had no qualms about commandeering a passing landspeeder or even a hover truck—had there been one to be had. But all they encountered were simple, traditional means of local transport, designed for carrying small quantities of goods through Cuipernam's maze of winding, narrow streets. Given the hectic mix of bulky commercial transports, Ansionians, visiting and resident aliens, and domesticated animals that crowded the city streets, a low-flying landspeeder might have been slower than walking, anyway. Cuipernam was an old city, with a commercial center that had never been designed with modern vehicular traffic in mind. That was one of its attractions to visitors, but it also meant that its transportation facilities were a throwback to a much earlier era.

At least, Luminara reflected gratefully, it was not far to the municipal complex, the weather was good, and it was something of a relief to be walking again instead of fighting for balance on the back of a lofty, galloping suubatar. She glanced sunward. They still had plenty of time to reach the municipal hall before the Unity delegates assembled to cast their critically important votes.

They were halfway there when Luminara felt the disturbance. Peering in its direction, it took her only a moment to detect the suggestive movement out of the corner of one eye. Extending a casual hand to her companion, she touched Obi-Wan's arm in a certain way, then Barriss's, while her fellow Jedi alerted Anakin. Kyakhta and Bulgan had moved out in front while the endlessly curious Tooqui darted inquisitively from stall to shop. None of the nomads noticed the subtle change that had come over their human companions.

Edging closer to Luminara, giving no sign that anything was amiss, Obi-Wan whispered a single world. "Where?"

She told him with her eyes, glancing upward and to their left.

Responding with a barely perceptible nod, he passed the information along to Anakin and their Alwari guides while she informed Barriss. It was decided not to tell Tooqui. He was unlikely to be a primary target, he would find out soon enough what was going on, and the last thing they needed was a hissing, panicky Gwurran running amok on the crowded streets.

When the snipers on the roofs that paralleled the avenue below opened fire, it was only to see their shots deflected by waiting, activated lightsabers. Not one of the shots that rained down from the surrounding rooftops came close to striking its mark. Emitting a collective cry of alarm in no less than two dozen distinct languages, shoppers and travelers, merchants and pedestrians proceeded to scatter in all directions. Jedi and companions ducked into the large trading establishment that dominated the far side of the street.

Mouth agape, Ogomoor stared down at the panic that had infected the street below. A moment earlier, the Jedi and their associates had been strolling along, to all outward appearances content and unconcerned, wholly innocent of the fate that was about to befall them. The next, they had not only repelled his carefully choreographed ambush but had taken refuge in the building opposite, out of sight of his chartered assassins. They were the best he had been able to find and hire subsequent to his bossban's incensed orders, but good as some of them were, they couldn't hit what they couldn't see.

Fear fighting frustration inside him, he pulled out his special closed-frequency comlink and ordered his ground troops to rush the trading compound where the quarry had sought shelter. If the Jedi could be driven back out onto the street, then his rooftop executioners could pick them off. Even Jedi would be hard-pressed to deal simultaneously with more than one axis of battle.

"This way!" Luminara led her friends toward the back of the establishment as customers and sales personnel alike dove for cover. It was good that they did. While the Jedi were concerned for the safety of innocent bystanders, the several dozen professional killers who came barreling in through the rear entrance labored under no such ethical compunctions.

Fire erupted within the compound as rifles and blasters blazed away. Inside the establishment's armored office, two managers and one of the owners bemoaned the destruction of store and stock as the two sets of combatants flailed away at one another. The authorities had already been alerted, but by the time they decided to put in an appearance the interior of the neatly laid-out commercial complex might well lie in ruins.

These were not the same garden-variety assassins and murderers she and Barriss had been forced to confront soon after their arrival on Ansion, Luminara decided. They advanced with much more assurance, took aim with far greater accuracy. Only Jedi skills enabled her and her companions to hold them off.

Someone, she mused, had gone to considerable trouble and expense to engage this bunch.

Dealing with two assailants at once, she did not see the small shape of the diminutive but well-armed Vrot rising slowly on her left from behind a pair of terrified customers. Knowing he would probably get only one shot at the elusive and difficult-to-target Jedi, the Vrot took careful aim. As he was about to pull the trigger of his weapon, something that was all bulging eyes, flailing arms, and kicking feet landed on his head and shoulders. Startled, the murderous Vrot went down beneath a volley of uniquely inventive invective.

"Tooqui kill! Bad bad foreigner! Tooqui choke with own entrails! Tooqui—*whup!*"

Throwing the lightweight obstruction off his shoulders, the infuriated Vrot whirled and brought his weapon to bear on the meddlesome Gwurran. As he did, he was struck again, this time by two much bigger and stronger bodies. Luminara saw that she was once more free to deal with her original assailants. Between the three of them, Kyakhta, Bulgan, and the effervescent Tooqui were cheerfully beating the living daylights out of the unfortunate Vrot.

But there were too many skilled attackers. To ensure the safety of innocent bystanders, of shoppers and sales personnel, Luminara and Obi-Wan decided that a retreat was in order. It would be more dangerous to continue the fight out in the street, where they would again likely come under close-in fire from surrounding rooftops, but that was better than seeing dozens of inoffensive citizens cut down by the callous gang of professional killers.

Ogomoor got the word from one of his hirelings inside the compound and hurried to alert his frustrated snipers. "Be ready!" he instructed them via voice and comlink. "The Jedi are retreating! Let them all back out onto the street before you resume fire." Returning his attention to the boulevard below, he added more softly but no less emphatically, "We don't want even one of them to get away."

Kneeling behind his sniper's rifle on the parapet of the building on which they waited, one of the assassins inquired casually, "What about the Alwari who are with them? The two big ones and the little one?"

"Don't worry about them. Our people on the ground will take care of them. Get the Jedi first, then their Padawans." Eagerly, Ogomoor leaned forward to enjoy the forthcoming slaughter while exposing as little of his own precious self as possible.

Below, a recognizable garment appeared, vanished back under cover, appeared again. *Come out, noble Jedi. Show yourselves. Step out in the street, into the clear, bright sunshine of Ansion. Step out where I can see you. I, and my very high-priced servants.*

There, he shouted silently. He could see both Jedi, fighting side by side, emerging with obvious reluctance but emerging nonetheless from within the cover of the trading compound. He could see the two kneeling assassins on his left tensing as they prepared to fire. With luck and good fortune, it would all finally be over in less than a minute or two.

Unfortunately, the blessings of Jiaguin, the god of guile, were not with him that morning. The Alwari who descended upon the pair of snipers might as well have dropped out of the sky for all the intimation they gave of their presence. Knives and other traditional weapons flashed repeatedly in that same clear, bright sunshine of Ansion that Ogomoor had been counting on to facilitate the work of his hired assassins. As he whirled and raced for the exit that led down and away from the rooftop, he caught a passing glimpse of the bold motifs on the intruders' garments. His eyes grew even wider than usual.

Situng Borokii—*and* Hovsgol Januul. Warriors of the two most important overclans. Ferocious fighters with reputations that extended the length and breadth of both hemispheres.

What were they doing *here*, in Cuipernam, interfering in a city brawl? He did not know and could not imagine. He knew only that the sunny rooftop was no longer a safe place to linger.

As he fled, he saw that similar scuffles were taking place on the roofs opposite, where other outriding Alwari were overpowering his remaining snipers. Without shooters on the rooftops to worry about, he feared the Jedi and their Padawans would make short work of his surviving workforce. Then there would be nothing standing between them, the city of Cuipernam's municipal complex, and the Unity delegation. Unexpectedly, he found himself faced with the prospect of having to report yet another failure to his master. An especially expensive failure. Soergg would be less than pleased and more than furious. He would . . .

Cuipernam was not the only city on Ansion, and Soergg the Hutt not the only bossban worthy of the majordomo's inimitable talents. Weary of having to report one failure after another, the redoubtable Ogomoor wondered as he descended the stairs three at a time if today might not be the right day for someone of his ability to think seriously about seeking employment elsewhere.

No, he told himself as he fumbled for the closed-frequency comlink. He might yet make his knowledge and experience pay. There was still one card left to play.

Neither Luminara nor Obi-Wan quite understood what had happened to the potentially lethal shooters on the surrounding rooftops until a familiar face appeared in the midst of the body-strewn street. As soon as they recognized it, they and their Padawans were in equal measure surprised and relieved.

"Hello, Bayaar." Placing one hand over her face and the other over her chest, Luminara greeted the Borokii warrior in the accepted Alwari fashion. Behind him, Borokii and Januul fighters were mopping up the last of the hired assassins. This wouldn't take long, she saw, since the remainder of their attackers were now desperately scrambling to flee in any and every available direction. "Though I didn't expect to see you again, I have to admit that your timing for a reunion is nothing short of admirable."

"What is this?" Obi-Wan gestured past him, in the direction of their other rescuers.

Bayaar's sharp teeth showed in a broad grin. "Your honor guard, noble Obi-Wan. Don't you remember being promised a 'present' by the twinned Council of Alwari Elders? This is it. They didn't want anything to happen to their new offworld friends." Had he been physiologically capable of doing so, he would have winked. "Especially not before the formal treaty between the Alwari and the Unity is put in place. We've been shadowing you ever since you left our camp; guarding your rear, looking for trouble, watching out for you." His tone and expression grew more serious. "We lingered almost too far behind you."

"We would have managed," Anakin told him. At a stern look from his Master, he added quickly, "Though your help was certainly more than welcome."

Bayaar bowed slightly in the Padawan's direction, and Anakin felt abashed. Would he ever learn to think before speaking? His training was making him more than overconfident: it was making him brash. Somehow, he was going to have to learn how to be as patient as Obi-Wan. Otherwise he would never stand a chance of equaling, much less surpassing, the skills of his instructor.

"We're no less anxious than your elders to conclude this matter." Making sure her lightsaber was resecured at her waist, Luminara started back up the street. Obi-Wan joined her, with the rest of their party following behind.

They were flanked on both sides, on both the ground and the surrounding rooftops, by warriors of the Situng Borokii and the Hovsgol Januul. Drawn from the best fighters of both clans, they presented an intimidating yet captivating spectacle as they escorted the offworlders through the city streets. Wide-eyed locals stopped in their tracks or emerged from shops to behold the procession, and visiting aliens from even sophisticated worlds were suitably impressed. The Jedi were not challenged again.

When they finally arrived, the municipal hall of the city of Cuipernam was as they remembered it. While Bayaar and his warriors stood guard outside, the visitors were announced and admitted. The makeup of the Unity's delegation was somewhat different than it had been before. Delegate Ranjiyn was there, of course, and Tolut, and five others Luminara recognized, but for purposes of the vote the delegation had been expanded to twelve members. In consideration, no doubt, of the importance of the decision they were to render. Of the twelve, eight were natives of Ansion and the others resident aliens like the humans Volune and Dameerd and the Armalat Tolut.

Though they watched and listened attentively, neither Anakin nor Barriss paid any particular attention to the welcoming formalities. Kyakhta and Bulgan sat proudly behind the visiting humans, while a bored Tooqui spent his time searching the floor for valuables that might have been dropped by the esteemed participants. So long as he stayed in the background and did not intrude on the proceedings, everyone ignored him.

Shocked apologies and genuine sympathy flowed from the delegates when they heard how unknown forces had tried to have the city's guests executed in the streets. In return, concern was voiced by Obi-Wan and Luminara for the health and resolution of the delegates. As some of them were new to the Jedi, and vice versa, introductions were deemed in order.

Before they could begin, a panting, wild-eyed figure burst into the chamber. "Honored representatives of the Ansionian Unity of cities and towns! I beg you to grant me a moment of your time. I have information that will be of great use to you in the rendering of your decision." The figure reached for a pocket. "I know whereof the—"

A burst of energy illuminated from the front of the chamber. Lightsabers were drawn but not activated. The individual who had fired at the intruder had not panicked, but had taken careful aim. His weapon was efficient. The intruder had died instantly.

Warily approaching the smoking corpse, Anakin bent over the shattered figure of the uninvited Ansionian. Extending a hand toward the pocket the lifeless visitor had been reaching for, the Padawan removed the single device that had reposed within. A quick glance revealed its function. He held it up for the others to see.

"A recorder." He gave the device a cursory inspection. "It's fried."

The shooter returned the blaster he had employed with such precise aim to the pouch that hung from his neck. "So unfortunate. Bursting in uninvited, ranting and screaming like that, there was no way of telling what this one intended. When he reached for his pocket . . ." The speaker left the implication unsaid.

Next to him, Tolut the Armalet eyed the smoking corpse curiously. "That's Ogomoor. I recognize him despite the damage. Wasn't he in your employ?"

The shooter gestured nonchalantly. "He performed some occasional functions for me, yes. Though I gave him every opportunity and treated him well, I always thought him a bit unstable." A hand gestured in the direction of the dead body. "I am truly sorry to see my early judgment confirmed."

Barriss all but bolted toward the delegation. So abrupt was her reaction that Anakin was tempted to activate his lightsaber. Halfway toward the long, curving table behind which the Unity delegates were seated, she began gesturing heatedly at the individual who reposed slightly off to one side.

"You!" she declaimed in a voice so ringing it might as well have been the Jedi Luminara doing the accusing. "*You* were the one!"

The object of her wrath gawked uncomprehendingly at the furious human, then spread his arms wide in innocent supplication as he regarded the assembled delegates.

Luminara gazed narrowly at her infuriated Padawan. "Barriss? Explain yourself."

"Explain myself? Yes, I'll explain myself, Master." Her hand was steady as she held it pointed at the individual in question. "I didn't recognize him at first because I never saw him, but when I was preparing to flee the room where I had been imprisoned, before we left Cuipernam, Bulgan let his name slip." She indicated the still-smoking body on the floor of the hall behind her. "It all comes together now." Her eyes bored into larger, slitted ones. They stared back impolitely, masking the unpleasant thoughts that roiled behind them.

"Soergg the Hutt, I accuse you of ordering my kidnapping, of trying to obstruct any reconciliation between the people of the cities and the Alwari of the plains, of directing at least one and probably two attempts on our lives, of offering to pay the clan Qulun and anyone else who could manage it to abduct and restrain us until after the vote that is to take place here today, and probably of being in the pay of the Commerce Guild to boot." Her other hand dropped to her lightsaber.

A glance from Luminara was enough to stay the Padawan, but not to mute her anger. "This is an important conference, Barriss. No matter how we may feel about certain tangential matters, there are protocols to be followed."

"Tangential! But he's the one who had me kidnapped!" Barriss protested vehemently. "And he's almost certainly behind all our troubles here on Ansion."

"This is not a court of law, Padawan." Luminara spoke gently but firmly. "Words like *almost* are even less admissible here. This is neither the time nor the place for addressing such concerns. Restrain yourself." Her tone hardened. "Or I will have to."

Slowly, reluctantly, Barriss sat back down. But her eyes never left the distended, bloated object of her resentment. Behind her and her friends, city attendants were removing the broken body of the Hutt's former majordomo.

Shaking his head regretfully, Soergg addressed the curious delegates. "Our offworld friends have clearly been under enormous strain. This is quite understandable. Spending so much time among the savage, uncivilized nomads of the plains would take its toll on any civilized person." At this insult, Bulgan started forward, and had to be restrained by Kyakhta. "I take no umbrage at the child's outburst. I can only imagine the deprivations she and her companions have been forced to suffer these past weeks out on the empty prairie."

"At least we didn't have to worry about 'savage nomads' trying to murder us from ambush," Barriss shot back. Luminara threw her a cautioning glance, but for once the Padawan ignored it. She was that angry.

One of the new Ansionian delegates peered down the ceremonial table at the well-known and highly respected member of Cuipernam's diverse business community. The delegation had allowed the Hutt to be present as a courtesy, to observe the vote on behalf of all the city's business interests. "This offworlder's words trouble me, Soergg. Could she be so mistaken?"

The Hutt spread his arms wide. "You all know me here. I am only an ordinary businessperson trying, like the rest of you, to survive on a world where I was not born. Thanks to the warmth and openness of Ansion's people, I have prospered here. Think now: would I really do anything to jeopardize all that I have accomplished, everything that I have built?" Casting a kindly gaze in the direction of the barely controlled Padawan, he all but wept openly. "Is this the kind of understanding we can expect from envoys of the Senate if we consent to accept this concordance the Jedi bring before us?"

Oh, but he was clever! Barriss saw. The fat slug was an expert at twisting words to fit the situation. He might be lacking in minutiae like a conscience, or scruples, or legs, but words he had in abundance. She understood now why Master Luminara had warned her to keep silent. One of the first things a true Jedi must do, she remembered reluctantly, was learn to control her temper. At critical moments such as this meeting, personal feelings and individual emotions could not be allowed to intrude.

So she held in the fury she was feeling, did not try to employ the Force to wrench the smug, bloated Hutt's eyes out of his swollen head, and sat still as a sculpture chiseled in stone while delegates and Jedi discussed the terms of the proposed agreement between the city and town folk and the Alwari of the open plains.

She took some small satisfaction in Soergg's obvious tight-lipped displeasure when the final vote went nine to two in favor of adopting the concordance, with Kandah and an Ansionian from the southern communities voting against it. She also drew some edification from observing how effortlessly and smoothly Soergg subsequently lied, blandly conceding the fairness of the vote and vowing to uphold the terms of the treaty.

Taking her cue from her training, as well as from what she had just observed, she made her way unchallenged through the congratulatory postvote crowd to confront him directly. He loomed above her, massive but slow moving. Though she did not show it, it did her heart good to sense the first stirrings of fear within him.

"I hope to meet you again some day, Soergg." She smiled flatly. "Perhaps in surroundings and under circumstances where diplomacy is irrelevant." She nodded tersely to where Luminara and Obi-Wan were conversing with several of the other delegates. "And where the expression of my inner feelings is not subject to external constraints."

His response was a shrug that sent repulsive ripples through his lumbering body all the way down to his lump terminus of a posterior. "I bear you no ill will, little Padawan. Business is only business." But his tone, she noted, belied his words. In reality, he was furious and upset.

"Who hired you to try to stop us?" she couldn't keep from blurting. "I know who *you* paid, but who's paying you?"

He laughed, a deep and thoroughly unpleasant *ho-ho-ho*. "Ah, little one, you may know much of Jedi secrets, but nothing of business or politics. Paying me for what? I do whatever I do because it is good for my trade. Always the Jedi seek wheels within wheels, complications in matters simple."

"There's nothing simple about an entire world voting to join a movement that would see it seceding from the Republic."

"Secession? Why, that is a dead issue. Was it not just voted down, in your very presence?" he boomed softly.

"Then you'll abide by the new treaty between the city folk of the Unity and the people of the plains? You won't try to subvert it?" She glanced suggestively back in the direction of the entrance, toward the spot where the frantic, shouting intruder had been cut down by the very being she was talking to. "I don't suppose the individual you shot could have been carrying any incriminating evidence with him, could he?"

Soergg looked away, an action that was suggestive in itself. "An insidious notion, little Padawan. One unworthy of one as attractive as yourself." Emerging from between rubbery lips a fat, mollusklike tongue thrust briefly in her direction.

While the Hutt's tortuous reasoning was not sufficient to cause her to break off the confrontation, the repulsive gesture and attendant compliment were more than enough to drive her away. She rejoined her colleagues.

"It's time we were all of us on our way," Luminara observed. Turning, she waited while Obi-Wan thanked the representatives for their consideration, and commended them on their wise decision to remain within the Republic.

Once outside, Barriss tried to put aside her anger as she sidled up next to her fellow Padawan. "How are you feeling, Anakin?"

He was studying the sky, clearly anxious to leave. "Much better, now that our work here is done." Seeing that she was still staring at him, he added, "Is something the matter?"

"No. It's just that I think I may have misjudged you. I've come to know, and to understand, you a little better in the time we've been thrown together, Anakin. I realize now that you're searching for something. Searching harder than most of us, I think." Reaching out, she put a hand on his arm. "I just want to say that I hope you find whatever it is you're looking for."

He glanced over at her in surprise. "I'm looking to become a Jedi, Barriss. That's all."

"Is it?" she challenged him. When he chose not to respond, she added, "Well, if you ever feel the need to talk to someone besides Obi-Wan about it, you're welcome to confide in me. If nothing else, maybe I can provide a different perspective on certain things."

He hesitated, then replied gratefully, "I appreciate that, Barriss. I really do. I know it would be easier to talk to you about—certain things—than to Master Obi-Wan." He nodded in the direction of the two conversing Jedi.

She laughed softly. "Anyone is easier to talk to than a Jedi Master."

In agreement on that much, they began chatting in earnest, conversing for the first time with the straightforwardness and ease of old friends.

Luminara eyed them approvingly. It was important for Padawans to get along, because one day they would have to get along as Jedi, sometimes under the most difficult circumstances. Like Anakin, she too took a moment to glance skyward. Beyond the pure blue sky of Ansion, the Republic was in ferment. To the ordinary citizen all would appear normal, but those who were privy to the larger picture knew that vast forces were stirring—and not all of them benign. There was evil afoot. It was the task of the Jedi to root it out and render it harmless. But how was that to be done, when not even the Jedi Council was sure of the source or positive of its intent?

Not for someone like her to decide, she knew. *All I can do is my job.*

No, there was something else she could do. For a little while, at least. Lengthening her stride, she moved to catch up with Obi-Wan Kenobi; to seek his opinion on certain matters of significance, to congratulate him one more time on a job well done, and last but hardly least, to delight in the pleasure of his company.

There were some small pleasures not even a galaxy full of contentious factions and rising conflict could take away.

The three had arrived at Bror Tower Three one at a time, so as not to attract attention. Turbolifts had carried them to the 166th floor. While not as secure as an aerial transport, neither were the rooms holding the exhibition of the work of several of Coruscant's most prominent luminos artists the place where one would expect a trio of the capital's elite to be planning sedition.

Shu Mai watched the Ansionian and the Corellian approach.

Except for the three of them, the exhibition rooms were empty. The expression on the Senator's face reflected concern. As for Tam Uliss, he made no attempt to disguise his displeasure.

"You've heard" was all the president of the Commerce Guild murmured. She already knew the answer.

It didn't stop the industrialist from nodding emphatically. "Ansion has voted to remain in the Republic." He glanced sharply to his right. "You didn't deliver, Senator."

Running a long-fingered hand through his mane, Mousul replied stiffly. "I did everything I could. The decision was not up to me. I vote here, in the Senate—not on the Unity Council. My ability to influence them is limited."

"This was not the Senator's fault," Shu Mai put in quietly. "If those Jedi had not made a peace between the town dwellers and the nomads, the Unity would have voted for secession."

"It doesn't matter." The industrialist's tone was curt, his manner impatient. "You've both already agreed. We move forward *now*—with or without Ansion's withdrawal."

"What about the Malarians and the Keitumites?"

Tam Uliss was unyielding. "Without their withdrawal as well."

Shu Mai let out a long sigh. "You know my opinion, and that of the rest of the guild. Without the impetus that would have been given to our movement by Ansion's secession, we cannot declare ourselves and our intentions openly. Without the provocation the withdrawal of Ansion and its allies would have provided, we cannot count on sufficient support for our actions."

Mousul nodded confirmation. "With Ansion, the Malarians, and the Keitumites still in the Senate, we have insufficient grounds for presenting our demands."

"That's not what you said last week." Clearly, Tam Uliss was not to be denied. "You remember what you agreed to?"

"Yes, I remember." Shu Mai started to her left toward a corridor. "I am not comfortable discussing this matter further here. Others may arrive to view this art exhibition. I've taken the liberty of arranging for a secure conference room in Bror Tower Four. Precautions have been put in place and personally checked by my staff. Security droids are now active on station. If you will follow me?" She smiled. "I'm sure we can resolve our differences."

"There's nothing to resolve." Uliss was adamant. "We decided this last week, during the conference in the aircar."

The fellow is so full of himself, Shu Mai thought disapprovingly as they moved out of the exhibition area and down the wide corridor.

Uliss spoke as they walked. "There comes a time when sentiment will no longer be denied. The others have been ready to declare the movement publicly for nearly a year now." He searched the Guild president's face.

"They would continue to wait, if you had not thrown your support to them." There was no anger in Shu Mai's voice, no rancor. Only a simple statement of fact.

Uliss shrugged diffidently. "I'm sorry for this disagreement, but it can't be avoided. You would have had us wait indefinitely."

"Not indefinitely," Shu Mai corrected him as she turned and led her companions toward the skyway that led to the next tower. "Only until the time is right."

"And when is that to be? After another year of waiting? Two years? Three?"

"Whatever should prove necessary, my friend." Their footgear clicked on the smooth floor. Removing a control unit from her waistband, she used it to scan the skyway ahead to make certain it was clear. It wouldn't do to have some wandering office functionary stumble into them. "I would hope it wouldn't be that long, but whatever it is, it is."

Next to him, Mousul was nodding. "What you and your friends fail to understand, Uliss, is that when it comes to politics, patience is one of the most powerful weapons one can wield."

The industrialist shook his head regretfully. "There is time for patience, and then there is a time to move. You're not going to win this argument, you know."

"If we reveal ourselves too soon, no one will win any arguments," Shu Mai replied with conviction. "I'm sorry we disagree on this, Uliss."

The industrialist smiled. "No hard feelings, Shu Mai. Not even you can win every battle."

They turned into the skyway. Beyond the transparent walls and roof of the pedestrian walkway that connected Bror Towers Three and Four, Coruscant shone resplendent in the scrubbed light of day. Strings of vehicles tracked traffic lines of force through the afternoon air. Automated service craft zipped among the soaring buildings on preprogrammed missions. A fine place, Coruscant. The center of modern civilization. Sooner or later any who sought power, be it political, financial, or artistic, came to Coruscant. Those who sought to influence the affairs of worlds eventually found themselves residing within or standing before the Senate itself, the greatest and most important deliberative body in the galaxy. Each sought to sway its members in his or her or its own way. A little guidance, Shu Mai knew, was all that was needed. A few appropriate suggestions.

But they must be made at the right time, and under the proper circumstances. She lengthened her stride. Alongside her,

Mousul did the same. Idly observing the city outside, Uliss fell a few steps behind.

Reaching the far end of the skyway, the president of the Commerce Guild whirled. Beside her, Mousul did the same. Raising the unprepossessing device she carried, Shu Mai touched a control.

Tam Uliss looked understandably surprised when he bumped up against the field. It was quite invisible, and quite impenetrable. The industrialist's face sped through a remarkable range of expressions in a very short time. His words, which to judge from his appearance were rapidly growing increasingly irate, did not penetrate the barrier that had unexpectedly materialized between him and his companions. Neither did his hands and body.

The president of the Commerce Guild and the Senator from Ansion contemplated their fuming colleague unblinkingly. The Ansionian's expression was blank, that of the Guild president thoughtful. A look of dawning alarm came over Uliss's face. Turning abruptly, he tried to retrace his steps back to Bror Tower Three—only to find himself blocked by a second barrier identical to the one that had materialized in front.

Stepping up to the barrier, Shu Mai studied the now panicky individual trapped within the skywalk. All the industrialist's money, all his important contacts, were of no use to him now. It was too bad. While she had not particularly liked Tam Uliss, she had respected him. Not a hand-length from her face, a furious and frightened Uliss was now screaming threats and imprecations at his fellow conspirators. The barrier continued to block the industrialist's words as well as his fists.

For a long moment, Shu Mai gazed into the face of her former associate. "Patience, my friend, is the one weapon we cannot afford to waste," she whispered softly, even though the object of her admonition could not hear her. Turning away, she walked back to stand alongside Mousul, who had retreated slightly into the hallway behind them. The Senator looked on as Shu Mai touched several small controls in quick, practiced succession.

A slight creaking noise filled the end of the hallway, quickly rising to a groaning. Uliss stopped pounding on the unyielding barrier. His rage turned to uncertainty, then to surprise. Metal failed, composite dissolved. Both palms pressed against the barrier, the industrialist was still looking at Shu Mai and the Senator as the entire skywalk broke away first from Bror Tower Three, then from Tower Four, and plunged toward the surface 166 floors below.

Walking right to the edge of the opening that had been torn in the side of the building, Shu Mai leaned over and looked down. Even amid the noise of the great city and given the distance to the ground, the skywalk still made a very loud splintering, shattering sound when it struck. The president of the Commerce Guild gazed thoughtfully down at the wreckage for a long moment before turning and moving back into the hallway that was now exposed to the air outside. Across the intervening gap, an identical hole had been torn in the side of Bror Tower Three.

"Structural fatigue," she murmured to Mousul. "Uncommon in this day and age, but not unheard of."

"Indeed," the Senator from Ansion replied noncommittally.

"Such an important person. A terrible tragedy. Terrible. I will deliver the eulogy for Tam Uliss myself." Long-fingered hands folded behind her back, she started down the hallway.

"That's thoughtful of you, Shu Mai." The Senator took a deep breath. "When they learn what has happened to Tam Uliss, after what happened to Nemrileo of Tanjay, I don't think any of the others will give us any more trouble."

"I agree. Our support should be more manageable once again."

The Senator gestured down the hallway. "If you don't mind, I think I will leave you now, as I have work of my own to do this afternoon."

The president of the Commerce Guild gestured understandingly. "I understand. I have work of my own to do as well."

They parted amiably; Mousul to return to his Senatorial duties, Shu Mai to her private office. There she locked herself in so tightly that nothing short of a small nova could interrupt her. Only when she was sure that everything was secure did she activate the special code sequence that put her in contact with the remarkable individual to whom she was charged with reporting the progress of the conspiracy on Coruscant.

When a familiar face appeared before her, she began speaking without hesitation. "There have been some—problems. The Jedi succeeded in making peace between the urban and nomad factions on Ansion. As a result, the Unity delegates on Ansion voted to keep their world in the Republic."

The voice on the other end was firm, confident. "That is too bad. It will force us to scale back our immediate plans." The face smiled. "I wouldn't have thought the Jedi could accomplish it. Not in so short a time."

"Something else. While Senator Mousul remains firmly committed to the cause, a number of our supporters were preparing to move forward despite Ansion's decision. It was necessary to deliver an—object lesson," She proceeded to explain.

The individual on the other end of the secure communication

listened quietly until Shu Mai had finished. "While I regret the loss of the industrialist Tam Uliss, I understand the reasoning behind your actions." Without quite knowing why, the president of the Commerce Guild felt much relieved. "It doesn't matter. Events advance, designs move forward. We can swallow the loss."

"The resolve of the Guild remains strong," Shu Mai told him.

Count Dooku smiled. "As does that of our other backers. I consider this nothing more than a temporary setback. The eventual outcome is inevitable, no matter what the irksome Jedi do. Great changes are at hand. Destiny awaits us, my friend. It comes, and soon. Those who are ready will be the ones to profit greatly."

It was a good thought to cling to, Shu Mai mused as the transmission was terminated. Deactivating the privacy shielding, she rose and left the room.

There was much to be done.